Praise for Jennifer Weiner

'Jennifer Weiner is a class act. She writes with confidence and style' Lisa Jewell

'Jennifer Weiner is a genius. Her books are totally gripping, beautifully written, heartbreaking and hilarious' Harriet Evans

'Witty, moving, stupendously well written and deeply perceptive' Jill Mansell

'Like Helen Fielding, Weiner balances romantic formula with fresh humour, deft characterizations and literary sensibility' *Guardian*

'Witty, compelling and utterly unforgettable' *Heat*

ALSO BY JENNIFER WEINER

Good in Bed
In Her Shoes
Little Earthquakes
Goodnight Nobody
The Guy Not Taken
Certain Girls
Best Friends Forever
Fly Away Home
Then Came You

JENNIFER WEINER
The Next
Best Thing

**SIMON &
SCHUSTER**

London · New York · Sydney · Toronto · New Delhi

A CBS COMPANY

First published by Atria Books, A Division of Simon & Schuster Inc., 2012
First published in Great Britain by Simon & Schuster UK Ltd, 2012

This paperback edition first published in 2013

A CBS Company

1 3 5 7 9 10 8 6 4 2

Simon & Schuster UK Ltd
1st Floor
222 Gray's Inn Road
London WC1X 8HB

www.simonandschuster.co.uk

Simon & Schuster Australia
Sydney

Simon & Schuster India
New Delhi

A CIP catalogue record for this book is available from the British Library

Paperback B Format ISBN: 978-1-47115-735-6
Ebook ISBN: 978-0-85720-960-3

Printed and bound in Great Britain by CPI Group (UK) Ltd, Croydon, CR0 4YY

For my brothers, Jake and Joe Weiner

"Please, please, please, let me, let me, let me, let me get what I want this time."

—THE SMITHS

PART ONE

—

Golden Girls

ONE

The telephone rang.

If it's good news, there's going to be a lot of people on the call, Dave had told me. Bad news, it'll just be one person from the studio, the executive in charge of the project. I lifted the phone to my ear, feeling like the air had gained weight and my arm was moving through something with the consistency of tar. My heartbeat hammered in my ears. My jeans and T-shirt felt too small, the sunshine in my bedroom stabbed at my eyes, and the atmosphere felt thin, as if I was working harder than I normally did to pull oxygen into my lungs. *Please, God*, I thought—me, the girl who hadn't been in a synagogue since my grandma and I had left Massachusetts, who'd barely remembered to fast last Yom Kippur. But still. I was a woman who'd lost her parents, who'd survived a dozen surgeries and emerged with metal implants in my jaw, the right side of my face sunken and scarred, and an eye that drooped. In my twenty-eight years, I hadn't gotten much. I deserved this.

"Hello?"

"Hold for Lisa Stark, please!" came Lisa's assistant's sing-song. My breath rushed out of me. Lisa was my executive at the studio. If she was the only one on the call, then this was the end of the road: the pass, the thanks-but-no-thanks. The no. I pushed my hair—lank, brown, unwashed for the last three days—behind my ears and sat on my bed. I would keep my dignity intact. I would not cry until the call was over.

I had told myself to expect bad news; told myself, a thousand times, that the numbers were not in my favor. Each year, the network ordered hundreds of potential new programs, giving writers the thumbs-up and the money to go off and write a pilot script. Of those hundreds of scripts, anywhere from two to three dozen would actually be filmed, and of those, only a handful—maybe four, maybe six, maybe as many as ten—would get ordered to series. My sitcom, *The Next Best Thing,* loosely based on my own life with my grandmother, had made the first cut three months ago. I'd quit my job as an assistant at Two Daves Productions in order to work full-time on the script, progressing through the steps from a single-sentence pitch—*a college graduate who's been laid off and her grandmother who's been dumped move to an upscale assisted-living facility in Miami, where the girl tries to make it as a chef and the grandmother tries to live without a boyfriend*—to a paragraph-long pilot summary, then a beat sheet detailing each scene, then a twelve-page outline, and, finally, a forty-page script.

For months I'd been writing, holed up in my bedroom, or carrying my computer to a neighborhood coffee shop, where I was surrounded by my more attractive peers, the ones who carried on long, loud telephone conversations in which they used the words *my agent* as often as possible, and did everything but prop tip cups and WRITER AT WORK signs in front of their laptops. I wrote draft after draft, turning each one over to the studio that had funded my efforts and to the network that would, I hoped, eventually air them. I considered each round of notes; I cut and edited, rewrote and rewrote again. I pored over books for expectant parents to give my characters just the right names, and spent days in the kitchens of local restaurants so I could nail the details of my heroine's job.

Two weeks ago I'd delivered the absolutely, positively final final draft. I'd brushed my lips against every single one of the pages, kissing each one lightly before I slid the script into the hole-puncher, then slipped the brass brads through the holes and pushed them shut. To celebrate, I'd taken Grandma out to lunch at the Ivy, at her insistence. My grandmother, a petite and stylish woman of a certain age, was a great fan of the tabloids. Any restaurant where the paparazzi were a regular presence on the sidewalk was a place she wanted to be.

When we walked up to the stand, the maître d' looked at me—in a plain black cotton shift dress and five-year-old zippered leather boots, with my laptop tucked under my arm—and gave a small but discernible shrug. My grandmother stepped toward him, smiling. If I dressed to maximize comfort and minimize attention, in shades of black and gray and blue, with a single necklace and sensible shoes, my grandmother had style enough for the both of us. That day she wore a black-and-white linen dress with a black patent-leather belt and black canvas espadrilles with bows that tied at her ankles. Her necklace was made of vintage Bakelite beads in poppy red, and she had a matching red patent-leather clutch in her hand and a red silk flower tucked behind one ear.

"How are you today?" she asked.

"Fine." The host's eyes lingered on her face as he tried to figure out if she was someone he should know, a screen star of yesteryear or one of the Real Housewives' mothers. "This is my granddaughter," said Grandma, and gave me a brisk poke in the small of my back. I stumbled obediently toward the podium with a *can-you-believe-her* look on my face, wishing I'd worn a necklace or a flower, or had thought to carry a pretty purse, or to have purchased one in the first place. "Ruthie is a writer." The man behind the podium could barely suppress his wince. *Writer*, of course, was not the magic word that would cause him to usher us to the finest table in the restaurant and send over a bottle of free Champagne. Maybe writing for TV was a big deal elsewhere in America. In Hollywood, it meant less than nothing. Television writers were as common as cat dirt, and anyone with a working laptop and a version of Final Draft on her hard drive could claim to be one. You could almost see the word *nobodies* in a balloon floating above the man's neatly barbered head as he led us to a table so far in the back it was practically in the kitchen. "Ladies," he said.

Grandma paused and rested her hand on the man's forearm. She tilted her face up toward his, batted her eyelashes, and gave him her gentle smile. "Would it be possible for us to have a booth? Or a table with a little more light?" Even at her age—seventy-six, although she'd have shot me if I'd said it out loud—her skin was still smooth, her eyes still bright, face vivid with rouge and lipstick, eyeliner and curling false lashes. Her waist was still slim, and her teeth were all her own. "We're celebrating."

He smiled back—it is, I have learned over the years, almost impossible to resist my grandma's smile—and led us to a booth halfway between the open front porch lined with white umbrellas, where the stars would pose and preen for the cameras, and the dim back room, where the nobodies were sequestered. We shared pasta and a chopped salad, had a glass of wine apiece, and split tiramisu for dessert. As we ate, Grandma told me stories from the set of *OR,* the medical drama where she'd been working as an extra that week. "The kids they bring in," she complained, running the edge of her spoon along the ridge of whipped cream that topped the tiramisu. "They're out partying all night, so by the time they get in their gurneys, they're exhausted. One of the

ADs has to run around set five minutes before every take just making sure they're not sleeping."

"Tough gig," I said. Grandma herself was spending eight hours a day sitting in the fake OR's fake waiting room. Every day, from ten in the morning until six o'clock at night, with union-mandated breaks for lunch and snacks, she'd get paid to do what she might have done for free on a normal day—sit in an uncomfortable plastic chair with a tote bag of knitting in her lap, looking somewhere between bored and worried as she waited for her name to be called.

"You have to respect them," she said, nibbling at the strawberry that sat on the side of the dessert plate. "Finding a way to get paid for sleeping. That's initiative."

"Nice work if you can get it," I said, and flagged down our waiter, and paid the bill. Then Grandma had gone back to the Radford lot in the Valley, a neighborhood ten miles away from and ten degrees hotter than Hollywood, where a number of television shows and movies were shot, and I drove back to Hancock Park, a pretty neighborhood with spacious sidewalks and green lawns, to our apartment in a Spanish-style building called the Moroccan, to wait.

The network had started picking up its comedies a week after our lunch. I'd spent my days with my phone in my hand, from the moment I opened my eyes to the moment I closed them. I would perch the phone on the edge of the sink while I showered or brushed my teeth, and sleep with it plugged in underneath my pillow. My thumb was permanently hovering over the keypad, hitting "Refresh" on *Deadline Hollywood* and *L.A. Confidential* and all of the websites that covered the industry. I'd quit going to the gym after I realized how much I was annoying my fellow swimmers by pausing at the end of each lap to check my phone, which I'd stowed in a waterproof plastic Ziploc bag and left by the deep end. I was too nervous to sit through a meal, but I was snacking constantly, eating bags of pretzels and dehydrated carrot chips and Pirate's Booty and sunflower seeds that I didn't really want, and ignoring my boyfriend Gary's phone calls, because there was, we'd learned, nothing he could say or do that would possibly calm me down.

Now here was my news, I thought, waiting for Lisa to get on the line, and the news wasn't good. Oh, well. At least I'd be disappointed in private. After I'd made the mistake of telling Grandma that I should be hearing something this week, she'd announced her intention of giving me my space. "You don't need an old woman breathing down your neck," she'd said, all the while hovering within five feet of my person, dressed in her at-home attire of lounging pajamas or a brilliantly embroidered silk robe, her slippered feet noiseless on the wooden floors as she found one task after another to keep her busy, and nearby. So far she'd polished the silver, rearranged the china, emptied, scrubbed, bleached, and refilled the kitchen cupboards and the refrigerator, and regrouted the powder-room tile. That morning while we drank the smoothies she'd made of pineapple and mango and Greek yogurt, she'd announced her plans to rent a steamer and replace the dining-room wallpaper, even though I'd begged her to leave that job to the professionals.

"*Nu?*" she'd ask casually, just once every night, as she served dinner to me and Maurice, her gentleman caller. As usual, her nerves were made manifest in the reemergence of her Boston accent and in her cooking. On Friday, when the first wave of pickups was announced, she'd prepared a standing rib roast, Yorkshire pudding, potatoes au gratin, and homemade horseradish sauce. On Saturday, she'd served a breast of veal stuffed with cornbread and sausage and studded with garlic and rosemary, and on Sunday, she'd produced an entire Thanksgiving dinner, complete with two kinds of potatoes and a turkey she'd brined in the hot tub (our down-the-hall neighbors, devoted fitness buffs, had howled when they'd gone up to the roof for a little post-hike relaxation and found, instead of clear water, a fragrant brew of bay leaves and garlic cloves and juniper berries, with a kosher turkey bobbing merrily in the middle).

I would pick at my food, then excuse myself, telling Grandma and Maurice that I needed to work, closing my bedroom door behind me. Of course, I wasn't working. I was staring at my phone, trying to will it to ring, and when I wasn't doing that, I was dialing the first nine of the ten numbers that would have connected me with Dave, the only person I really wanted to talk to.

"Ruth?" The voice on the other end of the line startled me so badly that I gave a little squeak. The assistant, who had probably grown accustomed to the quirks of neurotic writers, pretended not to notice. "I have Lisa on the line. Please hold for Tariq, and Lloyd and Joan from the network." I got to my feet, my heart lifting as quickly as it had sunk. The network. Oh God oh God oh God. *The network doesn't call unless it's a pickup,* Dave had said. They give the bad news to the agent, not the writer, and probably you'll read it online before someone has the decency to tell you to your face that your show is dead. But maybe Dave was wrong. It had been years since his own show was green-lit, years since he'd had to sit in breathless, chest-pounding agony, waiting for the call, this call.

Voices came back on the line, one after another, ringing like bells.

"I have Tariq," said Tariq's assistant.

"Holding for Joan," said Joan's.

"Ruth?" asked Lisa. "Still there?"

"I'm here." My voice was faint and quivery. I stood up, clenching my fists, my jaw, my abdominal muscles, trying to keep from shaking.

"Please hold," said a new voice, male and brusque and impatient, "for Chauncey McLaughlin."

I reeled back toward the bed. It felt like Christmas morning, New Year's Eve, a birthday cake blazing with candles, a man down on one knee with a diamond ring in his hand. Joan was ABS's head of comedy, and Chauncey McLaughlin (rumor was, he'd been born Chaim Melmann, then changed it to Charles, then gone full WASP with Chauncey) was the president of the network, a man I'd glimpsed once at a holiday party and had spoken with precisely never. Chauncey McLaughlin was the man who ultimately decided which of the pilots would get shot and, of those, which would make it onto the air in the fall and which would die quietly in the springtime.

"Who've I got?" he asked in a booming voice. Names were reeled off—Tariq, Lisa, Lloyd, Joan. "And Ruth, of course."

"Hi," I managed.

"Chauncey McLaughlin. I don't want to keep you waiting. We're going to go ahead and shoot *The Next Best Thing*."

I closed my eyes. My legs went watery with relief. "Thank you," I said. With the phone still pressed to my ear, I got up and unlocked the bedroom door to find my grandmother standing there. Evidently she'd given up even pretending that she wasn't waiting for the call. I flashed her a thumbs-up. She sprang into the air and actually clicked her heels together, a feat she couldn't have managed before her hip replacement two years before. Then she held my face in both of her hands. I could feel her hand on my left cheek and felt, as usual, nothing on my scarred right side as she kissed me, first on one cheek, then the other, before stowing her cell phone in her brassiere ("God's pocket," she called it) and hurrying off to the kitchen, undoubtedly to start giving her hundred closest friends and relations the news. A moment later, Maurice appeared in the living-room doorway, dressed for golf, with his tanned hands clasped over his head. He stood on his tiptoes to kiss me—Maurice, while not technically a little person, is a long way from tall, and a good six inches shorter than

I am—then turned back down the hallway. Maurice had two sons, no daughters, and even though he'd never said so, my sense was that he liked having a young lady in his life. He'd pull out my chair, hold doors open for me, ask me if my boyfriend was treating me well, and say that if he wasn't, he, Maurice, would be happy to talk to him about it.

As congratulations spilled over the line, from Lisa and Tariq and Chauncey, I found myself wishing not for my boyfriend, Gary, but for Dave. Dave, one of the Two Daves, was my boss and my mentor, the one who'd helped me craft the concept for *The Next Best Thing*, who'd overseen each revision of the script and assured me that I had just as good a shot at writing my own show as any other writer in Hollywood, even if I'd never been a staff writer, even if I was only twenty-eight. Dave's promise to serve as my co-executive producer had gotten me the meeting with Joan, and Dave's involvement, I was sure, had gotten the network to take a chance on an unknown quantity. A Hollywood veteran who'd co-created and run a successful sitcom for the past five years, Dave would know what to do next. And Gary. I'd have to call Gary and let him know.

"Ruth?" Chauncey's voice was deep and warm, the sound of your favorite uncle who'd come for the holidays with fancy barrettes and foil-wrapped chocolate kisses and the latest Baby-sitters Club book. "Did we lose you?"

"No, I'm still here. I'm just a little overwhelmed. I . . . oh, God, I don't even know what to say except thank you."

"And that the show will be brilliant," Lisa quickly added.

"We're counting on it," said Tariq. I could hear, or thought I could, the edge of desperation in his voice. Last year, Tariq had shepherded five pilots through the development process. The network had green-lit only one of them, a trippy hourlong dramedy set in an alternate universe where the dinosaurs were not extinct. The network had lavished millions of dollars on the sets and had cast a big-name former movie star as the lead. Even with all that, the show had lasted for exactly three episodes. Dave had told me, and the commentators on *Deadline* had confirmed, that if Tariq failed to improve his game, he'd be looking for a new job by the fall.

"Thank you," I said again. "Thank you all so much for believing in me."

"Of course," said Chauncey casually, "we might need you to make some changes. Nothing drastic, just a little rewriting."

"Oh my God. Of course. Absolutely. Whatever you need." I'd thought the script was perfect when I turned it in, but obviously I'd be willing to tweak or cut or change it in whatever way the network deemed necessary to get it on the air.

There was another round of congratulations, and Chauncey said, "Got more calls, kiddo," and, just like that, the call was over, and I sank onto my bed, clutching my telephone in one sweaty hand. I'd survived the first round of cuts. I would get to hire a cast, find my star, build the sets, shoot my pilot show. Instead of competing against dozens of scripts, I was up against maybe twenty-four . . . and even if *The Next Best Thing* never made it on the air, I'd have a lovely souvenir, a DVD of my dream made real.

I got to my feet, the same person I'd been ten minutes ago: average height and average weight (which made me practically obese in Hollywood), with thick, shoulder-length hair that could be coaxed to hang, sleek and glossy, when I spent the time or money to have it straightened. I had brown eyes, my grandma's full pink lips, features that might have been almost pretty before the accident, broad shoulders and curvy hips, a solid torso thanks to years of swimming, and olive skin that tanned easily and stayed that way, even in what passed for winter out here. Except for the scars, which my clothes covered, and my face, which my clothes did not, I was normal—even, from certain angles, pretty. It was a problem. Sometimes, people would react to me after they'd seen me from behind or from my good side. *Hey, baby, lookin' good!* construction workers would shout when I was walking with my gym bag over my shoulder and a baseball cap's brim shadowing my face . . . or, if I was meeting my grandmother at a restaurant, a man would approach from my left side at the bar and start chatting me up. I'd take care of things as quickly as I could, pulling off my hat, pulling back my hair. I would show them the truth, who I really was. The catcalls would stop abruptly, and the man at the bar would suck in his breath, then scowl as if it were my fault, as if I was somehow playing a joke on him. Once, a homeless man had asked me for change, ignoring my muttered "sorry" and chasing me down Sunset until I'd turned. His eyes had gotten big as he'd taken in my face. Then he'd pulled a dollar out of his pocket. And handed it to me.

I started to punch the button that would connect me to Gary. Then I stopped. Should I tell Dave first? I certainly could, now that I'd gotten the Call. He'd want to know. Maybe he'd even want to celebrate. Or maybe I should sneak out of the house, head to the airport, and buy myself a ticket to Hawaii, where he was vacationing, to tell him in person. I knew where he liked to stay, which flights he would have taken, his favorite restaurants on every island. Whether I'd be a good showrunner remained to be seen, but I had been an excellent assistant. The hard part would be getting past Grandma. "Fool me once, shame on you; fool me twice, shame on me," she'd say, and point out that I had already had my heart broken once by a Hollywood writer and that I should endeavor to make new and interesting mistakes rather than repeating the ones I'd made before.

She was right, I thought, and picked up the phone and called Gary. "Good news?" he asked, and I bounced on the bed, smiling as I said, "The best."

TWO

My love affair with television began when I was eight years old. It started—as so many things do—with *The Golden Girls.*

When I was three, my parents were driving on the Massachusetts Pike, on their way from their house in Framingham to dinner with friends in Worcester, when their station wagon hit a patch of black ice. The car skidded over the guardrail, flipped over twice, and then burst into flames. My mom and dad died, and my car seat broke free of its straps and went flying through the windshield. I broke an arm and a leg and most of my ribs on the right side of my body—the side I'd landed on—but most of the damage had been caused by going face-first through all that glass.

My mother's mother, Rae, had spent her life in Boston but was living in Coral Gables when the accident happened. She came north for the funeral and never left, arranging the sale of her condominium over the phone, having her furniture and clothes and dishes shipped up, moving into my parents' house, and taking over the business of raising me.

I'd spent chunks of my childhood in hospitals, undergoing and then recovering from various surgeries intended to repair the damage the accident had done. The longest stint was the summer between second and third grades, when I stayed at Shriners Hospital of Boston. The doctors there had big plans, a series of operations that would stretch from June to August. First, I was to have a titanium rod implanted in my jaw, to replace the shattered bone that had been reinforced with pins when I was five but was failing to grow properly. "You'll be like the bionic girl!" my orthopedic surgeon, a jolly man named Dr. Caine, had announced. Of all my doctors, I liked him best. He had a shiny bald head that glowed under the hospital lights. He carried peppermints and plastic-wrapped caramel squares in the pocket of his white coat, and when he looked at me, he looked at all of me, not just the parts he'd be cutting and sewing.

Three weeks after Dr. Caine finished up, I would have surgery on my face, a free-flap skin graft during which doctors would remove a rectangular piece of skin from my hip and sew it onto my cheek and chin. The danger there was reabsorption, the body taking the relocated skin and basically sucking it back into itself. I'd gone to the library after school, had snuck into the adult section and found medical textbooks there. In some cases, patients who'd had this kind of surgery looked almost normal—the new skin raised or stretched or discolored or lumpy, but the shape of their faces essentially correct. Others looked bizarre, grotesque, like they'd had bites taken out of their faces, the surgery grinding and swallowing bones and flesh. This, though, my grandmother told me in a phrase that never varied by a word, was "a state-of-the-art procedure." I would have it, and we'd hope for the best.

Finally, the ophthalmologist and the plastic surgeon together would work on my right eye, which drooped and watered and had a tendency to wander when I wasn't paying strict attention. By the first week of September, I'd be, if not healed, then "on the road to recovery" (another one of my grandmother's phrases). The doctors had talked about sending me back to school in some kind of protective plastic mask, which I had privately decided to pocket as soon as I was out of my grandmother's eyesight. *Hope for the best*, I told myself.

In those days, the television sets that patients could rent were boxy, outdated models that were bolted to the ceiling and got three channels. This might have been fine for regular folks, but Grandma decided it wasn't good enough for me. When I checked in on a sunny afternoon in June, I arrived with a twenty-four-inch top-of-the-line Zenith housed in shiny walnut paneling, with a remote control and stereo speakers. Grandma prevailed upon one of the orderlies she'd plied with baked goods to carry it into my room and set it up on a table that she'd convinced a friendly nurse to lend us.

The week before, Grandma and I had gone shopping together at Lord & Taylor downtown, buying pretty new pajamas and nightgowns, three new robes, slippers, and socks. We'd packed a reading lamp to plug into the wall, and board games: checkers and chess, Boggle and backgammon, decks of cards so we could play Crazy Eights. Instead of the ugly green plastic water pitchers most patients used, Grandma brought me one made of acrylic, with a candy-pink swirl that ran through it, and a matching drinking cup and a pink bendy straw to match. The night before the surgeries were to start, we went to the library and chose a dozen books: *Caddie Woodlawn* and *Little House on the Prairie, Anne of Green Gables* and *The Chronicles of Narnia.* "I'll read them to you," Grandma promised, because the doctors had told us there would be times when reading would be uncomfortable for me. My face would be swollen, stitched up, and bandaged after the jaw operation. I'd wear compression bandages once the plastic surgeon did what he could for my cheek, and I'd have a patch to let my eye heal, when I wasn't doing exercises to learn how to track and focus with it again. "Eye gym classes," Grandma called them.

I spent my summer on the fourth floor, in the bed by the window in a room for two, where a bulky air conditioner wheezed and rattled day and night. Most of the children on the floor with me were there for simpler surgeries. They were having their tonsils or appendixes taken out, getting tubes put in their ears, having broken bones set or birthmarks removed. These kids would come and stay for a night or two. Parents and siblings and grandparents and friends would crowd into the room with balloons and presents and get-well-soon cards, cups of Dunkin' Donuts coffee with the orange-and-pink logo, and sheet cakes from Stop & Shop. They'd draw the curtains and imagine I couldn't hear what they were saying through the flimsy cotton. *What's wrong with her? Jesus. Poor thing. Theah but for the grace ah God*, I heard somebody's mother say in a thick Boston accent. *Well, can they fix it?* a boy once asked, and his mother had shushed him and hadn't answered. Once, someone's little sister wandered through the curtains. She stood at the side of my bed, looking down at me thoughtfully.

"Do you have cancer?" she'd asked. She was, I guessed, maybe five or six years old.

"Uh-uh," I said, and shook my head back and forth the few inches I could move against the pillow. This was between Surgery Two and Surgery Three. Most of my head and face was swathed in tape and gauze. The left half of my mouth worked fine, but the right half was immobilized by the bandages, so everything I said came out of the corner of my mouth, sounding like a secret. "I was in a car accident. I'm having operations to fix my face."

She looked at me steadily, staring in a way grown-ups and older children wouldn't let themselves. "What's it look like underneath?"

"There's a scar." With my fingers, I traced the raw red line that extended from the corner of my right eye to the edge of my mouth.

"Does it hurt?" asked the girl.

Because Grandma wasn't there yet, I could tell the truth. "Yeah, it does," I said, "but it's going to get better."

She considered this for a moment. "My brother had food poisoning," she confided. "He's ten. He throwed up everywhere."

I smiled, wincing as the right side of my mouth tried to mimic the upward motion of the left. "Is he feeling better?"

She frowned. "He got a new bike! And he says I can't even use his old one!"

The side of my face was throbbing. It felt like the flesh was being squeezed by a giant invisible fist, a hand that would never let me go. A tear leaked out of the corner of my right eye and trailed underneath to soak the bandage.

"I wish I had food poisoning," the girl said. "I'd throw up if someone would give me my very own new bike. I'd throw up everywhere."

Rage rose inside me, swelling like I'd swallowed a balloon. I found myself suddenly furious at this girl, at her desire to be sick, to be here, and furious at her brother, who, I knew from experience and eavesdropping, would puke and poop for a few days and then go home a few pounds lighter, essentially fine. I was beginning to suspect that I would not ever be essentially fine. My face might never stop hurting, and even if it did, it would probably never look right, no matter what the doctors kept saying.

Just then, a woman pushed through the curtain, coming to collect the little girl. Her gaze touched my face; then she quickly looked away. "Katie, are you being a pest?"

Katie, who had clearly already decided that the universe was a cruel and unjust place, screwed up her face in preparation for a tantrum. "I'm not bothering her, I'm just telling her about how stupid Jared got stupid food poisoned!"

The woman gave her daughter a tight smile, then gripped her shoulders and looked at me . . . or, rather, looked in my direction without looking at me directly, with her gaze focused a few inches above my forehead. It was something I'd noticed grown-ups doing a lot that summer—some of the nurses, most of my roommates' parents. "I'm sorry if she disturbed you, honey."

" 'S okay," I said as clearly as I could with the half of my mouth that moved. Distaste flickered across the woman's face. I could see it before she turned away. I thought about how I must look, my head like a baseball, white and round, with stitches; my hair, normally long and pretty, in two greasy pigtails that lay limp and curled and crusted with blood and the reddish-gold stuff that oozed from my drains, because the doctors hadn't yet given Grandma permission to wash it. *It's human nature,* Grandma had told me when I asked her why people looked at me the way they did, why their eyes went cold, like they were insulted by my face, like it was my fault. *People don't like to see things that aren't perfect. It reminds them of what could go wrong in their own lives, I guess. Their own mortality.* When I'd asked what *mortality* meant, she had told me. *We're all going to die, but some people—most people—don't want to think about that. They want to think they'll live forever, but nobody does.* Grandma did not believe, as she said, in sugarcoating things for me. Life was hard. I'd learned that much already.

"We'll leave you alone, then," the woman said, and steered Katie back through the curtains, where I could hear the new-bike-owning Jared entertaining the crowd with details of how he'd been stricken. "I started feeling sick in fifth period, and I thought I could make it to the bathroom, but then . . ." He made an extremely realistic retching noise. "All over the hallway! Right in front of Mr. Palley's room!"

Everyone laughed. I closed my eyes, falling into a doze, waking to the *click-click* of Grandma's heels in the hallway at six o'clock sharp. It was dinnertime. Every night, a nurse would place my meal on my table, removing the tan plastic cover to reveal whatever the cafeteria had deemed appropriate fare for patients on a soft diet: grayish-brown meatloaf, gummy mashed potatoes, overcooked canned carrots and peas, all of it whirled in a blender and reduced to a paste . . . and every night, Grandma would replace the lid, take the tray, and carry it back out into the hall. Her reasoning was that I was suffering enough that I deserved to have only my favorite things for dinner, and so that's what she would bring me: macaroni and cheese, mashed by hand, matzoh-ball soup with the carrots and celery carefully strained out, corn cut off the cob, topped with a pat of salted butter, chopped up fine. When I could manage real food again, she'd bake cookies and rugelach for the whole floor, preparing tins of baked goods whenever one of the doctors or nurses had a birthday. She'd bring éclairs and glistening sugar-glazed fruit tarts from her favorite bakery on Newbury Street, and I'd tear them into tiny bites with my fingers, letting each bit of pastry or chocolate or cream dissolve slowly on my tongue, filling my mouth with the tastes: rich, salty, bitter, meltingly sweet.

Dinner would be served each night on the china she'd brought from home. There would be real linens, napkins and tablecloths in bright patterns. Grandma would sit in the green plastic-cushioned armchair next to the bed and pick at her own dinner, keeping up a cheerful conversation about what she'd done that day. When she was younger, after my mother was in school, she had worked as a saleswoman at Mills Fine Furniture, the store her husband had founded in downtown Boston. When he'd died, she'd become the owner, but, after a year behind a desk in the back office, she'd decided that she preferred being out on the floor, helping customers decide on the perfect lamp or chair or a just-right dining-room table. She'd hired a manager to handle the payroll and the paperwork, the hiring and the firing, the vendors and the taxes and the rent, and had gone back to work as a saleswoman until she'd retired and moved down to

Florida. There she had stayed, in the same gated community as some of the people she'd known in Boston, playing bridge and mah-jongg and canasta, going on power walks and attending water aerobics classes, until she came back to Massachusetts to take care of me.

Grandma told me how when she'd been, as she put it, "a working girl," she would unlock the store's front doors each morning at ten o'clock, with her hair, in its modified beehive, perfectly arranged, her lipstick freshly applied and her nails manicured and polished pale pink. She would position herself at just the right distance, never hovering or crowding but never too far away, smiling at whoever came through the door: young couples, single women, sometimes entire families, with babies bundled into snowsuits and great-grandparents with walkers and canes. *How can I help you?* she would ask, always managing to sound as if helping them would be the highlight of her day, even if it was 7:55 and the store closed at 8:00 and she'd been on her feet since lunch. *What do you love?* she would ask, instead of *What do you need?*

"Furniture's something people have to live with," she explained to me that summer in the hospital. "A kitchen table, a dining-room chair, the couch in their living room, those are things they're seeing and using every single day. It can't be enough that things are functional," she'd say as she plucked a wilted flower from the bouquet that stood on the table just inside the front door, or brushed a stray lock of hair from my eyes. "They have to be lovely. You have to feel good every time you look at them."

My grandma, I knew, was beautiful, even though she denied it. "Oh, you should have seen me at twenty. Then I was a looker!" She'd shown me pictures of herself on the beach in Atlantic City, in an old-fashioned swimsuit, modestly cut, but still displaying her tanned, rounded shoulders and the tops of her breasts. Her lips were dark with lipstick, and she smiled coyly, her brows lifted in a knowing expression and her hair thick and brown and wavy, the same hair my mother had inherited and passed down to me. Her figure was a perfect hourglass, full hips and bosom with a tiny waist between, and her face was heart-shaped, with generous features, wide-set eyes and full lips that looked pursed for a kiss. She loved clothes and dressed beautifully, in the cuts and fabrics she'd learned would complement her curves—A-line skirts and fitted jackets, narrow belts and blouses she'd have tailored to accommodate her chest.

"Here we are on our honeymoon," she would say, resting her fingertip on her younger self's belly. "And in there . . ."

"My mom!"

"Your mom," she would say, and pull me against her, settling my scarred cheek against the scented warmth of her clothes.

After the accident, Grandma had stayed home with me for a year, and then, when I was four, she'd enrolled me in nursery school at the JCC and gone back to work part-time at Mills Furniture, which she'd sold before moving to Florida. (My father's father had died when he was a child, and his mother, suffering a slow decline from Alzheimer's, was in a nursing home in Maine and in no position to help.) That summer, the summer of my surgeries, Grandma'd go home after work to pick up the food she'd prepared the night before, and then come to the hospital to feed me. "Let's get organized here," she would say, snapping a tablecloth over the table, then wheeling it over to my bed, positioning it over my chest. She'd adjust the bed until I was sitting up, fussing with the books and flowers and water pitcher, straightening my slippers, hanging my robe in the closet. She'd unwrap silverware and napkins, setting me a place even if I was drinking dinner through a straw.

"The Sitter came in again," she'd say, perfectly erect in her chair, with her legs crossed at the ankles, the tip of her right pump resting on the tiled floor and her gold bracelets twinkling on her wrist. She would wear tweed suits in cool pinks and beiges, with sheer stockings and high-heeled T-strapped shoes and, always, a vintage Hermès scarf elaborately wrapped around her neck, because, as she'd confided, "the neck is always the first to go." (*Go where?* I wondered, but I was twelve before I asked.)

"What did you do?" I would ask. The Sitter was a man— Grandma and her coworkers had never been able to determine whether he was homeless or just odd—who would come into the store and then proceed from one chair to another, until he'd sat in every single chair in the entire place. Armchairs, easy chairs, Parsons chairs, and La-Z-Boy recliners—the Sitter would position himself just so, then sigh, and close his eyes, and rock back and forth, "like a man," Grandma said, "who's having a hard time in the bathroom."

"Bite first," said Grandma. I lifted my straw to my lips and took a slurp of chicken-corn chowder, letting it slip down my throat, waiting until she pressed her lips together. "I offered him coffee."

"Really?" To my knowledge, the Sitter never spoke, never acknowledged the presence of other people in the store . . . he just moved from chair to chair, grunting his grunts, wiggling his hips deeper into the cushions, until it was closing time and one of the salesmen would take him by the shoulder and gently steer him out the door.

"Really. I could see him thinking about it." Grandma sank back into her own chair, letting her chin drift toward her chest, pooching out her lips and frowning, and, in that instant, she became the Sitter, a man I'd never seen but could easily imagine. It was a kind of magic she could do, a gesture, a shift in posture, a subtle rearrangement of her features that turned her into someone else. "I didn't think he was going to answer me—you know, he never talks—but after a minute, he said . . ." I leaned forward, all of my pain forgotten, until she said, "'Do you have tea?'"

"So what did you do?"

"Made him a cup of tea, of course, and I gave him some of those thumbprint cookies."

"Apricot or raspberry?"

"One of each," she said. Reaching into the Tupperware container she had in her purse, she put two of the cookies in question onto my tray. As I began to crumble the cookies into manageable bits, she performed her nightly ritual, touching my face gently, examining the bandages, running her thumb from my forehead to my chin on the unblemished cheek. "Is it bad today?"

"Not so bad," I would say, even if it wasn't true. I knew what would happen if I told Grandma it hurt. She would rise instantly to her feet. "Excuse me for a moment," she would say, her voice low, her face calm. I would hear the sound of her heels tapping briskly down the hall . . . and then I'd hear her voice, which would start off quiet and reasonable, then get louder and louder, her Boston accent growing more and more broad. *Why is my granddaughter in pain? Your job is to manage her pain. Now go do your job, or let's find someone who can, because this situation is unacceptable. Ruth is eight years old and she's been through enough.*

I didn't want the nurses or the doctors to be angry at me. I didn't want them to think I was weak. If I couldn't be pretty, in the manner of girls, I'd decided I could be brave, like a boy or a superhero, impressing strangers not with my beauty but by how much I could endure.

"I'm fine," I would tell her. It was my ritual response, and once she'd heard it, Grandma would clear my dishes, scraping or pouring the leftovers into the trash can, rinsing cups and plates in the bathroom sink and piling them into the tote bag she'd brought. Then, with the door closed and, if I had a roommate that night, the curtain around my bed drawn, she'd take off her shoes, turn on the television set, and get into bed beside me.

We would watch TV every night for an hour, from eight to nine, my daily allotment of what Grandma sometimes called "the idiot box." *The Cosby Show* and *Who's the Boss*, reruns of *Star Trek*, and *Murder, She Wrote*, my grandmother's preferred program . . . but our favorite, shown in reruns, was *The Golden Girls*. I loved them all, sarcastic Bea Arthur and sexy Rue McClanahan and sweetly clueless Betty White. I loved that they were friends, sharing a house, in an eight-year-old's fantasy of an every-night slumber party. I loved that Bea Arthur's Dorothy still lived with her mother, and nobody thought it was strange. In my fantasies or, sometimes, in the strange and oddly vivid dreams I'd have after the nurses would give me painkillers, Grandma and I lived in that house. We'd sit in the kitchen, drinking coffee (which I'd never tasted, only seen), making jokes, waiting for Blanche to come home from whatever misadventures she'd had the night before, or for Rose to tell us a story about life in St. Olaf, or Dorothy to talk about her ex-husband, Stan Zbornak.

In Florida, where the Golden Girls lived, the weather was always warm and the skies were always sunny, and no crisis could not be managed in twenty-two minutes plus two commercial breaks. In that happy land, not everyone was beautiful, or young, or perfect. Not everyone had romantic love. But everyone had friends, a family they'd chosen. It was that love that sustained them, and that love, I imagined, could sustain me, too.

That was television for me, a dream of a perfect world, one where I fit in, one where I belonged. It was homemade butter cookies with dabs of jam in their centers, the sun setting outside my window and the air conditioner wheezing away and my grandmother next to me, smelling of Aqua Net and Shalimar, with one arm around my shoulders, her cheek resting on my head. Some nights, exhausted and in pain, dopey with drugs, I would imagine that the glass of the TV set's screen would soften like taffy. I'd stick one finger through the screen, then two fingers, then my hand, my wrist, my arm, my shoulder. I would part the glass as if it was a curtain, and I'd walk into the Golden Girls' ranch house and emerge, in their kitchen or living room, dressed in my robe and pajamas and slippers, unbroken and unscarred, just a regular eight-year-old girl.

Dorothy, in her tunic and loose-fitting pants, would raise an eyebrow. "Well, where did you come from?" she'd ask.

"Oh, leave her alone," Rose would say, bustling over with a cup of cocoa. "Poor thing, she's up way past her bedtime!"

"Picture it," Sophia would begin. "When I was a young girl back in Italy . . ."

"Not this one again," Blanche would say, swooping into the room in a silk peignoir and high-heeled mules. She'd perch on the overstuffed couch, cross her legs, and then pat the cushion, inviting me to sit beside her. "Come here, honey. Take your shoes off. Stay awhile."

When the show was over, Grandma and I would make up stories. What if Sophia and the rest of the girls took a trip back to Italy? What would happen if Blanche got married again and moved away? What was Dorothy's son like, and would we ever get to see him? What if he moved to Florida, too, and fell in love with Blanche's daughter? (Dorothy's son eventually did arrive. He turned out to be gay, a revelation that sailed right over my eight-year-old head.) Grandma would bring me notebooks, leather-bound in robin's-egg blue and pale pink, sometimes with the words MY DIARY in scrolling gold script on the cover. She'd bring boxes of felt-tipped pens, black and red and blue. "Write it down," she would tell me. "Tell me a story." When I'd complain that I didn't know how to spell a word, didn't know how to say what I wanted, or that I was tired, she'd put the pen in my hand, open the notebook to a fresh page, and say, "You're not being graded. Just try."

So we would watch, and when I felt well enough, I would write the continuing adventures of the Golden Girls, sometimes guest-starring Grandma and me. Roommates would come and go, kids with broken legs or tonsil issues, just passing through. Once, I shared a room with a teenager recovering from her high-school-graduation-gift nose job. They wheeled her in just after a nurse had finished changing my bandages. The curtain was open, and, for a moment, we regarded each other. Both of her eyes were blackened, and her nose was in a splint, but, from her expression, I guessed that I looked even worse. "Jesus, what happened to you?" she asked in a froggy, nasal voice, taking in my eye patch and the bandages on my cheek. Her parents shushed her. Grandma glared and jerked the curtain shut. The next morning, the girl was gone, and Grandma and I and our television set were alone again.

The summer slipped by in a syrupy, pain-spiked haze. It was a season without weather, because the hospital always had an air-conditioned chill, a summer without any of the usual markers, picnics or fireworks or trips to the beach. On operation days, nurses would wake me up before dawn and wheel me into the operating room without so much as a sip of water. ("Why so early?" I asked, and my grandmother would make an uncharacteristically cynical face and say, "The doctors don't want to miss their tee times.") "You ready to go?" Grandma would whisper, bending close to me. Those mornings she didn't bother with her makeup. I could see wrinkles around her lips, fanning out from the corners of her eyes, and grooves in her forehead that stretched from her nose to the corners of her lips. Her hair was still dark then—she dyed it, I knew; when I was home, I'd help her brush the solution onto the spots she couldn't reach. She was old, and the doctors and fathers who'd give the pretty nurses appreciative looks all ignored her, but to me, she was beautiful. I knew how she had looked, the beauty she'd once been. That beauty, I thought, was still there, like a layer of a shell hidden under subsequent accretions of mother-of-pearl, but you could see it if you looked closely enough.

"Remember," she would tell me, "I'm going to be right there, waiting right outside." She would hold my hand as they pushed my gurney down the hallway, letting go at the last possible moment, when the doors to the operating room swung open to let me through. Someone would poke a needle into the crook of my arm; someone else would position my head underneath the bright lights. "Count backward from ten," a voice from nowhere would tell me, as the anesthesiologist put a mask over my mouth . . . but I'd never make it past seven. My eyelids would get heavy, my lips and tongue too thick to maneuver, and I'd be gone.

After my last operation I jolted awake, my arms and legs itching, not knowing how long I'd been unconscious—days? Weeks? The right side of my face felt as if it had been soaked in gasoline and set on fire, with the invisible hand back, squeezing, squeezing. My right eye was bandaged and my left eye was stuck shut, the lashes pasted to my cheek with tears and blood and Betadine. The inside of my mouth, where the surgeons did most of their stitching, was so tender that for days all I'd be able to manage would be puddings and ice cream and milk-soaked Life cereal. The television and the notebooks were my anchors, my constants. "Write it," Grandma would tell me, her blouses perfectly pressed, in spite of a day in the August heat. "Write it all down."

"It hurts," I managed, though it was agony to move my jaw and tongue enough to even get those words out.

"I know," said Grandma, stroking my hair. I picked up a pen with hands that felt as thick and clumsy as Mickey Mouse's gloved extremities. I remembered Katie and her mother walking through the curtains, bathed in the sunset's apricot glow, back to the world of normal people, where nobody stared, where girls got normal things I was already sensing would be off limits for me—friends, boyfriends, a husband, a home. I opened the notebook and wrote, *I will never be beautiful.* Then I shut my eyes, turned my face toward the wall, and pretended I'd fallen asleep.

That was the only night I ever saw my grandmother cry. She picked up the notebook, read what I'd written, closed it slowly, and turned toward the window. I saw her reflection in the glass, saw her shoulders hitching up and down, saw tears shining on her cheeks as she whispered, fiercely, over and over, *Not fair, not fair, not fair.* I made myself stop looking, aware that what I was seeing was private, not meant for my eyes. The next morning, her cheeks were dry, her eyes were bright, her lipstick and mascara as perfect as ever. The page I'd written on was missing from the notebook. It had been ripped out so neatly that it took me the rest of the summer to even notice that it was gone.

THREE

I moved to Los Angeles six months after graduating from Grant College, a small and well-regarded liberal-arts institution in Connecticut that had the benefit of being a mere ninety minutes from Grandma and from home. I'd finished with a degree in English literature that I'd earned with highest honors. It hadn't taken me long to realize that the degree qualified me to do precisely nothing except go to graduate school for more degrees. Instead of that, I set my sights on Hollywood, like plenty of people before me who were good writers, devoted viewers, and believed they could combine those skills into a profitable and glamorous career. What set me apart from my peers was that I was the only person I knew who'd made the trip out west with her grandmother.

I wasn't sure how Grandma would feel about my plan, so I'd broached it carefully, and only after doing weeks of research. I had money from the accident, more than enough to support me for the rest of my life, even if I never got a job, if I lived frugally. My parents might not have had the foresight to make out a will, but my father had two college friends who'd gone into the insurance business, and he had obligingly purchased policies from both of them. The settlement, carefully invested by my grandmother, had given me enough to pay all of my medical expenses, and for my college education, with plenty left over to launch me into a life of my own. I felt guilty about having it, knowing how many of my classmates had taken out loans to pay their tuition and were graduating with six figures' worth of debt, but the one time I'd said so, Grandma's lips had tightened, and she'd said, "Divide it by every year of your life you won't have your parents, and you'll see it's not that much." *Divide it,* I heard, *for every year I won't have my daughter.* After that, I didn't complain.

One Friday night in June I laid out my plan, complete with charts and spreadsheets, my best estimations of how much it would cost to live in Los Angeles, with food and rent and car payments, and how long it would take for me to find a job. "I'll give it a year," I told Grandma as she sat, legs crossed, in a pale-pink dress printed with red-and-orange hibiscus flowers, a gold cuff bracelet on one of her narrow wrists and a comb ornamented with pale-pink crystals in her hair. "If I haven't gotten a writing job by then, we can come back east and I'll think about something more practical. Business school or law school." It had never crossed my mind to go without her, to head west alone and leave her behind.

Grandma frowned. "Why a year? Why not two? Why not five? Business school." She shook her head, repeating the words as if they hurt her. "Why would you do that to yourself?"

I tried to explain. "I'm sure a lot of people think they can write television shows."

She shrugged. "Lots of people probably think it. But you actually can."

"Maybe."

"No 'maybe.' Do or do not. There is no try!" During moments of stress, Grandma had a tendency to sound like, or actually quote, Yoda. "I think you're a very good writer."

I shrugged. I'd written for the school paper all through high school, and had won prizes for fiction and poetry in college, but secretly, I'd wondered whether I'd won because I'd been the only one who'd entered. Most of my classmates had enjoyed more active social lives than I'd had, and had spent significantly less time in the library. What did it matter that I'd been named the top student in the English department if I was the only one who was even trying?

Grandma was still mid-soliloquy. "You're the most determined person I've ever met."

"You don't get out much," I countered.

Grandma ignored me. "If anyone can break in out there, it's you."

"Okay," I said. "I figure I'll give it a year."

"Give it two."

"Eighteen months?"

"Fine," she said. "But I'm paying the rent." She folded her hands in her lap, telling me that was that.

"We'll split it. I've got money—"

"I do too," she pointed out. "And I might not have long to live."

"Oh, boy," I said. "Here we go with this again." Whenever she was denied something she wanted—brunch at the Four Seasons for Mother's Day, a freshwater-pearl necklace, an early-morning trip to Provincetown so she could secure street-side seating for the Mardi Gras parade—Grandma would recite her "I might not have long to live" speech, although from all indications she was perfectly healthy and would probably live, as her own mother had, well into her nineties.

"At least let me enjoy my last days on this earth. Hollywood." She stared dreamily into the distance, possibly picturing movie stars and red carpets, limousines and premieres. "I think I've always belonged there."

"Did you ever want to act?" It was embarrassing, but I'd never considered what my grandmother might have really wanted to be, besides a housewife, then a mother and a furniture sales-woman, and then the one who took care of me.

She gave a little *pfft* through pursed lips and a single, dismis-sive shake of her head. "That wasn't an option."

"Why not?"

She was looking at me as if I'd asked why she hadn't spent her young adulthood growing a second head. "It just wasn't something you did. And I had to help my parents. And there was Miltie, of course." Her face softened, the way it always did when she mentioned her baby brother, ten years younger than she was, the one she'd helped raise while her own mother had worked as a cashier in a candy store. "Maybe we could stop and see him on the way."

I had a temp job in a Boston law firm that had started two weeks after I'd graduated, a summer position that stretched into fall. Grandma gave notice at the furniture store, and together, we began the process of picking through fifteen years' worth of possessions: the things my parents had bought, the things Grandma had shipped from Florida, the boxes of old clothes, report cards, and elementary-school art projects, rugs and dishes and pots and pans and hundreds of books. We held a tag sale at the end of September, and spent the following weekends driving trash bags and boxes to Goodwill and the Salvation Army, until the two-bedroom house stood almost empty, with a FOR SALE sign staked in the front yard.

We started our trip just before Thanksgiving, thinking we would meander our way across the country and arrive in Los Angeles the second week of December. I'd found us a short-term furnished rental in what the Internet had assured me was a safe part of West Hollywood, a one-bedroom apartment with a couch in the living room, a full kitchen, and easy access to the 101, the highway that would take me to the Valley. In a crate in the back of Grandma's Cadillac were printed stacks of my résumé and writing samples, the *Golden Girls* and *Friends* spec scripts I'd written, and a garment bag with two interview outfits that I'd bought at Filene's Basement. There was a navy-blue blazer with pants and a matching skirt, the short-sleeved sweaters I'd wear underneath, and the strand of pearls that had been Grandma's wedding gift to her daughter and were now mine.

We stayed at affordable places on the way, stopping off to see Yosemite, the Grand Canyon, and Milt, now well into his seventies, who lived in a condominium in Cleveland and left all three of his television sets on all day long, volume blaring, tuned to ESPN. We spent a single night in Vegas, where I treated us to tickets to see Bette Midler and a meal at a restaurant with actual Picassos on the wall. The next day we were in Los Angeles, where we stayed, at Grandma's insistence, at the Regent Beverly Wilshire—"the *Pretty Woman* hotel!"—for our first three nights in California, at a rate Grandma had bargained for after presenting the bemused clerk with her AAA card and her AARP card and, I suspected, the story of what had happened to my face, while I was out in the cobblestone driveway collecting our luggage (I had managed the trip with a single nylon duffel, while my grandmother had two vintage Louis Vuitton suitcases, a trunk, a hatbox, and three zippered garment bags). "One room," I'd told her, holding up my index finger for emphasis, before leaving her at the front desk. By the time I returned, Grandma was beaming, with the key card in her hand and a bellman waiting with a wheeled cart behind her.

We took the elevator up to the sixth floor of the Wilshire wing. The manager had put us in a suite, with a sprawling living room with a marble bar and a bedroom with two queen-size beds draped in crisp linen coverlets. He'd even sent up a tray of chocolate-covered strawberries, bite-size petits fours, miniature éclairs, and a bottle of sparkling wine.

"What a sweet man," Grandma said, bending down to unbuckle her shoes before sinking onto the gold-velvet-covered sofa with a sigh. The bellman had opened the curtains, and we could see the lights of Rodeo Drive through the windows. There were Chanel, Gucci, and Tiffany, and just up the street, I knew, were Saks and Barneys. I'd have to get Grandma's credit card out of her wallet before I left the next day, I thought as she patted the cushion beside her.

"We're here!" she said. I sat down and gave her hand a squeeze. I thought about what an odd pair we made, me in my jeans and navy-blue long-sleeved T-shirt, running shoes on my feet, my hair pulled back into a bun, and Grandma in her creamy white wool dress, her narrow lipstick-red patent-leather belt, a gold locket at her throat and gold bangles around her wrist and her husband's wedding ring, on its own gold chain, tucked against her heart. I probably looked like her helper, the paid companion to one of the frail little old ladies who lunched. The thought of it made me smile.

I rested my head on her shoulder, with all the miles that we'd driven humming through my body. Grandma could and did drive, but never on highways, not since my parents' accident. I'd have to find us a place to live permanently, one within walking distance of a supermarket and a movie theater and a park, one with a well-equipped kitchen—no dorm-size refrigerator or two-burner stove for my grandmother. Ideally, we would have our own space and our own bedrooms. I'd have to find doctors for the both of us, switch my driver's license from Massachusetts to California, and figure out which grocery stores sold Empire kosher chickens. Focusing on these details let me ignore, for now, the bigger picture: that I had left the only place I'd lived, the only home I'd known, that I had risked everything to come here and try to find work in an industry where there were many more applicants than jobs. But, in that moment, I squeezed her hand again and didn't complain when she picked up the phone to order room service, sliders and quesadillas, a cheese plate, a lobster Cobb salad, and a bottle of white wine.

I got lucky on the apartment hunt. Waiting in line at the DMV, I'd overheard a woman talking about how her brother and his wife had split and had to sublet their place. I excused myself for eavesdropping, then told the bemused woman that my grandmother and I were in the market for a two-bedroom, that we had excellent credit and would be wonderful tenants. The apartment turned out to be a beautiful bilevel in a ten-story building right where Hancock Park became Koreatown. It had a living room and dining room, hardwood floors, a good-size galley kitchen with white subway tiles, two full bathrooms—one with an ancient claw-foot tub—a wrought-iron balcony just big enough for a single chair and half a dozen flowerpots, decent closet space, and big windows to let in the light. The rent was more than I'd planned on spending, but I felt better about writing the checks when I came home on our second night at the hotel and learned that my grandmother had gotten a job.

"Ruthie, look at this!" she said after I'd pushed the door open and found her barefoot in the living room, waving a sheet of paper triumphantly over her head.

"What's that?" I'd asked.

"My call sheet!"

"Your what?"

She grabbed my hands, pulled me down to the couch, and explained. There were services, one of which was actually called Central Casting, where regular people without a single day's acting experience could register. They would submit a picture, give their height and weight and measurements, and list any special skills: juggling, or riding horseback, or even things like being able to speak with a Southern or a Southie accent, or owning a car and possessing a valid driver's license. "Then," Grandma said, "there's a number you call every day, and you hear what parts are available, and you submit yourself, and then . . . you get picked!"

"You got picked!"

"I got picked!" she confirmed. "I'm going to be an extra tomorrow on *Major Medical*."

"Wow." It sounded too good to be true. Grandma looked like she couldn't believe it, either, happy and almost dazed as she smoothed her skirt (black cotton, pleated, trimmed in black eyelet lace) and said, "I wonder if I'll get to meet Brock Cantrell." Brock Cantrell was the star of the show. He played a hunky neurosurgeon tormented by his wife's tragic death (she'd been beheaded by a helicopter's blades on a sightseeing trip to Hawaii).

"I'm not sure how that works." I didn't want her to expect too much. My suspicion, as yet unconfirmed by any real-life TV experience, was that extras were treated in the same manner as furniture and props, that they were kept as far away as possible from the stars and were actively discouraged from making conversation, or even eye contact, with them. But the next day, Grandma came home beaming, dressed in her very best Chanel suit, the one she'd bought for my bat mitzvah, with a signed headshot of Brock in her hand. "To Beautiful Rae," he'd written, then scribbled his signature. Better yet, she'd booked a week's worth of work on *Major Medical*.

As it turned out, senior citizens like my grandmother, the ones who were both ambulatory and with-it enough to get themselves to a set, read a script, and take direction, were in great demand as extras. For our first three months, while I looked for a job, she was the one who'd earned a steady paycheck, starting with background parts and working her way up to actual speaking roles. She made a bunch of extra-friends and learned to speak *Variety*. Words like *sides* and *stand-ins* and *blocking* began to pop up in her conversation. "Can't stay up late," she would announce, getting up from the table to begin loading the dishwasher. "I've got an early call." She knew the names of the men, and the handful of women, who ran the studios, who headed comedy and drama development, who had "ankled" their jobs at the big agencies to set up shop on their own, who'd had his or her development deal force-majeured during the writers' strike of 2008, and who, of the seven writers credited for a movie's script, had actually done the writing (as opposed to who had merely gotten his name on the credits because of Guild arbitration). It was like living with Walter Winchell, but I didn't mind.

In six weeks' time Grandma played a feisty old lady with a heart condition on *Grey's Anatomy*, a feisty old lady with an STD on *House*, and a feisty old lady with a shoplifting problem on *Law & Order: LA*. ("Let go of me, pig!" she'd cried when the security guards had nabbed her in Macy's.) Even on days when she didn't have a single line, when all she had to do was show up, spend an hour in hair and makeup, and then sit under the lights in a pretend restaurant mouthing the words *radishes cabbages broccoli* to the extra sitting across from her, she was happy to do it. She liked being out of the house, spending the day with her fellow extras, close enough to the business of making entertainment that she could have a whiff of the glamour and the fame. She also came home with stories: the tale of the actor who refused to learn writers' names and would make them wear numbered placards during table reads, or the executive who'd thrown a can of Diet Coke at her assistant's head when she'd booked a car service for the wrong day of the week.

While Grandma worked and cooked and established herself, I made the rounds with my résumé, hope in my heart and concealer on my scars. I would wear my Filene's clothes, my skirt and jacket and heels and, on my head, a fedora the color of coffee with cream, accented with an ivory ribbon around the band, that Grandma had found at a boutique on Melrose and bought me as a good-luck gift. She'd shown me how to wear it, tilted to cast a shadow over my disfigured cheek, angled just so. "There," she'd say, giving the brim a final tug before sending me out the door.

I applied to every show, network, and production company that might have use for a hardworking English major who loved to tell funny stories and did not mind fetching coffee or taking her boss's car to be detailed, or even doing the detailing itself, if it came to that. I'd provide my own toothbrush and Q-tips and Armor All for the wheels. I wasn't proud. Day after day, I'd present myself to receptionists and watch their eyes widen when they took in my face. I would find a seat in a room invariably filled with young men and women dressed in their best, although I quickly realized that in Hollywood what constituted one's "best" was jeans with no visible rips or stains and T-shirts without anything too obscene written on the front. I retired my lined navy-blue jacket and skirt and invested in a bright fuchsia cardigan, cropped khakis, and metallic-gold ballet flats. "Polished and pretty," Grandma decreed, nodding her approval.

I started my job search in January, acutely aware that I was looking for employment in a land where beauty was the norm and that, here more than anywhere else, my face might work against me. Sitting in the waiting rooms, listening to the rustle of résumés, the weight of someone else's body shifting in a seat, I'd sneak looks at my competition's faces and wonder, with a sinking heart, whether everyone out here was beautiful, whether they'd all started out wanting to be actors and decided to be writers only after that hadn't worked out. Who'd want to have to look at someone like me every day when they could hire an assistant who was bright and diligent and qualified and also easy on the eyes?

It took me four months to get hired as the assistant to the writer's assistant on a show called *The Girls' Room*. In spite of its name, the show, an hourlong soapy drama-with-jokes about four girls who attended a posh New England boarding school, was created, run, and written almost entirely by men, which nobody seemed to find problematic. "I'll do anything," I'd told Steve Deylin, the showrunner, when he interviewed me. Steve, I knew from the Internet, had started as a writer-producer and moved up steadily until, when the man who created *The Girls' Room* moved on, he was ready to be in charge of the whole thing—the other writers, the directors, the cast, and the crew. "Whatever you need, and I won't complain. I just want to learn."

I showed up early, stayed until the last writer had gone home, paid attention, and never remarked about how, as a graduate from a well-regarded East Coast college, I was surely qualified to do more than fetch sandwiches, schedule haircuts, book Steve's NetJets, and cover for him on the one afternoon when he mistook his NyQuil for DayQuil. The only favor I asked for was to be allowed to sit in the writers' room whenever I could, listening and taking notes and figuring out how a television show came together.

I worked on *The Girls' Room* for three years. I got raises and promotions, and eventually I got to write my own episode. By union rules, sitcoms had to farm out a certain number of episodes each season to freelancers, and after I bombarded my bosses with my spec scripts and pitched jokes whenever they'd let me, they agreed to give me a shot, as long as one of the staff writers signed on to supervise.

The writer who took the assignment was Rob Curtis. Rob was a few years older than I was. He had dark hair laced with gray, ironic oversize horn-rimmed glasses, and an assortment of leather jackets rivaled only by his collection of ex-girlfriends. By the end of my first week as an assistant, I'd learned that women who came to read for Diner Waitress One or Busty Woman on Subway were also unwittingly auditioning for the part of Girl Who Will Sleep with Rob This Weekend. I also learned that

Rob was not very good at closure. He'd love them and leave them, usually so abruptly that the woman didn't realize she'd been left. At least once a month, one of Rob's ladies would call the show's offices demanding, in tones that ranged from screechy to weepy, to speak with him. "Who?" Rob would ask when I'd relay the message. He'd stroke his chin thoughtfully, making a show of trying to remember Jane or Joelle or Jessica. "Can you tell her I'm in a meeting?" he'd ask in a winsome tone that stopped working on me after the first dozen times he'd used it. I decided that cleaning up a staff writer's romantic messes was not part of my job. "I'm transferring you right now," I'd say, and give Rob a hard look. He'd drag his feet as he made his way to his office, eyes on the carpet, and shut the door before picking up his extension. *Sweetheart! How are you doing? Yeah, I meant to call, it's just been crazy-busy over here . . . Hey, can you send me your new head shots? Because I really think you've got something special.*

Sitting at my desk, where the hole-puncher stood at right angles to my computer screen, where there were extra umbrellas and Advil and cell phone chargers and a binder full of take-out menus stowed in my deep bottom drawer, I would think, smugly, that I'd never fall for someone like Rob, with his smooth talk and his good looks and his obvious *Sure we'll cast you* lies. I wasn't that shallow, I told myself, and I wasn't that dumb. But Rob snuck up on me, not with his looks or his charm but with the seductive notion that we were both Hollywood outsiders, that the two of us had our faces pressed up against the glass as we stood in the rain and looked in at a party to which we hadn't been invited, interlopers in a world that didn't really want us there.

Rob had grown up in Los Angeles, but his parents weren't industry people. His father owned a car wash, his mother did hair in Beverly Hills. Rob went to not-great public schools and then got an athletic scholarship to USC. Like me, like almost every writer I knew, he'd started his career as an assistant . . . but because of his talent, combined with his visible indifference to the opinions of others (which, of course, made everyone work harder to earn his approval), he moved up fast. By the time he was twenty-eight, he was a co-executive producer of *The Girls' Room*. He had a house on Topanga Canyon with three bedrooms and a pool. He drove a black Audi with a series of numbers and letters after its name that meant something to people who knew about cars, and he sent his parents money every month, which I knew because I'd heard him mention it on the phone. By all visible signs, Rob had made it . . . but when we were together, he'd let me know he wasn't one of them, a child of privilege. He'd roll his eyes at one writer's mention of his prep school or another's stories about her parents, both psychiatrists on New York's Upper West Side. He made me believe that it was us against the world, that we were two outsiders plotting our takeover of an industry determined to keep us down.

"So what do you think?" he would ask the room as we worked on a scene where the girls of *The Girls' Room* were dealing with a romantic crisis, the way they did most weeks. Technically, he was asking the whole room, but his eyes would go to me first, as if he knew that I was the one who could be counted on to come up with something that would work. He'd rock back in his chair, long legs extended, taking up space while we pitched ideas. Maybe Cara could plan a surprise party for Lily? Maybe there could be some kind of Cyrano action, one of the girls hiding somewhere, feeding the other one her lines? He'd nod silently, or not nod, holding still, and we'd all try again and try harder, until we came up with the idea or scene or bit of dialogue that finally got him to smile.

When we have our own show, it'll be different, Rob would tell me when I'd mention, in as non-whiny a tone as I could, that there was something deeply suspect about a show about women, that starred women, that purported to tell women's stories, and was written almost entirely by men. *That's a one-percenter,* he'd say quietly after the yeast-infection joke I'd pitched was met with groans and grimaces instead of laughter (a one-percenter, in writers' room parlance, was a joke that only one percent of viewers could be expected to understand). Rob and I were united in our desire to change the world, or at least our little piece of it; unwavering in our belief that we could write something more true, more funny, more meaningful than the soap-opera antics put on every week by *The Girls' Room,* a show that depended largely on love triangles and a Mysterious Stranger from the Past showing up. In the three years the show had aired, all but one of the four starring girls had learned she'd been adopted. One of the writers' room jokes was that the show should have really been called *Which One of You Bitches Is My Mother?* We shared a common distaste for Taryn Montaine, the beautiful, stupid, black-hearted, and abusive star of the show.

"You know, she did porn," Rob told me, straight-faced and matter-of-fact, at the end of three painful hours the writers' room had spent rewriting a script after it became obvious that Taryn, like the presidents Bush before her, could not, under any circumstances, pronounce the word *nuclear.*

"She did not," I said.

"Well, not porn, exactly. Soft-core stuff. Like on late-night cable." Rob turned his laptop around to face me, eyebrows raised in a wordless challenge, and we spent the next hour online, slipping down the rabbit hole of blurry close-ups of what may or may not have been nipples. "That," he would say, tapping the screen with the cap of a Sharpie, like a historian reviewing the Zapruder tape; "that is, conclusively, her ass."

"How would you know?"

"Because she flashes all the boy writers whenever she can. You know that, right?"

I nodded. I'd never seen firsthand evidence of Taryn's much-discussed penchant for coming to her dressing-room door wrapped in just a towel (which would ride up or slip down) or showing up on set in tops that were low-cut, see-through, or both, but I'd been around long enough to know that it had made her a great favorite with the show's carpenters and electricians.

"Also, her name used to be Terry Mastrontonio."

"Shut up."

"Check it out," he said. "Next time you print the budget, take a look. We're still cutting checks to her name. And," he continued gleefully, "she's got a mustache." Fingers thumping over my keyboard, he logged on to *TMZ* and pulled up a picture of Taryn on vacation, sprawled on a beach in a remote part of Mexico, miles away from civilization and, evidently, her waxer.

"Oh, dear," I said, looking, as my heart lifted. Whatever was wrong with my appearance, facial hair wasn't one of my problems.

I knew it was ungenerous and unkind; that picking on Taryn made me no better than the people who stared at my face and whispered behind my back; but the truth was, it felt good to be part of a conspiracy of two writers bonded by their mutual loathing of an overpaid and undertalented TV actress. Rob and I could riff for days on Taryn's shortcomings . . . or, rather, Rob could riff, and I would laugh, all notions of sisterhood and solidarity abandoned because, really, would Taryn have defended me if the tables had been turned? Doubtful. This was a woman who hadn't bothered to learn my name; a woman who'd asked her agent to ask the showrunner if some other assistant could drop off scripts and wardrobe at her dressing room because—and I quote—"the one with the messed-up face kind of freaks me out? Like, no offense? But it's bad energy, y'know?"

Rob and I were sent out on script for ten days, which meant we weren't expected in the office and could just write. It was

Rob's idea that we meet each morning at the pool at the Regent Beverly Wilshire, where I'd stayed with Grandma when we'd gotten to town and where, it turned out, he'd worked as a busboy when he was a teenager. Each morning, we'd take over one of the tables for four and order lavish brunches (charged to the show, of course): lobster eggs Benedict, bowls of fruit salad and house-made granola and yogurt, berry smoothies and iced coffees. Then, with the plates cleared and our laptops open, we'd work until we hit our seven-page-per-day quota. Our episode was entitled "Gone to the Dogs." The premise was simple: Taryn and her classmates help out a teacher by dog-sitting her pup. On a trip to the park, they lose the dog. Hilarity ensues. The high point of the show, at least from my perspective, was that Taryn would spend the entire second act locked in a Porta-Potty. Petty, yes, but I'd take my revenge where I could find it.

"So how would she walk, exactly?" Rob asked me after I'd pitched a scene where Taryn's character was describing a too-ambitious bikini wax.

"You just want to see me look foolish," I said. Then I pushed my chair back, stood up, and made my way around the edge of the pool in a bow-legged waddle. Rob laughed and then grabbed my hand and waddled along with me. "Like this?"

"Perfect." He was flirting with me. No big deal. Rob flirted reflexively with everyone, including the sixtysomething cleaning lady named Dolores who pushed her trash can into our bungalow at eight o'clock every night, and the cashier at the commissary who'd dyed her hair the color of meringue and spit when she gave you your change. But I had never had a boyfriend, had never really dated, and I was so taken with him, his handsome face, his charm, that I decided, over the ten days we spent together, we were in love.

The day we turned in our script, we went back to the office and spent an afternoon in the writers' room, reading through what we'd written, with each writer playing a part (typically, I read Taryn's lines, in a not-nice Valley Girl drawl). "Good stuff," said Steve, which, from him, counted as a ticker-tape parade. Rob rummaged in the pantry refrigerator until he found a bottle of wine left over from our premiere party. Together, we drank most of it as the sun went down and the lot emptied, until finally I found the courage to make the move I'd rehearsed a hundred times in my head. We'd been talking about nothing—Rob's plans for the weekend, his parents' upcoming anniversary—when I'd crossed the room and kissed him, first his cheek, then his neck, then his lips.

"Hey, whoa there," he said, laughing, holding my wrists in a playful grip.

"I love you," I told him—words that would stab at me every time I thought about that night. Before he could answer, and before I could look at the expression on his face and see if it was shocked or, worse yet, horrified, I went down on my knees on the scratchy industrial carpet and proceeded to give him the first-ever blow job of my life (I'd perfected my technique by downloading some of the soft-core movies we'd surfed in search of Taryn).

He didn't say anything, but I heard him groaning and felt his hands in my hair, holding me in place. "Oh, God," he sighed as his hips thrust forward and he came in my mouth. I gulped— the porn hadn't told me that semen would taste like hot, salted Clorox—coughing and sputtering but determined to do this right. With my scarred cheek resting against his thigh, I tried not to think about how he hadn't said my name, or offered to reciprocate in any way, or how he hadn't even tried to kiss me. We were a couple. The sex—such as it was—proved it. Now we could launch our future together, our brilliant and funny future as writing partners and partners in life.

That was not what happened. What happened was that Rob

didn't show up at my grandma's party the night our episode debuted. When I got to work the next day, the showrunner called me into his office and asked if I'd heard the happy news. Rob and Taryn had eloped the day before . . . and Taryn, Steve told me as gently as he could, was pregnant.

I sat there, stunned, speechless, reeling, ashamed beyond comprehension. I had never suspected that Rob and Taryn had shared so much as a sandwich. (Not that Taryn ate sandwiches. Not that Taryn, as far as I could tell, ate anything—she was slim as a ribbon, with long arms and coltish legs and not a single ripple of cellulite.) "But he hates her," I'd said, thinking of the hours upon hours, the days upon days that Rob had spent making fun of Taryn: her complete ignorance of world history and current events, her inability to memorize any speech more than two lines long, the way she acted mostly with her hair and her cleavage, her default pose of breasts sticking east and ass jutting west.

"I guess maybe he doesn't hate her that much," Steve had said. The way he'd spoken, the look he'd given me, all of it announced, as clearly as if he'd said it out loud, that everyone in the office knew the way I felt about Rob. Maybe they even knew what had happened between us the night we'd both stayed late after the read-through of the script we'd written together.

I'd made my way back to my desk, trying to convince myself that it couldn't be true. It had to be some kind of elaborate writers' room prank, like the time Steve had told the writers that Trojan was giving away ten-thousand-dollar prizes to the person who made the best video about his first time using what he referred to solemnly as "the product." Steve had generously agreed to let the writers use his flipcam to tape their entries. Then, after they'd emailed their submissions to an in-box he'd set up, he'd compiled them all and posted them on YouTube under the headline "There Is Hope," with a note that read, "Attention, geeks of America. As this video clearly reveals, geeks grow up and have sex, too!" The writers had responded by having Steve's Bentley bronzed like a pair of baby shoes (the bronze was a special-effects shell that peeled right off, but when Steve saw his car, he fell to his knees in the parking lot, wailing, "My baby! My baby!" . . . a moment that the writers, of course, had captured on camera and posted on YouTube). Maybe it was finally my turn to get pranked. In five minutes, the door would swing open, and there would be Rob, with a pie box in his hands and a delighted grin on his face. "Fooled ya! Fooled ya!" he'd chant, and then he'd take me by the hand to a room at the Regent Beverly Wilshire and do to me what I'd done to him. I waited five minutes. I waited an hour. I waited all morning. The door never opened. Rob never came back.

FOUR

So tell me the timeline," my boyfriend, Gary, said as he walked out of the parking garage on Camden Street, on our way to the kickoff dinner the network was throwing for *The Next Big Thing*. I reached for his hand and was pleased and a little relieved when he let me take it and gave me a reassuring squeeze. When we stopped at the light, I looked at him, marveling, as I often did, that he was actually interested in me, that we were actually a couple. Gary had pale skin, dark hair and dark eyes, and a cleft in his chin that I would jokingly suggest filling with various dips and toppings for my snacking pleasure. He'd gotten dressed up—or at least his version of dressed up—for the occasion, wearing a belt with his jeans, black leather shoes instead of sneakers, and a sportscoat instead of a fleece. True, there was an ink stain on his cuff, but he was here and he was trying, and I felt lucky, loved and lucky, with him at my side. I had a show. I had a great guy. What more could I, could any woman, want?

"The timeline for tonight or the timeline for the show?" I asked. The light turned green. Gary dropped my hand and started walking, so that I had to half run to catch up.

"Show," he said.

"Okay. Well, let's see. We start pre-production next week, and for the next eight weeks I'll be working on the pilot. I'll have to cast it, of course, and hire a director, and a DP—a director of photography—and a line producer . . ." I paused, waiting for him to ask what a line producer did, so I could tell him that a line producer handled all the details related to the business side of shooting a show, but Gary didn't ask. My voice was high and chirpy, slightly breathless from hurrying, as I kept talking. "So. We'll hire people, and build the sets, and rewrite and rehearse, and then we'll shoot it over two days, and edit it, and turn it in to the network, and wait for them to decide if they're going to pick it up and order it to series . . . and if they do, we'll make more."

"How long will all that take?" he asked as we walked across Beverly. The dinner was at a steakhouse called Mastro's, a few blocks from Rodeo Drive, with its boutiques and jewelry stores, close to where Grandma and I had stayed when we'd first come to town.

"Depends. Six weeks, eight weeks, something like that." The wind gusted, threatening to blow open my wrap dress and dislodge my hat. I clamped one hand down on top of my head, and struggled with my skirt with the other.

"So you're going to be waiting all over again?"

"Yup," I said, trying to sound cheerful about the prospect. "The network will make holding deals with the actors, so they can't go off and work on something else. Say we get picked up in May. I'll hire writers and bring back everyone I worked with on the pilot, assuming I liked them and the network or studio doesn't want to replace them. We'll start shooting in June and shoot all summer, depending on the order: if they want nine episodes, or eleven, or thirteen. The new shows premiere in September, unless we're a midseason replacement, in which case January. And . . . that's it."

"That's it?" His voice was flat, his tone uninterested, his expression impossible to read in the darkness as he walked with his hands jammed in his pockets and his head down. He looked like a guy being led to the guillotine instead of to a party.

"That's it. Then you have to wait to see if you get good reviews, and if you find an audience, and if you get renewed."

"It's a lot of waiting," Gary observed.

"It's not so bad," I said, trying not to sound disappointed. All I wanted was for Gary to be happy for me, to be as thrilled as I'd felt since I'd gotten the pickup, and all he'd done was ask picky questions, pointing out the problems, prodding at the soft spots, how long it would take to hear from the network or the audience, and how brutally the odds were stacked against me.

It was January in Los Angeles, still warm enough to go out at night with only a light wrap. After a childhood in New England, I missed the seasons—the crisp fall air, the showers of dogwood and magnolia blossoms in May—but I'd grown to love L.A.'s weather—the warm winter days, the cool desert nights, the weeks that could pass without a cloud in the sky (except for the ever-present smog). Gary handed his leather jacket to the coat-check girl, I tucked my cashmere wrap into my bag, and we followed a hostess up the stairs covered in carpeting the color of rare prime rib, past a man playing Cole Porter on the piano and a line of beautiful women—escorts, I guessed—who were sitting at the bar, long legs crossed, glossy hair and perfect bodies on display. Every one of them had probably been the prettiest woman in her high school, her college, her hometown. Here in Los Angeles, though, beauty was as common as the oranges that grew on the trees everyone had in their backyards. As we walked past, I imagined their eyes on me, wondering what had happened to my face, grateful that it hadn't happened to them. The high-ceilinged room was noisy with the sounds of conversation, silverware, and the muffled pop of a Champagne cork, and the air smelled like seared meat.

"Here we are," said the hostess, dropping us off at the entrance to a wine room toward the back of the second floor. When I walked in, the executives started clapping and I bent my head, embarrassed. There was a sign on the wall that read THE NEXT BEST THING. I wanted to take a picture, freeze the moment, live in it forever.

"How about a toast!" said Lisa from the studio. She was dressed in her usual loose-legged trousers and high-heeled boots, a sweater and a chiffon scarf elaborately wrapped around her neck. Today the pants were pale gray, the sweater was black, and the scarf was shades of green from emerald to mint. There were ten of us at what had been billed as a small getting-to-know-you dinner, a celebration before we'd officially begin the work of building *The Next Best Thing*. Lisa and Tariq were there representing Lodestar, the studio that had produced my show, then sold it to ABS. From the network, there were Joan and Lloyd, who until the previous week had been Joan's assistant, but had since been promoted to vice president of comedy. Both of my former bosses, the Daves of Two Daves Productions, were there—David Lieberman, with his wife, Molly, and David Carter, with his girlfriend, an entertainment lawyer named Shazia Khan, who was possibly the most beautiful woman in the room, if not the entire restaurant.

Shazia's skin was honey brown, her wide eyes were accented with perfectly arched brows, and her teeth glowed a bluish white that made them look slightly radioactive. She wore a red dress with gold accents, an outfit that was not exactly a sari but that somehow managed to suggest a sari, and jeweled gold sandals on her high-arched feet. Shazia's father was Persian, a philosophy professor at Princeton, and her mother was Swedish, an actress in art-house films. Shazia was what you got when you combined those two exemplary gene pools. Not only was she beautiful, but she had an undergraduate degree from Columbia and a law degree from the University of Chicago, and was regularly named as one of the most powerful attorneys in town. None of the men in the room could take their eyes off her. David Lieberman—Big Dave—was especially solicitous.

"Is he ignoring you?" he asked Shazia, gesturing toward his partner, who sat in his wheelchair. Dave Carter—Little Dave— wore a tweed sportsjacket, a white button-down shirt, and khaki pants. His shoes—brown leather loafers—were perfectly pristine, because Dave had never taken a step in them. He was paralyzed from the waist down, the result of a boating accident he'd had the summer after college. Paralysis had not prevented him from becoming one of the most successful producers in Hollywood, or from dating a parade of women, each one more lovely and accomplished than the one before.

"Do you need anything?" Big Dave asked. Shazia gave him a patient, practiced smile, the kind of smile she must have dispensed a dozen times every day to parking-lot attendants, waiters, and deliverymen and just random male strangers on the street. "Another drink?" Big Dave persisted. "Something to eat? Want to wear my jacket? Take all my money? Anything?"

"Honey," said Big Dave's wife. "Put your tongue back in your mouth and get Ruthie some wine." Molly Lieberman smiled at me. Molly could afford to be indulgent. Her blond hair, blue eyes, pink cheeks, and Barbie-doll body might have made her looks a little more pedestrian than Shazia, but she was a former Miss Teen America who'd worked steadily on TV shows and in films, mostly horror movies, where she'd be chased through a dark house and murdered in the first ten minutes. At twenty-six, she'd married Dave Lieberman. At twenty-eight, she'd had twins and had since all but retired from acting. Like many Hollywood wives, she worked as a decorator. Unlike many Hollywood wives, who treated their job as a hobby and spent their time redecorating one another's houses, Molly was actually good at her job—she'd taken classes, done an internship at *Elle Décor,* apprenticed herself to one of the top commercial designers in town, and now made more money than she had as an actress. Molly moved with the confidence of a woman who never doubted her place in the world, her good looks, her husband's love and loyalty. That night, she was dressed in her usual surfer-girl chic, a floor-skimming halter-style maxi dress in a floaty chiffon, with a slightly threadbare lavender sweater wrapped loosely around her shoulders. She had Havaiana flip-flops on her feet, and a necklace bearing diamond charms that spelled the initials of one of her sons' names around her neck. Her hair hung in loose, beachy waves that floated down to the center of her back.

After she'd dispatched Dave to the bar, Molly reached over and adjusted the brim of my hat. I tried not to blush, or to grin like an idiot—a real live movie star, touching my things, treating me as if I belonged! "How are you?" Molly asked, sounding as if she actually cared. "Are you thrilled?"

"Thrilled," I repeated. The truth was, I was still in a state of disbelief that something I'd written, something I'd thought up in the privacy of my own bedroom, and on long walks, and while I was in the pool or the shower, was actually going to be cast and shot and might, if everything went well, someday be shown on TV.

Molly looked over my shoulder. "And how about you, Gary?" she asked. "Your girlfriend's blowing up!"

Gary managed a smile and bobbed his head in a quick nod.

"Who's going to be there?" he'd asked when I'd told him about the dinner. "Nobody special," I'd said, knowing that if he'd known that Molly and Shazia, both the Daves, and the head of comedy for the network were coming, he'd find a way to be busy, or sick, or out of town. "I'd really appreciate it if you'd come," I told him. "It'll be fun," I'd said. I'd emailed him reviews of the restaurant, which was supposed to have the best rib eye in town, extra-strong martinis, and warm butter pound cake for dessert, and I had been extra-solicitous in bed. Finally I'd given him what amounted to an ultimatum: *Please come. I need you there.* He'd squirmed, with his hands in his pockets and his eyes on the ground. "It doesn't sound like my kind of thing," he'd said.

"But it's my kind of thing," I'd pointed out, and added that I'd gone to his school's end-of-year potluck picnic, that I'd chatted with his colleagues and even gotten into the principal's swimming pool, scars and all. *Why is it not your thing?* I wanted to ask . . . but part of me didn't want to know the answer and just hoped that he'd be a good boyfriend and come with me.

Gary and I had met in the coffee shop where I'd retreated after things had fallen apart with Rob and I'd left *The Girls' Room.* I'd run ads on Craigslist advertising my services—for a fee, I'd help high-school seniors craft their college essays. Gary had watched me working and asked if I could help him with his personal ad on Match.com, where he was flying, unnoticed and un-dated, under the handle "Lonelyguy." ("Why?" I'd asked him. "Was 'Desperate, Creepy Stalkerguy' taken?'")

We'd agreed on a fee. I'd interviewed him and learned that he was a high-school teacher, the middle of three children from St. Louis, that he'd come to Los Angeles with a girlfriend, that things hadn't worked out but he didn't regret the move, because he loved the California weather, the chance to spend most of his time in shorts and sandals and see the ocean every day. The ad I'd written spelled out his good qualities, his patience and consideration, his dry sense of humor, and then I discovered that I had feelings for him, and, much to my surprise, that he had feelings for me, too.

Gary was my first real boyfriend, the first man I'd gone to bed with, and things had been wonderful. At least, they'd been wonderful when I was just the Two Daves' assistant. When I'd realized I was thinking about Little Dave more frequently, and in different ways than an employee should think about her boss, I'd told myself it was just a workplace crush, destined to go nowhere. David Carter was ten years older than I was, and in a wheelchair, and the women he dated were so far out of my league that they might as well have represented some evolutionary leap forward from human females as I knew them. Gary was steady and funny and reliably kind. We'd bring in a pizza and watch movies on a Friday night, take trips on the weekends to the zoo or the park or the beach. I thought—when I wasn't fantasizing about Dave dumping Shazia, or the gorgeous research cardiologist he'd dated before her, or the stunning actress who'd preceded the doctor, and declaring that I was the one he loved— that maybe someday Gary and I would get married. We'd buy a house in the Valley, where you could get more for your money, a place convenient to the private school where he taught, with a swimming pool and a guest house where Grandma could stay. I'd write screenplays, he'd teach history, and we would live out the non-glamorous Hollywood version of happily ever after. I would think about it . . . but it would be like thinking in outline, life as a series of occasions without any of the dialogue or description filled in. I could name the orderly procession of events—getting married, buying a house, having children—I just couldn't imagine actually doing them with Gary. There was no reason why this should be: I loved him, I enjoyed his company, his sense of humor, his good looks . . . but when I tried to imagine the specifics—standing under a chuppah with him, or greeting him with a positive pregnancy test—my mind would shut down. When my pilot had been ordered, it felt like a good excuse to stop thinking about why that was, to simply apply myself to the work at hand and hope that my romantic future would sort itself out while I tended to my show.

Ever since I'd gotten the call, though, things had gotten worse, not better. I'd thought that Gary, who'd always been supportive, my biggest cheerleader, my number one fan, would be thrilled for me, and that maybe I'd be able to picture more of a future together when I had the grown-up job title "executive producer and showrunner." Instead of being an assistant, I'd have assistants of my own, and responsibility for a staff of actors and directors, gaffers and grips, set decorators and stand-ins that would eventually number close to two hundred. None of this would change the content of my character, just the size of my bank account. I would be, still, the woman I'd always been: same personality, same dreams, same face. But Gary had changed, becoming quiet and sullen and hard to reach. I'd dial his number and be sent straight to voice mail. Or we'd make plans and then he'd cancel at the last minute. In the past few weeks, he'd taken on extra work at school, agreeing to coach the chess club, offering extra Spanish tutoring sessions. He'd said that he could use the money, but that made no sense: I'd be earning four times what I'd be making as an assistant if the show got picked up, and the pilot shoots alone would give me more than enough to pay for our usual entertainments, and even fund a few weekends out of town, if we found time to take them . . . but when I pointed this out, he got even quieter, and every time I'd started to ask my grandmother what it meant, and why he was behaving as he was, I'd stopped before I'd started, part of me convinced that I did not want to know the answer. *At least he's here*, I thought, and told myself that Gary's presence in a roomful of executives and showrunners meant that he was coming around to accepting my new role . . . but the look on his face before he brought his wineglass to his mouth and drained it strongly suggested that he'd rather be anywhere else, anywhere but in this room, with these people.

Waiters bustled to refill glasses and set out wooden platters of appetizers, sliced cured meats and house-made buffalata,
ceramic dishes of glossy rosemary-brined olives, warm Parker
House rolls with ridged pats of butter and silver-dollar-size
mother-of-pearl dishes of sea salt on the side. Lisa beamed at
me. "To Ruthie," she said, with her glass held aloft, "and to *The
Next Best Thing*. May it run for a hundred episodes."

"A hundred episodes!" everyone echoed. Glasses were
clinked. More wine was poured. Little Dave, sitting in his chair
with a glass of wine in one hand and his arm unself-consciously
around his date's waist, gave me a smile and lifted his glass.
"Enjoy this," he said. "It's as good as it's going to get."

I bent down to hear him better, glad for the excuse to get
close. "What do you mean?"

"I mean," he said in his calm, cultured voice, still with its
hint of a New England accent, even though it had been years
since he'd come west, "that they haven't made a hash of it yet."

"Made a hash of it?" I must have sounded skeptical, because
Dave gave me a wry smile.

"I forget. You weren't around when *The Girls' Room* got off
the ground. Or *Bunk Eight*. You don't know what it's like to
have your vision . . ." He paused, letting his gaze rest on each of
the executives as he sought out the right word. "Adulterated," he
finally said.

I took another sip of wine, conscious of Gary, who was standing in the corner with one of the waiters. "I know things change
once you're in production," I said. "I've been working in the business for five years, you know. Remember? I'm the one who sits
at the desk outside your office? Reads the scripts? Sets up your
lunches? Listens in on the notes calls? Goes to all the tapings?"

"Ah," said Dave. "But it's different when it's yours." Before
I could ask him to explain or tell him the seventeen reasons I
believed my show would not, in fact, be adulterated, the waiters

ushered us toward the table. Dave wheeled himself into the space left empty between Shazia and Lloyd. I took a spot at the foot of the table. In spite of Dave's warning, in spite of Gary's obvious unhappiness, I couldn't stop smiling. *My show*, I thought, picturing the sign taped to the door, as I chatted with Joan, discussing actresses who might be right to play Daphne Danhauser, the lead, and her Nana Trudy. *My show.*

There was roasted pork loin with fennel, seared rib eyes with truffle butter, and whole grilled branzino for the main course. Bottles of Riesling and Malbec were emptied and replaced and emptied again. Then came coffee and cordials and the famous butter pound cake, served with mounds of whipped cream, and salt-sprinkled dark-chocolate brownies on a wheeled cart. Afterward, groaning and vowing not to eat for a week, we all walked out to the valet stand, and I waited, thanking everyone, until the executives had departed and Big Dave had eased his frame into the tiny sports car he drove and Molly, who, sensibly, refused to contort herself into the passenger seat, had hopped into her Range Rover, and Little Dave had wheeled himself up the ramp of his Mercedes van, after holding the door for Shazia and closing it once she was in. Then, finally, it was just me and my boyfriend, standing in the windy street.

"That," said Gary, "was awful."

I turned toward him, the frustration I'd ignored all night bubbling up. "Why? What was so awful about being in a roomful of people I'm going to be doing my show with? People who are actually, oh, I don't know, happy for me?"

Gary ducked his head. "This isn't working," he said in a low voice.

I felt my chest contracting, as if I'd been punched. "What?"

Gary pulled off his glasses and blinked at me as he rubbed the lenses on his shirttail. "I'm proud of you. Or I'd like to be. I can't ask you to go backward, to just be an assistant for the rest of your life. You want bigger things." He spread his hands, smiling sheepishly. "Me, I'm just a teacher."

"What do you mean, just a teacher? That's the most important work there is." *No,* I thought. *Oh, please, no.* I was remembering our two-year anniversary, a trip we'd taken to Desert Springs. We'd taken side-by-side mud baths, giggling in the steamy, sulfur-scented weedy water, Gary grumbling about how he was going to be picking twigs out of various crevices for weeks to come. We'd had dinner in a fancy restaurant at what used to be Cary Grant's estate, sitting outside, and when I'd gotten cold, Gary had gone inside and come back out with a wool blanket for my lap.

The wind gusted. I yanked my hat down around my ears and reached for him. He stepped backward and then held my hands, taking pains to keep plenty of space between our bodies.

"You're important," I told him. "What you do is so incredibly important. It matters more than anything, more than any dumb TV show, and I'm sorry if I haven't been making you feel that way."

He shook his head and dropped my hands, running his fingers through his hair. "It's not you. It's not that. You haven't done anything wrong. Those people," he said, tilting his head up toward the restaurant, "they're, like, a different species or something."

"The women, maybe," I muttered.

Gary kept talking. "They're just so different. They don't care about the same things that I do."

"What do they care about?" I asked. I was simultaneously feeling panicky sorrow and honest curiosity. How did Gary see himself in relation to the executives and showrunners and Hollywood girlfriends and wives we'd just shared a meal with? How did he really see me?

Gary spread his hands wide again. "Ah, you know. They care

about making money. It's not about art, or drama, or telling the best stories, or trying to make the world a better place. It's just selling stuff. Selling airtime to the advertisers. Selling stories to the viewers. Like that."

I stared at him, wondering when he'd turned into a communist, or whatever he'd become, and how I'd failed to notice. "Is that what you think I am?" I asked. "That I don't care about art or craft or storytelling? That I'm just a sellout?"

He shook his head, but he didn't do it immediately, and he didn't do it very hard.

"I don't understand," I said. My voice was raw, and my belly was knotted. Everything hurt. "I wrote something people like, and now a network wants to put it on the air. What did I do . . ." I felt my throat tighten as I forced the words out. "What did I do that's so wrong?"

"Nothing," said Gary, sounding tired. "You didn't do anything wrong. It's me." He made a sweeping gesture, one that took in the restaurant, the road, the valet stand, the glitter of the shops, the high-end sedans and SUVs and sports cars stopped at the traffic light, cars that each cost more than he'd make in three years of teaching. "This isn't the kind of life I want for myself, and those aren't the kind of people I'm ever going to be comfortable with."

And now I'm one of them, I thought. *One of those people.* When I'd been an assistant, or when I'd supported myself editing kids' college essays about how their class trip to Paris gave them a new perspective on the world, or how the night their father won an Oscar had changed their lives, I'd been fine, just another L.A. striver with more dreams than successes. But now . . .

Gary took my hands once more. "I want you to be happy. I want you to find someone to be happy with, someone who wants all of this, who's going to be happy for you. But it's not for me. Do you understand?"

I thought I did. Maybe *I don't feel comfortable with these people* was what Gary told himself or maybe even what he really believed, but I thought the truth was different and far less flattering. The truth, I thought, was that Gary liked it when we were both in the same place, a just-starting-out teacher and an unemployed television writer, both of us trying to take that next crucial step forward. Now I'd leapt ahead, vaulting over him, and he didn't like being left behind, and I didn't know if I could face what was coming all by myself, all alone. It was too much. I couldn't do it without him . . . but I wasn't going to beg. Maybe the fantasy of Dave would be better than the reality of Gary. Maybe somehow it would be enough to sustain me.

"You know what?" I heard myself saying through numb lips. "Maybe it's for the best. I'm going to be so busy. Even if we don't get picked up. You know, so many of the shows get shot in Vancouver. I could end up in Canada for six weeks." *I could be with Dave,* I thought, and felt the knots in my belly relax incrementally, even though I knew how utterly unlikely that was.

Gary nodded, head down. The back of his neck glimmered, pale in the wash of the streetlights. I felt a moment of overwhelming tenderness mixed with frustration toward him, remembering how we'd made love for the first time, how slow he'd been, how careful. *Is this all right?* he'd asked me, holding his weight on his forearms, his body hovering over mine, the tip of his penis barely grazing the seam between my legs. *Okay? Am I hurting you? Should I stop?* I'd gotten so frustrated, because that kind of solicitousness, that caution, was not what I wanted at all. I wanted to be desired, fiercely; I wanted him to tear at my clothes, to kiss me like he was drowning and my mouth was air, to hold me like it would hurt him to let me go. *Okay?* he'd asked, easing himself inside me. His bedroom had been lit by a single flickering candle, and in that chancy light, with my breasts and the smooth skin of my belly and thighs exposed and my hair down over my cheeks, I could believe that he thought I was beautiful. And now he was leaving me. How could I stand it? How could I go on, get up in the mornings, go to work, do my job, without his love?

A car rushed past. The wind sent my skirt flapping up past my hips. Gary leaned toward me, with my hands still slack in his. I turned away and then told myself, sternly, to be a grown-up about this. I kissed his cheek. He squeezed my hands . . . and while I was trying to come up with a line—*Be well* or *Take care* or *I'll never forget you*—Gary took one long last look at me, then crossed the street and walked away.

FIVE

The day I found out about Rob's marriage, I sat behind my desk, holding very still, concentrating on the act of pulling air into my lungs, then letting it out, waiting until the writers and the rest of the assistants had made their noontime exodus to the food trucks. When they were gone, I'd opened up a fresh document on my computer and typed my resignation letter, giving my last day as precisely ten business days from that moment. I printed it out and left it, signed, on Steve's desk. "Is there anything I can do to change your mind?" he asked when he came back from lunch, and he hadn't looked surprised when I'd shaken my head. Rob was on his honeymoon, which meant I wouldn't have to face him before my time on the show was up. On my last day of work, I got a cardboard box from the supply closet and emptied my desk, packing up all those extra umbrellas and bottles of Advil and the dozens of scripts I'd printed out and studied and marked up with Post its and notes. I'd loaded the box in the back of my car, cleaned off my computer's desktop and erased the cookies on the hard drive, then gotten behind the wheel and driven off the lot. I'd tossed my ID badge into the trash can at the Poquito Más on Ventura on my way home, knowing I'd never be back.

"What happened?" cried my grandmother as I walked into

the living room with the cardboard box in my arms. I hadn't told her I was leaving. She'd only want to know why.

"Tough day at the office," I said. I locked my bedroom door behind me, stowed the box in my closet, and lay facedown on the comforter. It was too humiliating to think of, except in brief snatches, but even casual reflection showed me my mistake. I'd imagined myself as one of the normal people, the ones who walked off toward their happy endings in the warm glow of the sunset, a girl who could get a guy like Rob. Clearly I'd been wrong. How had I gotten it so backward? How had I fooled myself into believing that he would want me, that he thought of me as anything besides a friend? The tears came then, scalding hot on the one cheek that could feel them. Being rejected was one thing. Being shamed the way Rob had shamed me, being passed over in a way that let everyone I worked with know exactly how foolish I'd been, how far I'd overreached, was a pain I hadn't begun to imagine.

"Ruthie, what's wrong?" My grandmother stood in the doorway, apparently afraid to come closer. "You look terrible. Does something hurt?" It had been years since my last operation, but she knew how to deal with that physical pain, with ice packs and Advil, with hot baths and mugs of whiskey-spiked tea and urgent, whispered telephone calls to whatever physician or surgeon was currently in charge of my care. She could handle illness and surgeries. She was not equipped to deal with heartache. At least, that's what I thought as she crossed the room and perched on the edge of my bed. I heard the swish of silk as she crossed her legs beneath her lavender dressing gown.

"It's that Rob," she said, and didn't wait for my answer.

Grandma knew I'd been expecting him for the party, the night our episode had aired. She'd seen me pacing the apartment, jumping every time the doorbell rang, staring out the window, watching for his little black coupe to pull into the drive. I'd gone to sleep with my phone in my hand, checking it obsessively throughout the night, half-believing I'd get a call or a text from a hospital or the police somewhere, telling me that he'd crashed his car or suffered an out-of-nowhere heart attack or been the victim of some bizarre accident or crime. Certainly he'd talked about it enough. Mortality, especially his own, was one of Rob's favorite subjects. "Call me crazy," he'd begin, at whatever dive bar we'd stopped at for after-work wings and beers. He would wait obligingly until I'd said, "Crazy," before continuing, "But I just know I'm going to die in a way that's going to be in all the papers. Like, I'll be in a hot tub by myself one night—"

"Don't say it," I interrupted, having an idea as to where this might be going.

"And I'll just think, 'Hey! Maybe I'll stick my winkie in the outflow tube.' "

"Your winkie?"

"My man-gland. My throbbing member. My—"

"Okay, okay, I've got it." I was blushing, and I hoped he couldn't see.

"And then," he continued, sprinkling salt over the foam on his beer, "I'll be trapped, and I'll drown. Death by Masturbation. And the neighbors will find my decomposing corpse, with my winkie still stuck in the hot tub, and the next thing you know, I'm in *News of the Weird*."

"Simple solution," I told him.

"What's that?"

"Just promise yourself that you'll never stick your . . . thingie . . . in the outflow tube."

He shook his head. "I should just stay out of hot tubs. But I like them! Surely you see my dilemma." He'd looked at me searchingly, and I'd turned away, but not before giving him the line he expected: "Don't call me Shirley."

Grandma stood at the side of the bed, wringing her hands.

"There are other fish in the sea," she said. I didn't answer. "A bird in hand is worth two in the bush," she said. I didn't even know what that was supposed to mean. "You catch more flies with honey than with vinegar." I lifted up my head, glaring at her.

"What are you talking about?" I croaked.

She retreated quickly, moving backward across my floor in her slippers. "I'll just let you rest, then," she said, and closed the door behind her.

I stayed in my room all night long, flat on my back on my queen-size bed, replaying every conversation that I could remember having with Rob, every minute that we'd been alone together, writing or eating lunch or doing impressions of Taryn Montaine Tries to Unwrap a New CD, or Taryn Montaine Realizes that Her Hybrid Actually Does Need Gas After All. Maybe he'd just been using me as a constantly available audience, someone on whom he could try out his bits before bringing them to the writers' room. Tears ran down my cheeks, and I rubbed them away, letting my fingers explore the contours of my cheek, where the skin was stretched, where my eye drooped. How had I misread the signals so badly? How had I been so dumb?

I never told Grandma what had happened. As it turned out, I didn't have to. Rob and Taryn had sold their wedding pictures to *People* magazine, and the happy news had been spread all across the *Girls' Room* website, along with what was, in my opinion, an entirely fabricated tale about how the two had fallen in love over their seasons of working together. "I am so sorry," Grandma said as I lay with my head buried in my pillow, not answering, because what was there to say?

For the first week, I wanted to die. I thought about how to do it: the warm bath, the razor blade, the plastic bag, the pills. Then, with the first sort-of smile I'd managed since I'd gotten the news, I recalled Dorothy Parker's poem "Résumé." *Razors pain you / Rivers are damp / Acids stain you / And drugs cause cramp. / Guns aren't lawful / Nooses give / Gas smells awful / You might as well live.*

Might as well live. Besides, if I died, Rob would know just how badly he'd hurt me. All I had left was my pride . . . and I was determined to hang on to as much of it as I could. *He doesn't get to win this one,* I'd think, while dragging my leaden body and stiff limbs through some formerly unremarkable task, like showering or putting on pants. I would survive, if only to thwart him, to show him that I could succeed in spite of him. Ten days after I drove off the lot, I packed a bag, got into my car, and went to my gym and its big, brand-new swimming pool.

That first night, and on many nights to follow, I would swim, lap after lap after lap until my fingers were pruney and my goggles were fogged and my arms and legs were so heavy that I couldn't think of anything—not Rob, not Taryn, not what I was going to do next. Back at home, I'd fall into bed exhausted, my shoulders throbbing, my skin reeking of chlorine . . . and when I slept, I'd dream of swimming in open water, from Dover to Calais, or Miami to Cuba, with the taste of salt in my mouth and the waves lifting my body, the sun warming my back and shoulders and miles of empty water all around me.

Grandma kept working, leaving the house before eight each morning to take her seat on *Flight 152,* a romantic comedy set entirely on an airplane (she wore a polyester plaid pantsuit and sat, with a crochet hook that would eventually become integral to the plot, in seat 15-C). For three weeks, she put up with my impersonation of a silent, swimming, soup-eating ghost. When I sat down for dinner on the fourth Friday night, the table was empty. There was no soup simmering on the stove, no bread in the breadbasket, no wine in the decanter, no smells of roasting chicken or slow-cooked brisket or stewed fruit or honey cake or any of her other Shabbat-dinner standards coming from the tiled kitchen. I stared at the pristine white tablecloth, the crisply folded napkin, the silver that had been Grandma's wedding gift to my parents when they'd gotten married. "Do you want me to order takeout?" I finally called.

Grandma thumped her four-pronged cane on the floor as she made her way out of her bedroom and over to the table (the cane wasn't hers; it was a prop that she'd brought home for the night). She drew herself up to her full height and looked at me. She was, as always, impeccably dressed, that night in a vintage skirt of sky-blue linen embroidered with white loops and flowers, and a lacy white blouse, with bone-colored pumps and coral lipstick. "If you give a man a fish, he eats for a day," she announced. "If you teach a man to fish, he eats for a lifetime."

I blinked at the empty table. "So . . . you want me to go get fish? I could go to Bristol Farms." My brain felt like it had been wrapped in cottony insulation. My joints ached. My heart hurt.

Grandma touched my shoulder. With one fingertip, she traced the scars that lay underneath the cloth of my shirt. She'd let her hair go white when I'd been in college, and wore it pulled back in a sleek twist, and I could see the pale pink of her temples underneath as I looked up at her, the wrinkles around her eyes and her lips. "Life is hard," she said, not unkindly. "But you can't just lie there and let it kick you. Get up," she said. "Get another job. Find another guy. Go fishing."

I didn't go fishing that night. I didn't go swimming, either. I got in my car and brought us both burritos from Poquito Mas for dinner, shrimp for Grandma and carnitas for me. The next morning, I woke up with the sun and looked around the wreckage of my room, the piles of unwashed clothes, the streaked mirror, the dusty hardwood floors, the boxes of scripts and memos and printed-out emails from Rob that I'd hauled from *The Girls' Room*'s office. My cotton nightshirt was stuck to my chest, either with sweat or with tears, and my hair hung in chlorine-smelling clumps against my face. *You can do this,* I told myself, and swung my legs out of bed, first the right one, then the left, feeling the hooked wool rug beneath my feet, the one my grandmother had worked on in a series of doctors' offices and hospital waiting rooms during my surgeries when I was a girl. I had survived all of that. I would survive this, too.

I spent the weekend going through my closet, taking armloads of the work clothes I hadn't worn in weeks to the dry cleaner, tossing the swimsuits that had gotten so stretched and faded that they no longer covered my waterfront, then going online to order new ones. I swept my floors and stripped my bed and ordered a new flowered duvet cover, with sheets to match. I squeegeed my windows with ammonia and water and waxed the wooden floors, and while I worked, I invented a job for myself, a writing job that would pay the bills until I could handle a writers' room again. Grandma watched all of this wordlessly, but I thought I saw approval glimmering in her eyes, which were still bright and still missed very little.

I spent Monday morning composing the ad that would run on Craigslist. "College essays giving you grief?" I wrote. "Got the goods but not the words? Let a professional writer help you craft the perfect essay or personal statement for top colleges and universities. Reasonable rates. Happiness guaranteed." (I'd added that last part, imagining that I could guarantee they'd be happy with their essay but that, of course, I could not make any claims about whether they'd get admitted to the schools of their choice.) The ad went live at noon. By three o'clock, I had my first email. Ten minutes later, I'd made my first appointment, and by six, I was booked for the week. "You're doing what?" Grandma asked that night, one penciled eyebrow lifted.

"It's writing," I said after I'd explained, daring her to contradict me. She shrugged, muttering to herself, and went to her bedroom to begin moving clothing from one plastic bag to another, a trick that served as the Jewish woman-of-a-certain-age's version of meditation. The next morning, after blow-drying my hair and applying Dermablend to my cheek and putting on a skirt and boots and a jersey top, I packed up my laptop, got in my car, and staked out a table in the Coffee Bean and Tea Leaf on Beverly and Robertson, a perfect spot underneath a window and convenient to a power outlet. For the first time since that day when I'd gotten the news about Rob, I allowed myself to feel the tiniest hint of hope.

I spent the next six months working with tongue-tied teenagers trying to get into college and, eventually, lonely friends of my grandmother's who'd found only liars and heartache on Match.com or JDate.com and thought a spruced-up profile could change their luck. The senior citizens were my favorites (I'd start them off by showing them how to switch the font size on their screens to a clear and readable twenty-four points). Even Grandma asked for an ad, and insisted on writing me a check once I'd presented her with the finished product: "I Have My Own Teeth," read the headline. "Young at heart, with a sparkle in her step and a spring in her eyes, loves to laugh, cook, and watch *Desperate Housewives* on Sunday nights, seeks a gentleman with at least a few of his original parts, who knows the words to 'Bye, Bye, Blackbird,' appreciates a good roast chicken, knows the Lindy, and drives at night."

Grandma's ad produced a few duds and, finally, a lovely retired banker named Maurice, pronounced Morris, who lived in a sprawling colonial house in Brentwood, loved to ballroom dance, and drove a vintage Cadillac Lincoln Mark V the size of most studio apartments, which he'd lovingly restored and drove even at night. Maurice, who was all of five foot two on a good day, and had bought his suits in the boys' department of Barneys until he'd been able to afford bespoke clothing from London and Hong Kong, would squire both of us to his tennis club in Beverly Hills on Sunday mornings for brunch. He and Grandma would sit underneath an umbrella, sipping horseradish-spiced Bloody Marys and trading sections of the *New York Times* to the *thwack* of the tennis balls on the clay courts, while I'd do a shallow dive into the empty pool and swim laps, thinking about what adjectives could put the best possible spin on a pear-shaped fellow with a wispy mustache and a fondness for high-waisted jeans, or how to make the girl who'd confessed to never reading anything other than *OK!* magazine at the nail salon sound like she cared about the world as it existed beyond the tips of her eyelashes.

I made a decent amount of money and even a few friends, and learned that first impressions, and beauty, could be deceiving. One of my clients was a pretty high-school senior, all long legs and highlighted hair and sentences that rose up at the end, turning statements into questions. When we'd met, I'd dismissed Caitlyn as a Beverly Hills bubblehead, privileged and protected, who had as much chance of getting into Berkeley as I did of being tapped for the Miss America pageant. "Extracurriculars?" I'd asked, and Caitlyn, using her pierced tongue to shift a wad of purple gum from one side of her mouth to the other, had mentioned helping pet-sit for a friend who'd had a breast reduction, and volunteered that she sometimes babysat her little brother, which I'd bet her parents paid her for. Then, in the Beverly Center, an enormous shopping mall, I'd met the brother. He had cerebral palsy and sat in a candy-apple-red wheelchair with a computerized board with words and pictures in his lap, his head rolling from side to side, giving the occasional yelp or moan. "Shh, honey," Caitlyn said, pulling a folded napkin from her back pocket and wiping his lips with practiced, maternal efficiency. I watched her and marveled, burning with shame at the way I'd dismissed her, the way I'd seen all that glossy hair and tanned skin and heard her talk about tennis and Paris and thought *shallow* and *silly* and *dumb*.

I made small changes to my life, the way the experts advised.

Slowly, I would add or subtract one thing, one activity, one habit, each week. Instead of swimming for hours, I'd swim for ninety minutes, then just sixty, and some days I'd take a yoga class or go for a hike or just let my body recover and do nothing at all. I made myself stop Googling Rob and Taryn obsessively, but I was still aware of their lives, especially since a few of the gossip websites insisted on chronicling their every move and vacation and trip down the red carpet. I had read in *Us Weekly* about the postnuptial party they'd thrown at the Beverly Hills Hotel, and *People* had printed the news when they'd given birth to a little boy named Jack. I told myself I didn't care. I even considered sending a wedding gift, but when I went to their online registry and found myself browsing knives, I decided that maybe I shouldn't.

I had walked off the set of *The Girls' Room* in January. It was June when I finally forced myself to call Shelly, my agent, the woman who'd gotten me the job. I dialed her office number at eight o'clock at night, after she'd left for the day, so I could leave my apology on her voice mail instead of dealing with her in person. Reading a speech that I'd written out beforehand, I explained that I'd been going through a tough time (those were the words I'd chosen, after considering and rejecting the phrase "personal issues"). "But now everything's fine," I said, hoping I sounded cheerful and confident and, above all, sane, "and I'm ready to work again."

"Ruth Saunders," Shelly said when she called me first thing the next morning. "Look who's back on the face of the earth." Shelly was in her thirties, a tiny girl who'd been born in China and adopted by a Jewish couple on the Upper West Side in New York City. She had doll-size hands and feet and blunt-cut bangs and the most astonishing collection of purses I'd ever seen. She'd gone to Spence, then NYU, and if you closed your eyes when she talked, you could imagine you were speaking to an old-school theatrical agent, a fast-talking fella in a grimy fedora who'd call you *Toots* and say things like *such a bargain,* and she always referred to me by my first and last names.

"I'm sorry I've been out of touch," I began, even though I was sure Shelly knew what had happened, and why I'd stayed quiet for so long. "*The Girls' Room* turned out not to be the best fit." A total euphemism, and we both knew it, but there was no way I was going to spell out the specifics.

"And now I suppose," she said with a sigh, "that you would like to be gainfully employed."

"I'm not a flake," I said, even though it was precisely what a flaky *artiste* would say.

"Were you in love with him?" she asked me, her voice gentle.

I winced. There were no gossips like showbiz gossips, which meant that everyone in my little world knew, if not the specifics then at least the generalities, about what had happened and what a fool I'd been.

"Never mind," said Shelly before I could answer. "It's none of my business. I could try to find you a lady showrunner . . ." I laughed, knowing, as Shelly surely did, that women-run shows, especially comedies, were still a distinct minority. After all these years of feminism and presumed equality, there still wasn't a woman hosting a late-night network show, and only a handful of ladies were writing for those male hosts. Sitcoms weren't much better. Male writers and showrunners were the rule, women writers and showrunners were still the exception, and while every writers' room had a few females and at least one person of color, comedy was still very much a white man's world.

"Don't worry," I told my agent. "I can work with another guy. I promise, I can keep it zipped." We had ourselves a chuckle over that, even though I'd certainly worked (and I was sure that Shelly had, too) with a few guys who couldn't keep it zipped, guys who viewed the women they worked with as just as accessible to them as the bagels and doughnuts set out for their selection at craft services every morning.

"You'll probably have to start as an assistant again," she said.

I winced, even though it was what I'd been expecting. I'd never actually made it to staff on *The Girls' Room;* I'd just been hired as a freelancer to write my single episode. The assumption was that I'd make the jump to staff the next season, after my episode had aired. That, of course, was before my supervisor married the show's star and I'd taken my cardboard box and broken heart off to the deep end to heal.

"But don't worry. You've got great writing samples. You'll get on staff eventually. And believe it or not, I think I've actually got something that could be perfect for you."

SIX

There might have been places in the world where it was normal to see kids being raised by their grandparents, but Framingham, Massachusetts, in the 1980s was not one of them. In that suburb of Boston, it was the good old nuclear family, mom and dad and however many kids could be packed into the back of the minivan or SUV, at soccer games and school plays, Girl Scout camping trips, father-daughter pancake breakfasts. Even the couples who had divorced would put on a show of togetherness for the sake of the children, which meant that the children I saw moved in constellations of parents and siblings, where for me it was just the two of us: my grandmother, the sun, bright and fiery, and me, the little planet in orbit.

Grandma did what she could to make up for my lack of parents. After she went back to work, she hired a series of young women from the area colleges to take care of me, knowing that these babysitters, with their high-heeled boots, their sparkly eye shadow and feathered earrings, their scents of perfume and patchouli oil and cigarette smoke, and the boyfriends who'd drop them off and pick them up and call when they were over, would be a lure to my female classmates. After school, Kate or Melissa or Judy or Elaine would pick me up and walk me and sometimes a friend back home. Under the sitter's indulgent eye, we would make toasted-cheese sandwiches, do our homework, give each other manicures, or French-braid each other's hair. We'd watch the forbidden soap operas and leaf through the pages of *Seventeen* and *Mademoiselle* and *Vogue*, discussing whether we were high- or short-waisted, whether our faces were round or oval or heart-shaped, whether we could wear the latest layered bob, or if the newest shades of lipstick would work for us.

"You're so lucky," my best friend, Sarah Graham, told me. Sarah had moved to Framingham just before the start of fourth grade. By then, the rest of my classmates had more or less gotten used to my face. They didn't stare and they rarely teased. The cruelty-prone boys had figured out that Marissa Marsh, who had a weak chin and stringy hair and already wore an adult size twelve, was much more prone to tattling and tears when they called her Blubber than I was when they called me Frankenstein.

Sarah was a misfit, too. She had an overbite that was being corrected by braces and headgear, a body that was all knobby elbows and protruding knees, and a face that we had decided was heart-shaped, with brown eyes and brown hair and glasses. She was the first person I'd met who had allergies (wheat, eggs, dairy), and she sniffled year-round, except for a few brief weeks in the wintertime, when pollen season was over and before she'd caught her first cold.

Sarah's mother was a nurse who worked in a gastroenterologist's office, and her father was an engineer at MIT. They were strict with Sarah and her two older brothers. The Graham kids couldn't watch television unless it was PBS, they couldn't eat sandwiches that weren't made with whole grain breads . . . and, of course, fashion magazines were forbidden in the Grahams' house. "They reinforce gender norms," Sarah said gloomily, flipping through my grandmother's September issue of *Vogue*. She paused at a picture of an evening gown made of ecru lace, the model's eyes darkly shadowed, her short hair covered with a feathered cloche, and sighed, brightening only after Elaine, the day's sitter, asked if we wanted to toast marshmallows over the gas burner and make s'mores.

Sarah might not have been the friend I'd chosen if the choice had been mine to make. I loved to read and was deeply involved in the half-dozen television shows I watched. Sarah liked the Red Sox and video games, and could have happily spent all her free time and every quarter she could cadge at the Ms. Pac-Man machine in the back of Papa Gino's, where we'd stop after school for a slice and a soda. She got antsy and bored after half an hour at the mall, while I could spend entire afternoons there, pitching pennies into the fountain, watching people—teenage couples with their bodies tucked around each other, mothers wearily pushing infants in strollers, old men towing oxygen tanks, senior citizens with fanny packs and puffy white sneakers, pumping their arms as they did their daily laps. Sarah liked horror films and boy bands and spray cheese right from the can. I preferred romantic comedies and *Terms of Endearment* and thought spray cheese looked like extruded orange snot. Still, we were friends, spending afternoons and Friday-night sleepovers together, possessors of each other's secrets. I knew not only that Sarah had discovered her mother's vibrator, tucked under a pile of washcloths in a bathroom drawer, but that she'd been using it since her eleventh birthday. She knew that I had a desperate crush on Mr. Herman, who'd been our substitute science teacher for six weeks while Ms. Van Rijn recovered from a mastectomy, and that, in the top drawer of my jewelry box, I had six Polaroid pictures that I'd taken of just the good side of my face, wearing the lipstick and eye shadow and false eyelashes that Cheryl, my sitter, had helped me apply. She was the one who read the stories I'd write in the journals my grandmother kept buying me, my own versions of the Baby-sitters Club and Nancy Drew, stories about twelve-year-old girls with no parents and missing limbs, girls who were blind or deaf or otherwise disfigured who discovered they had superpowers, or sixteen-year-olds falling in love.

What happened to us was a classic story, one that most women have their own versions of: "The Tale of the Lost Friend." Sarah and I sat together at lunch, we played together at recess, we spent as many afternoons together as our schedules would allow. (Sarah had recorder lessons and, with her brothers, took fencing classes in Cambridge; I had piano and ice-skating lessons in the winter, and between my face and her allergies, there was usually a doctor's visit once or twice a month.) Starting in junior high, we'd call each other every night to talk about what we were wearing the next day, and whether Jared Marsh (my crush) or Jason Biller (Sarah's) had noticed what we'd worn the day before. The summer before high school, we spent afternoons in my backyard on towels, in bikinis, with Hawaiian Tropic oil on our bodies and Sun-In in our hair. I was planning on joining the swim team, and Sarah, still tall but much less gawky, with her braces off and her headgear reserved for nights, had traded her glasses for contacts and was thinking about volleyball or maybe basketball. "And then there's homecoming," Sarah said, as if I could have forgotten. The homecoming dance, the first dance of the school year, the Saturday night after the fourth football game of the season, in the school gym. Any student with the ten dollars for a ticket could attend.

On our first day of ninth grade we wore the outfits we'd shopped for and chosen together: Calvin Klein jeans, ribbed sweaters (red for her, plum for me), rubber-soled suede work boots—a fad that had swept through Framingham the previous spring—and oversize gold hoop earrings. My bus got to school first, and I waited for her by the front door, eager for her opinion: I'd gotten up at five-thirty to be sure that my hair, which I'd set in hot rollers, and my makeup were both perfect. I'd curled my lashes and smoothed on foundation under my grandmother's supervision, and she'd allowed me a squirt of her Shalimar. Following her instructions, I sprayed the perfume in front of me, then walked through it, allowing the scent to adhere to my clothes, my skin, my hair. Now I waited, squinting, peering over the tops of my classmates' heads, the boys in varsity jackets, the girls squealing laughter, smacking gum. I saw the top of her head first, then her ponytail, bobbing with each step. As Sarah drew closer, I saw she was talking to a boy named Derek Nooney, who lived in her neighborhood and rode her bus. Derek had gotten taller over the summer and had a juicy crop of acne spread over his forehead and his nose.

I pushed myself off the waist-high brick wall where I'd been sitting and stood by the door, where I knew she couldn't miss me. Sarah was wearing her Calvins and her red sweater, like we'd planned, and a floating silver heart around her neck that I'd given her for her birthday after saving up to buy it at Tiffany. "Hey, Sarah!" I said, and waved. She looked up. Her face was closed. "Ohhi," she said, running the words together like she was desperate to get them out of her mouth. She turned, bending her head back down to Derek, saying something I couldn't hear. Her remark was followed by the bellow of his goatish laughter. The two of them slipped past me as the bell rang, joining the throngs of students streaming through the doors.

Sarah and I didn't have lunch together. Rather than try to find people I knew in the wilds of the enormous cafeteria, a high-ceilinged room that clanged with the noise of a hundred different conversations, forks and knives, salad greens being chewed and sandwich bags unwrapped, I took my lunch to the lawn outside. It was mild and sunny, the temperature still in the eighties, and I had a copy of *Black Beauty* tucked into my backpack, which I'd bought with a birthday gift card at the L.L.Bean outlet store two weeks earlier, after Sarah's mother had dropped us off for a back-to-school shopping trip. My diary was in there, too. *Write it down,* I heard my grandmother say . . . but I couldn't think of the words I needed. Derek Nooney was in the remedial math class. Up close, he smelled like spoiled yogurt, and he used to throw clods of dirt at the short bus that took the handicapped kids to the vo-tech after lunch. The only thing he had to recommend him was that he was a boy. Maybe that was all that mattered.

That afternoon, for the first time, there wasn't a sitter waiting for me when school got out. I was almost fourteen—old enough, my grandmother had decreed, to be home alone for the hours between when school got out and when she'd be there to start dinner. I waited for Sarah by the school doors, in case that morning had been an aberration, a cruel joke, a mistake. She was with Derek again, the two of them walking so close their shoulders were touching. This time I didn't say anything to her, and Sarah, whom I'd seen naked, and crying, whose bikini line I'd helped wax, who'd slept in my bed and borrowed my pajamas and eaten a hundred dinners at my table, barely looked at me. I pulled my baseball cap low over my forehead (hats weren't allowed in school, but I put one on as soon as the last bell rang) and went back inside. No way was I waiting for the bus and watching the two of them ignoring me, maybe even laughing about me. The late bus, for kids who had after-school activities, came at four. I'd ride that instead.

I was wandering down the hall, looking for an empty classroom to sit in, figuring I'd get started on my homework, when Mrs. Seeley, my English teacher, called my name.

"Ruth? Ruth Saunders, right? Are you here for the school paper meeting?"

I shook my head. "I missed my bus," I mumbled.

"Room 112," she said, as if she hadn't heard me, and then stood there, watching, until I gave up and went across the hall to Room 112, where there were eight or nine kids who all seemed to know one another already. Mrs. Seeley followed me and shut the door. I looked around.

"Okay, everyone, I've brought you a new recruit. This is Ruth Saunders. What are you interested in? News? Sports? Current events?"

"We need someone to do the social calendar," said a girl whose fine light-brown hair was coming loose from its ponytail. She wore hot-pink elastics in her braces, which matched her shirt. "It's easy. You just talk about what's coming up. Dances, football games, cupcake sales . . ."

Great, I thought as she handed me a stack of announcements. So I'd join the school paper and spend my time typing up all the activities I'd never get to participate in or be invited to. On the other hand, Grandma had already started talking to me about the importance of extracurricular activities and how I should find something I enjoyed, something I was good at, something with writing, something that would impress the colleges to which I'd eventually apply.

Room 112 was the school's media room, with a dozen laptops on a long table against one wall. The ponytail girl, whose name was Brittany, helped me open a new document, gave me a word count, and showed me how to title the document, how to format the headline and the byline, and where to send it when I was through. I sighed, trying to put the image of Sarah and Derek out of my head, and started typing. *The JV cheerleading squad will be holding a bake sale to raise money for the library every day at lunch the week of September 20,* I typed. *Don't forget the Sadie Hawkins Dance on November 3. The Salvation Army welcomes your donations of winter boots and jackets. Please leave them in the bin outside the guidance office.* And then, when I was done and no one was looking, I wrote, *WHICH freshman has a zit on his or her forehead that rivals Mount Vesuvius, and WHEN will it finally erupt? Send your best guesses to the editor. Winner gets a cream-filled*

Hostess cupcake. I snorted and then hit SEND. A minute later, I heard Brittany's shout of laughter from across the room . . . and, for the first time since that morning, I felt as if the world might be a place I wanted to live in.

"We can't print this," Brittany said when she came back to my desk.

"Why not?" I was surprised by myself. Normally I didn't talk to strangers. I didn't like them looking at me.

"Because it's illegal?" Brittany said . . . but she didn't sound very certain. "Or libel. Or slander. One of those."

"Why? I'm not naming anyone. I'm not even saying if it's a boy or a girl. It could be anyone, really."

"Hmm." With the tip of her tongue, Brittany twanged the elastics that hitched her top braces to her bottom ones. "Let me ask Mrs. Seeley."

Mrs. Seeley, of course, put a stop to things, citing the school's anti-bullying policy. "How would you feel if someone wrote that about you?" she asked. I hung my head, blushing, thinking that kids were probably thinking worse things about me, and saying them to one another, all day long. I could walk her down to the girls' room at the end of the hall and show her what I'd seen on one of the stall doors. By 3:45 I'd turned in my copy, along with a typed-up list of the school lunches for the week ahead, and was trudging out to wait for the late bus when I heard someone calling my name.

"Hey, Ruth! Wait up!" There was Brittany, with even more of her hair flopping around her flushed cheeks, and a boy, a senior, whose name I didn't know.

"We have an idea for . . ." The boy looked around, even though the halls were empty. "An underground paper."

"What do you mean?"

"Instead of the official paper, it'd be something we did on our own and distributed ourselves," said Brittany.

"That thing you wrote," the guy continued. "About the zit. That was funny. We want to have a gossip column, and if we do them all as blind items . . ."

"You know, where you don't say anyone's name," Brittany said.

I nodded. I knew what blind items were. I'd seen them in Suzy's column in *Women's Wear Daily*, to which my grandmother subscribed (she was, she joked sometimes, the only woman in our zip code, possibly our state, with a subscription). "'WHICH very-married socialite was spotted on a very private Jamaican beach, cavorting with a man young enough to be her son, while her husband was stuck in Manhattan for Election Day?'" I quoted.

This time, the look the two of them exchanged was puzzled.

"Like that, but with kids who go here," I said. "Like, WHICH going-steady senior was spotted at Howard Johnson's sharing a sundae with a girl who's definitely not his girlfriend?"

"Who?" Brittany asked.

"Oh, I don't know. I just made that up."

"So you're interested?" Brittany asked.

I looked at the clock. There were five minutes until the bus came. "What if we get in trouble?"

Brittany and the boy exchanged a smile. "We'll cover our tracks," said the boy. "If you're interested, write something up, and give it to Brit by Friday. We'll be in touch."

The bus came groaning up to the curb. I took a seat in the back, yanked my cap down again, pulled out a notebook, and opened it to an empty page. When you looked like I did, people went out of their way to not see you, to act as if you weren't there. This was lucky—it meant that I could go almost anywhere, and that I saw and heard a lot that wasn't meant for my eyes or ears. I uncapped my pen and began. *WHO is the Goth girl who wipes off her black eyeliner and unlaces her Doc Martens once a week for*

Girl Scout meetings? WHICH cheerleader is doing more in the bath-room after lunch than freshening her lipstick? WHICH teacher, who's been telling everyone she did Weight Watchers over the summer, actu-ally had a gastric bypass operation over summer vacation? DID that varsity wrestler really get a fat lip during last week's meet . . . or did he get his mouth stuck on his old girlfriend's new braces? I was so involved in what I was writing that I almost missed my stop. It was mean, I knew. It made me no better than all the kids who called me Frankenstein and whispered about my face. But, I had to admit, it felt wonderful.

The next morning, I gave Brittany what I'd written. At lunch-time, when I was preparing to buy some milk, take my book, and sit outside by myself again, she found me in the cafeteria and grabbed me. I saw Sarah's eyes widen as Brittany whisked me past Sarah's table and over to her own, which was in one of the prime spots, underneath a window, and filled with other juniors and seniors. "So how much of this stuff is true?" she asked.

I squirmed, wishing for my hat. The Goth Girl Scout was Mandy Pierce, and I knew her secret only because we went to the same dentist and I'd seen her there one afternoon in her uni-form, sash and all. The teacher was Mrs. Gerlach, who taught typing. I'd heard her talking about Weight Watchers and get-ting to school early to walk on the track in the teachers' lounge, where I'd gone to drop off that morning's attendance count, but I'd seen a copy of *Eating Well After Weight-Loss Surgery* tucked in her purse, along with bottles of vitamins and a protein shake in a glass bottle. I didn't know any bulimic cheerleaders, but I'd heard enough gossip to figure I was safe in what I'd written, because there had to be at least one; and the wrestler was Sarah's older brother. I'd heard the story about how he'd hurt his lip from Sarah the week before, back when we were still talking.

I told Brittany what I knew. "Can you do this every week?" she asked, and I pretended to think it over before answering with a casual, "Sure, I guess," even though I wanted to jump up and down, to shout with joy, to march over to where Sarah was sitting, more or less in Derek Nooney's lap, and tell her that maybe she had a boyfriend, but I had friends . . . and a job.

"Do you have a title?" asked the guy I'd met the day before—he was the editor in chief of the school paper, and of this new, secret underground venture. His name was Joel Kingsbury, and he was handsome, in a thoughtful, pale, bespectacled way.

"How about 'Our Lips Are Sealed'?"

"I like it," Joel said, and smiled at me. Warmth rushed through my body, from my toes to the top of my head . . . and that was my *A Star Is Born* moment. Joel slid to one side, Brittany moved to the other, and just like that, like magic, there was room on the bench for me. It was like my dream of television: the glass softening and parting, so that I would have a place in the world.

The underground paper was called *Hellmouth*, because Brittany was a *Buffy the Vampire Slayer* fan, and it came out every two weeks, unless Joel or Anita, who wrote columns about politics, or Scan, who drew the cartoons, got busy or sick. We'd type it up on a laptop and print it at Brittany's, since her mother had a copier, and leave it in stacks in different places each time—under the bleachers in the gym, in the girls' and boys' first-floor bathrooms, in a corner next to the microwaves in the home-ec kitchens. We'd get to school at six in the morning on Drop Days, with piles of the papers in our backpacks, and creep around the building, delivering them, before piling into Joel's car and going to HoJo's for breakfast. In my four years of writing "Our Lips Are Sealed," only one person ever figured out that the anonymous author who signed each column "Kisses!" was me.

It was right before Christmas when I left my meeting at the official school paper, the *Framingham High Observer*, and found Sarah on the low wall where I'd been sitting when I'd first seen her and Derek. She must have been waiting for me. "You need to stop writing all that mean shit about Derek's face," she began.

"I don't know what you're talking about," I said coolly. After my first Mount Vesuvius reference, I'd instituted a regular feature in the column called "ZitWatch." When Derek's forehead zit had finally exploded, I'd taped a Hostess cupcake to the locker of the person who'd gotten the date right, and then turned my attention to the pimple on his chin.

"I know it's you," said Sarah. "You're the only one in ninth grade who'd use a word like *protrusion*. You're such a show-off."

I stared at her blandly. Maybe I was a show-off, but at least I didn't stuff my bra. Which Sarah did. Maybe I'd use that in next week's column.

The bus pulled up to the curb, and I started to walk past her. My throat felt swollen, and my eyes were burning. I wondered what she'd done with that Tiffany locket I'd bought her. I'd saved for weeks to buy it, and when my grandmother had offered to chip in, I'd told her no.

"You should cut it out!" Sarah's voice was loud and shrill, and she sounded like she might have been crying. "He can't help how he looks!"

Oh, I thought. *Like I can?* I turned around.

"You were supposed to be my friend," I said. Sarah stepped back. Clearly, she wasn't expecting me to say anything except that I was sorry, which I wasn't.

"You're just jealous," she retorted. "Because I've got a boyfriend, and nobody's ever going to want you."

I felt my eyes flood, and blinked fast, so the tears wouldn't spill down my cheeks. "I'd rather have no boyfriend than Derek Nooney," I said. "How can you let him kiss you? Aren't you afraid that one of his—what's that big word? Oh, right. *Protrusions*—one of his protrusions is going to explode all over you?"

"Bitch," said Sarah.

"Human Stridex," I responded.

Her face crumpled, and I could tell what she was thinking: that the next time she picked up a copy of *Hellmouth*, she might find herself on the receiving end of my attention, being called Human Stridex for all the world to see. Without another word, she turned, her shoulders slumped. Triumph surged through me, hot and heady. I'd won. It was undeniable. But it didn't feel good. All I wanted to do was to run after her and ask her why: why she'd dumped me for Derek Nooney, why she acted like she couldn't even see me anymore.

My grandmother was, of course, thrilled that I'd joined the school paper, that I had an activity, that I'd made friends. She clipped each story I wrote and had them all laminated and then bound in a scrapbook. I never told her about *Hellmouth*, but I was pretty sure she knew—at least once a month, I'd host a staff meeting in my bedroom, with the door locked and four or five senior staffers gathered around Charlie McKenna's laptop (his father worked in computer science, and Charlie was one of the first kids to have one). She would provide us with snacks—piles of sandwiches, bowls of popcorn, platters of cookies—and I'd hear her humming, moving past our room as we whispered and laughed. By the time I was a senior, editor in chief of both papers, I'd made up my mind: somehow I would find a way to write for a living when I grew up. I'd find a way to use my voice, funny-mean and observant, to earn my keep, to make my name, to carve out a place in the world.

SEVEN

The Monday morning after my conversation with Shelly, I pulled on my old navy-blue interview jacket—only by now I knew enough to pair it with jeans and a fedora, instead of heels and a skirt. I straightened my hair, painted my face, and proceeded, dry-mouthed and sweaty-palmed, to the Burbank offices of Two Daves Productions. I'd pulled into the lot a neurotic forty-five minutes early, parked my Prius, and established myself in the eighth-floor waiting room that, save for the *Bunk Eight* posters on the walls (tanned, white-teethed specimens of both sexes conducting a pillow fight in a picturesque cabin in the woods) and the copies of *Variety* and the *Hollywood Reporter* on the coffee table, could have fronted an insurance office, or a dentist's, or a bank.

I silenced my cell phone, crossed my legs, and opened up the folder containing everything I could find about the men I'd be meeting with, and began to reread.

The Two Daves were David Lieberman and David Carter. Friends since college (Harvard, of course), they'd been staff writers all through their twenties before landing a development deal, during which they'd created the sitcom *Bunk Eight*. Shelly had told me that their previous assistant had just left under mysterious circumstances, and that the Daves were eager to replace her immediately, if not sooner.

I was halfway through reading an interview the Daves had done with *The Onion* (they'd insisted on conducting the session in Big Dave's hot tub—*as you do*, I thought) when the door swung open and a little black-and-white dog came bombing out of the office, zipped past the receptionist, and hopped smartly up into my lap.

"Oh, hi there!" I said, startled. The dog looked at me with bright black eyes and then gave my nose a single lick and curled up in my lap as if it had known me all its life. One of its ears stuck straight up, the other flopped as it ran, and I remembered something I'd read somewhere—that when God sees a dog he likes, he folds one of its ears down to remember it.

"Pocket, off!" boomed a voice from inside the office. The dog lifted its head, sighed, and then hopped off my lap. I got to my feet as an extremely tall, handsome man stepped out of his office.

"Sorry about that, Ruth. You're Ruth, right?" I nodded, brushing dog fur off my legs.

"I'm Dave Lieberman. You can call me Big Dave. It's self-explanatory." He raised his voice, shouting in the direction of a closed door. "Hey, asshole! Your therapy dog tried to hump our job candidate's leg!"

"Oh no it didn't!" I cried as a calm voice issuing from behind a wall called, "Pocket, go to place."

The dog obediently trotted to a fluffy rectangle of padding in the corner and curled up. Big Dave winked at me. "It's a she," he stage-whispered. "You're not allergic or anything, are you?" I shook my head. I hadn't grown up with pets—my grandmother was not, as she put it, a dog person, and I'd never lobbied for a bird or a fish or a cat—but this dog, now regarding me calmly with its chin on its paws, seemed like an excellent example of its kind. Besides, plenty of showrunners brought dogs to work—it was one of the job's common perks or affectations, depending on your attitude and on the dog's behavior.

While Big Dave fished a treat out of a ceramic jar labeled TREATS, I took a moment to consider my possible new boss. True to his nickname, Big Dave was over six and a half feet tall, and everything about him was large. He had enormous hands, and feet the size of loaves of bread. His nose was a generous hook, his teeth looked slightly larger what most men I knew had in their mouths, and his chin jutted heroically, like a little kid's drawing of a superhero. Then there was his hair, a shoulder-grazing mop of glossy brown that he was constantly fussing with, combing with his fingers, pulling into an impromptu ponytail, and then releasing to hang in waves and ringlets against his cheeks.

Big Dave's hair might have said "rock star," but his clothes were strictly prep school. That morning he was arrayed in flat-front khakis, lace-up oxfords, a button-down shirt striped cream and lime with his monogram—*DAL*—on the cuffs, and a Lilly Pulitzer tie in an eye-watering pattern of hot pink and tangerine. He had a booming laugh and a winning smile, both of which, I would come to learn, he deployed regularly. The world delighted Big Dave, and why shouldn't it? I knew, from my reading, that Big Dave, at thirty-six, was rich enough to own five sports cars, one for each workday, and a sprawling glass box of a house that was perched in the Hollywood Hills, with a swimming pool and a hot tub and a sauna, a home gym and a screening room that sat twelve.

"Pleasure to meet you," Big Dave said, taking my hand. "Where are you from, Boston? I'm hearing Boston. You ever go to camp in the Berkshires? You look like a girl I knew once. Stacey Saunders? Played volleyball? Not you, obviously, but any relation?"

I shook my head, looking around as Dave helped himself to a Fresca and the little dog—Pocket—crunched up her treat, licked her lips, then began chewing on a cylinder of red rubber. The office, up on the eighth floor overlooking Alameda Avenue, was large and sunny, with big windows that let in plenty of light. It was equipped with couches and chairs and beigey-gray carpet that had most likely come from some office supply warehouse. The desks and bookshelves and telephones had probably been there before the Daves arrived and would remain after they left. But the furniture was the only thing signaling that we were in a place where work was expected to happen. Except for the couches and carpets, their office was a romper room, a ten-year-old boy's dream, if the ten-year-old boy had expensive taste and an unlimited budget. A soapbox racer painted red and white was parked against one wall. On a table beside it was a half-assembled four-foot-high Death Star made of LEGOs, alongside a variety of diagrams and Internet-procured cheat sheets. A Nerf basketball hoop was affixed to the back of the door, a felt golf green was rolled out along one wall, a giant tank filled with bright fish had been set between the two desks, and there was an old-school pinball machine underneath the window.

"Do you play?" Dave asked.

I shook my head. "Ms. Pac-Man was my game."

"Ooh, good one." He settled on a white leather sofa, underneath a row of movie posters—one for *King Kong*, another for *Attack of the 50 Foot Woman*, and a third with Tura Satana, of Russ Meyer fame, bursting out of her halter top as she confronted some unseen foe. The pièce de résistance, displayed in a Lucite box in the corner, was a gold wheelchair that it took me a moment to recognize as the one Woody Harrelson had used when he'd played the titular character in *The People vs. Larry Flynt*.

"Affectation," said Big Dave, following my gaze. The back door swung open, the little dog raised her head and gave a cheerful yip, and a man entered the room, his hands working the wheels of a far less glamorous chair than the one in the see-through box.

"Screw you," said the man in the wheelchair. He was boyishly handsome, with thick brown hair and mild hazel eyes, and he spoke to his partner with familiar affection. "I'm not the one who bought the Batmobile."

"You see?" asked Big Dave, arranging his features in a hangdog expression. "You see how he treats me? Besides," he went on, turning back toward the man I assumed was his partner, "I didn't buy the Batmobile. I leased it for my birthday. How many times am I going to turn thirty-five?"

"Bought. Leased. You're splitting hairs," said the man in the wheelchair—the other Dave, I presumed. Little Dave. "All I know is that when you look up *entitlement* on Wikipedia, there's a picture of you. In the Batmobile."

"I didn't actually drive it," Big Dave grumbled.

"Oh, well, in that case, I take it all back."

"Are you getting this?" Big Dave asked again, raking his fingers through his hair as he turned to me. "You see what I put up with?"

"Big white guy can't catch a break," I said . . . which turned out to be precisely the right thing to say. Both Daves laughed, Big Dave loudly, Little Dave with a dry, quiet *heh-heh-heh*. The dog looked from one Dave to the other, her bright black-olive eyes following each beat of the conversation, one ear erect, the other folded and floppy.

"Calling us out on our privilege," said Big Dave. "I like her already."

"I'm Ruth Saunders," I said after Little Dave had wheeled toward me, his hand extended. I had a bad moment, wondering what to do, before bending awkwardly from the waist and taking his hand, which was warm and dry and very strong.

Little Dave's attire was as unremarkable as his partner was

flamboyant. He wore jeans, pale-blue loose-fitting Levi's, the kind that would never go out of style because they'd never been quite in style, a Polo shirt in bluish-gray, and a pair of New Balance running shoes, which struck me as either deliberately ironic or a cruel joke: running shoes for a man who couldn't walk. Maybe they were comfortable, I thought, and then wondered whether he could feel his feet. If I couldn't feel my own, I decided that I'd wear the least comfortable, most beautiful shoes I could borrow from my grandmother—delicate, strappy stilettos with heels high enough to preclude normal walking. If I was going to be stuck in a wheelchair, at least I'd look good sitting there.

"Thank you for coming on such short notice," said Little Dave. "I like your hat."

"Affectation," I said, and he smiled. His hair was cut short and combed in a way that wasn't trying too hard to hide his small bald spot. He had a neatly trimmed beard and gold wire-rimmed glasses and a watch on a leather band on his left wrist. He could have been a suburban algebra teacher, a dad who'd coach youth soccer on the weekends, pick up paper towels and chicken breasts on his way home from work, and not complain when his wife instituted Meatless Mondays. I liked him immediately.

"Is Pocket actually a therapy dog?" I'd asked. I'd seen people in wheelchairs with dogs, but I'd never seen one quite so small.

Dave, frowning, shook his head and spoke to his partner. "I wish you'd stop telling people that. It sets up false expectations."

Big Dave grimaced. "What, like that the dog's actually going to do something useful?"

"She does things." Little Dave snapped his fingers, and the dog, instantly alert, bounded out of her bed. "Pocket, shake." She sat down and gravely extended her paw to me. I took it and shook it. "Pocket, play dead," said Little Dave. The dog lurched forward one step, then two, and then collapsed on her side with a realistic shudder, letting her tongue flop out of the corner of her mouth. I smiled and Big Dave said, "Pocket, executive!" The dog got up, trotted over to a stack of scripts piled in the corner, and lifted her leg as if she was going to pee. I applauded.

"I taught her that one," said Big Dave. Little Dave set his hands on the wheels again and rolled quietly behind one of the desks in the outer office, with the dog's eyes following his every motion. There he picked up what looked like a black plastic bullhorn and tossed it to his partner.

"What's that?" I asked, the way I guessed I was supposed to.

"Radar gun," said Big Dave, who had arranged himself underneath a poster for *Buck Rogers* and crossed his long legs.

"For what? Do you clock each other's pitches?"

"Pitches, land speed, whatever. Little Dave once achieved eight miles an hour on his way to the bathroom. Sometimes we just sit outside on the median on Ventura and point it at people."

"That's when there's nothing good on cable," Little Dave said.

Big Dave put down the radar gun, picked up a light saber from a basket next to the couch, and tossed it from hand to hand. "So. Can I ask a personal question?"

I nodded, wondering whether his inquiry was going to concern my appearance or my work history.

He touched his own cheek. "Can you tell me about . . ."

"Ah. Well, I should start by saying, 'You should see the other guy.' " The joke—one I'd used a few times before—worked. Both Daves smiled. "I was in a car accident when I was a kid. My parents hit a patch of ice and flipped their car."

"Oh, no," said Big Dave. He leaned forward to pat my arm. "Oh, honey, that's terrible."

I looked at Little Dave in his wheelchair and wondered if I was expected to reciprocate and ask what had happened to him, even though, of course, I already knew. Before I could make up my mind, Big Dave said, "He was in an accident, too."

"I'm sorry," I murmured.

Little Dave waved his hand, looking uncomfortable. "It was a long time ago," he said.

This, of course, was like catnip to his partner. "You guys should go out!" said Big Dave.

"Um . . . ," I said as Little Dave rolled his eyes at me and mouthed the words *Ignore him.*

Big Dave put down the light saber and plucked a Magic 8-Ball out of the basket. "Will Dave and Ruth find true love?" he asked, and shook the ball.

I looked at Little Dave. "Does he do this with everyone?"

"He does," he replied. "Also, it's a custom Magic Eight-Ball. Every side of the triangle says 'Fuck yeah.' "

"Don't tell her that!" Big Dave pouted. He put down the Magic 8-Ball and picked up a pen and a pad. "Do you think there's a show there? A dating service for accident survivors? Or maybe a supernatural show." He studied me carefully. "Did the accident leave you with any kind of psychic powers?"

"Mr. Sensitivity," Little Dave said, and I shook my head and told him that, sadly, I was superpower-less. I added, "No parents, though. So I have that whole Disney-orphan thing going for me."

"Oh, no," said Big Dave, looking stricken. "God. I'm so sorry. What is wrong with me?" He looked at his partner. "Why do you let me say these things?"

"When have I ever been able to stop you?" The other Dave turned to me, still with a pleasant, welcoming look on his face. "How long have you lived in Los Angeles?"

More questions followed, the two of them trading off. Where did I live? Did I like the neighborhood? Where had I grown up? Had I enjoyed my time on *Girls' Room*? Was I working on scripts of my own? Finally, Big Dave arrived at the elephant in the room.

"So what have you been up to for the past . . ." He glanced at my résumé, no doubt calculating the months between my departure from *The Girls' Room* and my arrival in their office. ". . . little while?"

There were any number of answers I could have given that would have been acceptable. I could have said something vague about a spec script, a screenplay, the dissolution of a writing partnership, or how I'd spent the time trying to put together a deal or rewriting someone else's script, and it would have been enough to satisfy the Daves. Plenty of writers went months and years between full-time situations, and while it was obviously preferable to stay steadily employed, I wouldn't be the first writer in Hollywood to have left one show and had to wait awhile for the next one.

Big Dave had swapped his 8-Ball for three juggling bean-bags, and he tossed them into the air, waiting for my answer. Little Dave was looking at me.

"I've been writing classified ads," I said.

Big Dave widened his eyes. "Really?" Little Dave asked. It wasn't a sarcastic West Coast *really,* it was a pleasant one, a tell-me-more-about-it invitation. "What kind?"

"Have you two ever spent any time on the Internet dating sites?"

Both men shook their heads. Big Dave cocked his thumb at his partner. "He prefers to order his hookers via text." Little Dave made a shooing gesture, shaking his head.

"Ignore him," he said again. "Everyone else does."

"Oh, c'mon," said Big Dave. "I'm just trolling you." He turned to me, looking worried. "Is that what the kids say? Trolling? Is that a thing? It's a thing, right?"

"On the Internet," I assured him. I was already aware of how much I wanted to keep talking to Little Dave, asking questions about his dog and his show and his life in a wheelchair. But the way he looked at me, that calm regard and impressed expression, reminded me, painfully and pleasantly, of Rob, and I was determined not to let any of that happen again. *Don't be the same fool twice,* I thought.

"So tell us," Little Dave said. "What's going on with Internet dating?"

"Well, for starters, the websites are full of people who don't know the difference between *you're* with an apostrophe and *your* without one," I said. "And everyone says the most generic things you can imagine."

"Likes funny movies, Mexican food, snuggling on the couch," Big Dave supplied.

"Likes a good sense of humor. Dogs and sunsets," said Little Dave.

"Exactly. I started up a business where I'd help kids write their college applications, and then someone asked if I could help with his dating profile. I'd meet people for coffee, do kind of an intake interview, ask them about themselves and what they were looking for, and then write them an ad."

"That's genius," said Big Dave.

"That's a show," said Little Dave, even though we all knew that dating-service sitcoms and dramedies had failed on every network.

"So what was your success rate?" asked Little Dave. "Percentage-wise?"

I answered him honestly. "I really couldn't say. I try to tell people that you can have the best bait in the world, and sometimes the fish just aren't biting. But I found my grandma a boyfriend, so, you know, I consider the whole thing a win." For some reason, I left out the fact that my business had also netted me a boyfriend. *Just being professional,* I told myself. No reason for them to know about my personal life.

Little Dave was looking at me when his handheld beeped. He glanced down, pressed a button, and made a face. "The network says we can't use lube."

Big Dave was indignant. "Who are they to tell us how to manage our sex lives?" He bent down, scooped up his juggling balls, and threw one savagely through the Nerf hoop that hung on the back of the office door.

"We can't say 'lube,' " Little Dave explained. "In this week's script. We need to come up with something else." The two of them looked at each other, then at me. I knew, without being told, that everything up until now had been small talk. This was the real test, the only one, ultimately, that would matter.

"Do you really think people want to hear the word 'lube'?" Big Dave mused.

"Personally, I do not," said Little Dave.

His partner grinned, baring oversize teeth. "Were you this much of a killjoy before you were a crip? I can't remember."

"Always," said Little Dave, apparently unoffended. "I've been a killjoy since birth. They wrote it under 'gender' on my birth certificate."

"What about love goo?" I suggested, and was rewarded with Little Dave's almost inaudible laughter.

"Passion slime," Big Dave parried.

"Or you could just go with the all-purpose 'marital aid,' " I said. "Sometimes less is more."

"That's very true," said Little Dave, and nodded at his partner. "It's news to this one, though."

"You know what I wish someone would write about?" I asked. "That gum that squirts in your mouth. You know, the stuff with the liquid center?" I'd been working on a bit about the ejaculating gum for weeks, scribbling lines about how the gum really didn't know me well enough to be doing that in my mouth without my permission, and that if the manufacturers were smart, they'd have the first piece in every pack just dribble its contents politely down your chin, in the name of good manners and social contracts, and at least buy you a drink before that.

"Squirting gum," Big Dave mused toward the skylight. "I wonder if that's funnier than lube."

"Anything is funnier than lube," said Little Dave.

"Lube's pretty funny," I said.

"Not if you've been listening to the largest Jew in captivity make jokes about it for ten days." He looked at his partner. "And you shouldn't talk about lube with female job candidates," he said. "Hostile work environment. Remember?"

Big Dave groaned and launched into the story of what had happened to the Two Daves' last assistant. The tale began with the studio installing new Internet firewalls to ensure that nobody could access anything pornographic, or even remotely offensive, online while on the studio's grounds. "So of course I went right to HR and told them that it was an awful policy; indeed, a dangerous policy," Big Dave said. "I told them it was a writer's job—not even a job, really; more like a calling, almost a holy obligation—to find the offensive, to seek it out, to wallow in it. I told them comedy's just pain expressed as laughter."

"It was very moving," Little Dave said. "I might have cried." I smiled. I was beginning to realize that, whatever they did for the network, whatever they technically got paid for, this was their real job, bouncing jokes off each other, one Dave topping the other in an all-day comedy show.

"So anyhow," Big Dave continued. "It's two weeks later, and I'm at a party, and I'm trying to show our assistant . . ."

"Our young female assistant," said Little Dave. "She had a name, too."

"Erica. See, I'm not a monster! Anyhow, I was showing *Erica* how terrible the new system is, so I pulled out my iPhone and I typed *anal*."

"But of course," I said.

Big Dave grimaced. He had, it emerged, been fully expecting that the iPhone would come back with the expected "restricted access" cartoon, with Foghorn Leghorn announcing, "I say, I say, I say, that website's off-limits, podnah!" Instead, what popped up on the screen—in living color and high-resolution video—had prompted Erica to flinch, turn pale, and run out the door. Only a swift promotion had staved off the inevitability of a sexual-harassment complaint.

"They made her a development executive," said Big Dave, in the mournful tones someone else might have used to announce that a dear friend had become a vampire or a Republican. "And we were told not to hire another girl."

"We were told no such thing," Little Dave said.

"It was suggested," Big Dave said.

"It was not," Little Dave told me.

"You don't have to worry about offending me. I'm down with anal," I said, and immediately began wondering what kind of treatment I'd opened myself up to with that statement.

"Writers' rooms are dirty places," Little Dave said.

"Oh, believe me, I know. I worked right outside of one for three years. I'm a dirty girl," I promised. I kept my legs crossed in case they were trembling and held my arms stiffly against my sides, convinced that I'd sweated through my silk blouse. "I can do gross, believe me. I once wrote a whole bit about how annoying it is when the adhesive from the maxi-pad sticks to your pubic hair."

Little Dave looked mildly repulsed. Big Dave looked actively interested. My face felt like it was on fire, but I pressed on. "Seriously. Whatever you guys need . . ." *Oh, God.* I shoved my hands against my skirt. "I mean, don't worry if you think it's, you know, demeaning . . ." *Oh, God. Ruth, stop talking.* "I've been an assistant before. I know the drill. I'll get coffee or lunches. I'll pick up your dry cleaning . . . photocopy your scripts . . . make your reservations. If you need notes dropped off at home, at night . . ."

Big Dave was chuckling.

"Okay, I realize that I'm babbling, and also that I sound like a whore. This is my first job interview in a while, and I'm a little out of practice, and that light saber's making me nervous . . ."

"Oh, it's not a working light saber," said Big Dave, not without regret.

"I'd work really hard. I'd be a good assistant. Thank you. That is all." And, with that, I finally managed to close my mouth.

Little Dave gave me a friendly smile. "I think she'll do," said Big Dave. He put down his juggling balls and headed into his office. Through the open door, I saw him open a a toy chest with his name painted on the lid and began looking for something else to play with. But his partner wasn't done with me yet.

"Your scripts were good," Little Dave said. He patted his thigh, and Pocket hopped out of her bed and hopped up into his lap.

"Oh! Thanks!" I'd submitted my episode of *The Girls' Room*, the dog-walking show where Taryn's character had been locked in the bathroom, and a spec script I'd written about a girl who goes off to college and meets the ghost of her dead mother.

"And I read your short story."

I had to work hard to keep my mouth from falling open. "You did?" I'd published a single short story, in an online journal called *Room & Board*, which had paid me in contributor's copies. The story had been rejected without comment from *The New Yorker*, but the fiction editor at *The Atlantic* had sent a brief handwritten note: "You're obviously a writer, but this isn't quite right for us." The story, called "Drive," was about a young woman, recently dumped and hitchhiking home from college, who gets picked up by a woman on her way to meet the death row prisoner she married without ever having touched him. As the miles pass, the two of them have a long conversation about love and obligation and the Meaning of It All while sharing a bag of Cheetos on the Pennsylvania Turnpike. As an undergraduate, I'd thought it was very profound . . . but it had only been published online, six years ago, which meant that Dave Carter would have had to have done some serious digging to find it.

"You liked it?" I asked, and he nodded.

"I liked the dialogue. Writing the way people really talk isn't easy. I thought you nailed it."

"Thanks," I said, blushing with pleasure.

Dave stroked his little dog's back. She looked at him adoringly, as if there was no place she'd rather be than curled in his lap, and I thought, and quickly made myself stop thinking, that I could guess at how she felt. "You probably don't want to be an assistant forever," he said.

"Maybe not forever," I said. "It's not such a good look when you're fifty."

He nodded. "How does this sound: Let's plan on you being around to help us when we need help. When we don't need you, you're free to do your own thing, write your own stuff. And if you want our help, we'll help you."

This was unexpected and generous. "You will?"

"We'll supervise," said Little Dave. "And if it's good, we can open some doors. Bring it to the networks. They'll take our calls." Of course they would—when you had run one of the most successful sitcoms on the air for the past five years, of course networks would take your calls. Probably the president would take your calls, too, if you came up with some ideas for peace in the Middle East and wanted to bounce them around.

"You'd do that?" I felt like I might cry. I'd wanted a job,

any job, and had found mentors—saints!—instead of mere employers.

"People helped us," called Big Dave, who'd left his office door open and had, I guessed, heard the whole thing. "We want to pay it forward."

"And in spite of what Mother Teresa back there will tell you, it's not entirely selfless," said Little Dave. "If we bring something good to the studio, and they sell it to the network, that works to our benefit. They'd attach us. We'd get paid."

"Makes us useful to keep around," said Big Dave, stretching his arms over his head and yawning noisily. "Even after we've stopped being productive and just show up in our offices to have a change of scene and use the bathrooms. Which Dave here does most mornings at around eleven. Just FYI."

"Ignore him," said Little Dave, wincing.

"That's . . . wow. That's incredibly nice of you. So . . ." I wasn't sure if I was hired or how to ask. Little Dave sensed my discomfort and stepped in.

"We'll have HR give you a call and send over the paperwork. Can you start Monday?"

"Of course," I said. "And thank you. So much. You won't regret hiring me," I told them, and promised myself that I would work as hard as I could to make it true.

EIGHT

I spent the next year discovering that the Daves were as good as their word. Being their assistant involved plenty of scut work: copying and collating scripts, picking up sandwiches and coffee, ordering holiday cards, fetching dry cleaning and food for the office pantry, and taking Pocket to the groomer's, but it also left me plenty of free time to work on the show that would become *The Next Best Thing*. Best of all, whenever there was an intern to watch the phones, the Daves would invite me into the *Bunk Eight* writers' room. There I'd have a seat at the table with eight other writers, and all of us would pitch jokes and bits. A few of mine even made it on the air. At least once a week, one of the Daves would make a point of asking me what I was working on, which meant I had no excuse not to start writing my own thing.

I'd had the idea for a long time, probably since I'd first decided to move to Los Angeles. I wanted to write about a girl who was kind of like me, and an older woman who was a lot like my grandmother, and describe their adventures, which would be fictionalized versions of our own. It would be a coming-of-age story, where the women coming of age would be twenty-eight and seventy-five, both of them falling in love, having their hearts broken, and learning, and mending, and moving along . . . and it would be set in Miami, as my own personal, secret homage to *The Golden Girls.*

The Daves encouraged me as I wrote, offering notes and feedback and, best of all, free time to work. As the months went by, my crush on Little Dave only intensified. Big Dave was fun and funny, but Little Dave was the one I daydreamed about. I'd arrive at my desk before eight-thirty most mornings so I could be there when he wheeled through the door, and I'd stay until he'd left for the night. At any moment of the day, I had a kind of preternatural awareness of where he was: onstage, in his office, on the phone, in the pantry, fixing himself a bowl of cereal or refilling his water bottle, and on weekends, when I didn't see him, I stored up observations, anecdotes, stories I could tell. I thought of him when I should have been thinking of Gary, even when I was with Gary. At the movies, holding Gary's hand, or at a restaurant, listening to him talk about his latest run-in with the head of the Language Arts department or the parents who'd tried to bribe him to raise their kid's B+ to an A−, I'd find myself imagining what it would be like to be with Dave: his calm regard, his reticent, tucked-in smile.

On the first Christmas I worked for Two Daves, I came to the office to find an elaborately gift-wrapped box on my desk. Inside, there was a five-hundred-dollar gift certificate to the Burke Williams spa (Big Dave's doing, I guessed) and a wrapped first edition of what I'd told Little Dave was one of my all-time favorite books: *Dinner at the Homesick Restaurant.*

I stretched my budget and bought Big Dave the state-of-the-art video-game remote controls he'd wanted and mentioned at least once a day since November. That was the easy part. I spent hours thinking about what to buy his partner, who was hard to shop for, even in the notoriously difficult category of single men rich enough to buy themselves whatever they wanted. Little Dave didn't care much about his clothes. He held season tickets for all the teams in town, so I couldn't wow him with box seats to the big game. He played poker in Las Vegas, where he'd travel via private jet, and the hotel would comp his rooms and meals. He had enough money to get himself whatever he wanted, to go anywhere in style, and I didn't want to go with the obvious choices: a scarf or gloves for his trip back east or, worse yet, a gift card for a bookstore or a restaurant.

After extensive deliberation, I picked out two books: a coffee-table collection of Francis Bacon's paintings, and one of my favorite novels, a book called *Body* by Harry Crews that I must have wrapped and unwrapped half a dozen times before deciding to just give it to him without comment or any kind of inscription beyond a generic, cheery "Happy Holidays." It was a provocative choice, given my face, given his wheelchair. *Body* was a book about freaks: a female bodybuilder, one of the best in the world; her enormously obese older sister; her boyfriend named Nail Head, who'd come back from Vietnam with a deep suspicion of humanity and a tattoo of a fly on the head of his penis; and a bulimic male bodybuilder named Billy Bat, who'd earned his nickname for having the best back in the business, latissimi dorsi that flared out like bat wings. *Body* also had one of the sweetest sex scenes I'd ever read. About halfway through the story, set at the bodybuilding championships in a Florida hotel, the heavy sister seduces the male bodybuilder, who adores her for everything her flesh represents, all the things she could enjoy that he was forced to avoid—or eat, then purge. It was about love transcending appearance, about how beauty was a shifting line, arbitrarily dictated, easily changed, and how two people could connect in spite of physical differences, how they could fall in love in spite of appearances that set them apart from the rest of the world.

"Hey," said Dave, wheeling into the office the day after New Year's. He was tanned from ten days in Hawaii, the hair on his forearms lightened from the sun, and as always, I felt my heart lift when I saw him. Any day when I got to see him, to talk with him or even just be around him, was a good day. "Thanks for that book. I really enjoyed it."

"You did? I know it's a little out there . . ."

"No, no, it was great. The voice was fantastic. I read the whole thing on the flight over. Couldn't put it down." I wondered how his traveling companion had felt about that. For the past few months, Dave had been dating Shazia Khan, who wore her black hair almost to her waist, along with killer spike heels that I knew I wouldn't be able to endure for fifty yards. Once, during taping, I'd seen her perched on Dave's lap, one leg slung over the armrest of his wheelchair, one arm coiled around his neck, her long hair covering his face like a veil as they kissed.

"Did you have a good vacation?" I asked.

He rubbed at his nose, which was slightly sunburned. "I did. The ocean was perfect."

"Do you swim?" I asked, surprised.

Dave nodded. "It's kind of a trick. Wheelchairs and sand aren't a great combination. But once I'm in the water, I can still . . ." He mimicked a paddling motion, and I saw how strong his arms were, and couldn't help but imagine him pulling me onto his lap, like he'd done with Shazia, and how it might feel to spread my hand against his neck.

"I've never been to Hawaii," I said.

"It's an easy trip. Quick flight. Let me know if you ever want advice on where to stay."

"Thanks." I got busy behind my desk, turning on my computer, straightening the stack of scripts, slipping on my headset so I could collect the voice mails that had arrived overnight. Dave would normally begin his morning by wheeling into the pantry for a cup of coffee, black with one sugar, and a Clif Bar, either the carrot cake or brownie flavor. But that morning, he stayed in his chair in front of my desk, watching me as I lifted the receiver.

"Do you need something?" I asked, setting the receiver back down.

He was looking at me so intently I wondered if there was something on my face. That had happened before. The nerve endings on the right side weren't as sensitive as those on the left, so I was always careful to check for stray toothpaste or lipstick or breakfast debris before I left the house and again before I got out of the car, but maybe I'd missed something.

"Dave?" I asked, feeling my skin getting hot.

He shook his head like he was trying to wake himself from a dream. "Sorry. Senior moment." He touched his forehead and then put his hands on his wheels, shifting himself backward, as if going to the pantry. Then he stopped and said, "You know I've got a pool at my house, right?"

"Right." I'd talked with his pool maintenance people a few times, arranging for cleanings and deliveries of chemicals.

"Maybe, if you wanted, you could come over for a swim."

"Really?" Dave knew that I was a swimmer. He'd spotted my gym bag, my goggles and suit tucked into its mesh pockets, and I'd told him how I loved the water, that I'd been a lifeguard for a summer on the Cape, that it had been one of the best summers of my life. (And also, although I didn't tell him, one of the worst. In my National Seashore–issued red racerback bikini and a baseball cap pulled low, between my tan and all the running and swimming I did to stay in shape, I looked as close to a *Baywatch* babe as I ever would in my life. Jogging across the beach sometimes, in that red bikini, tanned legs flashing, I'd notice the appreciative gazes of boys and men and the jealous glances of women—all gone the instant they got a look at my face.)

"Yes." He turned his chair so that he was facing the pantry. "I'm usually away most Sundays, playing poker. If you wanted to stop by . . ." He let his voice trail off, maybe wondering if this was a good idea, if it somehow crossed the employer-employee line.

"My gym has a pool," I told him. "So it's not like I've got nowhere to go."

"Swimming outside's different."

I found myself nodding in spite of myself. I swam at my gym all the time, of course, but the only outdoor swimming I'd gotten to do in Los Angeles was at Maurice's club, and the pool there was on the small side, more for kids, or for tennis players to take a dip in, too short for me to get a decent workout. Still, I loved the feeling of swimming in the outdoors, the contrast of the air and the water on my skin.

"You'd be helping me with my WASP guilt," Dave said. "I'm the only one who ever uses the pool. It feels wasteful."

"Shazia doesn't swim?" I asked casually, as if I wasn't angling for information about how much time she was spending at Dave's house and how serious they were.

"Not much. It's a hair thing, I guess," he said. "Anyhow. There's a key underneath the welcome mat . . ."

"I heard that!" Big Dave sang out from his office.

Little Dave shook his head fondly. "Just shoot me a text ahead of time."

"Thank you," I said. "That's really nice of you."

He ducked his head. "No problem."

I spent the rest of the week replaying the conversation, wondering whether he'd been serious or had just made the offer on the spur of the moment, never imagining that I'd follow through. I had a boyfriend, I told myself sternly, even though I suspected if I mentioned Dave's offer to Gary, he'd just shrug and tell me to have fun. On Friday I decided that Dave was just being polite . . . but then, on Saturday afternoon, I remembered how he'd looked when he'd been talking about *Body*, how intently he'd stared at me, and I felt my stomach do a slow flip-flop.

He wants to be my friend, I told myself. I could use friends. I'd made a few at *The Girls' Room,* but since my abrupt exit from the show I hadn't kept in touch, so now my circle was small: Gary, Grandma and Maurice, the Daves, the *Bunk Eight* writers, Caitlyn, who emailed from Berkeley, and a few of my college-bound clients who'd kept in touch.

I texted his cell phone at eleven o'clock the next morning, after telling Gary I'd be spending the day with my grandmother. "I'm actually in Vegas," Dave wrote back. "Stop by whenever you like—I won't be home until eight or nine tonight."

I thanked him, plugged his address into my GPS, and drove, trying not to imagine that Dave had invited me over for drinks, or dinner, or to watch a DVD of one of the Oscar-nominated films that he got each year as a voting member of the Writers Guild and cuddle on his couch. Dave lived in a sprawling single-story modern house perched high on a hill near the Getty Museum, just off the 405. The key was where he'd told me it would be, and the wooden door, set in a frame that I guessed had been widened to accommodate his wheelchair, swung open easily. Pocket gave me a welcoming yip before curling back up on her dog bed in a patch of sunshine in the living room. *Don't snoop,* I told myself . . . but it was hard not to stare, not to wander through the beautifully designed and decorated home and marvel at the way it had all been put together.

If the Daves' offices looked like a playroom designed by a ten-year-old boy with an unlimited budget, Little Dave's house looked like something out of one of the decorating magazines I'd buy at the airport to keep me entertained and envious until I landed. There was an actual Andy Warhol hanging in the entryway, and a painting I didn't recognize, a six-by-nine-foot panel of undulating blues and greens in swirls and waves, that dominated the wall between the front door and the living room. The Francis Bacon book I'd given him was displayed on a leather-topped coffee table in the living room, which had, on its hardwood floor, the most beautiful rug I'd ever seen, an intricately patterned design of flowers and sunbursts rendered in shimmering green and gold and turquoise. Waist-high built-in bookcases ran along three of the walls, filled with novels and books about art and photography, collections of screenplays and biographies of famous actors. The fourth wall was floor-to-ceiling windows that looked out at the backyard and the pool. Paintings and framed photographs hung on the walls, and everything was arranged by someone who clearly had an eye for balance and proportion and texture: a heavy wool blanket on a smooth leather chair, a rough sisal rug on a smooth wooden floor, a cushy cotton dog bed and a basket of bones and rubber chew toys next to Pocket's bed. Everywhere I looked, something invited my inspection or my touch—heavy peach-colored marble sculptures shaped like pears and used as bookends; a stuffed leather pig that sat on the mantel over the fireplace, its snout turned up at an insouciant angle; an orchid, thick with violet-and-cream-colored flowers, on an end table, next to a stack of those "Made on a Mac" books of photographs that I had to keep myself from picking up and reading.

Instead, I made myself walk through the white-on-white kitchen, with low marble counters and wide passageways. Like the entire house, it had clearly been designed for someone in a wheelchair and, judging from the way things gleamed, was more to be admired than to be used. Either that or Dave had a housekeeper, someone whose job it was to keep the floors and sinks and countertops immaculate. The back of the kitchen, like the living room, was a wall of glass, with views of a koi pond and a landscaped yard, with brick paths and wooden benches, lush grass and flowering vines. Beyond that was the pool, a narrow rectangle twenty-five yards long, lined with dark-blue tiles and a hot tub at one end, with chaise longues and white canvas umbrellas, a drinks cart and a table for four and a small pool house, a miniature of the main house, behind it.

I walked out back to continue my inspection. At one end of the pool house there was a gym, with weight machines and a hand-pedal recumbent exercise bike. At the other end was a screening room, with half a dozen theater-style chairs and a full-size screen. The bathroom was enormous, with creamy marble tile covering the floor, a ceiling fan spinning slowly overhead, and a giant walk-in—or wheel-in—shower with two overhead spouts the size of dinner plates and a handheld attachment and nozzles bristling from the walls. Beside it were wooden cubbies, built-in dressers, and padded benches covered in green-and-blue-striped fabric. There were wicker baskets of flip-flops by the door, and stacks of blue-and-white towels.

I walked around, letting my fingertips sample the surfaces and fabrics, looking at everything, before sliding open one of the dresser drawers. Inside, I found stacks of women's swimsuits, in all different colors and styles, everything from white string bikinis so skimpy they'd barely fit a toddler to a modest black tank suit in a size sixteen. Some looked as if they'd been worn; others still had tags attached. I wondered who they belonged to, who they'd been bought for. Girlfriends? Female friends? One woman whose weight fluctuated wildly? They definitely didn't all belong to his current love. I'd Googled Shazia somewhat obsessively, and in every picture I'd seen she was the same, tall and slim and elegant.

I picked up the stack of suits, feeling the slippery nylon and Lycra in my hands. I knew the basics of Dave's history: the bits that Big Dave had told me, what I'd been able to glean from gossip, and the profile that the *Hollywood Reporter* had done three years ago. I knew that Dave had been paralyzed in a boating accident right after he'd graduated from college, when his sailboat had been T-boned by a drunk guy in a powerboat near Province-town on Cape Cod Bay. I knew about how he'd deferred his admission to Yale Law School and decided to give Hollywood a try. He'd sold his first show three weeks before his self-imposed one-year deadline, and now went back east only for birthdays, his parents' anniversary, and one Red Sox game each season.

I replaced the pile of swimsuits, reached into my bag, and pulled on the one I'd brought from home. Then I stood in front of the mirror, in the flattering light of the lamps, imagining how Dave might see me. The doctors had spent most of their time and attention on my face, reasoning, correctly, that clothing would cover the worst of the damage most of the time. My right arm and shoulder were puckered and pitted with scars that made it look as if something had been chewing on me. *You look fine,* Gary would say—he wasn't one for compliments, and I tried not to do the needy-girl thing of asking for them. Now I considered myself, my legs tan and smooth with muscle from the swim-ming and hiking and yoga, my hair falling in thick profusion over my shoulders. I would never have one of those va-va-voom Hollywood bodies that balanced a tiny waist with improbably big breasts, but I had, as Grandma was constantly telling me, "a cute figure," decently proportioned and shown off nicely in the V-neck swimsuit I'd selected on the chance that Dave might come home when I was in the water.

Outside, by the pool, I sat on one of the lounge chairs, wrapped in the thick terry towel, feeling the sun warm my face and my feet, listening to the birds and the wind in the trees. If someone had handed me this piece of land and several mil-lion dollars to do whatever I wanted, to build whatever kind of house and garden would please me best, this was probably close to what I would have come up with. In its specifics, it was differ-ent from the little home where I'd grown up, but in its feel, the way it welcomed you, with its play of patterns and texture and color, it felt like the way a home should be. I could see myself cooking in the kitchen, serving meals to Grandma and Maurice and the Daves at the dining-room table, swimming in the pool first thing in the morning, and curling up on the couch as a fire burned late at night.

I wondered again what the deal was with Shazia, and how much time she spent here. I'd tried to keep from poking around too much, but from what I could tell, there didn't seem to be anyone else's stuff in the rooms I'd surveyed—no women's coats hanging in the closet by the front door (I'd broken down and peeked), no yogurt or cottage cheese or diet drinks or pomegranate juice in the refrigerator (I'd looked there, too).

So maybe Dave and Shazia weren't serious. Or maybe, for all I knew, he'd moved into her place, and they were currently not in Vegas at all, but back there, in bed together, doing things to each other that mere mortals would have to pay to see on cable. I pulled on my cap and goggles and eased myself into the water, which was not too cold and not too hot, and held me up like a lover's hands. Like the rest of the house, like every piece of furniture, like the rugs and the cabinets and the color of the walls, it was not too hot and not too cold . . . it was just right.

NINE

The actress stood onstage, in a circle of light, facing an audience I knew she couldn't see. Dressed in a fitted blue skirt, a frilly white blouse, and high heels, she breathed deeply, making her breasts swell against the shirt's buttons. Her nerves were palpable. In the hot stage lights, I could see the fine sheen of sweat on her upper lip. Finally she began.

"I think we can find a way to make this work," she said. I leaned forward in my seat, surrounded by executives, my hands pressed tightly together, knowing every word she'd say, because I'd written them and rewritten them and read them out loud dozens, maybe hundreds of times. The setting was an upscale restaurant in Boston; the woman, Daphne, was a waitress, a regular-looking girl who wore her heart on her sleeve and had big dreams of someday owning a restaurant of her own. In this scene, the first in the show, she was appealing to her boss to let her switch from the front of the house to the kitchen and work with the chefs. *The best pilots are the simplest,* the Daves had instructed me. *It's all about getting the audience to fall in love with your characters, so you tell as basic a story as you can.*

I had listened, and the pilot for *The Next Best Thing* was as stripped down and clean lined as I could make it. Act One: Nana's and Daphne's lives in Boston fall apart, with Nana losing her boyfriend and Daphne losing her job. Act Two: They move to Miami. Act Three: Nana goes on a date and realizes, at the age of seventy-two, that she needs to rely on herself before she can be in another relationship, with another man to support her. Daphne gets turned down for her dream job but then goes back and fights for it and gets the chef to take her on as an unpaid assistant for a week, with the promise to hire her if she can show him she's got the right stuff. Back at home, in the tag, the mini-scene that would run before the next show began, the ladies sit on the couch and review their progress. *We're all right for now*, Daphne says, the words that, in my mind, would end every show. And: *fin*.

Onstage Daphne was pleading with the Boston restaurant manager. "I know I don't have a ton of experience, but if you give me a chance . . ."

"I'm sorry," said her would-be boss, played on this night by Lanny Drew, the head of casting, the one who would give, or withhold, the studio's approval of our choices.

"I'm a good cook." She paused, and in that pause, I could hear her gathering strength to say what she was ashamed to say but knew to be true. She wiped her cheek and blundered on. "Maybe I'm not the prettiest girl in the world, but you've got to have someone who can manage the inventory and deal with the vendors and tell the homeless guys to get lost when they start scaring the customers."

"I'm sorry, Daphne," Lanny said. "I think you're a nice kid. But this isn't the place for you."

The girl on the stage lifted her chin. For a moment, she stood perfectly silent, poised in the light. "Then where is?" she asked . . . and you knew she wasn't asking just about that restaurant, just about that job. This was my question, the one I'd asked every day in the hospital, and in school, after Sarah had abandoned me, and then in college, when I'd thought my looks wouldn't matter and learned, to my sorrow, how much they did and always would. "Where is my place?"

Lanny-as-manager didn't respond. The actress paused and then turned and walked off stage left, putting an extra roll in her hips, letting him know that the war wasn't over and that she intended to win.

There was a moment of silence. I looked sideways at Dave. I'd never been to a network casting session before, and I wasn't clear on the etiquette. Then I decided, *To hell with the etiquette*, and started to clap. Dave joined me, and eventually, so did Lisa and Tariq from the studio, and Maya, the casting director for *Bunk Eight*, who was helping me find the actors for my pilot, and Joan and Lloyd from the network (Lanny, I noticed, had gotten very busy with his BlackBerry). I sank back into my upholstered theater seat, breathless and enthralled. As good as the actress had been in person and on tape, she'd been even better in front of real, live people. "She was amazing!" I whispered to Dave.

He nodded back, his face unreadable, his hands resting on his thighs. "We'll see" was all he said.

The girl's name was Allison Pierce. The previous June, she'd graduated from NYU . . . and, if I got my wish, she'd pack up her apartment, fly back to Los Angeles, and start preparing for a starring role in the pilot. Unless Polly, our next contestant, did a better job . . . but never mind that now.

"Can you give us a few minutes?" Joan called to Dave and me, from her spot a few rows behind us. The network held its auditions in an actual theater, with a stage and lights and auditorium seating and fringed velvet curtains—all of it designed, I suspected, to produce maximum anxiety in the would-be stars. I hurried up the tilted aisle, through the doors, and into the lobby, where our second girl was pacing, talking silently to herself. I found Allison in the ladies' room, standing in front of the sinks, crying.

"Oh my God," I said, hurrying to her side. "What's wrong?"

"I can't believe it's over!" She sniffled and wiped her eyes. Allison was African American, tall and busty, with warm brown eyes and dimpled cheeks. I hadn't imagined Daphne as a black girl. In my head, she'd been white, like me . . . but when I'd seen Allison's audition, I'd decided that I'd be willing to make whatever adjustments were necessary if the network picked her. She was the total package, pretty but relatable, a girl who could handle jokes and drama with equal skill. Best of all, she was a fresh face, a complete unknown, and that, I knew, would help. "Casting people love their shiny new things," Big Dave said. "They're like raccoons. Also, they really like to be the ones to find the hidden treasure and take credit for it."

In the bathroom, I put my hand on Allison's shoulder. "You were amazing."

She wiped the skin underneath her eyes delicately, with her index fingertip. "I still can't believe it," she said. "I can't believe this is happening. I can't believe I'm here!"

"You and me both, sister," I said, and instantly wondered about the propriety of a white woman saying that to a black one. But Allison laughed and gave me a hug.

"Thank you," she said. "Thank you so much!"

"No, thank you," I said, and walked her to the lobby, and told her to enjoy the rest of her time in Los Angeles. Maya had been so impressed with Allison that she'd arranged for her to meet with people at a few other networks and production companies for the remaining twelve hours she'd be in town. "I don't know if this is the show for her," she said, "but that girl's going to make it somewhere."

Dave opened the theater door. "Ruth?" he called. I tried to ignore the thrill that went through me when he said my name. "They're ready for us."

I hurried back down the aisle, waving at Joan as I walked

past. Joan, the head of comedy for the network, defied every stereotype I'd ever heard about women in Hollywood. Instead of being an ageless, aerobicized hardbody who wore designer suits and high heels and could be anywhere between thirty-five and sixty but would never, under penalty of death, look a day older than forty, Joan was unapologetically fifty-seven years old, with wrinkles bracketing her mouth, fleshy upper arms, and a body as slack and soft as a stack of pillows. She wore her white hair in a bun, had mild blue eyes behind glasses on a beaded chain, and never wore makeup other than tinted lip gloss. Joan dressed like a small-town librarian, in sweater vests and elastic-waisted skirts and clogs. I'd never seen her upset, never heard her curse or even raise her voice. But there must have been steel in there somewhere, because she had been on top of the network's comedy department for the unimaginable span of sixteen years, outlasting a half-dozen different bosses and regimes and more shows than I cared to consider.

Finding this handful of potential Daphnes had been an ordeal, a two-week-long slog through hundreds of hopefuls, who had read for us in the windowless room in the back of Maya's Larchmont studio. There were girls who could do jokes but not the poignant stuff, girls who could do drama but not comedy, girls who could do both but didn't have the right look—too old, too young, too skinny, or just, for some inexplicable reason, not what I'd had in mind. It hadn't helped that I was what Maya called, with a mixture of exasperation and affection, "tenderhearted." I wanted to cast every girl who came through the door. I wanted to give them all hot tea and butter cookies and bracing speeches about self-esteem; I wanted to offer them tips and advice and coaching, and bring every girl who evinced even a hint of a possibility that she could be "it" back for another try.

That attitude had lasted for the first two days, and the first forty auditions. After that, I'd gotten increasingly ruthless, ink-ing black lines through girls' names before they'd finished their first speech, tossing their head shots into the recycling bin without a second thought. There were just so many of them, lined up in Maya's waiting room, hanging over the railings on her porch, standing on the sidewalk, chatting, smoking, texting, an inexhaustible supply of young women of all races or ethnicities who were, as we'd requested, at least a size twelve (even though I was pretty sure I'd seen some tens and eights with strategic padding) and who could play twenty-five or younger.

Every day Maya and I would watch a few dozen auditions, with Maya's assistant, Deborah, standing quietly in the corner behind a camera, putting each girl on tape. While we were sorting through possibilities in Los Angeles, Maya's New York City–based associate, Val, was doing the same thing with actresses on the East Coast, and girls from Toronto and Denver and Minnesota were also putting themselves on tape for our consideration. At five or six every night, Maya and I would pick our favorites, and Val would email hers. We'd review the tapes and narrow our choices, arguing and rewatching and bringing in the Daves and sometimes my grandma for a consultation before we'd settled on our four finalists.

We'd brought those four girls in to read for the studio. The executives there, led by Lisa and Tariq, had approved three of them to continue on to the network, cutting the girl we guessed they'd cut, an actress named Susannah Reynolds, who could manage the comedy and the drama but wasn't a standout in either realm. Then Maya and I had spent hours debating the order in which we'd present the girls to the network. Allison, our New York City find, had gone first. Next up was Polly Calcott, who'd been working steadily for the past five years, landing a bit part here, a three-episode arc there, spending each summer touring with *Hairspray*, where she'd played the starring role of Tracy Turnblad. Her experience, especially with multi-camera sitcoms and onstage, would serve her well, I thought, but her body would work against her. When Daphne became a bigger girl in my imagination, I'd thought that she would have an hourglass figure, with plenty of sand on top and on the bottom. Polly was short and square-shaped, cute . . . but if she was good enough, we'd find a way to make it work.

I leaned forward as Polly glided into the spotlight. Her hair was purple—she was playing a corpse on the episode of *NCIS* they were filming that week—and one ear glittered with half a dozen studs. I rolled my eyes at Maya, who gave me a *What can you do?* shrug. We'd asked Polly to look as conservative as possible, as close to the girl she'd be playing, but maybe she'd forgotten.

"Honey, I'm home!" she called, slipping across the stage on stockinged feet (in the script, at the start of the second act, after she and her Nana had moved to Miami, she was wearing Rollerblades). Joan smiled. Lisa actually laughed out loud. That was good, I thought: that even the people who'd read the script a dozen times still thought the funny parts were funny.

"Look out," drawled deadpan Lanny, who, in this scene, was reading the part of Nana. "I've got a cake in the oven."

"And I," said Polly, with a nifty little twirl, "have got a job interview at Emeril's!" She skated up to the edge of the stage and dropped her voice. "Did you see the guy in 11E? Hair," she said temptingly. "Teeth."

"I didn't notice," Lanny droned.

"You like him," said Polly, and hugged herself. "Oh, this is perfect! It's all going to work out! I'll get a great job, you'll fall in love . . ."

Lisa cleared her throat and picked at her thumbnail. Joan, with her eyes still fixed intently on the stage, shifted in her seat. Lanny pulled out his BlackBerry. I snuck a look at Dave, whose face was maddeningly unreadable. Was this going well? Horribly? I watched as Polly finished her scene and took her bow. Again, the executives gathered, whispering and gesturing. I walked up the aisle again to say my good-byes to Polly, who was pulling on a leather jacket and a knitted newsboy's cap. "Gotta run," she said.

"Date?" I asked. It was, after all, Friday night.

She gave me a weary smile and pulled something out of her handbag. An apron. "I'm already late for my shift," she said. "Hey, you should come in sometime. We've got five-dollar small plates during happy hour." With that, she was gone, off to Dan Tana's on Santa Monica Boulevard, where she'd been working as a waitress when she wasn't singing "Good Morning, Baltimore," or pretending to be dead in a Dumpster. It was heartbreaking . . . but, I thought, it also meant she'd bring a certain verisimilitude to the part of a restaurant kitchen rat.

Joan stuck her head back into the hallway. "We're ready, Ruth."

My breath caught in my throat. Where was Carter? I looked around at the empty cubicles, the vacant couches, the quiet corridors. By the time I'd turned back to the doors, Carter DeVries was charging through them, red-faced and breathless, her hair pulled into a ragged ponytail, with her script in one hand and her cell phone in the other. "Oh my God, did I miss it? Are they still here? There was this huge accident on Barham, and I was going to ditch my car and, like, run here. Please tell me I didn't miss it." She wiped her forehead, then tugged at her hair. "I think I parked in a handicapped spot."

"They're waiting for you. But don't worry. Take a minute. Give me your keys," I said. Carter handed me her keys and then collapsed on her back on the couch, hot-pink Keds waving disconsolately in the air as she groaned out loud. Carter was twenty-two, the veteran of an improv troupe who'd won awards for a one-woman show she'd written and performed called *Time of the Month*. She was, in my opinion, the funniest of the would-be Daphnes. Every time she read Daphne's lines about the Walk of Shame, Senior Version, where Nana Trudy's peers made their way back to their condo in last night's clothes, with their orthopedic shoes in their hands, their teeth in their pocket, and last night's Depends in their purse, she found different inflections, different places to pause, a way to make each take fresh and funny. She struggled with the more serious parts—her natural inclination was to make a joke of everything—but Dave, in his quiet, persistent way, made the case that drama was easier to learn than comedy. "Let's give her a chance," he'd said. *Give me a chance*, I'd thought before I'd been able to stop myself, and I'd smiled and said, "How can I refuse you?"

My concern about Carter was that she was too offbeat looking for prime time. She had what I'd call an interesting face, lovely from some angles, plain from others. She was also significantly heavier than the other girls, a size 22/24 where they were in the 14/16 range . . . but again, as with Allison's skin color and Polly's proportions, if she impressed the executives, we'd adjust.

On the couch, Carter gulped from her aluminum water bottle, then re-capped it and grinned. "Come on, Captain," she said, hopping to her feet. "Let's do this thing." She held the stage door open for me, giving me a small, mocking bow, then bounded up onstage, hollering, "I'm going to Hollywood!" before turning, squinting into the lights, and saying, "Oh, wait, I'm already here."

I took my seat, crossing and recrossing my legs while she did her scenes, the Daphne-loses-her-job and the Nana's-got-a-crush. My heart was beating so hard, I was sure Dave could hear it. When I'd been watching Allison, she'd been my first choice. When I'd watched purple-haired Polly, I'd thought the same thing. But now, listening to Carter, the girl who'd probably shared more of my experiences than the other two, the one who, unlike gorgeous Allison or plucky, punky Polly, actually had been a bit of an outcast, kind of a freak, I could imagine her, for example, standing outside a high school where a girl she'd thought was her friend walked right by, and in that moment I wanted her to get the part, wanted it so badly that it made me feel almost dizzy.

"We're all right for now," said Carter—the last line of the last speech in the script. She glanced down at the pages she'd kept in her hands and then lifted her head and looked out at the crowd.

"Thank you," Lanny drawled, sounding monumentally ungrateful. Carter bobbed a brief nod and then walked quickly off the stage, leaving the room quiet. I hurried out to tell her how well she'd done. When I got back to the auditorium, the murmuring was still going on. After a few minutes of straining, and failing, to make out more than a few words, I turned to Dave.

"Do I say something?"

He shook his head. "They talk first." He patted my knee, unaware of the way that simple gesture caused chills to race up my spine. "Deep breath, Ruthie. There's no firing squad behind the curtain. The worst is over."

I nodded, looking around the room. Maya had picked up her phone and was huddled in the corner, probably calling other actors about parts on other shows. When she saw me watching, she gave me a keep-your-chin-up wave, and I made myself wave back.

"You okay?" Dave asked.

"I feel like their mother!" I whispered back. "I'm a wreck. I want them all to get it."

"Not going to happen," Dave pointed out. "There can be only one."

"I know," I said, practically moaning, "but I just wish . . ."

Raised voices interrupted us, Lanny saying, "It won't work," then Lisa, with "I disagree. I disagree completely."

I swallowed hard. "Does it always take this long?" I asked. I was hoping for another reassuring squeeze. I could barely keep still while Dave sat still, his hands in his lap, as if he was meditating and could stay that way, perfectly at ease, for hours, even for days. That was when Lanny started talking.

"Well. You've given us three very interesting choices."

I turned around to look at them, forcing a smile. In the world of television, *interesting* was not a word that you wanted to hear. Maybe on cable, things were different, but interesting was not a good thing at the networks.

"How old is Allison?" Tariq began.

"Twenty-two," I said. "She just graduated from NYU."

"She looks older," said Lanny. Lanny had a high, nasal voice, an Alabama accent, and a reputation, formed during his years in business affairs, of bedeviling creative types over the most trivial matters. He was, the Daves had told me, a guy who would scrutinize shows' expense reports and make a fuss about the ten-dollar line item that showed what you spent on toilet paper or ink cartridges every week. Most showrunners simply ignored him, but one, a man who had enough money to buy his own island after creating successful, long-running shows in the 1970s, 1980s, and 1990s, had gotten so frustrated with Lanny's carping over the high price of flavored coffees that he'd hired an espresso cart to visit the set each afternoon, dispensing lattes, loose-leaf tea, artisanal gelato, and a variety of fresh-baked pastries. *How do you like me now?* read the note that he'd faxed to Lanny, attached to a copy of the bill for the cart, the previous week's ratings, and what was reputed to be a Xerox of the showrunner's bare ass.

"I think Allison has a kind of gravitas," I said. I actually thought that her height and natural solemnity would play off her sweet smile and serve Daphne's character well. Even when she was dithering over the wrong guy, screwing up at work, or falling on her face on Rollerblades, you'd know that, deep down, Daphne was a girl who knew what she was doing in the world. Besides, she had dimples. How could you not smile when a girl with dimples was smiling?

Evidently Lanny could. "I just don't buy her as a comic lead," he drawled. "I mean, maybe Medusa . . ."

Medusa? "Medea," Dave corrected quietly.

"Right," said Lanny, entirely unfazed. "Big, dramatic roles, fine, I get it, but she's not an ingénue."

"Moving on," said Joan, who was seated in the row in front of Lanny. I tried to hide my devastation, to look professional as Joan opened the notebook on her lap (the notebook had kittens with sparkly fur cavorting on the cover). "I thought Carter was hands-down the funniest."

"I agree," I said quickly.

"I wouldn't fuck her," Lanny said. I stared at him. He lifted his chin with a smug *Yeah, you heard me* expression on his face.

I felt my jaw drop. *Oh, no,* I thought. *I did not just hear that.* Someone—Lisa, I guessed—sucked in her breath, but nobody said *Excuse me,* or *What did you say,* or *Hello, sexual harassment lawsuit,* and Lanny didn't apologize. The room had gone silent, except for the sound of my heart.

"What?" I finally managed.

"Her face," Lanny explained—not to me, though; to Dave. Lanny seemed to have decided that even though I'd come up with the concept and written the script, Dave was really the one in charge, and thus he addressed all his remarks to Dave. Maybe he couldn't stand to look at my face, or he was similarly dismissive to all young women, or to all women in general. As I sat there, stunned, Lanny picked up Carter's head shot, a picture of a perfectly nice-looking girl with long dark hair and a wry, thin-lipped smile. "She's got maybe two good angles."

A flush was creeping up my neck. Daphne as I'd written her was never meant to be a beauty . . . in fact, it was important that she not be a beauty. She had other qualities, and her nothing-special looks were one of the reasons the regular girls would root for her. "So we'll shoot her from her two good angles."

Lanny was shaking his head. "That's asking for trouble. Believe me. I went through this with Alyssa Rose." Alyssa Rose was a former network star who, indeed, looked lovely when shot head-on, but in profile resembled nothing more than a long-faced, large-nosed Abraham Lincoln.

"What I think Lanny's saying," Tariq said hastily, "is that you need the lead of a comedy to have a kind of universal appeal."

"What about Polly?" asked Lisa. "I thought she was solid."

"She's the second girl," Lanny said. Meaning, Polly wasn't a lead, but the lead's best friend, the girl our male lead would date for three episodes before realizing he was meant to be with the headliner.

"Look," I said. "As you guys know, I was going for something specific here. Daphne's supposed to be a regular girl—"

"TV-regular," Maya interjected.

I frowned, but kept going. "You know, an identifiable, relatable, normal—"

"TV-normal," said Lanny.

I blinked at them both. "Does TV-normal mean regular-world gorgeous?"

The room got quiet again. In the silence, I heard my answer. *TV-normal* did, of course, mean regular-world gorgeous. Polly and Carter hadn't been pretty enough, and Allison hadn't been young enough or relatable enough or, possibly, white enough, even though none of them would ever say so. Not out loud. It was just understood . . . by everyone except me.

My heart sank. I was afraid to look at Maya. *Back to the*

drawing board, except who could we possibly see who we hadn't auditioned already? What rock was left to kick over, what tree was left to shake?

That was when Joan started talking. "We have an idea," she said. I turned toward her eagerly, thinking, *Yes, please, anything, you're the experts, you fix this*. "We'd like to do the show with Cady Stratton," she said. "Pending our executive producers' approval, of course," she added, giving Dave and me a bright smile. "We've had a holding deal with her since she left *All Our Tomorrows*. We've been looking for the right project, and we think this might be it."

I kept my face immobile, trying to regroup as fast as I could. My sense of who Cady Stratton was—a pretty girl with Marilyn Monroe curves who'd been the costar of a long-running soap until a few years ago and hadn't worked since—was dismayingly vague.

"Will she read?" I asked.

Joan shook her head. "She's offer-only. We can send you tape . . ." She looked over at her assistant, who jumped out of her chair like it was spring-loaded and racewalked out of the room.

Dave put his hand on my arm and squeezed until I shut my mouth. While maintaining his grip on me, he maneuvered his chair so that he was facing the executives. "I'm sure," he said, "that Cady Stratton will be just fine."

Cady Stratton. I drove myself to the Two Daves' offices, trying to remember exactly what Cady Stratton looked like, how her voice sounded, whether she could, conceivably, be a decent Daphne, even though I knew that these were, more than likely, rhetorical questions. When the network said, "We'd like to do the show with X," even if X was a talking chimp or the executive producer's talent-free first cousin, you smiled and said, "Of course, what a brilliant idea." The chances were good that they'd had Cady in mind before the auditions had even started . . . which meant, of course, that all three of our picks were losers before they'd said a single word.

I waved hello at Bradley, the Daves' new assistant, and set up my laptop in the conference room. There, I provisioned myself with coconut water and energy bars from the pantry and devoted the next several hours to learning all I could about the star of my show.

Cady was easy to find on the Internet. She had a website, an IMDB page, and a Wikipedia entry. She was on Facebook, she was on Twitter, and a number of fans had set up their own sites in appreciation of her work—or, in the case of one terrifying Tumblr, in appreciation of her cleavage. In twenty minutes' time, I learned that Cady had been the lead actress's smart-mouthed, funny daughter on *All Our Tomorrows.* In her three years on the show, she'd been kidnapped by an Arab sheikh, struggled with agoraphobia, run off to join a cult (this, presumably, after conquering her fear of leaving the house), and given birth to her stepbrother's twins. Cady had a heart-shaped face framed with strawberry-blond hair, and looked about as Jewish as a ham sandwich, but I could deal with that. I scrolled through years' worth of reviews, articles that mentioned her expert timing, her wide-eyed cuteness, her combination of beauty and sass. She had the right body type, even if, at a curvy size ten, she wasn't as big as I'd hoped my leading lady would be . . . but was she ready to carry a show?

"She's funny," said Dave as we sat in front of his jumbo-size computer screen and watched a teenage Cady poke her head, accented with a banana peel, out of the trash can where she and her best friend were hiding from their mothers in a Nickelodeon movie of the week. It was clear that Cady knew exactly where the camera was positioned, and exactly how to angle her face to find the light.

"She's really good," I said. Except for the goyische-looking thing—the pale skin and blond hair, the button nose and pert chin that, combined, said Straight Out of Mankato—Cady was all I could wish for, adorable and charming and at ease in her skin. "Look at this." I tapped Dave's mouse and called up an interview from some women's magazine's "Body Issue." Cady had been featured and photographed in a red satin corset, her rounded bottom perched on the edge of an old-fashioned soda fountain stool, creamy-skinned breasts tilted toward the marble counter, cherry-colored lips wrapped around the candy-striped straw that was stuck into a chocolate shake. "It took me some time, but I've finally gotten comfortable with my curves," Cady proclaimed in the copy. "I'll never be a size zero, but as long as I'm happy and healthy, that's fine."

I snuck a look at Dave looking at her—those curves! that cleavage!—and was relieved when he didn't seem especially impressed.

"Promising," he said. He'd pulled his chair right up next to me, with Pocket curled in his lap, close enough that I could smell his scent—nutmeg and cloves, paper and ink, and the corn-chip smell that Pocket's paws and fur exuded—as I clicked through pictures of Cady in a low-cut dress at a movie premiere, tabloid shots of Cady holding hands in the airport with an aged-out Mouseketeer, and a Q and A she'd done with *TV Guide*.

"You don't think she's too pretty?" I asked. Dave stroked Pocket's back, and I watched the dog wriggle in pleasure. He shook his head.

"Visual medium," he reminded me, and I nodded. My heart was breaking for the girls I'd found on my own, but some of that was about me, not them. I'd wanted to be the fairy godmother, waving my magic wand over an unknown, transforming her pumpkin into a carriage and her rags into a ball gown, turning her into a star. In my imagination, the girl who won the role would be a girl like me, broken in some essential way, moving through a world that didn't want her. But even more than any of that, I wanted the show to succeed. I wanted the pilot to get picked up, to make it on the air, to be admired by critics and beloved by viewers, and eventually, to run for seven seasons. With Cady on board, the chances of all that happening would increase exponentially, and I was enough of a pragmatist to see it.

Pocket nuzzled at my wrist, lifting my hand. I imagined Carter and Polly and Allison hearing their phones ring, listening to the polite phrases I'd heard Maya recite a thousand times: *You're gorgeous. You were great, it's just that the network* (or the studio, or the producers) *decided to go in a different direction.* I remembered Allison crying in the bathroom, how Carter's face had glowed when she'd finished that last speech, and how brutally Lanny had dismissed her . . . and now here I was, supposedly their ally, their sister, dismissing all of them, like they'd never meant anything to me. Was I turning into a terrible person? Had Hollywood done this to me? Or had there been a heartless person inside all along, just waiting for a chance to crawl out into the light and start hurting other women the way I'd been hurt?

My cell phone trilled in my purse. Shelly, my agent, was on the line.

"Hey, Ruth Saunders. You okay with the Cady of it all? Good," she said before I could answer. "I've got another request from the network. They're wondering if we could call Daphne something maybe a little less . . ."

"Jewish?" I guessed.

"She can still be Jewish," Shelly assured me. "Just, you know . . ."

"Assimilated. You know what? We don't need to give her a last name for the pilot. We can just call her Daphne. I never heard back from legal about whether 'Daphne Danhauser' cleared or not." That struck me as a reasonable compromise to make for the time being. If we got picked up, I could go back and make her a true Jewess again, after I'd found some way to explain Cady's distinctly non-Semitic appearance. Maybe I could say she'd been adopted.

The office door swung open. Pocket, who'd been dozing, lifted her head from Dave's thigh and gave a brief yip as Shazia came striding into the room. "Hi, baby," she said, and bent down to kiss Dave. I turned away, but not before I saw their lips meet as she scooped Pocket off his lap and into her arms. "And how was your day, sweetheart?" she asked, snuggling the dog against her. I would have given anything for Pocket to growl, or to jump out of Shazia's arms and into mine, but the dog wriggled happily as Shazia scratched her chest. *Traitor.*

"You guys still working?" Shazia asked, setting Pocket down gently.

By then I was on my feet, collecting my purse and my notebook. "Just wrapping up. I should head home. More auditions in the morning." It seemed unreal, but in less than twelve hours I'd be back in the casting office in Larchmont, holding auditions for the part of Nana Trudy. Maya had already lined up a parade of where-are-they-nows, sitcom and movie stars of the 1970s who were willing to read for the part.

Shazia turned to me, brushing her hair back over her shoulders. "Why don't you come out with us? We were just going to grab sushi."

"Oh, no. Thanks, but I bet my grandmother's got dinner waiting for me." I almost groaned out loud. Could I have sounded any more like a ten-year-old?

"Are you sure?" Dave asked. "I think we could both use a drink."

"Thanks, but you two go ahead." Dave whistled for Pocket, who jumped into his lap, and rolled out the door with Shazia behind him, one hand resting lightly on his shoulder.

I waited until his car was gone and the office lights, on an energy-conserving timer, had gone out, and I was sitting in the darkness. Yes? No?

Yes. I slipped off my shoes and, in my bare feet, crept down the hallway and eased open Dave's office door.

The space was sophisticated and comfortable, a version of his home, only with a few more WASP-at-work touches. There were hardwood floors, with a single gorgeous Oriental rug in front of his desk, where two clubby leather chairs sat, a wooden table between them. His desk was a massive slab of teak, and on it was a computer, a wood-and-leather in-box that sat empty, a painted tin mug full of pens, and two photographs in frames made of driftwood that I'd caught only glances of as I'd come in and out to deliver him a sandwich or a coffee, to drop off scripts or usher people in for meetings. There was a *Bunk Eight* poster on the wall, a framed shot of the cast signed by all the actors next to it, and a vintage poster of the Boston MTA hanging on the wall behind his desk, and beside it, a framed poster reading VISIT BEAUTIFUL CAPE COD, with a painting of a cottage colony at sunset, the blue-gray waves dissolving in curls of foam.

One corner of the room belonged to Pocket—there was an organic cotton dog bed, slipcovered in chocolate brown with jaunty pink accents, and metal bowls for food and water, and a basket of rawhide bones and rubber chew toys. There was a couch for guests, a brass-and-wood bar cart with crystal pitchers for water and Scotch and vodka and brandy, a monogrammed silver ice bucket, cut-crystal glasses and cloth napkins, white linen embroidered with blue sailboats. Next to Pocket's bed, probably so she could practice playing executive, sat stacks of scripts.

I crossed the room, gliding on my tiptoes, settled my hip on the edge of the desk (there was, of course, no chair), and picked up the first picture. It was a family shot: a younger Dave, with more hair, on a beach with his arms around a young man and a young woman who, judging from the similar cast of their features, the color of their eyes and hair, were his brother and sister. There was a boat in the background, resting on its side, its yellow-and-white sail pooled on the sand, and the young woman's hair was blowing in her eyes and mouth. All of them were smiling. Dave wore a Harvard T-shirt and khaki shorts, and I could see his calves, his knees, tanned and strong with the waves frothing around them. His feet were submerged by the water. The girl had a metal pail in her hand, and I bet it was full of steamers or oysters, something they'd gathered for dinner. I imagined that later, they'd have a bonfire on the beach, and all the summer kids, the lifeguards and camp counselors, the ice-cream scoopers and lobster-roll sellers, would come. Someone would play a guitar, someone else would pass around a bottle of booze, and as the flames died down, couples would slip away into the dunes, carrying blankets or towels. I'd been to a dozen bonfires like that the summer I'd worked as a lifeguard, although, of course, no one had ever taken my hand and walked with me across the cooling sand into a secluded nook carved out by the wind.

I traced the edge of the picture with my thumb and wondered if that was the sailboat Dave had been on during the accident. Would you want a picture of that hanging around, confronting you every day? I couldn't imagine.

I set the picture down and picked up the one beside it . . . and there were Dave and Shazia, at some black-tie gala. Dave was in a tuxedo. Shazia, poured into a red dress with a plunging neckline, sat on his knee. Her head was flung back, eyes shut, mouth open, and she was laughing hard. One of Dave's hands rested on her thigh, the other was on the small of her back, and he was looking up at her like she was Venus, the goddess of love herself, come down from Mount Olympus and landed on his lap.

I put the picture back fast and, in doing so, brushed the computer's mouse. The thundering notes of the *Close Encounters* theme filled the office, and I leapt off the desk, stifling a scream, as the screen blossomed to life. There was a space to type in a password, same as on my computer . . . and before I could stop myself, I reached out and took my best guess, typing the letters that spelled POCKET.

Welcome, said the screen. The desktop opened . . . and there was Dave's in-box, just begging for my tap.

In for a penny, in for a pound, I thought, and tapped, and saw what I expected to see: emails from Big Dave about the current *Bunk Eight* script. Notes from the studio, notes from the network, notes from me about setting up a lunch with potential line producers next week. I scrolled halfway down the first page, through eighty emails, before I found one from Shazia . . . and because it had been opened, I figured I was safe. I clicked and saw that he'd written, "Nine o'clock?" And she'd written back, "I'll be there." Then she'd typed, "I adore you." And Dave had written back, "You're my girl."

I adore you. You're my girl. I closed the in-box, put the computer back to sleep, and sat cross-legged in the chair opposite his desk. Somehow, those endearments were more intimate, more specific, than *I love you.* Anyone could say *I love you* . . . but not everyone could make Shazia laugh the way Dave did. Beautiful Shazia.

I'd thought it before I'd walked into this room, but now I believed it, beyond any doubt. They were in love. I didn't have a chance. I turned off the lights, put on my shoes, locked the doors behind me, and drove home along the empty freeway, past the billboards for a half-dozen TV shows that would probably be off the air, canceled, before *The Next Best Thing* even debuted.

I got home just after eleven o'clock. Normally, Grandma would have been asleep. She'd leave dinner warming in the oven or wrapped in foil on the counter, with a note as to how it should be reheated and stored, and details of how she'd spent her day and what she planned to do tomorrow. But that night, she was sitting in the kitchen, in her dressing gown and the fur-trimmed mules that I'd bought her as a joke and that she'd decided that she loved and wore almost constantly when she was at home. There was beef-and-barley soup on the stove, fresh-baked challah on the counter, and Maurice's soft, somehow upper-class snores issuing from behind her closed bedroom door. The kitchen windows were cracked open. I could hear the low thrum of traffic and could smell Los Angeles at night, car exhaust and sun-baked pavement, citrus and salt from the sea.

"*Nu?*" Grandma asked. "Did they pick a winner?"

I slumped at the dining-room table, my spoon in my hand, my chin a few perilous inches from my bowl of beef-and-barley, so tired I could barely keep my eyes open. "They didn't want any of them. They're giving us Cady Stratton."

"Cady who?"

"Stratton. She was on . . ." I paused, yawning enormously. "A soap opera. Some Lifetime movies. She's funny. She has a good look."

Grandma frowned. "Did she audition? I don't remember her name."

I shook my head. "The network had a holding deal with her. They're giving her to us." When Grandma didn't answer, I told her, "This is how it works. It's collaborative. I bring something to the table, they bring something to the table." Even as I was reciting my lines, I was remembering what Dave had told me at our kickoff dinner, how I should enjoy the moment before the show became adulterated, before everyone else started imposing their visions on the world I had imagined.

Grandma carried two plates from the kitchen cabinet to the claw-footed table for six that she'd had shipped out from our house in Framingham. She sliced off a chunk of challah and covered it with butter and marmalade, taking her time, spreading jam right to the edge of the crust.

"She'll be great!" I said, trying to sound excited about a star I'd never met.

Grandma nibbled at her bread and said nothing.

"I mean, I'm sure the studio wouldn't have picked her if they didn't think she'd be amazing."

Wordlessly, my grandmother re-capped the jar.

"Maybe I'll get a better sense after I meet her." When I bent to kiss her, she took my hand.

"Ruthie," she said. "I have some news."

My skin bristled with goose bumps as I sat back down at the table, in the seat closest to the door, the one that had always been mine. Was she sick? Was that why she'd waited up, to tell me?

"What?" I said in a voice that was strangled and small.

She sat up straight, her hands folded in her lap, neck erect, face elegant in profile with her hair drawn tightly back. "Maurice has asked me to marry him."

At first I thought I'd misheard her. I was so tired, and the day had been so crazy, that maybe she actually had said something about breast cancer or heart disease and I'd missed it. I made my brain replay each word, one at a time, and I forced myself to smile, even though I felt as alarmed as if she'd told me that she actually was sick. It felt as if someone had pulled a plug and I was watching everything I'd counted on, everything I'd believed in—my grandmother, my boyfriend, the house and town I'd known—spiraling away until they were gone. This was not part of the plan . . . and in all the ways I'd imagined my life proceeding as I went through shooting the pilot and waited for the pickup, my grandma's tying the knot and, presumably, moving out, leaving me alone, had never been part of the picture.

"Congratulations!" I said in a kind of beauty-queen squeal, too high and too loud, patently false. I got up and hugged her with arms that felt frozen, all the while keeping a smile pinned to my face. Grandma hugged me back.

"We're going to move into his place," she said, and then took my face in her hands and looked at me. "You'll be fine," she said.

"What? Of course I'll be fine! I'm so happy for you!" I turned away, taking my seat again, certain that I looked as if I'd been slapped. *No, I will not be fine.* I could barely stand to think about it. I would be alone, completely alone. My parents had died, Rob had married someone else, Gary had dumped me, Dave loved Shazia and didn't think of me as anything more than a friend, and now my grandmother was ditching me, too?

Oh, grow up, I thought. Here I was, twenty-eight years old, with a great apartment and a more-than-decent paycheck and, of course, a pilot I'd be shooting, all the standard trappings of grown-up life, and I was freaking out because my grandmother had announced that it was time for me to live on my own. This could not possibly be normal. I forced myself to look pleased, tried to manage delighted, then pulled back to merely not miserable. "When is all of this happening?" I made myself ask.

"Maybe in the fall," she said. "I've got some work to do on that house, but once I get rid of the pictures of his late wife and throw out some of the potpourri, it'll be fine." She dropped her voice to a stage whisper that could have been heard on stages miles away. "You know that bathroom they added to the guest house is illegal."

"I knew he looked shifty," I said, half to myself.

"And upstairs, there's all of those bedrooms . . ." Her voice trailed off. I wondered whether she and Maurice had ever considered offering me one of those empty rooms, rooms formerly inhabited by Maurice and his late wife's children. But that was crazy. I wasn't a child. I'd lived in a single in a dorm for my last two years of college. I was a grown-up, with responsibilities. A job. A show. I'd be fine by myself. Still, I couldn't imagine this apartment without her: eating meals by myself, coming home at night without greeting anyone who cared about how my day had gone, waiting to ask who I'd seen, what I'd done.

"I hope you'll be happy," I said stiffly. "What kind of wedding are you planning?"

"At our age?" She widened her eyes to indicate the ridiculousness of my question. "Something small. Maybe here, in the lobby. Just a few friends." She then launched into a discussion about Maurice's sons, who, it emerged, had not been thrilled to learn that their father was taking a bride. "Worried about their inheritance," Grandma scoffed. She stood up and began loading the dishwasher as I sat, immobilized, at the table. Driving home, I'd been planning on having a glass of wine while I went through the Friday mail, which usually included my copies of *Us* and *People* and *Entertainment Weekly*. The stack was on the little table by the door and the wine was in the refrigerator, but I found I lacked the energy to stand, to sort, to pour. "Like I'm some kind of gold-digging floozy." Maurice, I knew, still fondly referred to his two sons as "the boys," even though one of them, a lawyer, was retired and the other was a podiatrist in Orange County, and both of them were married, with children and, in the podiatrist's case, grandchildren of their own.

"They're not happy for him?" For a moment I imagined calling them up, rallying them to my team, finding a way for the three of us to stop this marriage from happening. They'd keep the house they'd grown up in just the way they remembered it, complete with pictures of their mother on the mantel and dusty potpourri in the powder room, and I'd keep my grandma with me.

I shook my head at my own folly. "Well, I'm thrilled," I made myself say. I should have been thrilled. Maurice was a gentleman, considerate and generous and kind, and he worshipped my grandmother. It was evident in the way he looked at her, held doors for her, tucked a shawl over her shoulders when they watched TV, and sent back her soup and her coffee when he thought they weren't hot enough for her liking. "Maurice is great."

For a moment, Grandma didn't answer, and when she spoke her voice was low and thoughtful, with its usual merry, teasing quality absent. "I wonder sometimes whether I did the right thing, staying with you for all this time," she said. When I didn't say anything, she continued, "I wanted what every parent wants. The thing you never get: for your children to never be hurt. And you'd been hurt so badly . . ."

I noticed with alarm that she was crying—my grandma, who I couldn't remember crying since that long-ago night in the hospital. She raised her chin, brushing tears off her cheeks but not trying to hide them. "Hey," I said, reaching for her hand, handing her a napkin. "Hey, everything's okay."

She pulled away, turning so her back was to me and she was facing the open window and the dark sky. "It's not," she said. "It's not!" She took a deep breath, one hand on her chest, over the turquoise silk robe embroidered with red poppies. "I wanted you never to be hurt again," she said. "But everyone gets hurt."

Don't I know it, I thought.

"I'm like one of those mothers who makes their kid wear a helmet and knee pads to ride a tricycle down the driveway," she said. "I didn't do you any favors, living with you this long. I thought it was for your good, but really, I think it was for mine."

"What do you mean?"

She held up her hand. Standing in the kitchen, in her nightgown, under the overhead lights in their flea-market milk-glass shades, she looked every year of her age. *Overhead lighting,* she'd once told me, *is no woman's friend.* "I lost my husband. I lost my daughter. I didn't want to lose anyone else. I didn't think I could stand it. I didn't want to be alone, so I didn't let you go when

I should have. And Ruthie, that wasn't right." She said, "I told myself I was doing it to protect you, but I was just selfish. A selfish, foolish old woman."

"Grandma—"

She talked over me. "I should have pushed you out of the nest when it was time for you to go. I should have made you leave."

"So you're pushing me out now." I meant to sound light-hearted; instead I just sounded sullen and glum. Grandma must have heard that in my voice, because her own tone sharpened.

"It's not as if you're Moses in the bulrushes," she said. "I'm not leaving you on someone's doorstep in a shoebox, Ruthie. You'll have this place. Besides, you've got your TV show."

"That's right," I said quietly. "My show."

She closed the refrigerator and then the dishwasher, and turned off the lights. "So much to do!" she said as she made her way down the hallway, toward her bedroom. "We'll have to figure out the guest list . . . and find a caterer . . . and music, of course . . ."

I waited until she'd closed her bedroom door before I sat down on the living-room couch, in the darkness. Grandma getting married. It sounded like a punch line. I wondered if I could use it in *The Next Best Thing*. As to the bigger question, of how I'd live alone after years of being tended to, supported, encouraged, and fed—well, millions of women, some of them probably less equipped than I was, had managed that transition for thousands of years. I'd figure it out somehow. I curled on my side, closed my eyes, and tried to ignore that I felt exactly the way she'd described: a baby in a basket, like Moses in the bulrushes, abandoned on a perilous river, all alone.

PART TWO

~

The New World

TEN

The morning after my grandmother gave me her news, I was back at Maya's office in Larchmont, starting with auditions all over again, only now we were looking for a woman in her sixties instead of a fresh-faced funny girl. "Good morning!" Maya's assistant greeted me, handing me a bottle of water and a stack of head shots. "Wait till you see who we've got today!" I smiled back, even though I was having difficulty focusing on anything except what my life would be like without my grandmother.

From nine o'clock sharp until our first break at ten-thirty, I sat motionless in the little back room on Maya's uncomfortably itchy tweed couch (I suspected she'd picked an uncomfortable couch on purpose because it kept producers from falling asleep), watching the hopefuls read their lines. "You okay?" Maya asked after the appearance of an Oscar winner from the 1980s, who'd swanned through the door in costume and in character, wearing a silk robe and teetering heels, failed to earn even a smile. Normally I'd be dazzled and shy in the presence of the stars I'd grown up watching. I'd blush and offer flustered compliments and stare at them too hard, trying, in some cases, to determine if they'd had work done (most had), and if the work was working (mostly it wasn't). Another candidate, a woman whose posters had adorned many a dorm-room wall, seemed to have undergone a procedure that had severed all connection between the upper and lower halves of her face. As she read Nana Trudy's big speech, her forehead and eyes would move, and then, a split second later, her cheeks and jaw would catch up. It was very disconcerting, a kind of real-life time-lapse photography, and the actress's agent seemed to know that things weren't right. Prior to the audition, he'd called Maya with a heads-up, saying that the actress had had a recent bad experience with what he said was an "overly aggressive chemical peel." (This, I had learned, was Hollywood code for anything from "bad Botox" to "just got out of rehab" to "needs to go back into rehab.") While he admitted that, at present, she looked "a little strange," he wanted to assure us that the effects were temporary. "As if," Maya said, tossing the actress's ten-year-old head shot into the recycling bin before turning back to me. We were in a ten-minute lull between prospectives, and she wanted to talk. "So what's going on? Are you all right with Cady?"

I gave a firm showrunner-ish nod. "I think Cady will be fine." This was what I'd decided to tell myself after a troubled night's sleep and an early-morning swim. The truth was, any actress was a gamble. The ability to kill in an audition didn't necessarily mean that an actress could do the same thing on show night, in front of an audience . . . and even if she did great in front of the people, there were the cameras and the editors to consider. Drying off after my shower, I'd told myself that this was a case where the network knew best. It was, after all, their money on the line, their job to know which actress would get viewers to watch. And who knew? If Cady had consented to audition, it was entirely possible that she'd have been at the top of my list, that I'd have rooted for her as hard as I'd hoped for her competition the night before.

"So what, then?" Maya sat down on the couch beside me,

close enough that I could smell the lavender essential oil she rubbed on her wrists. I wondered about her interest. Was it a kind of professional courtesy she was extending, or had she come to think of me as a friend? We had traded the basics of our private lives, so I knew that she was single, that she had an eight-year-old, that her parents had sold their home and bought an RV that they parked for four weeks each summer in her driveway up on Laurel Canyon.

"Well, my grandmother's getting married," I began.

"Mazel tov," said Maya. Maya wasn't Jewish—at least, not as far as I knew—but in Hollywood almost everyone ended up what the Daves called Tribe by Osmosis, comfortable dropping the occasional phrase in Yiddish, and knowing better than to set lunch meetings on Yom Kippur or send a muffin basket during Passover. "Is that all?"

I hesitated.

"Not Cady," said Maya, lifting one finger. "Grandma getting married, that's a good thing." She looked at me slyly. "Is it a guy?"

When I didn't answer, she leaned even closer. "Gary?" she asked.

"No," I said. I'd given Maya the bare-bones version of our breakup right after it had happened. She'd nodded, brewed me a cup of chamomile tea, and said, "This probably sounds harsh, but honestly? Better that it happened now than in the middle of production."

"But is it a guy?" she asked me now.

I shrugged, thinking a guy would make more sense than explaining that I was upset about being abandoned by my grandmother. "Just a crush. Nothing serious. He doesn't even know."

Maya plopped herself down on the couch, sending a stack of head shots spilling onto the floor, crossing her legs, in their two-toned tights, and kicking off her red patent leather clogs.

Maya was in her early forties, a lifelong Los Angeleno with the wardrobe of an elementary-school art teacher who went every year to Burning Man: lots of loose, flowing tunics that she'd pair with natural-fiber skirts, cotton leggings, and clunky metal jewelry. Her brown hair was a frizzy corona, strands of which were constantly getting stuck in her lip gloss.

"Tell me everything," she said.

I shook my head, embarrassed.

"It is someone you work with?" she asked.

"Yeah," I admitted. "Which is the problem. I mean, I had a crush on a guy I worked with once. It didn't end well." I imagined that someone had probably filled her in on my history with Rob. It was too juicy a bit of gossip to remain in the small orbit of *The Girls' Room*.

Maya adjusted her serape. "It happens. People deal." This was true. I knew of a few formerly married couples, actors and agents and talent managers, who'd managed to continue running film production companies side by side even after they'd broken up. I also was remembering the rest of Maya's story, which I'd heard years ago from Big Dave. For ten years, Maya had dated an actor named Wes who spent half the year acting and auditioning in Los Angeles and the other half doing television and theater in Canada, where he'd been born and where he still maintained a residence (and got health insurance). Spotting this fellow in the shows Maya cast became an insider's game of "Where's Waldo?" He'd appear as a bartender, a party guest, a bouncer, a chauffeur, a well-meaning uncle on a Very Special Episode of a sitcom, the lead singer of the wedding band during sweeps week for a prime-time soap.

The year that Maya turned thirty-nine, she presented Wes with an ultimatum, in the form of a positive pregnancy test. He told her he wanted to take the weekend to think about the life changes a family would entail. "And you can probably guess how that story ended," Big Dave said. "He hightailed it up to Montreal and never came down again." Now Maya had a son named Andrew and was raising him alone. Somehow, none of this had made her bitter. She was still cheery, always smiling, energetic enough to greet every actor who came through the door with a hug and a kiss and a compliment on the last thing she'd done, even if the last thing she'd done was a showcase that played in the basement of the Scientology Center or a direct-to-video remake of the horror film *Swamp Thing*.

"A guy's a guy," she told me. "Whether you work with him or not. And be honest. Where else are you going to meet someone?" Maya asked. "Working the hours we do?"

I didn't answer. The truth was, I hadn't built much of a social life during my years in Los Angeles, even though I did what the experts suggested, putting myself in places where there were other young people around. I swam, I walked, I did yoga and went to the gym, but everyone I saw there seemed to have arrived with an existing circle of acquaintances, and I'd never figured out how to jump into conversation or even just say hi to the other women I'd see in the locker rooms, especially when we were all in the process of getting dressed, or undressed, and they could see my scars. I knew, too, from watching the Daves when *Bunk Eight* was in production, that my life was only going to get crazier when the pilot shoot began, and busier still if we got picked up. When shows were in production, showrunners had to keep a number of balls in the air. There was the episode that was being shot, the one you'd just shot and were editing, and the one being prepped for the following week . . . and it was almost a guarantee that if the network was okay with all three of them, the studio would have a problem, or the network would decide to flip the order, or the actor you'd cast for the crucial guest role who'd been so great during the audition would be awful in front of the cameras. There was always a crisis to handle, a fire to put out. Twelve-hour days were the norm, and it wasn't unusual to hear about a showrunner grabbing a few hours' sleep on an office couch, showering in the office gym, and not making it home for days at a time. If my life was a little empty, a little bereft of friends and confidantes, this wasn't the time to fix it.

"So who is it?" asked Maya, leaning forward, smiling. "Spill!"

But before I could decide if I wanted to tell her, Deborah knocked at the door. "Oops! Renée's here. More later." Maya hopped off the couch and swung open the door to admit Renée, an actress who'd jettisoned her last name in the early 1990s, back when she'd starred as the straight-talking neighborhood matriarch in the sitcom 'Round the Way.

"Ladies!" Renée sang, sashaying—that was really the only word to describe the way she moved—to the center of the room. She wore lizard-skin spike heels and a brilliant purple dress that clung to every curve of her ample figure. A mink stole draped her shoulders, and false eyelashes easily the length of my little finger fluttered against her cheeks. Renée was a woman of color—if she was great, the Daves and I had decided, we'd just say that Nana Trudy was a lifelong friend of the family rather than Daphne's actual grandmother. "Welcome," said Maya as Renée beamed at us. Glossy black curls—a wig, I figured—cascaded down her back. Her eyelids were shadowed in vivid purple, her lipstick was the shiny red of a Vaseline-coated stop sign, and beneath the mink, her V-neck dress was cut low, revealing a seam of cleavage deep enough to hide an iPad. Maya arched her eyebrows and pressed her lips together as Renée tossed her fur onto a chair in the corner. "You ready for me?" she asked. Her voice was the same girlish trill she'd had back in the day, and she was using all the cutesy-coy mannerisms that somehow still worked, even though she was old enough to be, and play, a grandmother.

"The room is yours," said Maya, spreading her hands wide with a welcoming smile on her clean-scrubbed face. In contrast with the women we saw all day long, Maya never wore makeup except a light lip gloss. It was as if, in response to all that artifice and beauty, the plastic surgery, the wigs, and the worked-on hair, she'd simply decided to take herself out of the game, wash her skin with Ivory, and go about her business.

We sat on the couch, both of us with a copy of the script in our lap. Renée took a seat on the chair in the corner, clasped her hands at her bosom—her nails, I noticed, were painted three different shades of purple and sparkled with glitter—and began Nana's speech to Daphne. "Hello, darling. Oh, now, what are you looking all downhearted about?"

"I don't think that interview went very well," Maya mumbled, in character as Daphne, downhearted after confessing that she'd been turned down at a fancy French restaurant where she'd applied.

"Sit down and tell Mama all about it," said Renée, and then glanced at her watch. "Actually, can you give Mama the hundred-and-forty-character version? No offense, but this whole traveling-pants thing you've got going gets a little tired."

Maya-as-Daphne sighed. "I don't know. Maybe Florida was a bad idea. Maybe we should just go home."

"What was that?" When no answer came, Renée straightened her shoulders, gave her glossy curls a toss, stood, and marched into the center of the room. "You're giving up on Miami after four hours and one job interview? I didn't raise you any better than that?" Without waiting for the answer, she said, "Your mother—God rest her soul—didn't want you to have a little life, Daphne. She wanted you to have a big life. She wanted you to go out into the world and push yourself, and get your heart broken, and fail, and fall down, and get hurt, and get up again."

"It's too hard," said Maya-as-Daphne.

"Too hard?" Renée repeated. "Too hard?" At this point, her voice had risen to the point that I would not have been shocked to see the windows shaking in their casings. I glanced at Renée's résumé and was unsurprised to see that she'd been touring with various Broadway productions since her show had been canceled. She was playing to the cheap seats, except there weren't any cheap seats in Maya's office, and there wouldn't be any on our stage.

Renée pulled in a deep breath. She tossed her head. One of her false eyelashes slowly unpeeled itself from her eyelid and fell, tumbling first onto her cheek, then into the crevasse of her cleavage. Maya pressed her lips together and leaned forward as if she'd suddenly been seized with a stomach cramp. I made myself look away, forcing myself not to laugh. "Do you think," Renée began, in pealing, bell-like tones, "that I gave up when that tramp Mitzie Yosselman beat me in the election for head of Hadassah?" I bit back a smile. This was a line, and an incident, I'd stolen from my grandma's life, although the names had been changed to protect the guilty, and it sounded very strange coming from Renée's shiny red lips. "Did your mother give up when your father said he wanted a small, intimate wedding? Did Barbra Streisand"—and here, Renée rested one hand on the vertiginous slope of her bosom and looked up, as if she'd invoked God—"give up when they told her that she needed a nose job if she wanted to be a star? No," she said. "No, they did not." She planted her fists on her hips, rolled her neck, and declaimed at top volume, "And I'm not letting you give up, either. Now, you wipe that poor-me look off your face, and you think about who you are and what you've got, and you get back out there and you use it."

"You're right," said Maya. "You're right. I will."

Renée held her pose for a beat and then relaxed, fanning her chest (she didn't seem to have registered the eyelash's escape). "Whew!" she said. "How'd I do?"

"That was great!" I said.

"Want it again?" she asked. "Any notes?"

Maya started shaking her head before Renée finished speaking, possibly because she was worried about the structural integrity of her office and whether it would withstand another go-round. "No, no, that was just fine. Any questions for us?"

"What's Hadassah?" Renée asked.

"Um, it's a Jewish women's organization," I answered. "They get together and, you know, raise money for charity." Renée stared at me blankly. "We'd be open to changing it to something else, obviously."

"Got it," said Renée. She pulled on her wrap and sailed out the door. My telephone buzzed, and Dave's face flashed on the screen. "Excuse me," I murmured. "Hello?"

"Good morning, Ruth. Do you have a moment to talk?" That was Dave—a little bit formal, invariably polite.

"Sure," I said. "Dave," I mouthed to Maya, pointing at my phone.

"Take your lunch," she whispered back. I pushed through the door, out of the dim hallway and into the sunshine.

There was the usual cluster of actors hanging around Maya's back porch: Today it was a clutch of reedy twentysomething guys in statement eyeglasses and scruffy plaid shirts who were probably auditioning to play Hipster Number One (or, barring that, his line-free friends Hipsters Two, Three, and Four) on the nighttime soap that Maya cast. There were also three little boys, ten-year-olds who could play seven or eight, bright-eyed and meticulously groomed, hair combed, fingernails clean, each with a parent nearby. The hipsters smoked and paced and muttered their lines. The boys bent over schoolbooks or gaming devices. The boys' parents ostentatiously fanned smoke away from their children's paycheck-earning lungs and worked their phones, having conversations with agents and spouses, looking for Junior's next gig.

I edged through the crowd, murmuring, "Excuse me." Kids and hipsters and parents parted, eyeing me hopefully: Was I a producer? Maya's new assistant? Someone worth flirting with or sucking up to? One of the moms, a streaked blonde whose spandex skirt strained over her hips, looked sharply at her towheaded son, who'd been staring at my face, until he gave me a lisping "Good afternoon." A hipster offered me an American Spirit cigarette. I declined, unlocked my car, and took a seat behind the wheel with the phone against my ear.

"I just watched Renée's false eyelash fall into her cleavage," I began. This had become my habit: I'd find an anecdote from my day, polish and smooth it until I deemed it Dave-worthy, and then have it ready for the next time we'd talk.

"Lucky eyelash," said Dave. "I got in touch with Cady's people to set up the meeting."

"Ah. The meeting." The one the network executives had promised us, so we'd at least get to say hello to the new star of our show before the pilot shoot began.

"I'm sorry to say that the news is not good," Dave continued. "She's out of town for the next two weeks."

"Doing what?" I asked.

"Her manager was a little vague on that point." I could tell, from his dry tone and the pause before he answered, that whatever Cady's manager had told him hadn't impressed him much. "The bottom line is, she's in Hawaii, and she's not coming back until the day before we're scheduled to start shooting. The best they can do is make her available for a drink that night."

I tugged at my hair, thinking. The meeting, as I well knew, was a formality. Cady would be our star, even if she showed up for the first day's filming having sustained a major head trauma and forgotten every word of English she'd ever known. But this bit of Cady's-on-vacation nonsense was also the first move in the Hollywood game that everyone played, the game of Who's Got the Power. Cady's team telling us that she could give us only thirty minutes' worth of her time less than twelve hours before we started taping was a preemptive strike, their way of letting us know that they mattered more than we did, that Cady's plans and desires were more important than ours. It was their way of establishing the hierarchy without saying a word.

"What do we do?" I asked.

"We could push back," Dave said. "We could tell them it's not good enough and that she needs to get off the beach, get on a plane, and at least sit down for lunch."

"Hmm." I wondered if I'd have to make that call or if I could get Dave to do it for me.

"Or," he continued, "we could let her win this round. Make her feel like she's got the upper hand, then use it as leverage when we really need her to do something."

"I think that's the way to go," I said, imagining what it would be like to start filming the pilot with a star who was already resentful about a vacation she'd had to cut short. Still, it was confusing. What exactly was Cady on vacation from? Wasn't her whole life a vacation? She had to have made plenty of money from *All Our Tomorrows*. If I were her, I'd spend my whole life going from spa to spa and beach to beach, with a retinue of friends and camp followers. I'd swim, and loll in the sunshine, and read all the classics I'd skipped in college . . . and probably be bored after three weeks, buy a laptop, and start writing something else. I knew myself well enough to know that I was not a girl made for lying around on beaches. I liked being busy, and I loved to write, and I'd panic about the money running out, no matter how much of it there was.

"I agree," said Dave. "Let her win the battles, as long as we win the wars. I'll let her pick the place and the time, and Bradley will go ahead and set it up. Unless you hired an assistant?"

"I'm getting there," I said. In fact, I'd been completely

daunted by the stack of résumés the studio had sent to my apartment. Every single person who'd applied to be my assistant was at least as qualified to run my show as I was, and many of them were more qualified. Most of them had gone to film school. They'd all had at least one assistantship, some to big-shot directors or successful showrunners, and although nobody was foolish enough to put his or her age on a résumé, I could do the math and guess that at least half of the candidates were older than I was. My plan was to pick three finalists, interview them all, and then hire the one who intimidated me the least, and be as generous to him or her as the Daves had been to me.

"Don't wait too long," Dave said. "You don't want all of the good ones to be taken."

"No, no, I'll find someone. And I'm going to help her, like you guys helped me," I said. I could feel my throat getting tight, and I was glad that I was in my car, with the windows up and the doors locked and the air conditioner humming noiselessly, instead of with Dave, trying to say this to his face. "I don't think I could ever tell you how grateful I am—"

"Hey," he said, cutting me off. "Give yourself some credit. This is all you. Dave and I might have sped things along a little bit, but this was going to happen eventually. You're talented, and the script's good."

"Thank you," I said, and swallowed, and wished for some knitting, something to do with my hands. Then I reminded myself of the email I'd seen, the picture of Shazia on Dave's lap. *I adore you. You're my girl.* I opened my purse and started rounding up stray receipts and gum wrappers, untwisting strands of hair from the ponytail holders I used when I swam, gathering breath mints and business cards as Dave talked through the scheduling. We'd have a week of preproduction, when we'd fine-tune the script, and the carpenters and painters and set dressers would build and furnish and decorate our sets, and we'd handle the thousand other chores that came along with getting a show on its feet. We'd have to have music written and approved, or buy the rights to existing songs, which could get expensive. The network would have to sign off on our casting, not just of the main roles but of anyone who had a single line, all the extras, and the clothes that every single person who appeared on camera would wear. There would be dozens of people to hire—everyone from the line producer and set designer to the caterer and the warmup comic. We'd work together for a single intense week—two days of rehearsal, a run-through apiece for the studio and the network before we finally shot the pilot. Then the crew would disband, I would go home, and all of us would wait for the network's verdict.

"One more thing," said Dave.

"What's that?"

"I heard from the network about rewrites."

"Oh?" My heart was pounding again, even though I'd been planning on revising the script to the network's specifications, making whatever changes they required. It was what you did, the price you paid for getting on the air . . . but I was terrified to hear what they'd want from me.

"Nothing too big," he told me. "It's just that, instead of finding out through dialogue about Nana Trudy's boyfriend moving into assisted living, they want to see that scene. That was their biggest note."

"Hmm." In addition to more writing, adding this new scene they'd asked for would require building a new set, and casting actors to play the boyfriend and the boyfriend's sons. "I don't suppose they're going to give me any more money?"

Dave gave a quiet, not unsympathetic chuckle. "Oh, grasshopper," he said. "You have much to learn. Anyhow, Lloyd—you remember him? The one who was Joan's assistant until about ten minutes ago?"

"The one who looks like he's twelve?" I asked, which earned me another chuckle.

"That's the fellow. He wrote up some notes. I think he might have actually taken a stab at writing the whole scene." Dave would never insult one of his corporate masters directly—he left that to Big Dave, who could insult his corporate masters all day long, using combinations of words and gestures I'd never imagined—but Little Dave's tone made it very clear what he thought of Lloyd's efforts.

"Well, send it along," I said. I tried to sound brave and cheerful, but I must have sounded sad or tired because Dave asked, "Hey, Ruthie, are you holding up okay?" His voice was so kind that I just blurted it out.

"My grandma's getting married."

"Wow," he said. "That's big news."

I nodded, feeling weepy and bewildered, wanting nothing more than to rub my eyes with my bunched fists and maybe take a nap in the sunshine.

"When's the wedding?" he asked.

"I don't know," I said. I cleared my throat, excused myself, and then said, "I don't know if they've gotten that far."

"Ah." There was a brief pause, and then Dave went back to the schedule, the meetings with potential line producers and directors of photography, the game of phone tag it would surely take to set up drinks with Cady. "Hang in there," he said. "I'll see you soon." I hung up the phone, rubbed my face, groaned out loud, hoping no one could hear me, and then went back into Maya's little office, where the next half-dozen hopefuls were waiting anxiously for their turn in front of the camera.

ELEVEN

I realized I was in love with Dave Carter on the Warner Bros. lot. The Daves were taking a meeting with Vincent Raymer, a producer who up until five years ago had run a network. After three dismal seasons he'd been fired and moved to Umbria, where he'd spent a few years growing and bottling his own olive oil. Eventually he'd returned to Los Angeles as a producer, developing his own shows and hoping that the newer, younger network president would look upon them with favor. Normally the Daves stayed away from outside producers, preferring to dream up and develop their own ideas, but Vince had been persistent, calling and emailing for weeks, telling me that he just needed five minutes of the Daves' time. Out of respect to the power Vince Raymer had once wielded, and because he'd told them, via email, that he had "something that I think you guys will really spark to," they'd agreed to a sit-down.

As usual, I'd called ahead to ask about parking arrangements and whether the offices we'd be visiting were handicapped-accessible, explaining, in the event that whoever on the other end of the phone didn't know, that Dave Carter used a wheelchair (that, I'd learned, was the preferred language—*used a wheelchair* as opposed to *was in a wheelchair*). Vince's assistant, Alice, who turned out to be a pudgy, pale, freckled young woman with lopsided eyes and a collection of too-short Ann Taylor sweater dresses, assured me in a hostile drone that we'd have nothing to worry about.

"Have you ever had anyone who used a wheelchair in your office?" I'd asked, and she'd sighed as if I'd just asked her to pack up her boss's entire wardrobe and have it shipped to Oahu for the weekend (a task that I myself had performed in my own early days on *The Girls' Room*) and said, "I have no idea. I've only been here for six weeks."

And I doubt you'll last six more, I thought. "Could you please check? It's important." She sighed again and promised that she would . . . but she hadn't called me back, and my three messages, two emails, and one text had all gone unanswered. According to the blueprints I'd found online, though, the building we'd be visiting had been built in 1953 and completely overhauled in the late 1990s, which meant that it should be fine.

Vince Raymer had an office befitting his former stature as head of a network, an expansive suite of rooms furnished with antiques, the walls hung with posters from the greatest hits of his network tenure. The floors were covered with Oriental rugs, and fresh flowers stood on the end tables. Instead of fluorescent lights, he'd installed chandeliers, and he'd mounted some kind of animal's bleached skull on the wall behind his desk. After waters had been offered and accepted, I took my place on the couch, and Alice, who gave off a vibe of barely suppressed hostility, plopped down beside me with a sigh. When we were all seated and waiting, a door toward the back of the office swung open, and Vince himself, an elfin man whose beard and cowboy boots and ears were all pointed, walked to the center of the room and held up a hand in the universal gesture for *Stop!*, waiting for silence. Once the room had gone quiet, he inflated his chest and, in a low and resonant voice, spoke two words: "Time-share."

We stared at him.

"Time-share," he repeated. "What do you think?"

"About time-shares?" Big Dave ventured.

"About a show called *Time-Share*," Vince said. "We take all the people who own a piece of a time-share in Florida. Or the Bahamas. Wherever. Doesn't matter. Those are our characters. We tell their stories."

"From the perspective of the time-share?" Big Dave asked, and the producer, apparently unaware that he was being teased, said, "Sure, if that's how you see it! The condo becomes a character! I love it!"

I bent my head, squeezing my legs together, hoping that, if anyone noticed, they'd think I was shaking because of some kind of gastric distress and not laughter.

"There could be a married couple that buys into the time-share as a last-ditch effort to save their marriage," Vince said. "And maybe an older woman . . . well, not too old, maybe she's thirty-five, but she's widowed, and her husband died in the time-share, and maybe his ghost is haunting it."

"A nighttime soap," said Little Dave.

"With a supernatural twist," said the producer. "Or, really, whatever you want. I just saw the time-share itself as, you know, the unifying thematic element." He rocked back on his heels, looking pleased with himself.

"What about continuity?" said Big Dave. "Is it a different story every week? Is it episodic? Because every week there'd be a different family in the time-share."

Vince frowned. "I hadn't really thought of that." He frowned some more, stroking his beard. "Tell you the truth, I hadn't really thought a lot beyond the title." He brightened. "But it's a great title, isn't it? *Time-Share*. It practically pitches itself!"

"I can see the poster," Big Dave said, and, with his big hands, sketched rectangle in the air. "*Time-Share:* The Times They Share."

I bent over again, biting my lip, shaking with laughter. Beside me, Alice yawned. I looked over and saw that she was busy tapping at her BlackBerry. Closer scrutiny revealed that she was playing FarmVille on Facebook. I mentally revised my estimate of how long she'd last on the lot from six weeks down to four.

"I bet we could get Moira Callahan," the producer said.

"For what?" asked Big Dave.

"For whatever part you write," said Vince. "The network's got a holding deal, and, you know, her last two shows died in development." He paused. "Dead in Development. You think that's a show, too?" He glanced at the couch, apparently noticing for the first time that his assistant was not assisting. "Alice, can you write that down?" The slug next to me sighed, put down her phone, and picked up a notebook.

The Daves and Vince spent ten minutes kicking ideas around. Maybe the time-share is actually a wormhole leading to other dimensions. Maybe an older woman left it to her young niece and nephew, who have to pretend to be married to live there. Maybe there's an evil developer who wants to tear down the time-share to make way for a shopping mall, and the residents have to band together to stop him. I scribbled down notes, knowing they'd amuse the Daves the next time they took me to lunch. *Time-Share:* The Times They Share.

Finally, the meeting sputtered to a halt. "We'll be in touch," said Big Dave.

Vince waved grandly. "I look forward to it." Hands were shaken; goodbyes were said. Lumpy Alice heaved herself off the couch and bent to gather up the water glasses. Big Dave zoomed away in his sports car to go look at a new sports car, and I began the trek to my Prius, which I'd been directed to park on the lowest level of the farthest-away parking structure. I was about halfway across the lot when my telephone rang, and I saw that it was Little Dave calling.

"Hello?"

For the first time in our acquaintance, Dave sounded flustered. "Hello. Ruth. Have you left yet?"

"No, I'm still here. Are you okay?" I said.

"I'm fine," he said. "I'm just sort of . . . stuck."

"Where are you?"

"In the men's room, at the end of the hall. Same floor we were on. I've been waiting for someone to come get me unstuck, but I think everyone's gone to lunch."

"Okay. Don't worry. I'll be back in a minute."

"Take your time," Dave said. I hung up, stashed my phone, and started trotting back across the lot, stopping to pull off my heels and trade them for the flip-flops I had in my bag. I'd dressed in what had become my work uniform—jeans and a T-shirt, for comfort, with a blazer on top, for polish, and a scarf around my neck and a hat on my head, for camouflage. In my mind, I was composing the letter I'd send to that idiot assistant who'd assured me that, *oh, fer shur,* the building was just fine for a man in a wheelchair. *The nerve of her,* I thought as I race-walked to the end of the hall, where, just as he'd said, Dave's wheelchair had gotten wedged in the doorway to the men's room.

I came up behind him, trying not to pant. "Hi."

"Ah," he said. "The cavalry." He sounded the way you'd expect a man stuck in a bathroom door to sound—stressed and embarrassed and trying to sound brave. I wondered how badly he needed the bathroom. Then I wondered how, exactly, Dave used the bathroom. Like normal people? With a catheter? Some system I'd never even considered? "Thank you for coming back."

"Oh, don't worry. It was no problem. So, um . . ."

"I think," he said, "if you just gave me a good push, I'd make it."

I looked down and saw that the hubs of each wheel had actually dug slightly into the wood of the doorframe. "Maybe if I tilted you backward a little . . ."

"Sure," he said. His lips were pressed together, his face was calm and relaxed, and I noticed how his shoulders strained the seams of his shirt, as well as the thick tracery of blue veins on his forearms as he rested them in his lap. I bet he looked like a superhero with his shirt off, I thought, and felt my heart beat faster at the thought of it.

There were no handles on the back of the chair—Dave had told me once that handles encouraged people to help, to push or guide him when he didn't need pushing or guidance. I gripped the back of the seat gently, gingerly tilting his weight back on the wheels, and pushed forward. Nothing happened. I pushed harder, and the chair inched forward with a screeching sound of metal on wood.

"I think I can get this," I said. Dave had closed his eyes. They weren't squeezed shut in an expression of misery, but they were definitely not open. It was as if he was meditating, as if he'd sent his mind someplace else while his body was trapped in this indignity.

I decided that small talk was in order. "So how about that meeting? *Time-share*? I wonder if that's what Vince Raymer does all day. Just sits around and thinks up things that sound like they could be titles."

Dave's eyes didn't open. "Shows have been sold on less than that," he said. Half a beat later, we both said "*Cougar Town*" at the exact same time. Dave smiled, and I felt warmth surge through me.

"Do you think anybody's ever pitched *Co-op Board*?" I asked. "Or *Air Traffic Control*?"

"Probably. I know last year there were three different shows making the rounds with *Fantasy League* in the title."

While we were talking, I was pushing the chair back and forth, back and forth, working it forward in incremental notches, as gently as if it was carrying a basket of eggs. I'd probably been this close to Dave before—at the table in the writers' room, shaking hands during my job interview—but I'd never seen him from so intimate an angle. I could smell him—warm hay, strawberries, hints of something dry and papery, like books in a library—and could make out faint freckles on the bridge of his nose.

"I'm going to murder that Alice," I said. "These buildings are supposed to be up to code. How is this fair to people who use wheelchairs?"

"Take it easy, Gandhi." Still with his eyes shut, Dave sounded faintly amused. Finally the wheels spun free of the wall. I set the chair down gently on the tiled bathroom floor. He opened his eyes and said without looking at me, "Thank you."

"I'll wait." I gestured vaguely toward the hallway, long and dim and strangely empty. What was going on here? Had there been a fire drill that I'd missed? Where was everyone, and why hadn't anyone helped him? "Take your time. I'll be right here."

He nodded, hands on the wheels, and pushed himself deeper into the bathroom. I walked down the hallway, trying to catch my breath from my half-walk-half-run over and the effort it had taken to free up the chair. My face felt hot. *Gary*, I told myself. *Think of Gary*, who was sweet and good, and who loved me. I tried . . . but my mind kept wandering back to Dave, sitting so still in his chair, the calm expression on his face, the sweetness exuding from his pores . . . and I could remember, too, how my grandmother had known her husband was the man for her. "He smelled right," she'd said. That was when I'd known. Never mind that he was older, or that he couldn't walk. Dave was the one I wanted; the one, I thought, I loved.

TWELVE

C ut!" yelled the director, and turned to me, teeth bared in an
approximation of a smile. "We good?"

I knew my lines. "We're good!" I was supposed to say. As
soon as I'd said it, we'd move on to the next scene, which we
desperately needed to do. We were almost two hours into the
pilot shoot, and we'd gotten through precisely three pages of the
pilot forty-page script. At this rate, we were on schedule to finish
somewhere around three in the morning.

The problem was, I wasn't happy with what we'd done, and
I wasn't sure I knew how to improve the situation. Tentatively I
reached out and put my hand on the director's shoulder. It was
like touching a side of beef in a linen shirt, all sweaty muscle,
even though the stage, with its ceilings that stretched forty feet
high, was so vigorously air-conditioned that I could almost see
my breath. The room was awash in noise—the warm-up comedian's patter, the audience's chatter, the calls of the assistant director, and the whine of a blow-dryer. Somewhere, in the crowd
of about a hundred people, tourists and Cady Stratton fans and
people who'd been pulled in off the streets to come watch us
tape, was my grandmother—I'd cast her as an extra, a customer
in Daphne's restaurant, in the first scene we'd shot, and when
it was over she'd taken a reserved seat in the audience to watch

the rest of the show. "I don't know. I just . . . I think it's still a little . . ." I groped for the right words, looking around for Dave. When I spotted him, he was talking with the DP. I watched as Dave gestured up toward a light, and then pointed back down at the script, and I knew that if I fetched him, the director would lose whatever respect he had for me.

So I straightened up and said, "It's too big."

The director's face didn't move. He was a laconic fellow named Chad, a veteran whom the network had been ecstatic to hire. Now, two hours and three pages into what was shaping up to be an all-night adventure, he stared down at me, expressionless. "You understand," he finally said, "that it's hard to be small when you've got your star on Rollerblades and an old lady who's talking about fucking a man to death."

I tried not to wince at his language, either the *old lady* or the *fucking*. Putting Daphne on Rollerblades had been my idea, added at the studio's urging, their insistence that I needed some big physically funny moment in Act One. The joke about Nana Trudy's sex life was courtesy of the network, which had wanted something broadly comic enough to play in the previews and commercials. I'd fought, thinking that the inference was broad to the point of being disgusting, but I'd lost. "I know. I get it. But if maybe we could just try it with Cady doing a little less of a pratfall?" As it was, Cady had turned what was supposed to be a cute little tumble into a Cirque du Soleil–style split, prompting hollers and wolf whistles from the audience. Dave had grabbed me the first time she'd done it. "Don't let her get away with that," he'd said. "Pull her back." I was trying to do it, trying to tell her as effectively as I could that her gestures were too big, her voice was too loud, that all of the eye-bugging and neck-rolling she was doing made her look like a cartoon, not a real person. But the director, who was obviously ready to go to the next scene and send the stunt double and the stunt coordinator home for the night, wasn't helping. He'd laughed appreciatively at each of Cady's whoopsies, and the bigger they'd gotten, the more amused he'd become.

"One more time," I said as firmly as I could. "Less vaudeville. More nuance."

"You got it, boss," he said.

He turned on his heel, and I walked over to Cady, who was perched on the edge of the set's sofa, her legs crossed and Rollerblades swinging, waving to the guys in the front row who were whooping, "We love you, Cady!"

"Hey there!" she said, all shiny eyes and stage makeup.

"You're doing great," I said. "I'm just wondering if we can do one more take a little differently."

"Sure," she said. "Whatever you want."

I told her what I wanted. I reiterated my wishes to the director. I told Annie Tait, who was playing the part of Nana Trudy, to pull it back by about thirty percent. When Annie agreed, I knew that thirty percent was exactly what I'd get—not twenty-nine percent, not thirty-one percent, but a precisely calibrated performance that would be exactly thirty percent more subdued than what she'd done in the previous take. Annie Tait didn't resemble my grandmother at all. She was statuesque where Nana was tiny, and her features were patrician and WASPy— pale-blue eyes and a narrow, high-bridged nose, in contrast with my grandmother's larger features—but somehow, none of that had mattered. When she'd given what I'd come to think of as the *Buck up, li'l camper* speech to Daphne, it was like I was in the room with my grandmother, like she was talking to me. "She's fantastic," I'd said as soon as she was gone . . . and everyone, from Maya to Dave to the studio to the network, had agreed.

In her canary-yellow silk robe and heeled slippers, with a feather hair clip in her wig, Annie had once again become my grandmother, a funny and for-public-consumption version of my grandmother, the woman I'd written as a response to the stereotypical dirty-joke-spouting senior who afflicted the average sitcom. Nana Trudy was, I hoped, something new, a lady of a certain age with heart and a history and a genuine sense of humor and a sex drive that wasn't a punch line, a quirky woman with demons to conquer and wisdom to share.

Annie patted my arm. "Hang in there. It's always a little rough, starting out."

"Thanks," I said, and hurried back to my director's chair behind the monitors that displayed the footage each of the four cameras was shooting. The hair and makeup people fussed over Annie. The props assistants came onto the set with a new fake vase for Cady to shatter. The warm-up guy brayed jokes at the audience. *Hurry up and wait.* That was TV. "Ready . . . and . . . *action!*" the director finally called. Cady glided into the living room, dressed in what a Boston girl would think of as Florida clothes and Florida colors—yellow shorts, a cream-colored bodysuit, a turquoise headband in her hair. "Okay," she said. "My new commitment to healthy living begins . . ." She staggered, elbows flailing, catching herself on her grandmother's antique desk. The vase resting on the desk fell to the ground and shattered. Nana scowled. The audience howled. And Cady, unable to help herself, responding to their cheers like a flower turning toward the sunshine, launched herself into the same kind of crotch-on-the-floor split she'd been doing, only this time she pressed her hands against her mouth and said, "Oopsies!"

I held my breath, waiting for Chad to yell, "Cut," thinking, *No, that's not what I meant, that's not what I wanted.* The director, chuckling from his chair, kept the cameras rolling. "Careful, dear," said Annie Tait, "you still want to have children someday, don't you?" The line prompted more laughter from the audience, which led, inevitably, to more mugging from Cady . . . and was

I imagining it, or was the director actually slapping one oak-trunk-size thigh? "Hey," I said, and tapped Chad's shoulder. He ignored me. I tugged at his sleeve. "Hey!"

He gave me a *What can you do?* shrug. "They're locked in," he said. My heart sank. Was he right? Cady hadn't been nearly this broad at the run-through . . . but I knew that this happened sometimes when a live studio audience is involved. "They can't help themselves," Little Dave had said, as if the actors were a bunch of addicts and the audience members, mostly superfans and tourists bussed in from Hollywood Boulevard, were their drug. At our taping the audience was packed with Cady groupies. She'd used her website and Twitter account to invite her fans to her "triumphant return" to the world of TV. The bigger she got, the louder they got, on and on in a spiraling loop of awfulness. I could almost hear the critics from *Variety* and *People* sharpening their knives, waiting to cut into this tempting pie.

Chad called, "Cut!" again, and turned to me, his face expressionless once more. "Are we good now?" he asked. I looked at the clock, feeling sick as I saw how much time had passed. If I didn't keep things moving, we'd never finish. The audience would leave, the actors would start flagging, the executives would freak—already, Lloyd had emerged from the greenroom twice, once to ask when we thought we'd be wrapping the scene, and again to warn the editors not to use any of the takes where you could see Cady's underwear.

Lloyd was another thorn in my side. He was technically an executive, but so far, I'd found him hard to take seriously. The scene he'd written—"Just a few ideas," he'd said modestly, in the attached email—had been all but unreadable, the dialogue flat as cardboard, the jokes juvenile and cruel. Even worse, Lloyd seemed to have decided that the key to being respected by the studio and its employees was to deliver all of his remarks at a volume that could blow your hair back, even when all he was doing was saying hello. After ten minutes of his company, the Daves and I had nicknamed him Loud Lloyd.

"Everything okay?" he bellowed, and stared at me. The director, still working his wad of gum, stared at me. The cameramen, all four of them, stared, too.

"Good," I said, and tried to muster a smile. "We're good." *Maybe one of the earlier takes wasn't as bad as I'd remembered,* I thought, as pop music came booming out of the speakers and the warm-up comedian cried, "We are moving on!" and started pulling pretty girls out of their seats to dance. Besides, even if it was a bad scene, it was just one scene, and maybe the rest of the show would be so good that the viewers and the critics wouldn't notice. I slumped in my chair as people bustled around me, moving cameras, adjusting lights, the hair and makeup people hurrying onstage with brushes and blow-dryers in leather belts slung around their waists like gunslingers. The director was chatting with the cameramen about cars, if *chatting* could be applied to a discussion conducted entirely in shouts. Onstage, Annie Tait was deep in conversation with her wig wrangler, and Cady, still in her Rollerblades, had glided over to the front row to sign autographs. In the front row, Grandma waved.

"Ruth." I looked up. Dave was sitting next to me in his chair, with his hands folded, Zen-like, in his lap.

"When the student is ready, the teacher appears," I said. It was one of our old office jokes, something I used to say to him, typically when he wheeled himself out of the bathroom.

He smiled and said nothing.

"This isn't going well," I said.

"Oh, no, it's going fine," he said.

I stared at him. Was he watching the same show I was? Was he teasing me? "They're finding their levels," he said, patting my knee. "And remember, you can't look at each take as its own

thing. As long as you've got the right moments, it'll come together in the editing room."

I let myself feel a spark of hope. I had seen it happen a hundred times on *Bunk Eight*. You'd do three okay-to-terrible takes,
but in every one of them there'd be a flash of greatness, or at least
decency. The editors would snip those moments out, stitch them
together, and voilà: a perfect scene.

"I don't think Cady and I are communicating," I said. It
was frustrating, because I felt that if I knew her better, I'd have
more of a sense of how to modulate her performance. Unfortunately, prior to tonight's shoot Cady and I had spent only thirty
minutes in each other's company, when we'd finally had that
hard-to-arrange drink the night before. My leading lady had arrived fifteen minutes late, making a true movie-star entrance, in
sunglasses and bee-stung red lips, a white chiffon dress with a
sweetheart neckline that put the skin of her shoulders and the
tops of her breasts on display, with half her face hidden behind
dark glasses, wearing heels so high I knew that even my grandmother in her prime would have looked at them, shaken her head
regretfully, and put them back on the shelf. When I'd climbed
off my barstool, waving at her, Cady had embraced me as if we
were the very best of friends.

"Ruthie!" she squealed. Her eyes flickered over my face as
she kept her own expressionless. I guessed her agent or manager
or someone had told her about the situation and urged her not
to stare. "Come on," she said, and grabbed my hand, "they make
the yummiest sidecars here!"

At the bar, I spent ten minutes listening to her murmured
conference with the bartender about exactly how to prepare
a yummy sidecar. Finally she snapped a picture of the drink,
posted the picture to Twitter and Facebook, took a single sip,
then swiveled her stool so that our knees were bumping, and
gave me a Serious Listening expression, head tilted, eyes wide,

like she was playing a hard-hitting journalist interrogating a crooked politician. "So. Tell me all about you."

"Oh, there's not much to tell. I grew up in Boston—"

"Boston! Like, Harvard? Pahk the cah in Hahvahd Yahd?"

"Right."

"Did you go to Harvard?"

"Nope."

She patted my arm in a consoling fashion. "That's okay." Glancing down at my lap, where I'd been perusing scripts on my e-reader, she said, "Is that one of those e-book things? A Kendall?"

"Kindle," I said. Was she kidding?

"Kindle," she repeated. "Do you like to read?"

"It's my favorite thing," I said.

Cady considered this remark. "Not me, so much. I mean, I like self-help books. Deepak Chopra? Have you ever heard of him?"

"Yes," I said. I wondered again if she was kidding and decided that probably she was not. "Yes, I have."

"He's really good. Oh, and *Skinny Bitches Don't Get Fat.* Did you read that one?" She looked at me, wide-eyed, lips slightly parted, waiting for an answer. When none came, she grabbed my hand.

"You need to read it. It's, like, amazing." She pulled her phone out of her bag and started typing. "There! See! I just tweeted about it!"

I checked my phone and there it was, hashtag and everything. "I highly recommend it," Cady had written. "Good one," I said.

"You follow me!"

"I'm one of your minions," I said. "You're really dedicated to the whole social-media thing." This seemed like the most diplomatic way I could tell her that I was both impressed and slightly horrified at the eighty thousand random thoughts and photographs she'd sent out into cyberspace in the two years since she'd joined Twitter.

"Oh, you know how it is," she said. "You've got to keep your fans invested. You have to let them into your world." As if to prove her point, she struck a pose, painted lips pouting, cheeks sucked in, and snapped a picture with her phone. "There! Tweeted!" she said, and waited until I'd dutifully picked up my phone, checked out the shot, and told her she looked beautiful.

"So, I know you like to cook," I said, having read, in numerous magazine profiles, of Cady's love for whipping up the scrumptious Swedish cookies her mother and aunts had made.

She blinked at me. "What?" It turned out that the story of Cady in the kitchen, her love for baking, was just something her publicist told her to say—"especially when I'm being interviewed by *Ladies' Home Journal* or whatever." The recipes that ran with the stories weren't even her own, but were provided by the editors, or by what Cady referred to as her "people." I felt my heart sink. Daphne was an aspiring chef. It would have helped if Cady had actually known something about cooking . . . and I would have felt better in general knowing that my star wasn't a liar.

"So what do you like to do?"

Cady opened her jeweled minaudière, pulled out a mirrored compact and a lip brush and a tin of gloss, and started repainting her lips. "Oh, you know. Listen to music. Go out. I love the beach!" I tried not to wince or to flash back to every high-school senior whose essays had been similarly bland. She snapped her compact shut. "Tell me where Daphne came from." When I answered, talking hesitantly about my own childhood, my parents' death, my grandmother, she gave me listening eyes and tried to pay attention, or at least look like she was paying attention, but I caught her glancing at her iPhone as it thrummed constantly on the bar top. "Hey," I said after she'd checked the clock for the third time in as many minutes, "do you need to be somewhere?"

"No!" she said, but eventually she admitted that her boy-friend was outside, waiting in a cab at the curb. He'd fetched her at the airport and delivered her to me.

"Invite him in!" I said. "We can all have a drink."

She frowned at something on her telephone's screen and then gave me a brilliant smile. "Actually, I do need to run. We're having drinks with my manager. Five minutes."

"Oh." We made more awkward girl talk, moving from the brand of jeans Cady liked best ("Joe's Jeans are the bomb," she said, eyeing me critically. "And they're great if, you know, you're kind of on the hippy side") to the restaurants Cady favored, none of which I'd ever visited, how her parents were divorced and how her father, who had once been her manager-slash-dialogue coach, "isn't really a part of my life anymore." At ten-thirty sharp, precisely thirty minutes after our meeting had begun, Cady had hopped off the barstool, given me a merry wave, and vanished, leaving me with the check and with very little idea of who she really was or what kind of performance she'd deliver, and how—or if—I could work with her. It was like trying to race a horse you'd never ridden, with no idea what kind of touch or talk it would respond to, and the whole thing had left me uneasy. The cast of *Bunk Eight* weren't friends with the writers, exactly, but they were colleagues, and we'd all gotten to know one an-other over the seasons, from run-throughs and show nights to craft-service snacks. I had a sense of them. I had no sense of Cady Stratton at all.

"Let her settle into it," Dave said from his chair. "It's her first time back in, what, three years?"

"Two and a half."

He worked his wheels back and forth an inch, frowning. "Did you eat anything today?"

"Um." I'd had breakfast—Grandma wouldn't let me leave the house without it—but I'd skipped lunch, running over to the set to sign off on costumes at noon, and I'd been too nervous to manage a bite of the staff meal served in the commissary before the shoot had begun. "Wait here." He wheeled away and came back a minute later with a paper plate in his lap.

He'd made a turkey-and-swiss sandwich, with the cheese protruding from the edges of the bread. There was a handful of pretzels, an apple, a bottle of water, the kind of wholesome lunch you'd send a kid off to school with . . . the kind of lunch, in fact, that my grandmother had sent me to school with.

"You're going to be a good father," I said.

"What?" he called back. My words had been lost in the blare of the music, the laughter of the crowd.

Instead of yelling, I smiled, mouthed *thank you*, gave him a thumbs-up, and took a bite of the sandwich. I'd just finished my late-night dinner when the assistant director, a brusque woman in jeans and a denim workshirt, walked fast across the stage, calling, "Hold the work, please, hold the work . . . okay, quiet on the set," letting us know that we were ready to start filming the next scene, in the office where Daphne's soon-to-be-ex-boyfriend worked as a member of Nerd Alert, my script's version of the Geek Squad. (This scene took place in the first act, but we were shooting out of order, doing the Rollerblade business first so the stunt people wouldn't have to hang around, on the clock, all night long.)

The designers and set dressers had built and furnished Nerd Alert's offices perfectly, a cheerless, charmless space that spoke to the employees' soullessness, their limited lives. "I want it to look like a *Dilbert* cartoon, only more grim," I'd said, and that's what I'd gotten.

Now Cady, pretty and anxious in a ponytail and the trying-too-hard clothes I'd decided she'd wear for the breakup, stood on one side of his counter, and Phil, the ex-to-be, in khakis and a short-sleeved shirt and ironic clip-on tie, stood on the other.

"On your mark . . . get set . . . action!" Chad bellowed.

"So you see," Cady began, "I have to go do this. I have to go. Because if I don't, I'm going to spend the rest of my life wondering what could have been. Wondering, if I'd just found the courage to go out there and try, if maybe I could have been someone."

"I just don't want you to get hurt," said Steve Levenbaum, the actor we'd cast as Phil. Steve was a twenty-eight-year-old actor-slash-waiter who'd had to switch his shifts at Home Depot to shoot the show. In my early drafts, Phil had been a two-dimensional asshole, a lazy guy willing to settle for whatever plums landed in his lap, but as I'd rewritten, I'd come to think of him as scared, a man who would hurt before he could get hurt himself, who kept a veneer of hipster cynicism and false bravado shellacked over his own insecurities. Phil would never be more than a middle manager, never move out of the town where he'd grown up, a guy who'd live in a featureless two-bedroom condo in a new development off the highway, with a mortgage and a car loan that he'd struggle to pay. In other words, he was a starter guy. I hadn't consciously modeled him on Gary, but now that I heard the lines coming from an actor who bore a certain resemblance to my ex, I wondered if that had been my intention all along, if I'd written this scene as a way of telling myself to move on, that sweetness and compatability and a shared taste for sausage and mushroom pizza would get a couple only so far.

"Why are you assuming I'll get hurt?" asked Cady-as-Daphne. "Maybe I'll be fine."

"And maybe I'll be the pope."

Cady turned away, stung. Steve reached across the counter and grabbed her hands.

"I love you, Daphne," he said. His voice was raw. "I know maybe I haven't said that as much as you needed to hear it, but it's true. And maybe I'm being selfish . . ."

"Maybe you are!" Cady said.

"But I don't want you to get hurt," he continued. "Miami's not the right place for a girl like you. It's a place for people who are plastic . . . and, and stupid . . . and . . ."

"Beautiful," Cady said softly. I could feel the audience leaning forward, listening. She extracted her hands from Steve's grip, and straightened, and turned, cheating slightly so that the camera caught her profile. "Do you think I haven't thought about that? You think maybe the mirrors in my house don't work? I know what kind of girl the world likes, and I know that maybe I'm not exactly her."

I got to my feet, slipping off my earphones, watching her on the monitors, reciting the words along with Cady, remembering being in my hospital bed, sitting on the low wall in front of my high school, or curled up on the office floor with Rob's hands on my shoulders, recognizing the *no* in his touch.

"But maybe I've got something those other girls don't. Talent." Cady spoke the word crisply, hitting the *T*'s hard at each end, delivering it like a benediction. "I'm a good cook, and I've done the work. I know I can run a restaurant, and make it a place people want to be, if someone gives me a shot. I have to go there. I have to try. I have to see if what I've got is enough. It's what . . ." She swallowed hard. A flush crept up her cheeks, and her eyes were shining, and in that instant she was Daphne, with all of her doubts and all of her dreams, Daphne and me, too, getting ready to move to a strange place, jump out of the nest and take flight. Her voice thickened. My own throat got tight. "It's what my mom would have wanted."

"You're making a mistake," Steve said. "Six months from now you're going to come crawling back home, and you know who's got two thumbs and won't be waiting?" He cocked his digits back at his own chest. "This guy."

Cady's shoulders slumped. Her lips quivered. Her eyes brimmed with unshed tears. The audience was absolutely silent as she made her way slowly to the door. "Oooh, girl," I heard someone murmur. Cady put her hand on the doorknob, and it seemed in that moment like she'd leave with his insult still hanging there, unanswered. Then she spun around, just as we'd rehearsed, looking Phil right in the eye.

"I might be back," she said. "But I won't be crawling. And I won't be coming back to you." Then she turned again and, as the audience clapped and hooted, walked through the door.

"And . . . cut!" The director turned to me. "Good?"

"Very good." I was hopping up and down, hugging myself, practically dancing. "Really good." Cady walked off the set, carefully stepping over the camera cables, and stood in front of me, eyes shining, breathing hard.

"Oh my God, that was amazing," I said.

She smiled more widely. "Do you think so?"

"Oh my God," I said again. "Perfection!"

She tugged at her hair and twirled her toe. "It wasn't too . . . I mean, do you think we need, like, a joke at the end? So the audience knows she's going to win?"

"They know you're winning," I assured her. "Did you hear them? They're on your side! You've got them eating out of the palm of your hand!"

Cady nibbled on her lip. "Like, what if I say, 'Guess who's got two thumbs and won't be coming back to you?' Or, you know, my nana's there with me, and she says, 'You go, girl!' "

I winced. I couldn't help it. *You go, girl?* Was anyone still saying that? Were white people even allowed?

"Or, okay, maybe not that." She gave a little laugh. "I know

I'm not a writer, but I just feel like there needs to be something else there so they know that he didn't get the best of me."

"Trust me," I said, parroting a line I'd heard the Daves give, over and over, to actors through the years. "Trust the words. Trust your performance. When you see this played back, you aren't going to believe how powerful it is."

"I just think . . . ," Cady said. If I'd been Big Dave, I would have cut her off right there, saying, "Thinking is not your job," and Cady would have laughed, and then gone back to her mark, comfortable in the hierarchy and her own place in it. Big Dave could get away with a line like that because Big Dave was, well, big, and a man, a veteran producer and a powerful Hollywood player, and who was I? The showrunner, true, but also a woman, and not a pretty one, either, a young woman on the very first episode of her very first show, which meant that Cady probably believed she could get away with things that more experienced showrunners wouldn't have allowed.

"I mean, I just want . . . ," Cady continued. She toyed with a lock of her hair and spun one toe on the floor, giving me a sampling of the repertoire of little-girl gestures she'd probably deployed to great effect with male directors and producers over the years.

"Listen," I said. The conversation would have been easier if I'd been slightly more fluent in girl talk . . . but if I couldn't pull off the alpha-male stuff that the Daves did, I'd have to find my own way to deal with my star. I led Cady into a quiet corner of the stage and stood still, waiting until she'd stopped fidgeting and I had her full attention. "What you just did was so power-ful. Every girl who's ever wanted something and worried that she wasn't good enough to get it is going to watch that and feel affirmed . . . and proud of who she is . . . and beautiful."

She looked at me long enough for me to wonder if she knew

what *affirmed* meant. I put my hands on her shoulders again, copying something the Daves had done, and then turned her gently and steered her back toward the set. "Trust me," I said again, and she moved away without looking back.

Twenty minutes later, we were in the Boston house set shooting another pre-Miami scene. Annie Tait was giving herself a manicure on the couch when Cady, shoulders slumped, walked through the door.

"Looks like that went well," Annie observed.

"Phil says I'm gonna get eaten alive," Cady mumbled—but of course it was an actress-y mumble, each word clear and distinct and audible even to the people sitting in the farthest reaches of the back row.

"Phil," said Annie without looking up from her nail file, "is going to spend the rest of his life having his mother sew labels into his underpants. You're better off without him."

"What if . . . ," Cady began. "What if this is a mistake?"

Annie set her file down on the coffee table. "What if what is a mistake, dear?"

"Miami," said Cady. "What if I can't get a job in a restaurant down there? What if I'm not that good? What if I never make it?"

Annie Tait stood up. She crossed the room in one, two, three steps and hit her mark, right in front of the armchair where Cady was slumped. She reached down, touched Cady's chin, just the way I'd written, and lifted the younger woman's face up toward hers. When she spoke her voice was the perfect mixture of sweetness and steel, and even though I'd heard the speech maybe fifty times from fifty different actresses, it still made me want to cheer.

"Now you listen to me, Daphne Michelle. There are no quitters in this family. Do you think that I gave up when that tramp Mitzie Yosselman won the election for head of Hadassah?" I smiled—I couldn't help it—as, from the front row, I heard my grandmother laugh. "Did your mother give up when your father said he wanted a small, intimate wedding? Did Barbra Streisand"—and here Annie did the same thing that Renée had done during her audition, resting her hand on her breast, just above her heart, and turning her eyes toward the heavens—"give up when they told her, after *Funny Lady,* that she needed a nose job if she wanted to be a star? No," she said. "No, they did not." She looked into Daphne's eyes, holding her gaze. "And I'm not letting you give up, either. Now, you wipe that *poor-me* look off your face and you think about who you are and what you've got, and you get back out there and you use it."

"I will," Cady whispered. She straightened her back and raised her voice. "I will."

"And . . . *cut!*" yelled Chad, bouncing to his feet as the audience burst into applause.

We ran the scene twice more, but I knew we'd gotten it the first time, the heart and soul of *The Next Best Thing,* the love between the two women, Nana's role in her granddaughter's life, and the journey of the series, in which Daphne and her grandmother would master the world they had chosen, finding fame and fortune and love . . . everything I wanted for my grandmother and myself.

The rest of the shoot zipped by as if the film had been sped up—Cady's rejection and eventual triumph at the chichi Miami restaurant, Nana's charming the building superintendent and sweet-talking him into moving a spare refrigerator up to their kitchen, and the final scene, with the two women at the end of their first day in Miami, together on the couch, and Cady delivering the final line of the pilot, the line I'd labored over for what felt like half my life: "We're all right for now."

The director looked at me. "We good?" By then it was almost one in the morning. Most of the audience—my grandmother included—had drifted out the door. I had opened my mouth to tell him it was a wrap when Loud Lloyd came bustling out of the greenroom with a sheaf of papers in his hands, in a blue suit that looked as if it had been bought for a bar mitzvah . . . possibly his.

"I have a request from Joan," he announced importantly.

Chad rolled his eyes at me and said, "What's that?"

Lloyd pulled some folded pages from his clipboard. They were, I realized with a sinking heart, a version of the scene he'd written where Nana Trudy got dumped. When he'd emailed it over, I'd thanked him politely, had myself a laugh about his gross jokes about Viagra and Boniva and Nana's sex life, then emailed it to the Daves, imagining they'd be just as amused by his clumsy jokes and leaden dialogue as I was. They were amused. They were also worried. "Beware the executive who thinks he can write," Big Dave had said, and added in all caps, "DO NOT LET HIM ANYWHERE NEAR YOUR SET ON SHOW NIGHT." But I hadn't figured out how to keep Lloyd away . . . and now, here he was, script in hand, and a look on his face suggesting that he would not be stopped.

"Joan wants to see it once this way," he said, and tapped the pages. "The way I wrote it."

"I think we're fine with what we've got," I said. If I'd ever been this tired in my life, I couldn't remember when. Every part of my body ached, and all I wanted was something hot to drink and then about twelve hours of sleep, and my grandmother and Dave to tell me that I'd done my job well; followed by more food and more sleep, and then maybe a massage.

Lloyd was undeterred. "She thinks we need some bigger comic moments," he said.

Stalemate. I could fight him, could go back to the greenroom myself, find Joan, confirm that this was what she wanted, and try to talk her out of it . . . or I could indulge the Boy Wonder, shoot his stupid scene once, and pretend it had never happened. I certainly wouldn't be using it in the final cut.

"Okay," I said, so softly that I could barely hear myself. The director whistled quietly under his breath.

"What was that?" asked Lloyd.

I lifted my head and said it again, louder. "Okay."

Forty minutes later, we were finished once more. The warm-up comedian used that tired old line: "You don't have to go home, but you can't stay here!" The DJ played "Hit the Road, Jack," the executives applauded and then quickly filed out the door.

I congratulated the actors and the writers and talked to the executives, including Loud Lloyd, who patted my back and told me, "I really think we've got something special here." I conferred with the director about his availability for reshoots. "Honestly, I don't think we'll need 'em," he said, tucking a fresh piece of gum into his mouth. "I've done a million of these, and I've gotta tell you, this was pretty tight."

I hung back in the greenroom as the props crew retrieved their stunt vases and Rollerblades, and the craft-services guy packed up the leftovers, and the janitors swept the floor. I waited until I was the only one left on the stage. Then I walked onto the apartment set and sat on the couch with my legs curled underneath me. The cork floor in the kitchen was a replica of what Grandma and I had had in the house in Massachusetts. The couch, upholstered in beigey-gold velvet, was a twin of the one that Grandma had found at a flea market in Santa Monica and wrestled onto a U-Haul to drive home. Next to the couch, on a little table in a simple gold frame, was a picture of my parents on their wedding day. I'd put it there to stand in as a picture of Daphne's parents, and for good luck. There was my mother, her light hair falling from the widow's peak high on her forehead, her pale eyes trusting, and my dad, one arm around her waist, grinning like the whole world had been spread before him. It all looked so real, like an actual house, until you looked up and saw that there were no ceilings and no roof: just empty space and metal walkways, lights and cords and cables.

I picked up the photograph, wondering what my parents would have made of this: their daughter the showrunner, sitting at the center of a world she had dreamed up and called to life. "We're going to get picked up," I whispered into the darkness. Nobody answered, but still, I was convinced. The actors had been great; the story was solid; the executives even looked happy. I pulled off my hat, slid the elastic band off my hair, and shook it loose over my shoulders. Then I sat there, nerves singing with exhaustion, muscles quivering, a smile spread over my face, knowing that I was going to get to live in this world, this perfect world, for years to come. "We're all right for now," I said, and imagined Daphne and Nana, asleep in their beds, Daphne with a new job, Nana with new friends, and how I would guide the two of them like ships, like sailboats on a stormy sea, guide them until they reached port, guide them until they were safely home.

THIRTEEN

It took me a week in an editing bay to stitch together the pilot, picking the best takes of each scene, adjusting the laugh track and the music, arguing with and, for the most part, giving in to my friends at the network when we disagreed on a scene or a shot or a line reading. In the weeks since I'd delivered the final cut, Tariq and Lisa had been diligent about keeping in touch. *Looks good,* they would tell me. *Still in the mix,* they would say—a phrase that I knew from prior experience and the Daves' counsel meant nothing, because shows that were "still in the mix" toward the end of pickup season could wind up on the reject pile as surely as shows that had gotten turned down on Day One. *Chauncey really loves it. Everything seems positive.* I would pass the good tidings along to my actors, talking to Annie on the phone, leaving texts and Twitter direct messages for Cady, who told me that she rarely checked either her email or her voice mail but could always be reached that way. *Hang in there,* I would tell them. *Think good thoughts.*

Meanwhile, I was doing my best to keep busy. There was no point in trying to write something new while I was still waiting to learn the fate of the pilot, and going back to work for the Daves, even if they hadn't replaced me, felt like a giant step backward, a premature admission of defeat. "Take a vacation," Grandma said, but I was horrified by the idea of spending money without knowing for sure where my next paycheck would come from. So I banked the checks I'd gotten from the pilot and booked a daylong "intense relaxation" package at a local spa, even though *intense relaxation* sounded like an oxymoron. In the treatment room, I amused my masseuse by checking my BlackBerry not once but twice during my hourlong hot-stone reflexology session. "You seem a little tense," she observed as she squeezed my toes and I peered at the screen.

"Waiting to hear about my pilot," I said, and she nodded, like I wasn't the first would-be showrunner she'd worked on and I wouldn't be the last.

Back at home, smelling like sage and eucalyptus, I checked my messages again, then reposted my old Craigslist ad. For the next three weeks, I scheduled a client or two every morning: anxious teenagers who swore their lives would be over if they didn't get into Amherst or UPenn, lonely singles who were always more interesting than their dating profiles made them seem. The guidance department at the public high school in my neighborhood was happy to accept my services for kids who needed help with their essays but couldn't afford my fees. "A mitzvah," Grandma called it, but I knew that it was less of a good deed than an offering to the Gods of the Network: *Accept my good deed and pick up my show.*

I kept my phone in my bag while I conducted interviews in a coffee shop filled with my peers, writers thumping away at MacBooks or texting or tweeting. On a Wednesday afternoon, after I'd spent an hour with a skittish, gorgeous high-school junior who ran cross-country and was desperate to get into Brown, I pulled it out and saw that I had three missed calls—one from my agent, Shelly, one from Lisa at the studio, and one from Joan at the network.

I straightened my hat, a gray fedora with a bright blue-and-red plaid brim, while my Converse-clad feet did a fast shuffle on the floor. *Shelly first,* I thought, and punched in her number. "Ruth Saunders," she said. "Hey there, Miss Too-Fancy-to-Answer-Her-Own-Phone," she said.

"I was working."

"Uh-huh. Hang on, let me round up the troops. I'm gonna put you on—"

Before she could say the word "hold," I blurted, "Just tell me. Please. Are they . . . did we get . . ."

"Good news," she said. "But you didn't hear that from me. Hang on now." I sat there, stunned, joyous, feeling like I was flying. Somewhere there would be a girl, maybe in a hospital bed, maybe sick or hurt or lonely, maybe a girl without parents, and she would turn on the television set, and there would be my show, which would become her show, and she would lose herself inside it and dream that she belonged.

One by one, the executives got on the line. Tariq, then Lisa, then Joan, and then Chauncey McLaughlin.

"So," Chauncey began. "How do you feel about making a TV show with us?"

"I would be thrilled to make a TV show with you," I said. My voice was solemn, normal-sounding, but it was all I could do to keep from yelling or bursting into song. The pair of writers at the table next to mine lifted their heads like lions at a watering hole and glared at me in unison. I ignored them, tugging my blue-and-white-striped jersey down over my jeans. *My first haters,* I thought. "Thank you," I said into my telephone. "All of you. Thank you all so much."

"No, thank you," said Chauncey.

Joan took over. "It's a nine-episode order. I'll be sending you the schedule, but the plan is, we start shooting in May and premiere in September. And we'll be screening the pilot, so we'll probably have some notes from that."

"Of course!" I said. "Absolutely!" At that moment, they could have told me that the whole girl-and-grandma concept just wasn't working for them and asked if I could possibly make the whole thing the story of two twenty-three-year-old strippers in Vegas, and I would have happily, joyously, eagerly agreed.

"Congratulations," said Joan, and I thanked her.

"Don't tell *Deadline*," said Lisa, and I promised that I wouldn't say a word to the media until the network had issued its own press release.

"But I can call the actors, right? And the Daves?"

"Of course," said Chauncey, avuncular as ever.

"This is going to be fantastic," said Tariq in a tone suggesting that he was trying to convince himself that what he'd said was true, and I swore that I would do whatever I could to make the show a success. A minute later, the phone call was over, and I was sitting there by myself. Nothing had changed. The same battered computer with its TRU (for Truro, where I'd been a lifeguard that long-ago summer) sticker was on the table in the same spot it had occupied ten minutes ago, along with the same watery cup of iced coffee, the same canvas tote bag I'd used during my lifeguarding summer, same sneakers, same hat, same me . . . but everything was different now.

The laptop guys were still staring. "My show just got picked up," I told them, because it seemed rude not to say something. "Don't tell *Deadline*," I added, even though they didn't know my name or the name of the show.

"Congratulations," one of them muttered, and the second one managed a halfhearted thumbs-up. I picked up my phone. It wasn't even a contest, deciding who, among my stars and relatives and loved ones, I would call first.

"Two Daves Productions," said Bradley.

"I think that's my line."

"Hey, Ruth!" he said. "Congratulations."

"What?"

"I just saw the news on *Deadline*."

Unbelievable. "Are Themselves around?"

"They are not," he said. Of course they weren't. *Bunk Eight* was still in production, which meant the two of them were not lounging around the bungalow waiting to take calls from the likes of me. "Big Dave's on set, and Little Dave's in the editing room. Want me to grab 'em?"

"No, no," I said. "Just have them call me when they can."

"Will do. And seriously, way to go. How many did they order?"

"Nine."

He whistled. "You're going to have to hire your staff pretty fast. When's preproduction start?"

I told him that I wasn't sure, that all I knew was what Joan had told me—film in May, premiere in the early fall. "You probably know more than I do," I said with a laugh, and he did a quick search of the pertinent websites and said that in fact our premiere date had been announced as the second Wednesday of September.

"Shit. I need to call Cady before she sees this." Cady, and Annie, and Steve all deserved to hear about the pickup from a live human person, not the Net.

"You got it," said Bradley. "See you soon."

None of my actors were answering their phones. I left voice mails for Annie and Steve, tapped out a text for Cady with the words CALL ME in all caps, followed by—I cringed before hitting send—a smiley-face emoticon. Then I hopped in my car and drove off in search of Grandma. She'd told me in the morning that she hadn't booked any work that day, which meant that I could catch her on her way to the water aerobics class she took at the JCC. I wished it was nighttime, so we could celebrate properly—wine with dinner, maybe even Champagne, after which we'd retire to the couch with a few of the episodes of *Desperate Housewives* or *Grey's Anatomy* or even old-school *ER* that we kept stored on our TV's hard drive for special occasions.

I drove to the JCC and waited in the hallway, underneath posters advertising craft fairs and book clubs, until I spotted her with her tote bag looped around her upper arm, dressed in a hot-pink tracksuit, a silver silk head wrap, Maurice's enormous diamond on her left hand, and white mesh water shoes on her feet. I stood as she approached and flashed her a silent thumbs-up. She dropped her bag and started to cry.

"Oh, no," I said. "Oh, don't. It's good news!" I said, hugging her.

"I can't believe it!" She wept. "Your own show! Oh, Ruthie!" I hugged her hard, remembering my high school graduation and my graduation from college and the day I'd gotten my first television job, all the times I had wished for my parents and had only my grandmother instead . . . and how, in my mind, that had always been enough.

"Ordered to series!" She sniffled, wiping her cheeks. I smiled, thinking that I couldn't speak Girl, but somehow, my grandma had become fluent in *Variety*. With my arm around her shoulders I could feel how thin she was, in spite of her diet, and the water aerobics and the Pilates for Seniors classes. Grandma lived in fear of becoming one of the eggshell-frail ladies you'd see mincing through the supermarkets and movie theaters and museums in terror of breaking a hip. She exercised, she ate right, but she knew that none of it would stave off the inevitable. *I won't live forever,* she would say, and I'd brush her words away, not wanting to think about them, not wanting to imagine a life without her.

"I always knew," she said. "I always knew you were special." We sat together on a bench, holding hands, as little old ladies, some with canes, others with walkers, made their way past us toward the pool. Her voice thickened. "I wish . . . ," she began.

Then she stopped herself, even though I knew what she'd been about to say: that she wished her daughter, my mother, had lived to see this.

"I know," I said, and rested my cheek against the top of her head. I was thinking, as I'd often thought before, about deals: I do some work for charity, and the network picks up my show; I lose my parents but become a successful television producer. Was that really the way things worked? Was it a fair trade?

While I'd waited for my news, I'd read one of the books I'd pulled off of Big Dave's bookshelf and had never gotten around to reading: *You'll Never Eat Lunch in This Town Again*, by Julia Phillips. Phillips had been one of the first female producers with any power, the first to win an Oscar, for *The Sting*, and had been pitiless when it came to describing the types she'd encountered in Hollywood. Of female comedy writers, she'd noted:

> She was fat in high school. Whether she is still fat doesn't matter. It had already colored her point of view and made her very mad. She will always be fat inside. She beats you to death with her brains, but you don't know you're being killed because you're laughing so hard. Try to remember all humor starts with hostility (cf., comedy writer).
>
> She goes through a lot of therapy. Trying to get in touch with all those feelings nestled beneath all that fat. When she gets to them, and discovers she is as hideous on the inside as the outside, she becomes truly furious. The finding of these feelings gives her total permission to forget about yours.
>
> She makes serious money with some clever writing. But money is more often the scorecard for men. Sex is her scorecard, critical to her self-image, probably because she was laid so infrequently when it was first coming on . . . Now

lots of men who eschewed her company in high school sleep with her to curry favor, but she never knows if they love her for herself or her one-liners. Too afraid to find out, she sharpens her skills, often on other women.

I'd never been fat, although I was definitely bigger than the average actress (to be fair, out here in Hollywood, stop signs were bigger than the average actress). Still, I thought that Phillips, unsympathetic as she'd been, had correctly noted the essentially broken nature of most of the people—male and female—who'd ended up in the entertainment industry. If my parents had lived, if I'd grown up unscarred, with a mother and father who loved me and a grandmother I saw on school vacations, who's to say what I would have become? Maybe Sarah and I would have stayed best friends, and I would have been her maid of honor when she'd gotten married (this had happened a year ago, and God bless Facebook for letting me and the rest of the world know). Maybe my grandma would have been congratulating me on my wedding or the birth of my first child. Maybe I'd still be in Massachusetts, with a husband and a starter house and plenty of friends, my sarcasm confined to emails I sent to the other moms in my kids' nursery school, my relationship with TV limited to the shows I watched at night and talked about the next day, like a million other viewers.

No point in dwelling. I hugged Grandma, kissed her temple, and then steered her toward the dressing room so she could tell her ladies. "What do you want for dinner?" she asked. "Whatever you want! I'll make a feast!"

"Breast of veal," I told her, and drove home. There, in my sunny bedroom, with a glass brimming with ice and water and slices of lemon I picked from the little tree that grew in a pot on the porch, I took care of business.

First: Twitter. Gone were the days when it was enough to

make a good show and hope that viewers would find it. With cable and the Internet, with on-demand access and Hulu and television shows you could watch from your telephone, there were literally thousands of options and dozens of outlets, all clamoring for the viewers' attention. If you wanted to get noticed, you had to interact with your audience on show nights and between shows. You had to keep them hooked and in-the-know, tantalizing them with behind-the-scenes details, Tweeting pictures from the set and discarded jokes and stories—preferably with pictures—about how your stars spent their spare time.

So far, *The Next Best Thing*'s account had a scant ninety-two followers: my grandmother, of course, and then other writers, and network and studio executives. Cady didn't follow us, but her manager did . . . and every one of them counted, and word would spread. I had tweeted, so far, four times: once when we'd gotten the green light, once when Cady had been cast, once when we'd landed Annie, and then, at three in the morning, when we'd finally wrapped the pilot shoot, I'd typed, "It is done." Now I tapped out 140 exultant characters: *The three most beautiful words in the English language are not* I Love You *but Ordered to Series.* I hesitated a minute, then hashtagged it #thenextbestthing. My show's first hash tag. It was almost enough to bring tears to my eyes.

I @-signed Cady, who, I noted, had not yet shared the news with her three hundred thousand followers, although so far that afternoon she'd found time to send out four pictures of herself posing in the mirror, one hand in her rumpled hair, wearing a sequined minidress, her mouth in a Betty Boop pout. I didn't understand why so many people would want these breathless, minute-by-minute updates of the minutiae of Cady's life, especially because it had been years since she'd been on TV . . . but clearly, plenty of them did. They welcomed her tweets about "Just got up! Coffee, please!" and "I am in a BAD MOOD," her

Spotify playlists and the links she posted from gossip websites, prefaced by smug declarations like "Knew that," and "Toldja," and "Not surprised," and her endless series of self-portraits, typically snapped in bathroom mirrors.

I hit refresh, waiting to see if I'd been retweeted, if Cady had replied, if I'd gained any new followers, if anyone on the Internet had noticed my good news. So far, nothing.

Worry about it later, I told myself as my phone started ringing, flashing the name PETE on its screen.

"Hey, Pete!"

"Yuh?" he said, sounding confused and like he'd just woken up. It was four o'clock in the afternoon. This was troubling but not entirely surprising. Plenty of the television people I'd known back on *Bunk Eight* kept strange hours.

"Pete? Hey, it's Ruth." No answer. "You called me back?" Still nothing. Pete Paxton hadn't appeared in the pilot, but he'd been cast, pending a pickup, and would appear in a few scenes we'd add to the pilot later, after Chauncey had decided that the show needed more male energy. "Write a part for a guy," he'd said, via Loud Lloyd, and I'd said, "Absolutely."

So, in between the college applicants and the senior singles, praying that the request meant that we were, in fact, getting the nod, I'd written the part of a handsome, salt-of-the-earth sort of guy, the hunky neighbor who lived down the hall. I'd decided to make him a construction worker, because what's more manly than that? I'd named him Brad Dermansky and given him tattoos and a clingy ex-girlfriend, and I'd decided that when they met, he'd think of Daphne as a little sister, not the kind of girl he'd ever date. They'd be friends, and then her wit and smarts would wear him down, until he realized that she was all he'd ever wanted, that he was hopelessly in love.

For the first season, I figured, I could do will-they-or-won't-they, *Moonlighting* style. Brad and Daphne could date in the middle of Season Two and break up over a misunderstanding in Season Three. In Season Four I'd give Daphne a new boyfriend and Brad a new girlfriend, and Daphne would get engaged, and I'd write an episode where she'd be walking down the aisle, about to say her vows, and the officiant would ask if anyone had any objections, and Brad, unable to stand it a moment longer, would spring up from his folding chair in the back of the synagogue (or the church, depending on how Jewish Daphne could be) and declare his love in a scene that would leave not a dry eye in the house and possibly win him his second Emmy. They'd be engaged by Season Five, which would end with their nuptials, and which would bring the show to its hundredth episode, at which point *The Next Best Thing* would be eligible for syndication, and I'd be able to do whatever I wanted for the rest of my life.

"Hey, Ruthie," Pete slurred.

"Hi there, Pete. We got picked up!"

There was a long pause, followed by a rustling sound. I could hear giggling of the female variety in the background, which meant that Pete had company. "Oh. Oh, hey. That's . . . um. Wait, who is this? Is this Ruth?"

I took a deep breath. "Ruth Saunders. Executive producer. Brown hair, hats? Thing on my face?"

"Oh. Ruthie!"

"There you go." Like the character he'd be playing, Pete was lovely to look at, but unlikely to win the *Jeopardy!* Tournament of Champions anytime soon.

Pete yawned and then cleared his throat noisily. "Wow. Cool. Um."

I knew better than to ask, but I couldn't help myself. "Were you asleep?"

"Kinda."

"Up late watching that *Real Housewives* marathon?" That was what I'd been doing the night before . . . that, and pacing the length of my living room, hitting refresh on *Deadline Hollywood* once per lap. I should have told him I was out partying at a club (after, of course, I learned the name of the right club to mention). Maybe that's what it would take to earn his respect, or at least get him to see me as a peer, instead of a scolding old lady with a Boston accent. Although maybe scolding old lady could work for me. Maybe Pete would be more likely to take my notes if he didn't see me as an equal.

No answer. "Pete. *Pete!* Are you there?"

He managed a mumbled assent.

"Are you okay?"

"Oh, yeah! Fine! You bet!"

I wondered if he was on drugs, or if this was just the way most twenty-four-year-old male actors sounded. "Well, listen. Congratulations, and I'll see you soon!"

"Uh-huh." Pause. "Ruth-bo-Booth."

"Right. That's me."

"Boston."

"There you go." I could almost hear the pieces clicking together—Ruth-bo-Booth, Ruth from Boston.

"That's awesome. Your first show!"

"Thanks."

"No, thank you," said Pete. "I'll see you soon."

"You bet."

I hung up the phone and saw that my email was blinking. "Potential Writers" read the memo line of the email that Tariq's assistant had sent me. There was an attachment, which, when opened, yielded more than three hundred names and five dozen scripts, hundreds and hundreds of pages of work. "You'll need to hire a staff in the next two weeks," the note said.

"Oof," I murmured as my phone rang again, with Pocket's picture flashing. Dave. I grabbed it, punching the green button, lifting the phone to my ear.

"Hey, you!"

"Ruthie! Congratulations!" From the echo, I could tell that he'd put me on speakerphone.

"Way to go, sister!" called Big Dave.

"We're so happy for you."

"Don't forget about us when you're big," Big Dave cautioned. "You still have to take our calls."

Tears were running down my cheeks. I wiped them away. "I can never thank you guys enough. Thank you for believing in me. Thank you for thinking I could do this. I want to take you to dinner."

"We'll put that on the books," said Little Dave. "How are you? Did you tell your grandmother yet?"

"Remember when *Bunk Eight* got green-lit?" Big Dave asked his partner. "My mother hung up on me."

"She did?" I asked.

"Yep. She kept saying, 'Oh, I can't believe it, oh, I can't believe it,' and then she hung up." He paused. "We have a difficult relationship."

"I know." He'd told me, and many, many therapists, all about it.

"How about your parents, Dave?" I asked.

"They were pleased," he said.

Big Dave snorted. "They gave him a golf clap." To me, he said, "Sidney and Sandra are not what you'd call demonstrative."

"But they were happy for you, right?"

"They were," said Little Dave.

Big Dave snorted again. "Bitch, please," he said. "They're still waiting for you to quit playing and go home and take the LSATs."

"Can we focus?" asked Little Dave. "This is about Ruthie."

"We're thrilled," said Big Dave. "We couldn't be prouder."

"Seriously, Ruthie," said Little Dave—my Dave. "Anything we can do, just let us know."

Anything, I thought to myself, and imagined what my version of *anything* would be: Dave and I in the water, his arms strong around me, his voice in my ear, saying *Ruthie, you're the one I always wanted, you're the one I love.*

Thanks to my experience with *The Girls' Room* and the Daves, I knew the rules of putting together a writers' room, or at least the most important one: *Don't hire yourself.* You wanted people whose strengths and skills and senses of humor would complement your own, not echo them. In my case, that meant no broken girls—well, maybe just one. Or two. Maybe two. It could be my own form of affirmative action. I would not hire anyone who'd been stuffed in a locker . . . although, given the way most comedy writers tended to be refugees from the Island of Misfit Toys, formerly fat girls and currently gay guys, people who looked like Ewoks and ate like Wookies, wouldn't that eliminate ninety percent of the pool?

"I liked this one!" Grandma said brightly on Saturday morning as we made our way down Los Feliz Boulevard. On the East Coast, word was that nobody in Los Angeles ever walked anywhere, that it was all cars and underground parking structures and valets, but my grandmother had been a walker all her life, and a new city wasn't going to stop her. She had her recycled shopping bags slung over her shoulder and her shopping list tucked in her purse. We were off to the farmers' market, where she would gather supplies for the coming week, and then we'd have brunch.

She reached into her bag and handed me the first script she'd read. I saw that she'd purchased gold stars somewhere and had affixed one to the script's title page.

"Thanks!" I said, hoping that she'd be more discerning than I was.

"These were good, too," she said, passing me scripts two, three, and four. She'd spent the previous evening in her armchair, with an afghan on her lap, classical music playing softly, flipping through the pages with a red pen in her hand, sometimes clucking her tongue, sometimes laughing out loud, with a mug of tea at her elbow and a plastic binder labeled WEDDING on her lap, practically buried beneath hundreds of pages of sitcom. I felt a pang of guilt at the sight of it. I'd promised that I'd help her plan the menu, find a band, taste cakes, and narrow down the guest list, but so far, I hadn't done a thing. *Next week,* I told myself, and had gone back to my reading, with the increasing awareness that I was in trouble. Most of what I'd read had been good, and some of it had been great. A few of the scripts had been written on spec, for demonstration purposes only, to show that a writer could build and populate a world, but others had been written and developed under studio deals. They'd been contenders once. These shows, about divorced guys moving back in with their parents, and teenage girls in fat camps and senior citizens discovering they had superpowers, had once had the same chance as *The Next Best Thing* of actually getting cast and shot and making it onto TV. Reading them was like spending hours each day in a graveyard, visiting with the restless corpses of characters who'd never lived out their brief, imaginary lives. It was also depressing, because some of those scripts, maybe even most of them, were at least as good as what I'd written.

I bought an iced Thai coffee, made with condensed sweetened milk, and, while Grandma poked at bunches of basil and cilantro and quizzed the vendors on the diet of their chickens, I sat on a bench, flipping through my script stack. It was another gorgeous Los Angeles morning, the sky clear blue, a light, dry breeze swaying the fronds of the palm trees, the day a total contrast to my mood, which was depressed and heading quickly toward terrified. As an icy droplet made its way down my spine, and another curled from behind my ear to run down my neck, I plucked my phone out of my bag and called Little Dave.

"Did you ever read a script called *Scared White Girl*? By . . ." I flipped back to the title page. "Nancy Johnson?"

"Nope." He sounded cheerful and distracted. Probably there was a game on—Dave was a big Red Sox fan. Maybe he had friends over. I pictured his movie-screen-size TV broadcasting the game in an image crisp enough to see the stubble on the players' faces, aproned caterers in the kitchen, whipping up platters of sliders and wings. Shazia would be in the office, one hip perched on Dave's sleek white desk, her long black hair loose, telephone pressed to her ear, her tanned legs and painted toes bare. "Why? Is it any good? And where are you, by the way?"

"Farmers' market on Vermont. And the script's kind of amazing. I can't believe . . ." I paused.

"Oh, boy, here we go," he said. "Somebody's circling the drain."

"What?"

"You've been reading scripts all week, right? And, oh, about ten minutes ago, you started losing your mind because you can't see how your script's any better than the thirty-seven spec scripts you just read, and your show's going to bomb?"

I tugged my hair over my cheek. "More or less."

"Here's the truth, Ruthie. Nobody knows anything. William Goldman said that. He wrote *The Princess Bride*. Nobody knows anything. Repeat."

"Nobody knows anything," I said through numb lips. "But how can that be true? The network's already spent"—I looked to make sure that Grandma was busy inspecting a basket of beets, so she wouldn't hear and collapse on the spot—"two million dollars to shoot my pilot." I'd known that figure since I'd signed off on the budget, but it still astounded and scared me, and I tried not to think about it any more than I'd gaze directly into the sun. "How can they not know if they're going to spend that kind of money?"

"Nobody. Knows. Anything," Dave said again. "Those scripts you're reading might be perfectly fine, and have gotten passed over for reasons that have nothing to do with quality."

"Nothing to do with quality?" My stomach lurched. I got to my feet and dumped my iced coffee, only half-empty, into the trash. At these prices, the fees studios paid for scripts, not to mention the actual cost of shooting something, shouldn't the question of which scripts got picked up have everything to do with quality?

"For example, say you pitch a sitcom about a gynecologist who hates kids." I nodded mutely. I'd read just such a show that morning. "Now, it could be that it's a smart, well-written script, but maybe the network has one already, or maybe it's got a show about a child psychologist who hates kids, and Jenna Elfman's attached."

"Ah."

"Or," Dave continued, "you turned in your show about vampire cop partners who can't get along right after another network picked up a show about werewolf private detectives."

"Got it," I said. Grandma waved at me, beckoning me over. I tucked the phone under my chin, lifted her brimming bags over my shoulder—I could smell dill and leeks, and see a bouquet of sunflowers—and smiled as she introduced me to the farmer, a man about my age with weathered hands and an Amish-style beard.

"This is Ruthie, my granddaughter. She's the creator and showrunner of *The Next Best Thing*."

I covered the mouthpiece, narrowing my eyes at her. "We haven't premiered yet," I told the farmer.

Grandma ignored me. "I inspired the character of Daphne's grandmother," she said. "Be sure to watch for it!" She gave him a wave, and I followed her down the street.

"Hello? Dave, are you still there?"

"What was that?" he asked, sounding amused.

"That, evidently, was our PR department." We waited at a red light. A bus went by with a poster for *Walk-up*, a new sitcom, on its side. Grandma pointed at the bus and then at me. "Soon it's going to be you on that bus," she stage-whispered.

"Better on it than under it," I whispered back as Dave continued.

"Sometimes it's just a question of what resonates with whoever's calling the shots. Max Dubrov—you never knew him, he used to run comedy at Paragon—he had this thing about teachers. Any show with a teacher, any show that had anything to do a teacher, he'd just toss it."

"Why? Was his mother a teacher or something?" Men in comedy, I had learned, tended to have mother issues.

"No clue," Dave said. One network head had it in for a certain type of long-legged brunette who reminded him of his first ex-wife; another had been burned so badly by a show starring three children that he hadn't green-lit a single project involving an actor under eighteen in six years.

We crossed Vermont Avenue and stopped in the vestibule of a French café. The hostess walked us to a table on the sidewalk that was shaded by an umbrella. "Coffee?" she asked.

"Orange juice," I whispered, settling the bags underneath the table. Grandma pointed at the phone, eyebrows raised.

"Work," I whispered. She nodded, reached into her purse, pulled out a script, a red pen, and a coil of gold star stickers, and began to read as Dave talked about the question of trends.

"One year, something dark and edgy does well, so it's *I want comedies about cancer! I want to do a show about a support group for men with erectile dysfunction! I want a show about two kids switched at birth who meet their biological families right before they start high school!*" Dave said. "Then, when all those dark, edgy, ironic shows fail—and most of them will, because they're derivative copycats—the executives decide they want family comedies, with moms and dads and two cute kids . . ."

"Where Dad's a stay-at-home goofball, and the mom's a type-A stress-muffin, and one of the kids is a hot girl or guy, so you can appeal to the thirteen-to-eighteens, and everyone talks to the camera."

"Right," said Dave. The waitress put a menu in my hands. I pointed at the brioche French toast. She nodded and took the menu away and noticed Grandma's script.

"Are you a writer?" she asked.

"Oh, no, my granddaughter Ruthie is," Grandma announced, loudly enough for all the patrons at the other outdoor tables to hear. "Her show was just picked up by ABS. She's staffing her writers' room."

I cringed, praying that the waitress wouldn't have a brother or a boyfriend or a dad who was a screenwriter or, even worse, a script of her own tucked into her locker in the restaurant's back room. I thought about the stack of pages, two feet high, waiting for me back home, and realized again how lucky I was that all the variables—the whims of the executives, the desires of the viewers, and the availability of the actors—had aligned, for one brief moment, in my favor.

Dave's voice softened. "If you're worried that the people you'll be meeting with are going to resent you because they think their script should have been picked up, that they should have been the one doing the hiring, I'm not going to say you're wrong. But everyone knows the deal out here, and how much of it is luck. And honestly, writing for someone else's show isn't like a prison sentence."

"I know." I'd loved my time in the writers' room for *The Girls' Room,* and had occasionally felt guilty that I was actually being paid to spend my days with funny people who basically sat around telling jokes. It didn't feel like a real job. A real job was being a teacher or a nurse, or selling furniture, like my grandma had. Scrubbing floors, growing food, helping the sick, all of that was real work, and I'd endure pangs of guilt, or a sense that I was getting away with something, every time I got paid.

"You sound like you need a break. Want to come over?" Dave asked. Before I had time to get my hopes up, he said, "Pool's all yours. Shazia and I are going to Malibu this afternoon."

Of course they were, I thought, with my insides crumpling. I pictured them driving on curving roads along the cliffs, the top down, Shazia's hair in the wind, her short skirt riding up her long legs.

"I've got to keep reading," I said.

"Good luck," he told me. "And don't worry, you're going to pick a great room."

"I am?" I asked.

"People like you. They want to be around you. You'll do fine." Then as if he was worried he'd said too much, he gave me a quick "Gotta go" and hung up just as the brunch arrived.

My grandmother watched me as I put the phone back in my purse and then spread my napkin on my lap.

"You like him," she said. Lifting her knife, she sliced off a bite of poached egg and smoked salmon. She was dressed in what, for her, were casual clothes—white cotton capris, a loose linen blouse in lemon yellow, pale-blue laced-up Converse sneakers.

"Dave's a good boss," I said, taking a bite of my own breakfast and then quickly reaching into my own bag to retrieve a script before she could ask me anything else.

FOURTEEN

I'm sorry," said the patient voice from the speakerphone in the center of the table in the writers' room. The voice belonged to Eric Fein, the Standards and Practices lawyer who'd been assigned to *The Next Best Thing*. In our three weeks of work, I'd gotten familiar with his voice, and with his opinions on what was encouraged and permissible on network TV. "You can't say *ass-munch*."

There was silence as six writers absorbed this. "Ass snack?" offered Sam, brushing his long hair out of his eyes. Sam was one of my baby writers. He'd had one job so far, on an MTV show that had lasted a single season, and he supported himself by tweeting in the persona of Softie, the anthropomorphized roll of toilet paper who was the brand ambassador for SilkSoft toilet tissue. "We love your ass" was SilkSoft's slogan. During his job interview, Sam had told me, with a mixture of pride and embarrassment, that he'd thought of it all by himself.

"We'd prefer no *ass* at all," Eric replied.

"I don't get it," said Ginger Fairfax, the most senior of the writers. "Didn't they say 'douche juice' on *Cougar Town* last night?"

"I definitely heard 'bitch, please' on *Two Broke Girls*," offered George, my Harvard guy. George was African-American, which meant that the network was paying his salary as part of its diversity initiative. This, in my opinion, made no sense. George's mother was a surgeon, his father was a professor, both of his sisters were doctors, and George, who'd attended boarding school in New Hampshire before following both sisters to Cambridge, had grown up wealthy and well educated, in an atmosphere where racism and discrimination were the worst sins another kid could commit. I was glad to have him, even if he was funny in more or less the same way the privileged white Ivy Leaguers I'd known were funny, with his riffs about how his high-achieving relatives were scandalized by his decision to spurn the world of medicine and write jokes instead. "I'm the black sheep," he'd told me during our interview. "Pun intended."

"There were dingleberries on *Whitney*," said Nancy, who then covered her mouth with her fingers, like she was embarrassed to have even uttered the word. Nancy was my other baby writer, and I'd been thrilled to hire her and rescue her from Lanny Drew's clutches. For the past two years, she'd been toiling as Mr. I-Wouldn't-Fuck-Her's assistant, and while she was far too discreet to bad-mouth a former boss, my guess was that she was as relieved to be out of there as I'd been happy to have her.

The speakerphone sighed. "Guys, listen. I'm not responsible for those shows. I'm only responsible for you. And also, the action line on page three?" Thumbs flicked over iPads as we all flipped to page three. "Nana cocks her finger?" Eric read. "We need to make sure that doesn't resemble oral sex."

I frowned at the script. " 'Cocks her finger' just means pointing."

"Ah," said Eric. "Oh, okay. Got it. Sorry. Our software's a little sensitive about the word *cock*. Moving on," he said before we could start teasing him about his software's sensitivity. "When Veronica's standing over the heating vent and her skirt blows up, make sure we can't see anything." He cleared his throat. "We'd like it if she could be wearing shorts under her skirt."

"Who does that?" asked Claire. Claire and her husband, Paul, were my writing team, married with a two-year-old daughter. They'd met in college and moved to Los Angeles right after they graduated. As a writing team, they counted as one entity and would be splitting one paycheck, which made them a bargain: two bodies for the price of one.

"Sorry?" asked Eric.

"No adult woman wears shorts underneath her skirts," said Ginger. Ginger was the daughter of a television actress and her onetime director of photography, and, at forty, the most senior writer in the room. Friendly and easygoing, she'd been working for years and knew all of the executives and lots of the other writers on the lot, and what was worth eating at the commissary. "That's more of a second-grade-girl-on-the-playground thing."

"Fine. No shorts. Just make sure we can't see anything."

"No problem," I told him, and wrote myself a note to call the stunt coordinator and be sure that Veronica's underpants would remain invisible.

"Okay, then, I think that's it. Oh, one more thing," said Eric. I braced myself. This was how Eric operated, with his "one more thing" usually being the problem that would demand the most effort and time to solve. "The scene where Nana's joking about Barbra Streisand buying James Brolin from human traffickers?"

I smiled. That joke was one of my favorites.

"We'd prefer you replace Barbra Streisand."

I stopped smiling. "Seriously? Why?"

"She's notoriously litigious," Eric said primly.

"But we're obviously kidding. I mean, nobody actually believes that we think she bought her husband at a souk, or whatever."

Eric's silence implied that, indeed, people would believe we thought that.

"Can we say Hillary Clinton?" Nancy ventured.

"Laura Bush," called Sam.

"Why would Laura Bush want to pay money for George?" asked Paul. "The point of the joke is that it's a woman buying something she wouldn't be able to get on her own."

"Have you seen Laura Bush?" Sam asked. "Fat ankles."

"Hillary's are worse," said George.

"Do men actually care about ankles?" Nancy wondered out loud. "Because I've been told by many women's magazines that all you really care about is seeing a woman naked, and that we're the ones obsessing about our flaws. Like, are you seriously going to kick a woman out of your bed because you don't like her ankles?"

The men looked at one another. "Probably not," said Sam.

"I'm going to let you creative types sort this out," said Eric, which was how he ended every phone call. "Peace," he said, and we went back to what we'd been doing before his call: talking about our sex lives. This was how it went in most writers' rooms, which were like rolling group-therapy sessions. You brought it all to the table: your family history, your relationships with your parents and your kids, the story of how you'd had your heart broken, met your spouse, discovered your mother was having an affair with her costar (in Ginger's case) or your father had a secret family (in Nancy's). All of that material became fodder for the show, stuff you could repurpose and use as your characters' background, and none of it ever left the rooms, which existed under a cloak of secrecy. The writers' room is a safe place, the Daves had always said, a line I'd heard echoed by other writers and showrunners through the years.

That morning we'd been working on a scene where Nana Trudy goes on Date Number Three with a man she's met at the shuffleboard court, and learns he's got a penchant for rough sex . . . and, unfortunately for him, a heart condition. Ginger had been telling us the story of her college boyfriend, who had similar tastes but, sadly, not enough upper-body strength to fulfill his desires.

"So his big thing was, he wanted to rip my panties off me, right?" Ginger began.

"As you do," said Sam, biting into his third Clif Bar of the morning. Sam was tall and lanky and ate more than any human being I'd ever seen. He'd start each morning with two packets of instant oatmeal topped with half-and-half and strawberries, a toasted bagel with butter and cream cheese, and hot chocolate. Then he'd munch granola bars and trail mix until lunchtime. At two o'clock he'd break for a yogurt topped with a fistful of almonds and a cup of granola, and at four he'd have a triple-decker peanut-butter-and-banana sandwich. If he'd been a girl, I would have assumed he was bulimic. Because he was a twenty-four-year-old guy, I figured he was just still growing.

"Right," said Ginger. "But he couldn't actually, you know, rip them. So I'd have to pre-rip my own underwear. Just, you know, to get things started for him."

"That's pathetic," George scoffed.

"Yeah," said Ginger, spinning back and forth in her seat. "I guess it was kind of sad."

"I had a girlfriend who used to buy underwear a size smaller than what she wore, and if she went home with a guy, she'd leave them in his bed," Nancy volunteered.

"Thus making him think he got luckier than he actually got," said Paul.

Claire swatted his upper arm. "You're a pig," she announced.

"Yeah, but I'm your pig. And you have to sleep with me. The *ketubah* says so." This was an ongoing joke between the two of them: that Paul had gotten the rabbi to write up a wedding contract in which Clare promised to do all kinds of things, including give him blow jobs whenever he wanted them, and allow him to spend up to five percent of their combined income on sports betting.

"One day I'm going to get that thing translated," Claire muttered.

"So what happened to the guy?" I asked Ginger. "The panty-ripper?"

"He started working out. Then he got strong enough to rip my panties by himself. Then he moved on to T-shirts. Then we broke up." She made a face, remembering. "By that point, he was so built, he could've had any girl he wanted. But it was kind of a relief. I couldn't keep asking my parents for money for new clothes."

Sam's stomach made a noisy grumble. He patted it fondly. "Patience, my pet." Then he looked at me. "Can we order Thai for lunch?"

"Streisand first." I got up and stood in front of the whiteboard, which we'd divided into a grid. The vertical columns were for each episode, one through nine, with working titles. The horizontal ones named each character—Daphne, Nana, Brad, Veronica—and described what they'd each be doing. "Five minutes," I said. "Oh, and we also need alts for Brad's line in the A scene." That was where Daphne expresses her appreciation at Brad's scent—he'd spent the day repairing frozen-yogurt dispensers—and he replied, "Good thing you didn't meet me that summer I was working in the fish cannery." *Fish cannery* had gotten a decent laugh in the room, as had *mortuary,* but I thought we could do better. The writers bent down over their iPads as Amanda, my assistant, poked her head into the room.

"Hey, Ruth, I've got Joan and Lloyd from the network for you."

"Ginger, you're in charge," I said, and went to my office to take the call.

"Hello?"

"Ruth!" bellowed Lloyd. I winced. Speakerphone again—I could hear the staticky echo. I'd come to hate Speakerphone, knowing that the executives all surfed the Net and checked their email during calls, so you never really had their whole attention. "How are things going?"

"Really well." So far we were on schedule. We'd written one episode, were working on our second, and had gotten the studio's and the network's blessings for the outlines for Episodes Three and Four.

"It's all good on our end," said Joan. "We're getting ready to take the pilot out for testing, and we had a thought."

"Okay," I said, hearing Big Dave's voice in my head. Dave had kept a Sam's Club–size jar of KY jelly displayed on his desk, and when he got calls like this, calls that included the dread phrase *we had a thought*, he'd make a show of uncapping the bottle, putting the call on "Mute," and saying, *Bend over, here it comes again.*

"You know the alt we shot at the end of pilot night?" Joan asked. I grimaced, remembering. That had been Lloyd's scene, complete with gross sex jokes about how Nana Trudy had basically fucked her boyfriend into the ICU, with the intention of taking over his house and taking all of his money. How could I forget?

"We went ahead and showed it to Chauncey, and he was a big fan," said Joan. "So we cut a version using that scene, and that's what we'd like to take out and test."

"We're having it messengered over to you this morning," said Lloyd, sounding like he was doing me a big favor.

"I'm not comfortable with that," I blurted . . . which, I figured, was more diplomatic than saying, *I hated it, it's awful, and if you use it, you're going to ruin my show.* Even as I said the words, I knew they wouldn't do any good. Chauncey had spoken . . .

and once the president of the network decided he liked a line, or a scene, or an actress, as surely as day followed night, the showrunner would be stuck with that line, that scene, that actress. Still, I needed to make my case. I drew myself up tall in my chair, set my feet on the floor, and said, "If we've got people making fun of Nana Trudy in the first act, basically calling her an elderly nymphomaniac . . ."

Lloyd chuckled. "Elderly nymphomaniac. That's a good line. We should have used that."

I shut my eyes and pressed on. "The important thing in a pilot is telling the audience who they're supposed to root for. If you're making Nana a joke, they won't want to root for her. They'll just want to laugh at her."

The silence on the other end of the line told me that my executives were perfectly content in a world where viewers were laughing *at* Nana instead of with her. I could feel my throat tightening as I imagined my own grandmother's reaction to the scene, in which Annie Tait was called fat and ugly, an over-the-hill gold digger intent on getting her claws into any man who'd pay the deductibles for her doctors' visits. "Did you guys ever watch *The Golden Girls*?" I asked.

"Of course," Joan said promptly.

"I've seen it in reruns," Lloyd said.

"Those women . . ." I pressed my fist against my right eye, then my left one. "They were the heroes of the show, you know? You loved them. You wanted them to win. If we start off the show with . . ." *Lloyd's scene*, I almost said, and stopped myself just in time. "If we start *The Next Best Thing* with the scene you're proposing, it makes it so that Nana's not a hero. She's just a punch line." I paused and then added, "And it would break my grandmother's heart."

There was another beat of silence, during which I imagined Lloyd and Joan weighing possible ratings against one old woman's broken heart—one old woman who didn't even have a Nielsen box. "Why don't you take a look at what we're sending over. It's probably not as bad as you remember it," said Joan.

It was, I knew, just as bad as I'd remembered it, and possibly worse . . . but I could hear in her voice that the battle was over, and that I'd lost.

"I think this is a mistake," I said. My voice sounded high and wobbly, and I was, I knew, about ten seconds away from actually starting to cry. "I just need to be on record as saying that. I think it's a betrayal of what this show's supposed to be about." *It's a betrayal of me,* I thought. *My grandmother. My life. Everything we've lived through to get here.*

I heard the *beep* of call waiting. "Ruth, I need to take this," Joan said in her soft and placating voice. "Take a look at the cut. I hear that you're upset, but I think that when you watch it back and take some time to sit with it you're going to feel much better."

Wrong, I thought. "Okay," I said. When the call ended, I put my forearm on the desk and rested my forehead against it, breathing in the scent of fabric softener and my own skin, hearing a lyric from *Les Misérables* in my head: *There was a time when it all went wrong.*

"Ready?" I asked, and tried to smile. I had put off showing the pilot to my grandmother for as long as I possibly could. *I only have a rough cut,* I'd told her. *They haven't temped in the music. We're still making changes,* I'd said long after the point when we'd stopped making changes. *There might be reshoots,* I told her—true, but that didn't change the fact that for the past ten days I'd had a close-to-finished copy of the pilot in my possession . . . and I didn't want to show it to my grandmother.

She'd asked. Then she'd wheedled. At the dining-room table, draped in its white cloth, with my favorite dishes all in a row, she had employed reverse psychology, airily claiming that she wasn't interested, that she'd wait for the September premiere, just like everyone else. Finally, she met me at the door one night when I was coming home from work and said, "The longer you don't let me look at it, the more worried I'm going to get."

"There's nothing to worry about," I answered reflexively, even though I knew, or at least strongly suspected, that this was not the case. Lloyd's scene was just as hateful as I'd remembered. It went against everything I believed about the Nana character, everything I believed, more generally, about comedy for women and comedy for older women especially. It turned Nana into a caricature, the cliché of a raunchy, sex-starved senior citizen . . . but I had stalled for as long as I possibly could. I couldn't put this off any longer. "You can see it whenever you want to," I told Grandma over dinner. She clapped her hands together with glee and announced her intention to throw a viewing party.

"Keep it on the small side," I'd told her as she'd all but danced down the hall, talking to herself about menus and the guest list in between telling me, again, how proud she was. "I'm really not supposed to be screening it for people. I can't have it leak."

She stopped and turned, gazing at me, looking incredulous and hurt. "You think my friends would do that?" she demanded. "Bring their phones to our house, and tape your show, and put it on the Internet?"

"No, no," I said, turning back toward the table and gathering an armload of dirty dishes. "It's just, you know, they made me sign something . . . they take this all really seriously . . ."

Grandma stared at me a moment longer. I looked back and then put the dishes in the sink, turned on the hot water, and started rinsing. In that moment, I could have told her the truth: *They made me add a new scene, and you're not going to like it; it's going to hurt your feelings, and I'm sorry, but I didn't know how to stop it; I didn't know how to tell them no.* Instead, I ducked down to open the dishwasher, listening as Grandma got on the phone to tell Maurice she was having a party.

For days, I'd tried to warn her. The morning of the viewing party, I'd found her out on the balcony in clam-diggers and a loose cotton blouse and her gardening gloves, weeding and watering her container garden. "Grandma," I began. She looked up at me, with her gardening shears in her hand.

"I'm so excited," she said. "I can't even tell you." She snipped a stalk of basil and added it to the pile in the wicker basket resting beside her. There was a dab of sunscreen she hadn't blended on the tip of her nose and, ripening in a paper bag in a corner of the balcony, a dozen avocados that one of her friends had dropped off two days earlier so Grandma could make her famous guacamole.

"I have to tell you—" I said, but before I could get another word out, she shook her head and held up her hand to stop me.

"No, no, don't tell me anything. I was there when they filmed it, of course, but I want to pretend that I don't know anything . . . that I'm seeing it for the very first time, just like anyone else."

"Okay," I said, and slunk back inside, telling myself that I'd done my duty, that I'd tried to warn her, and if she didn't like what she saw, she had only herself to blame.

Now the moment had arrived. In the bathroom, I gulped down an airline-size bottle of vodka: liquid courage. Then I opened the door and found my grandmother, in one of her old furniture-store suits, a scarf at her neck, her hair shining from an afternoon trip to the beauty parlor. "Can I borrow you for a minute?" I asked. It was her hair, secured with the mother-of-pearl combs that had been the last birthday gift her husband had given her, that broke my heart. The combs meant that this was an occasion on the grandest scale . . . and she was going to be so disappointed.

She grabbed my hands. "Look! You won't believe it!" She pulled me into the living room. Bowls and platters were set up on the coffee table, my favorite olives wrapped and baked in cheese dough on a tray, alongside skewered shrimp and chicken . . . and on the wall, draped in a sheet, was what appeared to be an enormous new flat-screen TV.

"Oh. Oh, wow. That's really . . ."

"Maurice got it for me," Grandma said. "It's an early wedding gift. He didn't want me to miss a thing!"

The words I'd meant to say, everything I'd planned on telling her about the pilot, shriveled and died in my mouth. Grandma eyed me. "Don't you want to change?"

I had on the same jeans and loose-fitting tunic and scarf and clogs I'd worn to work. "I'm fine," I said, and took a seat in the corner as the doorbell rang and Grandma hurried to answer it.

Ten minutes later, the crowd was assembled, with Grandma established in the center of the couch. Her friend Elsa sat beside her, along with Georgia and Joe, a married pair of extras who frequently played spouses in the various hospital waiting rooms and restaurants where they worked. There was Martine, our across-the-hall neighbor, and Chloe and Sybil from water aerobics at the JCC, and Ernesto, who managed the meat counter at the Whole Foods on Fairfax. The dining-room table was draped in an embroidered cloth and spread with platters of appetizers: shrimp ceviche, fresh-made chips and tortillas, salsas made with smoky roasted peppers, tiny grilled lamb chops and mole-marinated drumsticks, fresh guacamole Grandma had made that afternoon.

"Come in, come in!" she said, shepherding her guests into the living room. I swallowed hard, trying to vanish into the armchair in the corner as people took their seats in front of the big new set. "Ladies and gentlemen!" Grandma said, beaming. "The Next Best Thing!" There was nothing to do but push the power button and then, with the remote in my hand, listen to the audience as they watched what I had made.

The first scene, Daphne losing her job, played fine. When Daphne went back and forth with the chef, the picture was so crisp you could see the instant when her cheeks began to flush, and the glitter of a tear well before it fell. Grandma slipped across the room to squeeze my hand. "I love it," she said. Her eyes were shining, her face wreathed in a smile.

"Thanks," I croaked. *Wait*, I thought. *Oh, just wait.*

The next scene took place in the house Nana Trudy had shared with her beloved. As Annie Tait made her grand entrance down the staircase, dressed in a flowing silk robe and fur-trimmed mules, one of the actors playing the boyfriend's sons snickered. "She looks like she's been ridden hard and put away wet," he said.

I heard the hiss of my grandmother's inhalation. Across the room, I saw Maurice take her hand. I couldn't imagine what he was thinking. Nor, I found, did I want to.

On-screen, Annie Tait walked gracefully toward them, eyes narrowed as she considered the three middle-aged men in suits waiting for her at the dining-room table. "Huey, Dewey, and Louie," she said, her voice arch and teasing. "What can I do for you this fine morning?"

"We want you out," one of the men said.

On-screen, Annie Tait stiffened. In the living room, I stiffened, too. "Why, I don't believe that's for you to say," Annie told them. "This is your father's house."

"Dad's done with you. As soon as he gets out of the hospital, he's going into a nursing home," the second son told her. "He left us power of attorney. Us, not you. We're putting the place on the market. You've got until the end of the day to pack up your broom and your Viagra and hit the road."

From the couch, somebody—it might have been Ernesto—

gave a snort of laughter. I cringed against the wall, afraid to look at my grandmother.

"I'll thank you not to speak to me like that," said Annie Tait.

"Oh, we'd be happy if we didn't have to speak to you at all," said the actor playing the first son, an incredibly nice man named Gabriel Arden, who had worked on TV and in movies for decades because of his ability to compress his mouth into an especially cruel slit. "We never could figure out what Dad saw in you."

"I mean, an Anna Nicole Smith, that, at least, we could have understood," said Son Number Two.

Annie lifted her chin. "I know things that woman would have taken another decade to figure out."

"Oh, yeah?" leered the third son. "Like how to get around Boston by horse-drawn carriage?"

The laugh track cackled and blared. I snuck a look toward the couch. Grandma was holding herself perfectly still, spine straight, head erect. "Oh, they're being so awful to her!" she whispered.

Annie licked her lips slowly and said, "You want to know something about your father? He didn't really need that cane he used." She waited until the three brothers had exchanged a puzzled glance and then leered at the camera as she spread her hands a good eighteen inches apart. "I take it you boys didn't inherit his talents?" she asked. Their looks of confusion turned to shame and fury as she said, "Or maybe you did, and it's just been divided in thirds . . ."

"Get to steppin'," said the first brother.

"And don't let the door hit your ass on the way out," said the second.

"Like the door's even big enough," said Son Number Three. More shrieks of glee rose up from the laugh track. Had it always been this loud, or did it just sound that way in the dead silence of the living room?

Annie's hand tightened on the banister. "What do I do now?" she asked. "Where do I go?"

"Go put on something low-cut and hang out by the VFW hall," said Son Number One. "You'll probably find someone else by dinnertime," said Brother Number Two.

"Which is at five-thirty," said Brother Three.

The laugh track brayed its approval. Annie Tait's shoulders slumped. Without another word she began to make her way back up the stairs. Then she turned—I imagined I could feel my grandmother tense—and uttered a line that had struck me as, if not funny, then maybe as at least close to funny and the best I could do with what I'd been given, the dog's dinner that Loud Lloyd had handed me: "Bite my Boniva!" There was more laughter, and applause, as the show's temporary track, Sara Bareilles's "King of Anything," started playing, and the picture faded into the space the editors had left for commercials.

I sat in my chair, legs folded, hands clenched in my lap, telling myself that what she was seeing on the screen wasn't that different from what I'd written. Sure, there were a few more double entendres, a couple of not-so-subtle hints that Nana Trudy might, in fact, have been either a sex addict or an alcoholic or both, a joke about how she didn't actually know the name of her only daughter's father because she'd gotten pregnant during what she referred to as her "Long Lost Weekend," but other than that, things were pretty much as she would have remembered them from the night of the shoot. Nana Trudy loved Daphne. Daphne loved her right back. Best of all, the show ended just the way it had in every version of the script that I'd written: with the two of them together in the home they'd made, comfortable and happy, with Daphne saying the line I hoped would close each episode: "We're all right for now."

I remained seated until the credits played, and forced myself to breathe as the words—"Created by Ruth Saunders"—flashed on the screen. Once they had faded, I hazarded another look at my grandmother. Still seated on the couch, in her beauty-parlor coif, and her combs glittering in her hair, she raised her head, the way she'd told me to do a thousand times, since I was old enough to walk, old enough to understand her. *Chin up!* she would tell me, brisk as a drill sergeant. *Never let them see you looking mopy.* "Well!" she said, and tried on a smile that did not touch her eyes. "Wasn't that something?" She crossed the room, plucked the remote from my nerveless fingers, and clicked the set into silence. Then, without looking at me, she sailed into the dining room, calling, "Who's ready for some dinner?"

I had been on the receiving end of my grandmother's silent treatment only a handful of times in my life—once when I was fifteen and I'd borrowed her gold bracelet without her permission and lost it, and again when I was sixteen and I'd taken the T to Boston for a concert I'd been forbidden to attend. What I'd learned from those instances was that my grandmother was capable of ignoring me in the midst of a roomful of people without making anyone else uncomfortable, or even noticing the tension. But I noticed. "Great job!" said Ernesto, through a mouthful of mole. "You must be so proud of Ruthie!" Instead of answering or agreeing, Grandma gave him a tight smile and then turned to Martine and started talking about whether the city council had done anything about changing the traffic patterns to Griffith Park during the summertime concerts. "I'll bet you're excited!" said Georgia, and Grandma gave a little sniff that only I could hear, excused herself, and took the half-empty guacamole bowl to the kitchen for refilling. Sybil wanted to tell me about her nephew, a recent art-school graduate who was hoping to get a job as a film editor, and I promised to pass along his résumé the moment it hit my in-box. "It was very funny," said Chloe, and Grandma, who'd just emerged from the kitchen with a platter of sugar-dusted churros, set it down on the table and asked Maurice if he wouldn't mind stepping onto the balcony with her. "I think," she announced, "that I could use some fresh air."

I nibbled at my ceviche and chips and drank too much sangria, alternately looking forward to and dreading the moment when the apartment was finally empty and Grandma and I would be alone. By ten o'clock the last of the guests had made her way down the carpeted hallway to the elevator, with Maurice to guide her and drive her home. My grandmother went to the living room and started gathering up plates and cups and napkins.

"So!" I said. I'd decided to play it straight. Maybe I'd been wrong. Maybe I'd imagined her shock and dismay when she'd seen the finished product, and had misread the way she'd been ignoring me all night. "What'd you think?"

"I think," she said, without looking up, "that Bea Arthur would be ashamed of you."

I felt my face redden as if she'd slapped it. I had expected a harsh review, but not that. Never that. "I think you're overreacting," I said, struggling to keep my voice even.

"Am I?" Her voice quavered as she held her armload of plates. "Because I've watched a lot of television in my time . . . oh, never mind," she said, pushing past me into the kitchen. "Why would you want to listen to—how did you put it again?—some dried-up old sack who wants you to bite her Boniva?"

I winced. I hadn't been proud of myself, writing that line, but it had gotten a big laugh in the room when Annie had read it, and God knew, it was funnier than the three jokes Loud Lloyd had proposed, all of which had to do with erections. "I'm not sure that line's going to make the final cut," I said. "We're still waiting to hear back from the Boniva people."

"Wonderful," she said, yanking out the drawer containing the trash can harder than she needed to. "I can't wait."

"Listen," I said, scooping up a few dirty plates and joining her in the kitchen. "It's a process, you know?" I was trying to remember what Dave had told me, to parrot a few of his most reasonable-sounding lines. "You have to give a little to get a little. I know right now it feels maybe a little bit big and jokey . . ."

She glared at me, hands on her hips. "Do you know how it feels?" she asked. "I don't think you have any idea. It feels like . . ." She drew a shuddering breath, and her voice caught. "It feels like you think that I'm a joke," she said. "Like I'm a joke, and you're putting me out there for the world to laugh at."

I felt my heart crack open as I realized the enormity of what I'd done, the awfulness of it . . . and that, in a few months' time, if everything went well, this awful thing I'd done was going to be on television for all the world to see. Critics and random viewers and teenagers whose worldviews would be shaped by what they saw would all be tuning in and feasting on the tele-vised version of my grandmother's debasement, laughing (or not) at a character who was just one more version of the oversexed, foulmouthed granny. *Bite my Boniva.* What in the world had I been thinking? The answer came, almost immediately. *Anything. I will do anything.* Write those lines, change the character, let Lloyd replace my words with his own, let the network insist on the actors and the scenes that it wanted, even if it meant selling out my own grandmother, the woman who'd raised me, who'd loved me? Sure thing. Why not. As long as it gets my show on the air.

"I tried to tell you," I said.

The look she shot me was full of pain and scorn. "You didn't try very hard."

"Listen," I began. "You always knew it wasn't going to be just us, on the show, right? I mean, Daphne doesn't have scars. Nobody's going to think she's me, and maybe nobody's going to think the grandmother's you." She raked me with her gaze, without bothering to utter a word . . . and then I was done.

"You're right," I said. My voice was a ragged croak. "That scene with Nana is awful. I didn't even write it, Lloyd did, the only thing that's mine is the Boniva joke, and I didn't want to shoot it, but he insisted, and then he was the one who had the editors cut it in, and they sent it to the network before I signed off, and then Chauncey saw it . . . what can I do?" I asked her. "I'm not the one in charge. They are."

I could hear her sigh from all the way across the kitchen.

"I can try to fix it," I said . . . but I wasn't sure any change was possible. I could try to plead my case to the network, to tell them, paraphrasing T. S. Eliot, that *this was not what I meant, not what I meant at all* . . . but I didn't think it would matter much. If Chauncey liked it, that made all other opinions irrelevant.

"I swear to you, I'll try as hard as I can," I said, and crossed the kitchen to hug her. "I am so, so sorry." She stayed stiff in my arms. "Are you okay?" I asked.

"I'm tired, Ruthie," she told me . . . and then, without looking back, still impeccable in her suit and scarf and heels, she walked to her bedroom and quietly shut the door.

FIFTEEN

The elevator that whisked me up to Chauncey McLaughlin's office moved so fast that it felt as if my stomach was still on the ground floor by the time the rest of me arrived on the fortieth. The views from the reception area were spectacular, stretching all the way to the sea. The receptionist was pretty spectacular, too, with almond-shaped eyes and high, gorgeous cheekbones, tawny skin, and a body that, when she stood to greet me, made me want to jump right back into the elevator, find a cab, and demand to be taken to the closest plastic surgeon's office.

"Ruth Saunders for Mr. McLaughlin," I said as firmly as I could. She gave me a professional smile. Her white teeth gleamed; the space-age metal earpiece in her left ear flashed green, then blue.

"Have a seat," she offered after I'd refused water, tea, or coffee. I did, and picked up an issue of *Variety*, and tried not to fidget with my hat or yank my hair over my cheek.

Ten minutes later, the door swung open. "Ruth Saunders," boomed Chauncey. I wondered briefly whether Loud Lloyd had learned volume management from him. Chauncey wore suit pants, a dress shirt, and a tie, but his sleeves were rolled up, his tie was askew, and his face was flushed a red so brilliant that I feared an incipient cardiac event, and quickly reviewed the CPR procedures I'd learned as a lifeguard while he led me into his office.

"Sorry about this," he said, fanning at his face before taking a seat behind a desk roughly the size of a city bus. He gestured at a comfortably upholstered chair across from the desk, and I sat down with my purse in my lap and my leg muscles tensed to keep them from shaking. "W-O-D."

"Excuse me?"

"Workout of the day. Cross-fit. You don't do cross-fit? I thought everyone did cross-fit! *Rolph!*" he hollered. A door from somewhere in the back of the office swung open, and a man the size of a telephone booth emerged, dressed in skin-tight bike shorts and a T-shirt with the legend PAIN IS WEAKNESS LEAVING THE BODY printed across his impressive chest. "Give Ruthie here your card." Wordlessly, Rolph dipped into his fanny pack—yes, he was wearing a fanny pack, and somehow he was making it work—and handed me a card that contained only two words: ROLPH. CROSS-FIT, followed by a website and an email address. Evidently Rolph did not deign to communicate by actual voice-to-voice conversation.

"Thanks," I said, and slipped it in my pocket.

Rolph gave me a terse nod and then pointed two fingers at Chauncey. "Protein," he said.

"Protein," Chauncey repeated. The two of them exchanged a complicated handshake, and then Rolph walked out of the office. It took him, I noticed, a very long time. He was fit, but that office was enormous.

"Now, Ruth," said Chauncey. "What can I do for you?"

I'd written out what I meant to say—about how the scene that Lloyd had written set the wrong tone, how it relied on painful stereotypes, how it was broad and unfunny and damaging to women, and I had rehearsed that speech, first in the privacy of my bedroom, then in front of the Daves. They'd been supportive but not encouraging.

"You can try," Big Dave said, but he sounded dubious.

"Chauncey might like your moxie," offered Little Dave, who sounded equally skeptical. I heard the truth in what they weren't saying: *Once a network president makes up his mind, good luck to you, lowly showrunner.* Still, though, this was my grandmother. She'd raised me; she'd loved me; she'd sacrificed her life for mine. I had to try. I wouldn't be able to live with myself if I didn't.

"It's about the A scene in the pilot," I said.

Chauncey stared at me blankly. A bead of sweat trickled down his cheek and darkened the knot of his tie.

"*The Next Best Thing*," I said quickly. "Girl and her grandmother move to Miami? Cady Stratton's starring?"

He gave a sudden, booming laugh. "I know that. You think I don't know that? You think I don't know my own shows?"

My face flushed. "No, no, of course, I was . . . I mean, I thought . . ."

He boomed more laughter at me. "Don't worry. Man, I love messing with creatives. You're so gullible!" He reached into a glass apothecary jar on his desk and extracted a bright-red gumball. "Sugar free," he announced, popping it into his mouth. "Aspartame." He lowered his voice to a whisper. "Rolph doesn't approve. Want one?"

"Sure." My gumball was the brilliant yellow of Tweety Bird. I wondered if it meant something and then scolded myself for overthinking.

"Look. I understand the arguments you could make about why that scene works," I said, breaking Little Dave's first rule: *Don't negotiate against yourself.* "The idea that Nana Trudy has basically, um, had sex with her boyfriend until he ended up in the hospital, and his sons aren't happy with her. I get the joke, and I know we need something big and funny right at the top, something that will play in the ads and establish the characters and their world, but I just feel . . ." And here, I froze. I knew how I felt, I'd practiced the words, but with Chauncey's red-faced, intense gaze on me, in this football stadium of an office, I found myself speechless. "It's my grandmother," I finally blurted. Chauncey stared at me, sweating, silent. "She hates it," I said. "She thinks it's mean. And because the character's kind of based on her . . ."

There was a pause. A long, painful pause. From somewhere far away, in the outer office, I could hear laughter, and I wondered if Rolph was flirting with that beautiful receptionist.

"Sometimes clichés are clichés because they're true," Chauncey said.

I nodded before I could stop myself. "But the stuff about early-bird specials and Viagra . . ."

"I hear you," he said. Which was, I knew, executive-speak for *I know you have a problem, but that doesn't mean I'm going to fix it.* "Tell you what," he finally said. "Let's see if we can come up with a compromise."

I felt faint with gratitude as the room swam in front of my eyes. "Whatever you think," I said. "I can rewrite it today."

He waved his hand. "Nah, let's just talk it out. The 'bite my Boniva' line stays. Pending the approval of the Boniva people."

I nodded, trying not to wince. I'd hated that line, but I would learn to live with it, and my grandmother would, too.

"How about this," he said. "We'll let the boys get in their digs about how she's basically been trying to fuck him to death and take his money."

I found myself nodding like a broken bobblehead, not letting myself think about how my grandmother was going to feel about being portrayed as an overage gold digger who used sex as a weapon.

"But . . ." He leaned back, staring at the ceiling, before pulling a monogrammed towel from his desk drawer and dabbing at his still-magenta face. "What if we looped in a line about how much she loved him?"

"Yes!" I yelled, and then lowered my voice. "Yes. That's it exactly. The sex stuff's all funny, I get that it's funny, but I think, for the emotional heart of the show, for us to care about Nana . . ."

"She has to love him," he said, completing my thought. "Which makes it even scarier when she gets kicked out of his house and has to find a way to start all over again."

"Right!" I bent my head. "Thank you. I'll go . . . I'll start writing . . . we can do the reshoots when we do the first episode . . ." The director was probably going to murder me, but never mind. Maybe I'd hire Rolph for protection. I'd bet anything he freelanced as a bodyguard. "I can't thank you enough for this. If there's ever anything I can do for you . . ." *Oh, God,* I thought, as Chauncey wiped his face again, balled up the towel, and tossed it toward a wicker basket in the corner. *As if.*

"We're good," he said. There was a knock on the door, and the gorgeous assistant came in with a bento box set on a black lacquered tray. I looked at the food: six miniature slivers of raw pink fish, a tiny lacquered dish of edamame, a stingy scoop of seaweed salad, and a teaspoon of brown rice. Chauncey winced. "I would kill my own mother," he announced, "for a goddamn cheeseburger."

"I can get you a cheeseburger," I offered. "Have you ever been to Umami Burger? They do this one with truffle butter . . ."

He cringed and waved me toward the door. "Happy writing!" he called. "Oh, and check in on your actors."

"Beg pardon?" I said—a line I'd adopted from the Daves.

"It's been a few weeks since you've seen them, right?" he asked. "Best make sure none of them went and got their faces tattooed." He grimaced, undoubtedly remembering the long-ago action-movie star who, between negotiating his film deal and the first day of principal photography, had gone to Australia and had a Maori tribesman do just that.

"I'll call them all right now," I said, and scampered toward the elevator before he could change his mind.

The next morning, I met with Pete at a batting cage in Santa Monica. "Ruth!" he called, squinting at me through the sun. I felt relieved that he'd remembered my name, and that he looked fit and sane and relatively stable, free of fresh piercings and tattoos, as he whacked the balls across the field and into a green mesh net. "Everything good?" I asked him.

"I'm being replaced, aren't I?" he asked without looking at me, and gave the next ball an especially savage whack.

"Huh?" I asked, startled that he'd think of it, though I knew that actors in pilots did get replaced on a regular basis. "You haven't shot your first scene, and you're already worried about being replaced?"

"Everyone worries," Pete said. This, I knew, was true, although I didn't think Pete had much to worry about. Chauncey loved Pete, insofar as Pete represented an antidote to the quippy, reed-thin, perfectly clad, meticulously groomed metrosexuals presently populating his shows. "These guys make Chandler Bing look like John Wayne. We need manly men!" he told his underlings. The word went down to producers and writers, all of whom quickly filled their scripts with a smorgasbord of blue-collar, big-shouldered, salt-of-the-earth types: plainspoken plumbers, down-on-their-luck professional wrestlers, former football players, bus drivers, and beat cops, none of whom would know Karl Lagerfeld from Karl Malden. Pete fit the template— he was big, he was brawny, he was handsome . . . and one sensed that he did not spend his evenings with the collected works of Flaubert. "Take care of yourself," I told him. I thought about warning him explicitly against piercings and tattoos, and then decided it would be best not to put any ideas in his head, even though there was obviously plenty of room.

The next day, Annie Tait and I had lunch at the Polo Lounge in the Beverly Hills Hotel, where we nibbled Cobb salads and people-watched. At a table by the window sat Stan Harris, a major movie star, with his sunglasses on and his shirt unbuttoned almost down to his navel, signaling to one and all that he was, indeed, Someone, and that the regular rules about things as mundane as shirt-buttoning did not apply to the likes of him. Stan had been in the news a lot lately. Three months ago, when the police came to his Bel Air estate to tell him to turn down the music, he'd gone off on what was widely assumed to be a cocaine-fueled rant, one that made reference to everything from the size of his bank account to the size of his penis (both, per Stan, substantial), and concluded with his sneeringly asking the (young female) officer if she was Jewish, and if it was true that Jewish girls hated giving head. His team had gone into full spin mode, at first denying that the actor had made such hateful remarks. When a tape surfaced on *TMZ* (one of Stan's party guests had pulled out a phone and recorded the whole exchange), a crisis manager, hired special for the occasion, said that Stan was "wrestling with some demons" in the wake of his recent divorce, and would be going away to seek treatment and address them.

Stan had dutifully done a month at a facility in Montana. Now he was back, and all of Hollywood was waiting to see what kind of impact, if any, his tantrum would have on his career. Most people's guess was none. As long as Stan was bankable, as long as his aquiline profile and lean, muscled torso put butts in movie-theater seats, he could say whatever he wanted to young female cops. "You don't really get in trouble until you start up with someone who's got more money or more power than you," said Annie.

"Really?"

"Sad but true. Remember Tim O'Shea?" Tim had been a sit-com star who'd struggled with a cocaine habit and what could delicately be called "anger issues" for years. He'd held a girlfriend at gunpoint, assaulted one of his wives in their car, and tried to drown a date in the hot tub after, it was whispered, she'd declined his request for anal sex. A few years ago, one of the gossip web-sites had obtained a frantic 911 call from a ladyfriend who'd bar-ricaded herself in a bathroom while Tim raged outside. Nothing ever happened to him—at least, nothing permanent. He'd get arrested; his grinning mug shot would be all over the Internet the next day; and then, a week later, he'd be back at work. "You know why?" asked Annie. Before I could answer, she said, "Because the women he hurt were disposable." She waved one elegant, manicured hand. "Escorts, porn stars, wannabe actresses just as messed up on drugs as he was. You can do whatever you want to girls like that, but when he started insulting executives . . ."

"Ah." I was remembering that Tim had finally lost his job, not after being jailed for assaulting a girlfriend with a pair of barbecue tongs, or being arrested when he was out on bail for threatening to throw a different girlfriend off a balcony, but for tweeting that his boss, the head of the network, wore a toupee. Which was true . . . but, evidently, saying so was a fireable of-fense. In a tersely worded statement, the network said that it "wished Mr. O'Shea the best in his future endeavors" but would no longer be working with him.

Annie looked toward the corner where Stan was holding court at a table full of supporters and employees and hangers-on: a young female assistant with two BlackBerrys, an agent I recognized from the trades, and a young man in a suit and tie who sat quietly next to the star, saying nothing, doing nothing, while the agent talked and the assistant texted and Stan ate his burger, chewing with his mouth open, just to show, in case the unbuttoned shirt didn't quite prove it, that he'd attained a level of being where the rules of civility and good behavior no longer applied.

"Know who that is?" Annie asked, nodding at the guy in the suit.

"Son from the first marriage?" I guessed.

"Good try, but nope. That's his sober friend."

"His what?"

"The guy they hired to stay with him twenty-four-seven and make sure Stan doesn't drink, or drug, or look at any porn." She gave me a wink. "I hear that's one of his many problems." Annie dipped the tines of her fork in her pitcher of dressing and then speared a chunk of turkey and a lettuce leaf. "Did you know that *I Love Lucy* was shot where we did the pilot?" she asked.

I nodded.

"So you know the story, right?"

"Which one?"

Annie gave a lascivious grin. "Okay. The way I heard it is, they're shooting an episode, and they break for lunch. Everyone's gone, except for one grip up in the rigging, hanging lights, and he looks down and sees Desi Arnaz getting"—she leaned in close and dropped her voice—"orally pleasured by an extra. So, he's looking down, and Desi looks up and sees him, and there's this moment of silence, and then . . ." Annie flapped her arms, waggling her brows, becoming, in that moment, Lucy's beleaguered husband. "Desi looks down at the extra like he's never seen her before in his life and says, 'What are you DOOO-eeeng?' "

I laughed. Annie beamed, then reached across the table and squeezed my hand. "I like you," she said, and I said, "I like you, too," and I smiled, thinking how putting a show together was sort of like building a family, and if you were lucky the way I'd been lucky with the Daves, at least some of the people you'd spend your days with would be people whose company you enjoyed.

Finally, there was Cady . . . or what Maya, my casting director, had taken to calling the Cady of It All. Setting a meeting with her proved, once again, complicated. Unfortunately, said her manager, a breathy-voiced fellow named Justin, she was busy all week, not free for lunch, or breakfast, or drinks, or a late-night snack. *Busy with what?* I wondered for the umpteenth time, and for the umpteenth time, I restrained myself from asking. "How's Sunday morning?" he'd asked.

"That could possibly work," Justin allowed. I'd actually made plans on Sunday to accompany Grandma to the county arboretum, to see if it might be suitable for her wedding, after which I would take her to her favorite Mexican place for lunch, with hopes of thawing the chill that had grown between us since the night she'd seen the pilot, but we could reschedule. "Brunch?" I asked.

There was a pause. "Sure!" Justin finally chirped. Given his mannerisms, the way he dressed and moved and spoke, I'd assumed he was gay after my first fifteen seconds in his company, and had been surprised to learn that he was, in fact, married to his high-school sweetheart, and that they had three kids together. "We'll do brunch."

"Um," I said, unclear on just who "we" was, and suspecting that Justin had just invited himself along. "I was hoping that Cady and I could just sit down together. You know," I said, and attempted a giggle. "Girl talk!" The more time Cady and I had together one on one, I'd reasoned, the more chance I'd have of figuring out what made her tick, and whether she'd respond to praise or pressure when it came time for me to help craft her performance.

"And I understand *completely*," said Justin. "I just think Cady might be more comfortable if I'm there."

Pick your battles, I told myself. "Okay," I said. "That will be fine."

* * *

On Sunday morning, I gave myself a pep talk as I dressed for the encounter. "Stars," I murmured. "They're just like us!" I opened my copy of *Us Weekly* and looked at a picture of Jennifer Aniston feeding a parking meter as supportive evidence. Then I wrapped my scarf, blue-and white stripes, around my neck, hiding as much of the scars there as I could, and gave my makeup one final check. Grandma had spent the night at Maurice's again, which meant I was on my own. There was no one to tell me that I'd gotten my outfit right, to run a thumb beneath my eyes to make sure my liner hadn't smudged, and to tell me that I didn't need to be scared of Cady. We were both, after all, young women trying to make it in Hollywood. True, only one of us had a grammatically incorrect ankle tattoo that had been featured in *People* magazine, but there had to be some common ground.

Ten minutes later, I'd pulled up to the curb in front of The Alcove and relinquished my key fob to the valet, who'd looked me up and down before visibly dismissing me as no one worthy of a greeting, let alone a call to the paparazzi. I bought myself a cup of tea, found a table in the front courtyard shaded by an umbrella, and sat there, sipping and waiting.

Cady and Justin were late, of course. Just as I was finishing my second mug of milky tea, sweetened with agave (a place like this knew its clientele and offered an array of non-sugar sweeteners), a black SUV rolled up to the valet stand. Justin got out first, dressed, as usual, in dark-rinse jeans and suede sneakers and an ironic T-shirt. Today's was bright green. I CAN DO ANY THING! it read, with a trefoil logo and the words GIRL SCOUTS OF AMERICA underneath. The passenger-side door opened and a wraith in high heels eased herself out of the seat and down to the sidewalk. Denim leggings clung to her stick-thin legs. Beneath them were five-inch stilettos, the kind that would turn even a casual stroll into an oversexed, swivel-hipped strut down an invisible runway. The young woman wore a shirt made of fine cotton that clung to her torso, the better for viewers to appreciate every bone of her rib cage. A dozen thin steel bangles chimed and rattled around one wispy forearm, and she wore a straw hat with a red satin band, a hipster's wink that said, *I'm too young and too cool for this hat, but look at me wearing it anyhow!*

The stranger whispered something to Justin, and then came teetering toward me with a smile on her fleshless face. It wasn't until she'd thrown her arms around me that I realized this starveling ghost-girl was my formerly robust star. I was hugging Cady Stratton.

I rocked back on my heels. My throat clenched, and I made a strangled sound, my attempt to say, then swallow, the words *What the fucking fuck?*

"Hi, Ruth!" she said, and let me go. She smelled like cigarettes, and was so emaciated that I could see veins pulsing on the undersides of her pale wrists.

"Cady?" I said. Out of the corner of my eye I saw Justin standing off to the side, hands clasped in front of his groin as if he thought I'd try to kick him, with a timid, placating expression on his face. "What happened?"

She danced away from me and whirled in a circle. "TrimQuick! I'm their new celebrity spokeswoman!" She dropped her tiny bottom into a metal chair—given the lack of padding, it must have hurt—and smiled. "I haven't been out in, like, forever, because nobody's supposed to see me until they unveil the new ads. It was like I had the plague or something. I missed three different premieres . . ."

"Coffee?" asked Justin, that dopey, please-Hammer-don't-hurt-me grin plastered to his face, his body still hunched in a defensive crouch.

"Espresso," Cady rapped. I shook my head. Justin pranced away. Cady leaned forward, the better to regale me with the details of her diet.

"They sent me this trainer who was, like, completely sadistic. Do you know what a kettlebell is? Anyhow," she prattled, either ignoring my silence or failing to notice it, "obvs, not everyone who does the program gets a trainer twice a day, so they'll, like, have to put a disclaimer at the bottom of the ads. 'Results Not Typical.' Something like that." She eyed me. "Hey, you know, I bet I could get you on the program for free."

"Cady." My voice was low, and it must have sounded, if not scary, then arresting enough to get her to quit babbling about resistance bands and the glycemic index. "Why did you . . . what did you . . ." She was staring at me, obviously confused. She'd been expecting compliments, and I was failing to deliver. This constituted an inexplicable glitch in her personal Matrix. "This isn't going to work."

She blinked, with the first hint of a frown marring her smooth brow. "Huh?"

"The character you're playing. Daphne. She's supposed to be . . . you know. A normal-looking girl. A regular girl. An everygirl." I felt my fingers moving to my cheek, my scars, and made myself rest them in my lap. "That's why we cast you."

"You cast me 'cause I was fat?" Now she wasn't frowning, she was full-on scowling, her pretty features pretzeled in a sneer. "Wow. Really? Because I thought you hired me because you liked my acting. Because you thought I was funny."

"Of course I liked your acting. Of course I think you're funny. I've been a fan of yours for years." Her expression softened with an actress's reflexive pleasure at being praised, and I was amazed at myself. I lied as if I'd been living in L.A. for decades. "But this . . ." I waved my hands at her body, or what was left of it. "I don't know what we're going to do. We start filming next week, and you can't . . ."

"I'm not gaining the weight back." Cady spoke flatly, in a tone that left no room for compromise. Justin, who'd been approaching with a dainty espresso cup in one hand, veered off sharply to the left, like a pilot who'd just gotten word from air traffic control about an explosion on the runway. *Thanks for your help,* I thought. "Do you know how long I've been the fat chick?" Cady demanded.

"Oh, come on! You were never fat! You just looked . . ." *Normal,* I was going to say, but Cady didn't give me a chance to say it.

"Do you know how many movies I went out for where they'd say, 'You need to lose twenty pounds'? Do you know how long I've been hearing that?" Her lips trembled. Her eyes filled with tears. It could have been acting, or it might have been actual pain, an up-close look at what happened to a Hollywood dream deferred. "I want to work, you know?"

My lips were numb as I forced out the words. "You are working. You have work. I gave you a job."

She swiped one hand through the air, dismissing the show, my baby, my dream. "That's nothing. That's not where it's at. The real money's in movies. Endorsement deals. Do you know how much that bitch Kim Kardashian gets to tweet shit about her trainer on Twitter?"

I shook my head. I was not one of Miss Kardashian's numerous Twitter followers.

"Fifty . . . thousand . . . dollars," Cady said. She crossed her arms over her chest and sat back smugly. "That adds up."

"I'm sure it does. And you can do whatever you want with yourself after the show. But for now, for the show, I need you to look the way you did when you were hired," I said. Even as I spoke in my scolding schoolteacher's voice, I knew it was impossible. Network executives could move Cady into a Krispy Kreme shop and make her drink lard for dinner, and there'd still be no way she could gain enough weight back in time for the show's start date . . . and that date, I knew, was nonnegotiable. If we didn't start filming on time, we wouldn't wrap on time, we wouldn't deliver our episodes on time, and we'd have to give up our premiere slot, which had already been announced and published all over the Internet.

"I don't see what the big deal is, you know? Whether the character's a size ten or a . . ." She shot an admiring glance at her diminished hips and thighs. "A zero. She's still, you know, the same girl."

Oh my God. This was bananas. Did she really not understand the problem she'd created? How every single show, every scene we'd pitched, every joke, every line, would have to be rewritten to reflect that Daphne no longer had any reason to be insecure, to doubt her own beauty or her place in the world? And how on earth would we handle the pilot reshoots, the scenes where we'd add in Pete? How could she not see what she'd done? Maybe, I thought, she was in the grip of some weight-loss-induced delusion. Maybe during one of her twice-a-days she'd bonked her head with a kettlebell.

I stared at her as she sat, arms crossed, glaring, one foot bobbing rapidly up and down, and considered my options. I could wrap her in a blanket—even the towel that I kept in the back of my car for swims would do the trick—pick her up, drive her home, and let Grandma cook for her. I could have her jaws wired open and force-feed her like a foie gras goose. I could tell the network that she'd been kidnapped, or that she needed to go to rehab; I could force them to change our start date . . . but even as I conjured increasingly far-fetched possibilities, I knew they'd never happen. Time was money, and I couldn't waste either one.

"Cady," I croaked. My hand was at my cheek again, and I

could feel myself blushing. What I was going to try to tell her felt as fundamental to me as explaining why humans needed to keep breathing or sleep at night. "The way you looked when we shot the pilot. It meant something."

She stared at me, eyebrows raised. Even her eyebrows were thinner than they'd been when I'd last seen her. I kept on.

"The world is full of girls who don't look like"—I groped for a name that would mean something to her—"Blake Lively, girls who never see themselves on television. For those girls, seeing you would mean something. Watching you get the guys, and wear the great clothes, and have the funniest lines, and be the leading lady . . ."

Cady reached across the table to seize my hand with her skel- etal fingers. "I hear you," she said, sounding like a very young, very thin network executive. "I hear what you're saying. But the thing is, out here, there's only one right way to look, and I was never it. I never was, and now I am."

Justin took that moment to waltz over to our table with a cheery "Hi-i-i-i!" He set down the espresso as if it were a gre- nade and eased himself into a seat. I gave him a black look, a glare promising that he and I would be discussing this later, one that implied that he'd had a duty to tell me what was going on, and that he'd dropped the ball. Then I returned my attention to the star of my show.

"Cady," I said. I realized that I was using her trick of saying my first name all the time. Maybe it would work. Maybe she'd be flattered enough to actually hear what I was saying. "Cady. This is going to create some problems."

She gave me a sullen look from beneath the brim of her hip- ster hat. "I don't have any problems. I feel great." I could practi- cally hear the *click* as she remembered something she'd probably meant to tell me at the start of our conversation. "You know, I did this for my health." *Bullshit,* I thought. *Bull-fucking-shit you did this for your health.* "Diabetes runs in my family. My doctor told me I was pre-pre-diabetic." She pulled a pack of cigarettes out of her bag, looked at them wistfully, and then replaced them. *Ah yes,* I thought, *Healthy Living's new poster girl.*

"We're going to have to do pilot reshoots," I said, thinking out loud.

Justin made his first contribution to the conversation. "Oh? Did you end up recasting Annie Tait?"

"What?" I asked, startled.

"Oh, nothing, nothing," he said, and gave a fluty giggle. "I just heard the network's not happy with her."

"If it's true, they haven't told me," I said, filing that news nugget away for future contemplation. "But now . . . how are we supposed to match shots?" We could put Cady in the same costumes, put her on the same sets, film her with the same cameras underneath the same lights, and of course, she wouldn't look anything like she had the night we'd shot the pilot.

"Padding?" Justin suggested.

Oh, sure, I thought, and gave a hysterical giggle. Pad her. But padding wouldn't turn her into a big girl any more than concealer could make me a pretty one. Before I could say any of that, Cady turned her evil glare at him.

"Hello! I don't think so! I worked too hard to get here. I'm not going to wear a fat suit and pretend I'm that girl again." She shuddered at the thought of being *that girl,* the girl she'd been six weeks ago, even as a fake.

"We're going to have to do something. Or else it's going to be a mess," I said.

"Let's just shoot the whole thing again!" Pleased with her solution and, apparently, ignorant as to how much implementing it would cost, Cady ripped open a packet of sugar substitute and tapped it, with ritualistic precision, three times over her espresso cup. I sat back, certain that my mouth was hanging open and that I looked, as Grandma would put it, like a stunned trout. *Call the network.* I had to call the network. Or, no, maybe I should try the studio first, they'd help me think of a game plan. Or maybe Dave would have some ideas about what to do if your lead actress had completely transformed her appearance. Maybe this had happened on *Bunk Eight* in the years before I'd arrived, and he'd know exactly how to handle it.

"Wait a minute," I blurted. Too loud. The couple cooing over their toddler at the next table stared at us. I lowered my voice. "Isn't there a clause in your contract about changing your appearance? Didn't you have to promise not to get tattoos, or dye your hair, or . . ."

"No clause," said Cady.

"We checked," said Justin.

Of course, I thought. Why would there be a clause? Cady's appearance hadn't changed at all in the years she'd been working. She'd always been bubbly and bouncy and noticeably bigger than the other actresses. She'd talked about it in interviews, laughing about how she was descended from a line of Scandinavian farmers' wives, and how, in her family of proudly plus-size women, she was actually the thin one, and how she'd worked hard to become comfortable in her own skin. *My hero,* I'd thought when I'd read those quotes and seen her pictures. Silly me.

Now Miss Comfortable in Her Own Skin was glaring at me, bony shoulders hunched, lean legs crossed, one narrow foot twitching like a metronome, the better to burn calories, even while seated. "It's too late," Cady said. "It's done. Cat's out of the bag." She giggled. "So to speak."

Justin reached across the table to give my hand an unwelcome squeeze. "There's a plus side to all of this."

"Pun intended," I said. Neither one of them laughed.

"You would not believe the press interest," Justin gushed.

"*People, Us, TMZ, Life & Style* . . . they all want to do features on Cady."

"On Cady's body," I corrected. "On Cady's weight loss." I felt as if someone had parked a bus on top of my heart. Daphne had been the lantern that I had wanted to hold up to all the girls in the world, the girls who weren't thin, the girls who weren't pretty, the ones who never saw anyone who looked like them on television unless they were the best friend or the butt of a joke. I had wanted a show like *The Golden Girls*, where it wasn't about being thin or young or beautiful, but about who you were underneath your skin, and whether you were loyal, funny, smart, compassionate, a good friend. And now my light had extinguished herself. The actress chosen to represent all the invisible girls of the world was going to be cavorting on the pages of the tabloids, showing off her brand-new bangin' bikini body and, undoubtedly, giving interviews about how miserable she'd been back in the dark days when she'd looked just like them.

Justin was watching me uncertainly. "She'll plug the show, of course," he said. I looked down at my lap, unwilling to trust myself to answer. I was imagining myself at eight years old, face bandaged, an IV needle in the back of my hand, a travel alarm clock in a pink leather case on the bedside table, counting down the minutes until *The Golden Girls* came on and I could see my friends, and visit a world where nothing hurt. "Barbara Walters's people called," he said. "They want her on *The View*."

I pushed myself away from the table. "Excuse me," I said. As I got to my feet, I saw a girl sidle across the bricked courtyard and work up the nerve to tap Cady's shoulder. She was maybe ten years old, with a rounded belly poking at the front of her plum-colored T-shirt, and she held an iPhone in one hand.

"Excuse me?" she said in a voice barely above a whisper. "You're Cady Stratton, right?"

Cady's face, formerly pouty and blank, lit up as if someone had clicked a switch. She gave the girl a brilliant smile. "I am!" she said with more animation than I'd ever heard from her when she wasn't onstage. "What's your name?"

"Ava," the girl whispered.

"Hi, Ava!" Cady smiled and reached across the table with one of her bony claws to take the girl's free hand. "Do you want a picture? You and me together? What do you say?"

Ava could barely say anything. She handed me her phone and got into position, cheek to cheek with Cady.

"Say cheese!" Justin caroled. *Cheese* was said. Cady smiled brilliantly. Ava looked faint. I snapped the shot and handed over the camera, which Ava accepted as if receiving a holy relic.

"You look so pretty," she whispered to Cady, who looked at me with an *I told you so* smirk. Ava hurried off, clutching her prize.

"You see that?" Cady asked. "They love me."

"I wonder if she'd love you more if you'd looked the way you used to." It was a clumsy thing to say, but why not put my cards on the table? I had nothing to lose.

"You'd think that, right?" said Cady. "But you'd be wrong." She flicked her hand at the patio, at the couples sharing pancakes, the single ladies lingering over lattes and mimosas, the children poking at plates of scrambled eggs, the women in yoga pants sipping smoothies. "All the girls. They don't want me to look like they look, they want me to look the way they wish they could look." She took off her hat, shook out her hair, and took a single tiny sip from her espresso cup. "You thought you were doing them a favor, giving them what they wanted. But that's not what they wanted." She ran her hands along her diminished torso, down to her narrow hips. "You'll see." She smiled merrily and then raised her head, looking past me. Evidently, Ava had told her friends. More girls were approaching, girls and young women and a few hand-holding dads and boyfriends. They came carrying cell phones, iPhones, flipcams, and BlackBerrys. They were whispering to one another when they weren't looking down at their devices, fingers flying, texting and tweeting the news into the world.

I pushed a five-dollar bill at Justin and dug my valet ticket out of my pocket. "I have to go. We'll talk soon," I said.

"Bye-eee!" he called, waggling his fingers. I handed over my ticket, tipped the valet, drove to the end of the street, and then pulled into a parking lot in front of a supermarket and collapsed with my head on the wheel, my heart pounding, eyes stinging. The network first? The studio? No, Dave. Before I could stop myself or overthink, I dialed his number. "Can I come over?" I rasped as soon as he'd said hello. "I need to talk to you."

"Sure," he said. He must have heard something in my voice, because he said, "Is everything okay?"

Nothing is okay, I thought. "I'll tell you in person," I said, ending the call. Maybe he'd have answers, or at least some funny anecdote about the time one of his stars had tried to pull a stunt like this . . . or maybe he'd just wipe off my tears and hold me, and I wouldn't have to think about any of this anymore.

I'd been to Dave's house maybe a half-dozen times to swim, each time using the key, never ringing the doorbell. It was almost enough to get me to smile when I pushed the button and heard a mellow chime play the opening notes of the theme from *The Jeffersons. Well, we're movin' on up*. A moment later, the door swung open, and there was Dave in his chair, dressed, as usual, in a short-sleeved shirt and jeans, with Pocket standing beside him, an inquisitive expression on her face, one ear up and one ear down.

"Hey, Ruthie." I could guess how bad I looked by the concerned expression on his face. "Are you okay? Here, come on in."

His wheelchair whispered across the polished wood floors as he led me to a low sectional couch. There was a baseball game on TV before he flicked it off, and I hoped that Shazia wouldn't come strutting out of the bedroom, all smiles and solicitousness. A minute later I was sitting, with a cold bottle of water in my hand, rocking back and forth like an old Jew at prayer and trying not to moan out loud.

"What happened?"

"Get me your laptop. I'll show you." Dave's chair purred across the floor as he went to fetch his MacBook. It didn't take long to find what I was looking for. The shots of Cady at the Alcove were already online. "Get the Skinny," one of the gossip sites invited. "Starlet Cady Stratton unveils DRAMATIC NEW LOOK at Sunday brunch! The star of ABS's upcoming sitcom *The Next Best Thing* showed off her STUNNING WEIGHT LOSS while posing with fans at The Alcove in Los Feliz on a sunny Sunday afternoon. How'd she do it? Cady was mum on the details. 'Wait and see,' she said."

Wordlessly, I pointed at the screen. Dave maneuvered his chair to my side and took a look at the photographs—Cady sitting, Cady standing, Cady cheek to cheek with one girl after another, grinning her skeleton's grin.

"Well," he said after a minute. "At least they got the name of the show right."

"What are we going to do?" I said. "She can't play the part anymore. She isn't Daphne."

For a moment, Dave didn't answer. Then he sighed. In that single exhalation, I heard the verdict. I heard the future. I heard the sound of dumpy Alice at her computer, tallying every mention of Cady as news of her DRAMATIC NEW LOOK spread across the World Wide Web. Network bean counters would log every tweet and retweet, every blog post and comment, and they would inevitably arrive at the conclusion that all publicity was good publicity, that any mention of Cady was good for *The Next Best Thing*. They'd liked Cady well enough twenty-five pounds ago, but they'd probably love her now that she was the obligatory Hollywood size zero and was getting all this attention for her STUNNING WEIGHT LOSS. I could bitch and moan, I could protest and complain, I could even go on social media and make my case to the public, and none of it would matter. Cady had won the war without a single shot being fired. She'd won the war and I'd lost my show.

I dropped my face into my hands. Dave inched his chair backward, then forward, his version of pacing. "Hey, Ruth," he said. "Hey, now. I know that this probably feels like the end of the world. But think about it. Was Daphne's weight really the most important thing about her?"

"It mattered!" I said tearfully, because of course I was crying by then.

"It mattered. Yes. But it wasn't the only thing that mattered. The girl you wrote is a real, funny girl."

"She looks like P-P-Paris Hilton!" I wept. "And I hate Paris Hilton! She has dead lizard eyes!"

With my face buried in my hands, I didn't see it, but I could imagine that Dave was smiling. "Okay," he said. "I'll admit there's a resemblance. But Daphne can still be real. She can still be funny. You can just think of other ways to tell the story you want to tell. Maybe you give her a best friend . . ."

I raised my head. My nose was running, my eyes were red-rimmed, and the tears had undoubtedly washed away the makeup I'd applied so carefully that morning. "I am not," I said, enunciating icily, "going to do a show with a fat best friend." My lips were quivering as I pushed the words out. "I wanted Daphne to be her own best friend, you know? I wanted her to save her own life." I meant to tell Dave about the viewers I'd imagined, the girl I'd been, the hospital beds, counting the hours until my next pain pill, how alone I'd felt, how television had saved me, but I was so choked up I could barely speak at all. I'd lost Gary. I'd lost the grandmother's character, and my real-life grandmother was barely speaking to me. Now I'd lost the heart of the show, the only thing left. I'd lost myself. Now I had nothing . . . nothing at all.

"Ruth." His hand was warm on top of my shoulder. "Hey. Listen. This is all part of the game out here. You know that. It's all about compromise. Nothing ever comes out just the way you imagined it."

"My heart is broken," I said. It sounded silly, cheap, and melodramatic, but it was also the truest thing I could say, and when I heard it out loud, it made me cry even harder.

Dave sighed. He wasn't an I-told-you-so kind of guy, so I knew he would never remind me of what he'd said at our kickoff dinner—how I should savor that golden time after a project had been green-lit and before it started shooting; how, from that moment forward, my show would no longer be mine.

"I thought I was ready for this. You know?" I'd worked long enough in Hollywood to know that nothing got done without compromise, that you had to give to get. I could handle disappointment. I could do what was necessary. I could smile at the actors who came to audition and thank them for coming, then draw a line through their names before the door had closed behind them. I could be tough when toughness was required; I could bend when bending would help. I could handle it when the executives rejected all of my potential stars and wanted, instead, a girl that they'd hand-picked; I could swallow hard and take it when they insisted on a scene that made Nana look more broad and crass than I'd intended. I could do it all as long as I felt like my toughness was in the service of something important, that I was protecting the essential heart of my story. But now . . . "If Cady's just some pretty girl, then I don't even know what the show's about," I said. "I should quit. I will quit. Let someone else make *The Next Best Thing*. It isn't mine anymore."

I got to my feet, intending to go to my car, drive right to the studio, and sit there, stewing in the parking lot, until Lisa or Tariq or someone showed up so I could turn in my resignation.

Dave's grip was stronger than I expected as he pulled me back down to the couch. "Hey," he said. "Let's not do anything hasty."

"Like what? Like lose half my body weight?" My laughter rang off the walls and all of his important art. "Do you have anything to drink?"

"More water?" Dave offered. "Or a nice cup of tea?"

I snorted and then crossed the room. I'd spotted a drink cart, a twin of the one in his office, on my first trip to his house. One of the cut-glass decanters had the word VODKA on a silver plaque hanging from a chain around its neck. I picked up a glass, poured a shot, and then went to the kitchen for tomato juice and ice. Dave's wheels purred behind me. "Hey, Ruth, take it easy."

"It's a Bloody Mary. A brunch drink. Perfectly acceptable. Want one?" There was, of course, horseradish in the refrigerator, some artisanal, locally produced brand I'd never heard of, probably made by hipsters in Silverlake with ironic mustaches. I found Worcestershire sauce, olives, and toothpicks. The ice cubes, I noticed, were in the shape of Han Solo, frozen in carbonite at the end of *The Empire Strikes Back*. Of course they were. Everything to the Daves was a toy, a game, a joke—even their show, which wasn't about them, the way mine was. I'd been stupid enough to take it all seriously, to invest myself, to imagine, idiotically, that a show could be a vehicle for change, or that it could help girls like me feel less lonely.

"Big Dave gave me those," Dave said. I ignored him. Facing

the refrigerator, I stirred my drink with my finger and swallowed half of it in three gulps. My face flushed as the vodka traced a fiery path down into my belly. I felt the muscles of my thighs and shoulders unclenching, and for one brief euphoric moment, I thought, *Maybe this isn't so bad. At least I got a show on TV.*

Then a wave of despair rolled over me again. "You know what it is?" I asked. Because I was still looking at the stainless-steel refrigerator and not at Dave, I could say it out loud. "I hate that she can fix herself. Just like that. She loses thirty pounds and now she's beautiful, and I . . ." My throat was closing. I lifted the glass to my lips and took another swallow before I felt Dave's hand on my hip.

"Hey," he said. "Hey, Ruth."

"I can never . . ." I said. I didn't have to tell him the rest. I could starve myself until I was Hollywood's ideal, submit to another dozen surgeries, and none of it would matter in the end. My face would always announce me as the funny best friend, the punch line, the freak. What I'd written in my notebook that night in the hospital was, always and forever, the truth: *I will never be beautiful.*

Dave's hand, I noticed, was still cupped around the curve of my hip. His feet were bare, pale, dusted with brown hair on top. He had hairy toes. Hobbit-y toes, I thought, and took another swig of my drink.

"Take it easy," he said, in his calm voice. "Let's take a step back and think this through. Why don't you go for a dip?"

It was May, with the temperature already climbing toward the nineties. "I don't have my suit," I muttered. *Go for a dip.* What a WASP he was. Nobody in his world ever died; probably they just *passed* or *passed on.*

"I've got extras in the pool house." I feigned surprise at the news, even though, of course, I'd found Dave's swimsuit stash already. Maybe this was what it was here for—writers and ac-tresses who'd show up at his front door, unannounced and weep-ing. He'd shoo them into the water and wait it out while they got themselves together.

"There's towels and sunscreen. I'll be out in a minute." Gently but firmly, he pried my glass out of my hand and then wheeled away down the hall. I went through the sliding glass doors, out back to the pool house. There was a light-blue suit with thin straps and a kind of corset detail, with underwire anchoring the bustline, that fit me fine. The neckline dipped low enough to show some cleavage, and its modest leg openings meant I didn't have to worry about not having had time to shave, or wax, or notice what was going on down there, in weeks . . . not since Gary. The water was perfect, the way it had been every Sunday I'd come over and done laps. I held my breath, pushed off the tiled wall, and swam all the way to the shaded end of the pool. I flipped, came to the surface, took a deep breath, and swam back. When I surfaced again, Dave was sitting at the edge of the pool. He was in a different wheelchair from the one he used at the of-fice, and he had a swimsuit on, baggy red board shorts. I'd never seen his legs before, pale and thin but otherwise unremarkable. They looked like the regular legs of a guy who hadn't been in the sun for a while. You'd never guess they didn't work. There was a towel around his neck, draping his bare chest, and I could smell coconut-scented sunscreen.

"Mind if I join you?" he asked.

"Hey, it's your pool," I said. I was, I realized, a little bit buzzed. I tried not to stare as he wheeled his chair to the edge of the pool, put the brakes on, and used his arms to lift himself up and off the seat and onto the ground. He scooted to the edge of the pool and eased his legs into the water. I swam another lap, thinking I'd give him some privacy. By the time I came back he was perched on the steps, wearing his typically bemused expression, his gray-blue eyes bright in the sunshine as he watched me.

"You're a good swimmer."

I planted my feet and tipped my head back, feeling water pour through my hair, aware of my bare arms and shoulders, the skimpy bathing suit that was the only thing keeping me from being naked. "I used to be a lifeguard."

"I know," he said. "I remember."

I felt his eyes on me, imagined him considering the possibilities, weighing the consequences. Maybe it was the vodka that made me so reckless. Maybe it was my disappointment. Maybe it was the feeling that, after what had happened with Cady, after what I'd told him in the kitchen—*I will never be beautiful*—I had nothing left to lose.

I swam toward him with clean, sure strokes, until I was standing right in front of him, close enough to see the beads of water on his eyelashes and in his beard. Underwater, I was just the glimmering shape of a body—hair, swimsuit, skin. No scars. For a long moment, Dave looked at me from his perch on the steps leading down into the water. "Ruthie," he said in a voice so quiet I could barely hear it. Then he stretched out one hand, cupped the back of my head, tilted my chin up, pulled me toward him through the water, and kissed me.

I felt him groan against my lips. It was the sound of a starving man who'd just walked into the world's grandest buffet, and gathered me against him, deepening the kiss as I wrapped my arms around him, feeling his flesh, sun-warmed and glistening with droplets.

I love you, I thought but somehow kept myself from saying, pressing against him until not even a seam of liquid could make its way between our bodies. Dave cradled me in his arms, kissing my forehead, my lips, my scarred cheek, my jaw, the spot underneath my ear, as if it was all the same to him, as if it was all beautiful. I heard the water lapping against the side of the pool, and when I tried to pull away, he held on tightly.

"This is maybe not a good idea," I managed.

"Maybe not," he answered . . . but his voice was rough, and he showed no signs of letting me go. Thoughts were spinning in my booze-fogged brain: my conversation with Maya about dating coworkers, and how she'd said, *Where else are we supposed to meet people?* The stack of swimsuits in the pool house, and what they might mean. Shazia Khan, driving up in her Mercedes-Benz coupe and finding me and Dave entangled in the water. Things could end badly. God knows they had with Rob.

Dave's mouth, hot and open, was on the hinge of my jaw, then my collarbone. I could hear his breath, harsh in my ears, as he hooked his thumbs into the swimsuit's straps and pulled it down to my waist. "Oh, God," said Dave before bending his lips to my breasts. "Ruthie. I thought you'd be beautiful, but not like this."

The pleasure of what he'd said jolted through me. He'd thought about me! He set one hand at the small of my back, then used the other to pull the swimsuit over my hips and then toss it toward the deep end. I laughed as I heard it splash in the water, then groaned as he settled me on his lap and bent his head toward me again. "Oh, my," he said. Then, "Ruthie."

He turned me so I was sitting on the top step, with the small of my back rested against the top step, and he was sitting on the step below me. I shut my eyes as his hands pushed my legs apart. I felt the water lapping at my skin, his hot tongue tracing a path from my breasts down my belly, then between my legs, licking urgently with his fingers tight on my thighs. At one point, the sensations almost became too much, and I tried to squirm away, but he held me tight, and lifted his head, and said, "No. Stay with me. I want you right here." I shut my eyes and let my legs fall open again, hearing the water splash and tremble against the tiled walls, hearing my voice in a spiraling cry as my orgasm burst through me.

Afterward, he sat on the steps and held me, floating, in his arms. I could barely open my eyes. I felt as lazy and sated as a cat asleep in the sunshine, or little Pocket, curled up and dozing in one of the cushioned lounge chairs. My bathing suit was drifting in the center of the pool, and everything that had happened with Cady and the show seemed very far away. I wrapped one arm around his waist and thought about dipping my fingers beneath the waistband . . . but what would I find? And what if, like Rob, he told me no?

I couldn't stand that. I couldn't risk it. I'd barely survived that kind of rejection once. I couldn't go through it again. So I turned, hopping quickly out of the water, grabbing a towel and wrapping myself up, leaving my swimsuit floating in the water. Never mind. He probably had people to pick up after him.

"Ruth?" Dave was looking at me, his expression puzzled. "Is everything all right?"

"Fine! Great! Everything's fine!" Even as I was speaking, and trying to ignore the look of hurt and surprise on his face, I was coming up with a plan. I would pretend that this was a casual encounter, a fling, a one-time-only event. I would pretend that I was a girl who had casual encounters and flings. I wouldn't tell him how I really felt, or how wonderful it had been, there in the water, the slow liquid lapping of his tongue, his hands strong against my skin. Heaven. It had been heaven. And, I realized, with my heart wrenching, it would be a heaven I'd never experience again. "You're really good at that, you know."

I made myself look away, remembering a term I'd heard in the *Bunk Eight* writers' room—*pity fuck*. Probably, that's what this had been—pity head. He couldn't be heartbroken. Probably he was just relieved that I was leaving with so little fuss, leaving him to the quiet of his afternoon; to Shazia. "Years of practice," he said, looking at me steadily. He was looking at me, puzzled, patient, and it was all I could do not to drop the towel, get back into the water, swim to him, and let him hold me, the way he had so many times in my dreams. But no. I knew what I wanted, and I strongly suspected it was much, much more than he was prepared to give me. Besides, there was the not inconsiderable issue of his beautiful girlfriend. What would she do if she found out? *I adore you,* he'd written. What if I ruined that for him?

I gave my body orders, short tasks that I could accomplish, one by one. *Dry off your arms. Now your legs. Wrap the towel around you. Now sit down on one of the chairs. Make sure no skin is showing. You're colleagues. That's all.* With each step, the events of the day, and then the month, came crashing back: Cady's weight loss. My grandmother's heartbreak. That terrible scene that Lloyd had written and the network had forced me to shoot and then include. Justin's tittering revelation about how they were planning on replacing Annie Tait, the only thing in the show that was working. I could remember the feeling of Rob's hands on my shoulders as he hauled me to my feet, the way his face had tightened as he'd kissed my cheek but not my lips, and I could hear my grandmother's voice: *Don't be the same fool twice.*

By the time I was sitting, wrapped in a towel, Dave had worked himself back into his chair, with his own towel in his lap. Beads of water glistened on the light coat of brown hair on his chest, and for a moment, I could feel my palm there, flat against the muscles. He was so strong, and his kisses had been like nothing I'd experienced, nothing I'd even imagined. Then I remembered Shazia on his lap, head thrown back, and Taryn Montaine, all long, tanned legs and cleavage in a hundred pictures in *People* magazine. Those were the girls who got guys like Dave. Not me. Never me.

"So what are we going to do about Cady?" I asked, and was proud when my voice came out steady. We could have been in the writers' room after we'd shared lunch, instead of him in a swimsuit and me naked under a towel, still weak-kneed and swoony from my orgasm.

"You aren't going to like it," he said after a moment. "But the truth is, Cady's going to get a ton of press about this, and the network's going to be thrilled."

I knew that he was right. I also suspected that any effort I could mount would be worthless in the face of free publicity.

"The thing is . . ." I crossed my legs, taking care not to let the towel slip. "If Cady's skinny, then I don't know what the show's about anymore."

"Beg pardon?" My heart broke a little bit at his words, the sound of his voice. Other guys would say *huh?* or *what?* or *how's that again?* With Dave you got *beg pardon*. He'd hold doors, I knew, and introduce you to strangers at a party and make sure your drink was always full (Gary had an unpleasant tendency to leave me on my own at parties and drift away toward whoever had the pot).

"There're three major themes in literature, right? Man versus man, man versus nature, and man versus himself, or herself."

Dave nodded. "That's what I remember from English class." He folded his towel in halves, then quarters. I watched his hands moving, remembering them on my thighs, pushing them apart as he lowered his lips to the slick seam between my legs. Oh, God. My face was getting hot. I made myself turn away, furious at myself. How had I let this happen? And how could I go on with my life, knowing it would never happen again?

"Right. So this show was supposed to be man—woman—versus herself." I waited for his nod before I went on. "It was Daphne's coming-of-age. Would she find the strength to make the kind of life she deserves? And her obstacle was herself. Her looks. Her weight. Her crappy self-esteem. Not being able to get out of her own way." The words came slowly because, while

I was talking about Daphne-maybe-Dannhauser, really, I was describing myself. Daphne Dannhauser, *c'est moi*, with the fractured family, the absent parents, the grandmother, the romantic missteps, the brokenness . . . only instead of scars, I'd given her pounds. "If she's thin, Daphne has no obstacles," I said. "She has no reason to feel insecure. There's nothing keeping her from getting what she wants. So what's the show about?"

Dave shrugged. "Sometimes baggage can be internal. There are pretty girls who can't get out of their own way."

"But nobody identifies with them," I said. "And nobody believes it, either. Not really. You can put Drew Barrymore in glasses, but nobody actually thinks she was a nerd in high school. Not anyone who actually was a nerd, anyhow. It's a Hollywood lie."

He drummed his fingers on his knees. "So maybe the show's a little less specific than you intended. Maybe it's more a girl and her grandmother coming of age than woman versus herself."

"Anyone could write a show about a girl and her grandmother," I said. Dave didn't answer. In the silence, I heard the hum of traffic in the foothills, the rustle of something creeping in the underbrush beyond the pool's fence, a skunk or a coyote or a raccoon, one of the wild things that lived out here. "Anyone," I repeated, and squeezed my eyes shut. When I opened them, Dave had wheeled himself into the shade of the pool house. It was a scene David Hockney could have painted—the slanting shadows, the cool blue rectangle of the pool, the man in the wheelchair looking out over the water.

"I should go home," I said. Dave nodded without speaking, without trying to stop me, confirming my belief that when you were a man who could get women like Shazia Khan, you had no romantic use for a woman who looked like me. I walked toward the pool house, wondering why I'd wanted this life in the first place. It was so fraught, so hard. *I should have been a pair of ragged claws* . . . or a cook, in chef's whites and clogs, my hair pulled back under a bandana, hidden in a kitchen, far from diners' eyes, following recipes where things always turned out the way they were supposed to and nobody from the network or the studio came along and said, *Try it like this* or *Do it like that* or *We want it with gravy on top.* I could have stayed in Boston, maybe had a boyfriend and a blog. Maybe that would have been enough for me.

The shower in the pool house had a wide plastic stool inside, its metal legs centered on the tiled floor, with a showerhead wide as a dinner plate hanging from the ceiling, a handheld nozzle attached to a hook at chest height, and more nozzles bristling from the walls. I found a shelf full of shampoo and body wash, a pink mesh sponge hanging from a cord, shaving gel, razors, everything a girl could want. On the marble counter were makeup remover and moisturizer. Glass jars of cotton balls were arranged next to a lighted mirror; toothbrushes, still in their plastic wrappers, were lined up in a stainless-steel cup. I slipped a file and a razor and a toothbrush into my pocket. I shouldn't leave without a parting gift, I told myself, feeling low and mean and miserable.

Dave was waiting for me by the pool. He'd put on a shirt but was still in his swimsuit, dark hair clinging damply to his pale legs. "You okay?" he asked.

"I guess."

"I'll give Tariq a call in the morning, just to give them a heads-up."

I nodded, even though I was sure that the network, the studio, and the entire rest of the world already knew what had happened.

"We'll come up with a plan," he said.

I nodded again, although I knew there would be no plan. The network would be as thrilled as I was heartbroken by Cady 2.0. Maybe they'd even be willing to suck up the expense and reshoot the entire pilot, like she'd requested. The show would turn into something different, something that was not what I'd intended, not what I'd meant at all.

"So . . . ," I said. I was hoping for reassurance, maybe even a kiss, a sign that, in spite of what he'd said, there was hope after all; for the show, and maybe even for the two of us, even though I knew better.

Dave turned his chair so that he was facing away from me. "Take care of yourself," he said. I waited until I was sure he wasn't going to say anything more or do anything else, and then, without another word, I let myself out the front door.

PART THREE

~

The Next
Best Thing

SIXTEEN

W
e have a few suggestions," Loud Lloyd boomed.

Big surprise, I thought, picturing Big Dave's big canister of KY jelly, hearing him say, *Bend over, here it comes again.* It had been a week since I'd seen Cady's transformation, a week since the episode in Dave's pool. Now I was in a conference room in Burbank, where executives from the network and studio had gathered to go over the test results for the pilot.

"No Dave?" Lisa had asked when I'd walked through the door.

"No Dave," I said shortly, knowing my response was probably on the wrong side of rude, but also aware that I couldn't say anything else without my voice cracking or my face turning red. I'd sent Dave an email the day after our afternoon in the pool, telling him, in a fourteen-word message that had taken me two hours to compose, that it would probably be best if I handled the meeting on my own. Dave's response had trumped mine for brevity. "Okay," he'd written . . . and that had been that.

I pulled out my laptop—unnecessary, but I felt the need for a prop—and got ready for what I knew would be one of the less enjoyable parts of the development process. Last week, emissaries from a research firm had taken DVDs of the pilot of *The Next Best Thing* to fourteen malls in medium-to-large cities all over the country, and had shown it to audiences consisting mostly of women ages eighteen to thirty-four, who'd been lured to a conference room with the promise of pizza and soda and gift certificates. These women had watched the show with dials in their hands, dials they could turn down when they were bored or displeased by what they were seeing and turn up when they were amused, and turn off entirely when they decided that the show was too horrible to be endured, even for free pizza and twenty-five dollars' worth of free stuff from the Gap.

The comments had been compiled, the numbers crunched, and now everyone was looking at a graph projected onto a screen at the front of the room, a graph with a line that rose and dipped and rose again, charting viewers' second-by-second reaction to *The Next Best Thing*.

"Hey!" said Tariq, hurrying into the room. He glanced around the table before taking a seat. "Is Dave coming?"

"No Dave," I said, hearing the edge in my voice.

The test results had been okay. Good, not great. The show's overall score—the percentage of viewers who'd said that they would definitely watch or would be likely to watch *The Next Best Thing*—was in the seventies. The low seventies. Shelly, my agent, had called with the news. I hadn't said anything except for a quiet "Okay" when she'd told me the numbers, but they'd felt like a punch to the gut. A seventy-two was the worst grade I'd gotten since a pop quiz in tenth-grade geometry after I'd been out for a week with strep throat. Shelly was quick to reassure me, explaining that, in TV land, a seventy-two wasn't that bad. *Friends*, one of the most successful sitcoms of all time, had clocked in at forty-one. In contrast, the best-testing show in network history, a post-*Seinfeld* spinoff starring Michael Richards and another bunch of bold-faced names, had notched an unheard-of ninety-one and still had lasted for only three episodes. A seventy-two was fine. And I'd be fine, too, with whatever the research revealed, and with Dave as nothing more than a colleague and a friend. I'd survived worse.

"Shall we begin?" The vice president in charge of the research firm, a middle-aged, heavyset lady named Marcia, got to her feet. She wore low heels, pale-blue eye shadow, and a strand of pearls. Her suit had shoulder pads the size of throw pillows, her lipstick was the bright pink of cheap bubble gum.

Joan, who'd been on a call, slipped her telephone into its pink knitted cozy, put the cozy into her blue felt purse, and peered around the table. "Maybe we should wait for Dave."

"Dave's not coming," I said.

Joan smiled at me, holding her hands up, palms out, in front of her, as if I'd thrown something at her face. "Easy, easy."

"Sorry," I said as Marcia stood at the front of the room, smiling benignly, as if she'd seen this all before.

"People enjoyed *The Next Best Thing*," she began. "They liked the central dynamic, the relationship between the grandmother and her granddaughter. Seventeen percent of viewers compared it favorably to *The Golden Girls*. As you know, there's a great deal of residual affection from people who remember Cady Stratton from *All Our Tomorrows* and are curious to see what she's been doing." As I smiled, she clicked a button and read off some of the viewers' comments that appeared on the screen. "'Funny!'" Marcia read. I felt myself relax. "'It could be funnier,'" Marcia read. My hands clenched into fists. Marcia hit a button, and more comments filled the screen. "'Cady's character complains too much,'" she read.

"But they're funny!" I protested. "Funny complaints!" Marcia gave me a look. "Sorry," I said again, feeling my face burn. "Sorry."

"Let me get right to what our audience identified as our biggest issue." Another click, and Annie Tait's face—warm, weathered, familiar, kind—filled the screen. I smiled, feeling my shoulders descend from where they'd been hovering, tensed, around my ears. I loved Annie.

"Here's our problem," Marcia said. Around the table, heads were nodding—network heads, studio heads, and the lank brunette ponytail of Alice, who was no longer Vince Raymer's assistant and was now the assistant to the vice president of comedy for ABS, despite having no discernible sense of humor.

"Annie?" I said. "Annie's our problem? Annie's great!"

"She was fine," said Loud Lloyd. "But we think that we could be getting more bang for our buck."

"A bigger name," amplified Joan, who'd dressed for the meeting in a sweater vest of alternating pink-and-blue stripes, with a turtleneck patterned with tiny whales underneath. She looked like she was ready to lead a group of preschoolers in a singalong. I wondered again how someone who seemed so sweetly inoffensive could have attained and held a position of power in such a cutthroat world.

"You've written a great part," said Tariq, running his palms over his bald head. He was dressed as sharply as ever, in a perfectly creased shirt made of finely woven cotton, with dark-blue pants and a black leather belt with a rectangular silver buckle, but one of his shoelaces was untied, and he'd spilled something sticky on his iPad's cover. "There are probably a hundred actresses the right age who'd kill to play it."

"Okay." I spoke slowly, but my brain was churning as I tried to figure out how to make the case for Annie. "But we went to all the big names when we were casting the pilot. Are we sure there's going to be new interest, given our budgetary constraints?" "Budgetary constraints" was code for "cheapness." ABS was notoriously parsimonious in launching its new shows, paying actors as little as possible for as long as it could. Which was why, of course, all those big names had turned us down in the first place.

"Signing on to a pilot's different than a show that's been or- dered to series," said Loud Lloyd in the scolding tone he might use to remind a kid who should have known better that two times two is, indeed, four. "We're fishing in a different pond now that actors know they'll be getting a guaranteed nine episodes' worth of work."

"Hang on." My armpits were getting clammy, and I could smell the acrid tang of flop sweat. If Annie was replaced, that would mean that all her work was for nothing. The great perfor- mance she'd turned in would serve as a first draft for the actress who would eventually be cast as Trudy. It also meant that hor- rible Justin was right. One of my stars was being replaced, and I, the showrunner, the woman ostensibly steering the ship, was the last to know.

Choose your battles, I told myself before raising my chin. The Daves, had they been here, might have told me otherwise, but as far as I was concerned, this was a battle worth fighting. "Annie was fantastic," I said.

"People don't know her," Marcia countered.

"Here's what we'll do," said Joan. "Let's make a wish list of, say, six actresses we think would give us the kind of buzz we're looking for. We'll put the word out—"

I interrupted. "Do we tell Annie this is happening?" Think- ing: *Do I tell Annie this is happening?* It was a conversation I couldn't imagine having: *You were amazing, everyone loved you, but too bad, so sad, you're just not quite famous enough.* "Listen, I know she's not the biggest name," I said. "But she was hands- down the best person for this part. She killed it in the room. She nailed it onstage. And if the show's a hit . . . I mean, who was Estelle Getty before *Golden Girls*?"

"Estelle Getty," Lisa mused, and tapped at her handheld be- fore turning to Tariq. "You think we could get her?"

"She's dead." My voice was shrill. How on earth would I tell

Annie she'd been axed? And how would I tell my grandmother, who'd adored Annie Tait since her debut in the 1960s and had been thrilled to have Annie playing the television version of herself, even a radically and unpleasantly altered version?

"Annie will understand," said Joan. "Annie's a pro. She's been through this before."

But I haven't. I sat there, fuming, as Marcia proceeded through a minute-by-minute dissection of the show, pointing out each instance where the dials had dipped down. "People really responded to the physical humor," she said, tapping the graph where Cady did her Rollerblade split.

"And we'll have that in every episode. I promise. But it's not going to be all just girl-stuck-on-a-balcony. Or girl-trapped-in-a-closet. Or girl-with-her-butt-sticking-out-of-the-doggie-door."

Loud Lloyd boomed laughter, until he noticed that no other executives were laughing, at which point he clamped his mouth shut. Alice yawned. Tariq rubbed his head wistfully. "Could we maybe do girl-with-her-butt-stuck-in-a-doggie-door once? Like, for sweeps?"

"No," I said, a little too sharply.

"We had another thought," said Joan. The room got quiet. Joan hadn't said much so far—she had, in fact, spent most of the meeting tapping away at her BlackBerry, causing me to wonder if she'd already given up on *The Next Best Thing*. I leaned forward, waiting.

"We've been tossing around the idea of Daphne having a friend."

"Hmm." It was the perfect noncommittal noise, a sound that said, *I'm listening*, but not necessarily *I agree*. I'd learned it from the Daves.

"Right now, her world feels a little small," Joan said. "There's Nana, and Brad, and the restaurant crew, but they're more frenemies. We're thinking she could use an ally."

We're thinking the show could use more eye candy, I translated, and gave another one of the Daves' famous *Hmm*s.

"We've got someone in mind," Lloyd boomed.

"Who's that?" I asked.

Marcia pushed a button. A familiar face flashed on the big screen. I jolted upright, rising halfway out of my chair, my toes curling in my shoes. "No." The word burst out of my mouth before I had a chance to think about it.

"You have a problem with Taryn Montaine?" Joan asked.

My hands had flown off the table and were waving around in the air like spastic birds. I made myself fold them in my lap and forced myself to sit. "No, it's . . . it's not that, exactly, it's just . . . I mean, I'm not sure . . ." Deep breath. Calm down. Focus. Speak their language. "Given Cady's appearance," I said carefully, "I'm not sure we want another pretty, skinny blonde."

"Taryn Montaine is not just another blonde," said Tariq. He looked indignant, like I'd insulted his country of origin or his mom. "She's hilarious."

She's an idiot, I thought. "You know I worked with her on *The Girls' Room.*" Joan nodded. Tariq nodded. Alice, my lumpy friend, favored us with another yawn. "She was . . . well. I hope I'm not telling tales out of school here, but she could be difficult."

"Difficult in what way?" asked Tariq, who probably thought I was just jealous, and was not entirely wrong.

"She had trouble with pronunciation. She couldn't say *nuclear.*"

"Neither could two of our presidents," said Tariq.

"We had to rewrite the scripts so all the stage directions said either 'sexy' or 'angry.' Those were the two adjectives she knew."

"Think of her as seasoning," said Joan. "A little goes a long way."

"People love her," said Tariq. "We're lucky she agreed to this."

"Wait. She already agreed?"

Down at the other end of the table, I saw Lisa and Joan exchange a guilty look. "We'd talked about adding a best friend," Joan reminded me . . . and it was true that, weeks ago, we'd had a five-minute, extremely general conversation about the possibility, at some point, down the road, of adding a confidante for Daphne, a Shirley to her Laverne.

"I thought it was weird that Daphne didn't have friends." This was Yawning Alice's contribution. Another country heard from. "I mean, what kind of girl has no friends?" She gave me what would have been a pointed look had her mushy features, her double chins and lopsided eyes, been capable of doing pointed.

"According to our research," Marcia said, hitting another button, putting another graph on the screen, "fifty-two percent of women under forty-five said they'd be 'very likely' or 'somewhat likely' to tune in to a show where Taryn Montaine had a role."

I wanted to groan out loud, to throw things, to bang my head against the table like Don Music on *Sesame Street* bashing his skull against his piano keys . . . but why bother? Again, the decision had been made without me . . . now I'd just have to figure out how to fit yet another character I'd never imagined or wanted into the pilot.

"I'll let you all hash this out once I'm gone," said Marcia. "Meanwhile, we need to have a conversation about the speech."

I sat up straight. The speech. The big grandmother-to-granddaughter speech that came at Minute Fourteen. The speech that was the heart and soul of that first episode and, really, the entire show: the speech told you everything you needed to know about the two characters, the obstacles the two of them would face and, hopefully, conquer.

"We got the highest number of tune-outs during those

thirty-eight seconds," Marcia reported, using a laser pointer to indicate the problem area.

I didn't answer. I'd never been good at hiding my emotions, and at that moment what I was feeling was that any asshole who'd tune out during that part of the show wasn't someone I wanted as a viewer in the first place. Of course I knew better than to say that. I'd take viewers wherever I could find them: teens, tweens, bored housewives, single moms, hermits, pyramid schemers under house arrest, even prisoners with viewing privileges, especially if they were between the demographically desirable ages of eighteen to thirty-four and there were Nielsen boxes in jail.

"We can take a look at it," Tariq said in a placating tone. "I'm sure there are places we can trim."

"Look," I said, trying to backtrack. "Nobody had a problem with the speech in the script. We've all read it, what? At least a dozen times? I realize that it's one of the quieter moments in the story, but I don't think we should change it. We're going to tell stories that have quiet moments every week. That's the nature of the show."

Tariq was rubbing his head like he was trying to massage an idea into being. Lisa squirmed in her seat, looking as if she would have given a kidney to be someplace else. Joan tapped calmly at her phone. There was my answer, in the silence. My beloved scene was history.

I breathed in, remembering again how I'd paced my bedroom floor, waiting for the call, praying to be green-lit, how I'd thought, *I will do anything to make this happen*. Here I was at my Rubicon. This was my anything. Time to step up, put on my big-girl panties, time to play ball. Besides, what was left to fight for? My real-girl leading lady, the "me" character, was about as real as a pinup poster, and practically as thin. The grandmother character was a sex-crazed caricature, like Blanche on *The Golden Girls* if she'd been mainlining Spanish fly. My dreams of love were in pieces; my personal life was a mess. Did any of it matter? "Okay," I said. My voice was so soft that nobody heard. I cleared my throat, raised my shoulders, and tried again. "Okay."

SEVENTEEN

I'm not comfortable with this," said Grandma. She smoothed her skirt, crossed her hands in her lap, and looked straight ahead as we sat in the drive in front of our apartment building.

"Believe me, I'm not thrilled, either," I said, putting the car in gear and flicking on the turn signal. "But you don't have to do anything. Just sit in the car and wait for me." Ten days had passed since the screening results meeting, and I was on my way to tell Annie Tait that, in spite of my best efforts, how I'd fought hard to get the network to change its plans, she was going to be replaced. After I'd delivered the news, I was going to do what I should have done weeks ago and spend the day with my grandmother, helping her with her wedding preparations. We'd made appointments for her to try on dresses, and then we'd be going to Sweet Lady Jane for lunch and a cake tasting. Fire an actress, eat dessert. Just another average day in Hollywood.

Even though I hadn't said anything specific about why I wanted to see her when I'd called, I suspected that Annie knew what was up. Yes, she said, she'd be home all morning. "Got nowhere else to be," she'd said lightly before giving me her address, which was on a little street off Mulholland. As we followed the twisting roads, higher and higher up into the hills, Grandma sighed.

"What?"

"Nothing."

I didn't want to push. Ever since the night I'd shown her the pilot, we'd been treating each other with exaggerated care, so I asked, "How's the guest list coming?"

She brightened. "Just fine. Frieda Yoloff's coming up from Coral Gables, and Martin McGuire—remember him from the store? He's flying in from Framingham." She talked, first slowly and then faster, about who else had RSVPed, what they'd serve and where they'd seat people, until I pulled into the driveway that my GPS assured me belonged to Annie. The house was a ranch, one story, white with green shutters, with orange trees in the narrow front yard and a gravel path that led to the door.

"Wait here."

"Hold on." Grandma reached into the tote bag at her feet and pulled out something round and wrapped in foil.

"You baked a cake?"

"It's never polite to show up empty-handed," she said without looking at me.

"I really don't think coffee cake is going to fix this," I muttered, without bothering to tell her whether I was talking about fixing things with her or fixing things with Annie. The parallels were hard to miss—here I was, in spite of my best intentions, selling out another old lady because that was what the network wanted, and I didn't have the guts or the power to tell them no.

I took the cake, got out of the car, and rang the doorbell. Annie answered, dressed in jeans, a button-down plaid shirt, and worn-looking cowboy boots. "I'm sorry to interrupt your weekend," I began after I'd handed her the cake.

"Come on in," she said in a tone that made it clear she knew this wasn't just a social call. "Want anything to drink?"

"Oh, no thanks." This was going to be awkward enough.

There was no need to compound things by having to navigate returning a coffee mug or a water glass after I'd delivered the bad news.

Annie's house continued the Western theme of her clothes. I spotted Georgia O'Keeffe prints on the wall, Navajo rugs on the floors, and a feathered dream catcher hanging in front of a window. The house smelled strongly of coffee and cat—I spied a litter box in the corner in front of a door leading to the garage. It seemed to be empty except for Annie. I didn't know, had never found out, whether she was married or had kids, and now seemed like the wrong time to ask.

She led me to the living room, where large windows overlooked the steep verge of a cliff, sat down on a brown cowhide-covered couch, and indicated that I should take the bentwood rocking chair. "I'm so sorry to have to tell you this," I began. Before I could continue, she raised one hand to stop me.

"Was it my performance?"

"No!" I was shocked that she'd even have to ask, and relieved that she'd already figured out what I'd driven up here to tell her. "Absolutely not. Your performance was great. Everyone thought so. You were fantastic. I couldn't have asked for better." I was gushing, I realized, and made myself stop, knowing that praise, however deserved, would not make her feel any better. "Honestly, it's just that the network wanted someone with a little more of a name, I guess." I hadn't meant to append that qualifier—I didn't guess; I knew—but *you're just not famous enough* seemed like such a bald and heartless thing to say.

Annie's forehead furrowed. She leaned forward, picking a bit of cat hair off one denim-covered thigh, and muttered something into her lap.

"I'm so sorry," I said, without asking her to repeat herself. "Really. From the bottom of my heart. I loved you from your very first audition, and you were a pleasure to work with, but . . ."

She lifted her head and repeated what I hadn't heard. "I thought you were different."

I didn't answer. *Yeah,* I thought. *So did I.*

"You're a bright girl, so maybe you can tell me this. The networks only want you if you're famous already, and the only way to get famous is to star in a show. But you can't be the star unless you're famous already. So what am I supposed to do?" Her voice was level, her face calm, but I could hear the anguish underlining each word, and I knew that I didn't have an answer.

"Oh, never mind," she sighed before I could come up with something to say. "It's not your fault."

But it is, I thought, getting to my feet. *It's my show. It's my fault.*

"I think you can find the door."

I nodded. I wanted to tell her again that I was sorry, that I'd done all I could. When Joan had asked for a list, I'd deliberately picked six actresses I thought would never have been interested in the part. I had no way of knowing that Penelope Weaver, the fifth of our sixth potentials, had lost all her savings in the stock market's most recent crash and was so desperate for work, any work, that she'd chosen our show over doing a voiceover gig on a straight-to-video Disney fairy movie. I could tell Annie that the whole thing made me feel lousy and small. I could tell her that I was ashamed of myself. But I didn't say anything. Words were just words, and what good would they do her?

"I think you're great," I said, with my hand on the doorknob. "I know that doesn't mean much, coming from me, but it's true. I hope that someday you'll get to work with people who deserve you."

She'd been walking a few yards behind me. "Don't be so hard on yourself," she said. "It happens."

"Yeah," I said, "but it shouldn't be happening to you." My eyes filled with tears. I blinked hard, looking away, and then opened the door. Annie stepped outside with me and squinted, shadowing her eyes with her hand. "Is that your grandma?" Of course, she'd met my grandmother, at the table read and the pilot taping. They'd posed for pictures together, which I'd snapped with my grandmother's cell phone and tweeted from the show's account.

"I cracked the windows, and she's got plenty of water," I said. Annie didn't smile. Instead, she quoted the Rolling Stones. "'What a drag it is, getting old.'"

"I'm sorry," I said one last time. She gave me a thin-lipped smile, stepped back inside, and shut the door.

"Well," said Grandma once I was back in the car. She'd pulled out her crochet hook and a bundle of thread. "That looked like it went well." I imagined what she was thinking: *Another old lady, thrown under the bus. Nice work, Ruthie. Didn't I raise you well.*

With my hands on the wheel, I bent my head. *Maybe it's a rite of passage,* I thought. Your first green-light, your first read-through, your first day of photography, and the first time you had to fire someone you didn't want to fire for a stupid reason, because the network made you do it.

"I feel like a monster," I said, steering the car down the hill.

Grandma kept her eyes on her wool. "You know what they say. It's not show friends, it's show business."

I waited until we were at a red light before turning to her. "What did you say?"

"You've never heard that?"

"Oh, I've heard it. Just, you know, not from you."

"It's true," she said as the driver behind me, a guy in mirrored sunglasses and a convertible, leaned on his horn. I waved at him to calm down, yanked at my hat, and started to drive again. "Show friends," I muttered, and then kept my mouth shut all the way to Beverly Hills.

*   *   *

"Hel*lo*!" caroled the saleslady, swooping toward us, quickly smoothing away her expression of concern at my scars and my grandmother's age and putting a welcoming smile in place. She had that Los Angeles agelessness that could have put her anywhere between thirty-five and fifty, skin tanned the color of Tang, body toned in the gym and improved in an operating room. Her ribbed sweater showed off the jut of her breasts and her narrow waist. The sweater was tucked into a short, fitted skirt, tight at her hips and knees, that turned her walk into a quickstep hobble. Glossy beige pumps with needle-sharp heels and elaborate eye makeup completed the look. Her hair was dyed a fashionable ombré, dark at the roots, shading to auburn at the ends. Her name tag, perched on top of her right breast, said FELICIA.

It was almost funny, watching her gaze dart from me to my grandma and back again as she tried to figure out which of us would be worse to deal with—the disfigured girl or the old woman. She finally made up her mind, and took both my hands in hers. "So when's the big day?"

"She's the bride," I said, nodding toward my grandmother, who lifted her left hand and waggled her engagement ring. "And it's in late September."

Felicia clutched both manicured hands to her chest and gasped as if she'd been shot. "Sep-*tember*? Oh, dear. That doesn't leave us much time at all."

"I don't want a wedding gown," my grandmother said. "I'm looking for something off the rack. Elegant but appropriate." That could have described her attire that day, a Diane von Furstenberg wrap dress in a dark-blue jersey with a pattern of silver and green, navy-blue ballet flats, and a matte gold clutch. The clutch, I knew, would hold her credit cards, her cell phone, a single Estée Lauder lipstick in its heavy gold case, and a tiny spritzer of the L'Occitane lemon verbena scent she wore in the summer. There would be a compact full of pressed powder, sheets of rice paper for blotting, tissues, and a comb. When I was little, investigating what I called Grandma's Magic Bag had been one of my favorite waiting-room pastimes. I knew each photograph she kept in her wallet, the specific scent of each bag's interior, and how there was usually a Hershey's Kiss or a square of Ghirardelli if I looked hard enough.

"Celebratory but subdued," I told Felicia, who'd started gnawing on one glossy lip.

"I'll know it when I see it," said my grandmother, gliding past Felicia to the racks, which she considered with an educated eye.

"She will," I said. "She's got exquisite taste."

"So, is this a second wedding?" Felicia asked faintly.

"Second wedding," I confirmed. My grandmother plucked a short, shimmering white dress made of crisscrossing Lycra straps off the rack and held it up against her.

"That's an Hervé Léger," said Felicia, pronouncing the French with great flair. "The bandage dress."

"It's a little racy," Grandma decreed, returning the hanger to the rack.

"I'm not sure—" Felicia began. My grandmother fixed her with a withering gaze. I turned to hide my smile as Felicia snatched something else off the rack.

"There's this!"

We looked. The dress was a bright orange-red, with a feathered slit that went almost up to the crotch and, hanging from an attached hanger, there was a limp fistful of fabric and feathers.

"Is that a cape?" I asked.

"A cape-lette," said Felicia.

"It's red," Grandma observed.

"We can order it in, ah, butterscotch," Felicia said, reading from the tag. "Or ivory crème. It's a very popular choice with, ah . . ."

Women who wanted to cover their arms, I guessed as Felicia opened and shut her mouth, then opened and shut it again. *Old women.*

"That is hideous," said my grandmother in a voice that was high and full of emotion. If you'd closed your eyes, you might have imagined that you were talking to a young bride getting ready for her first wedding, a woman with her whole life ahead of her, to whom men, and the world, were still mostly a mystery.

"Why don't you ladies have a seat?" Felicia stammered, evidently remembering that there was a protocol for these visits, a script she could stick to, even if the bride was fifty years older than the ones she usually saw and accompanied by a freakish-looking granddaughter. "May I offer you still or sparkling water?"

We both asked for water and then took seats on a tufted beige velvet love seat. I gulped my drink when it arrived, wishing it was something stronger. I couldn't get Annie's face out of my mind, her quiet resignation when I'd told her she was being replaced. I suspected I wouldn't have felt so torn up if she'd yelled, or been angry, or even just surprised . . . but her acceptance, her complete lack of indignation, her assertion that this was nothing new all drove home just how unfair the system was, and how complicit in that system I'd become. Should I have fought harder? Was it a fight I could have won?

My grandmother pulled her crocheting out of the tote bag she carried along with her clutch. I got up and wandered around the store, ending up in front of a three-way mirror with a raised, carpeted stand in front of it. I could imagine the bride-to-be in the dressing room, zipped and pinned into a dress, eyes closed, her mother holding her elbow, guiding her up onto the platform, whispering, *Keep your eyes shut. Don't look,* until the young woman was positioned in front of the mirrors. Then the bride-to-be would open her eyes and look at herself, radiant and blushing, her mother beside her, saying, *This is it. This is the one.*

I looked at myself, in my striped jersey, my scarf, my hat pulled down in its jaunty tilt, casting a shadow that was not big or dark or deep enough to hide the whole side of my face. The mirrors were unforgiving. There was my left side, pretty enough, there was my body, strong and fit, and my hair, shiny and light brown. There was my right side, sunken and scarred, the eye that drooped, the jaw that looked foreshortened and wrong, the cratered pink skin that would cause grown-ups to stare and kids to whisper about Two-Face, the *Batman* villain. There was the truth of it: I would never stand on this podium with my mother, in a wedding dress, with my face bare and unblemished. *All brides are beautiful*, went the saying . . . but that would never be true for me.

"Ruthie?"

I turned to see my grandmother with a short gold dress in her arms. The dress had beading on the front, a pattern of black and gold and white beads that formed . . . I looked more closely for confirmation. Yep. A cougar. A crouching cougar, to be specific, a cougar that was poised to strike. I wondered if you'd turn the dress over and find a young man on the back, running away as fast as his feet would carry him.

"Oh my God," I managed . . . and I felt my heart unfold as Grandma smiled at me, fashioning her hands into claws.

"Rrrawr!"

I started laughing. I couldn't help it. "Oh my God, do people buy that? And wear it?"

"Ladies!" Felicia called. Grandma gave me a conspiratorial grin before we returned to the couch, as Felicia wheeled a rack of dresses in front of her.

"Now," she said. "This is actually a bridesmaid's gown, but I think, in candlelight or a pale peach, it would be lovely." She pulled out a slip-style, spaghetti-strapped dress with a plunging neckline that was made of silk so clingy that you'd have to have been a Victoria's Secret model—or, better, a mannequin—to make it work. It was a dress for a sylph or a mermaid or a sixteen-year-old supermodel.

Grandma shook her head. "Sleeves. I'll need sleeves."

Felicia blinked as if she'd just heard a brand-new word in a brand-new language. "Beg pardon?"

"Sleeves," said my grandmother. "You know? The cloth that's attached to the shoulder?"

Felicia rifled through her rack again and came out with what appeared to be the store's only garment with sleeves—the bandage dress that Grandma had considered and rejected five minutes ago.

Grandma frowned. Felicia gulped. I cringed, knowing what was coming. Beside me, my grandmother drew herself up until she was at her very tallest, and started to speak.

"Listen to me, missy," she said. "I am an informed consumer. I have money to spend. And I've watched *Pretty Woman*."

"Many times," I said.

Felicia nodded, a frozen smile on her plasticized face.

"I know my rights," said Grandma.

"She reads *Consumer Reports*," I said.

"And I have money," she concluded.

"Lots," I said. "More than she needs."

Grandma pulled her American Express Platinum card out of her clutch and brandished it at Felicia, who cringed in the manner of a vampire confronted with a crucifix. "Do you have anything—anything at all—that I should spend my time trying on?"

"Let me go take another peek," Felicia said, and fled, taking her wheeled dress rack with her.

My grandmother got to her feet. "Let's go," she said. "There's nothing for me here."

"Thank you for your time!" I called as my grandmother

heaved at the heavy glass-and-metal door until it opened and admitted us onto the Rodeo Drive sidewalk. We walked to the corner in silence. Then my grandmother turned to me.

"I should have bought that cougar dress."

"You think?"

"Can you imagine Maurice's face? If I'd come down the aisle in that?"

"It was a lot of look," I acknowledged. This was one of my grandmother's pet phrases, one she'd use about a young actress who'd show up at an awards show in an unfortunately slit or sheer gown, or when I'd shown her the picture of Cady from the Alcove, all bony cheekbones and hipster hat. *That's a lot of look.*

For the first time since I'd shown her the pilot, she took my arm. "Ruthie," she said. "Are you really okay?"

Before I could answer, she steered us across the street and into Le Pain Quotidien, where we took a table by the window. "We've got some time, don't we?" she asked. I nodded.

We ordered lemonades, just like we did when I was a girl. After my surgeries, my doctors' visits, the times I'd have stitches removed or bandages replaced, we would go to a French patisserie on Newbury Street and order one dessert and two lemonades.

Grandma crossed her legs and looked at me. "I'm worried," she said simply.

"Why?" I hadn't told her anything about what had happened with Dave, or that I'd been requested-slash-forced to give Daphne a friend who would be played by Taryn Montaine. "I'm fine with you leaving. I'm happy for you! I know you and Maurice will have . . ." *Many wonderful years together* was what I was thinking, but I didn't say it, because, given her age and his heart, who knew? "I know you'll be happy," I said. My words hung in the air as a waitress came over, holding a sweating metal pitcher of water aloft in one hand.

"You ladies doing all right?" she asked. She had a curvy,

compact body, in a black T-shirt, denim skirt, black apron, and clogs. Her hair was in a short bob. Her nose was pierced with a tiny, glittering stud. It took me about ten seconds to realize that she was one of the girls who'd come in to read for Daphne, and by the time I figured it out and had prepared a greeting that was equal parts professional and apologetic, she and her pitcher were gone. I looked away. How many women had I thrown under various buses since this process had begun, I wondered as I sipped my drink and nibbled at the apple-pear turnover my grandma had ordered. How many actresses, and my grandmother, too?

"Ruthie," said Grandma. She put twenty dollars on the table and took my arm, pulling me onto my feet and then out to the sidewalk and the sunshine. We drove to the delectable-smelling bakery, where we sat at a glass-topped table and sampled slivers of a dozen gorgeously iced wedding cakes. It should have been wonderful . . . but all I could think of was the calm acceptance on Annie Tait's face, her recognition that the world was ever thus and that Ruth Rachel Saunders was unlikely to change it, and all the flavors, lemon-poppy and vanilla and chocolate-pomegranate, tasted like ashes in my mouth.

EIGHTEEN

"Pete?" I knocked on the dressing-room door, gently at first and then more firmly. "Hey, Pete, you in there?" It was Wednesday morning, ten minutes after the table read for the pilot reshoots was supposed to have begun. The executives had already gathered on the stage, in folding chairs in front of the set that depicted Daphne and Nana's Miami apartment. Craft services had set out hot coffee, breakfast sandwiches, granola and yogurt and fresh fruit. Everyone was eating and chatting and waiting for us to begin.

Cady Stratton, in leather leggings and a lace vest that let the world know that she'd lost even more weight since I'd last seen her, had teetered through the doors on skyscraping heels at nine-thirty on the dot and taken her place at the U-shaped arrangement of tables behind the placard that read CADY STRATTON/DAPHNE. Taryn Montaine had sauntered into the room a strategic thirty seconds behind her, in a white voile maxi dress that skimmed her flat gold sandals, with her honey-blond hair in a messy bun that had probably taken her twenty minutes to arrange, and an oversize pair of sunglasses shadowing her eyes. "Hi, baby," she'd said, putting her hands on my shoulders and giving me a cool, impersonal brush of a kiss on the good side of my face. I'd worried about what it would be like when we saw each other again, how she'd look and what we'd say, but I saw immediately that I shouldn't have wasted my time. Taryn clearly had no idea who I was, no recollection that we'd worked together, and no idea that I'd been in love with her husband. Maybe that was the beauty of self-absorbed people, I thought, as Taryn worked the room, dispensing hugs and kisses and squeals of greeting to the executives. Every time you met them, you got to start over again.

Penny Weaver, Annie Tait's replacement, had shown up next, with a basketful of homemade cranberry scones, which she'd distributed to the executives, and a handwritten note she'd given me that told me how thrilled she was to have the opportunity to play Nana. My grandma was in the audience, sitting just behind the executives, whispering into Maurice's hearing aid, telling him who was who. Chad the director, as tanned and muscular as he'd been on pilot night, was working his morning wad of Dentyne and making notes on the script, and the women in charge of props and costumes were in the front row, scripts in hand, waiting to make their own notes, figuring out what clothes the actors would wear and what things they'd need on hand: a cell phone and laptop for Daphne, a teapot and iron for Nana.

We had everyone except Pete. Five minutes before start time, I slipped off the stage to find him. I knew that he was on the lot, because Cliff the security guard, at my request, had called to tell me when he'd arrived. "Keeping him on a short leash, huh?" he'd said, and I'd given him a weak smile and said, "You know it." Pete's car was in its assigned spot, but his dressing-room door was locked. He hadn't answered my calls, texts, or emails, and now he was even ignoring my knocks. This wasn't good.

I banged at the door some more. "Pete? Are you in there? Is everything all right?"

Silence. I could feel my tea sloshing in my belly. We had precisely seven days to redo the pilot, at which point we'd start our normal workweek: table reads on Wednesday, rehearsals and run-throughs on Thursday and Friday, pre-shoots on Monday, live audience shoots on Tuesday nights. The network had graciously given us an extra week to add the new scenes to the pilot. Of course, the network couldn't exactly refuse, because it was responsible for all the new stuff we'd be shooting—the new characters of Brad Dermansky and Veronica King, the new actress playing Nana.

It would all work, assuming that I could keep things moving . . . which depended on my ability to get my star out of his dressing room. "Pete? Hey, listen. If there's a problem with your lines, or wardrobe, or whatever, we can talk about it, but I need you to . . ."

Come out of there, I was about to say, when the door swung open and there was Pete, in khakis and a polo shirt, combed and clean-shaven, looking like he was on his way to play a round of golf. He held the script in his hand. It looked, I noticed, with the first stirrings of unease, like he hadn't so much as opened it, even though a PA had driven it to his house on Friday night, and I'd emailed him a backup copy myself the following morning. "Hey, Ruth!" he said.

"Pete. Hi. What's going on?"

"Oh, nothing," he said, still making no move to start covering the hundred yards between his door and the stage. "Just getting into character."

"Listen, I want to respect your process," I began. After all my time working in television, I still had a hard time saying that phrase without laughing. Big Dave used to tell stories about Lorin Chatsworth, a classically trained Shakespearean actor who'd appeared on one of the dopiest sitcoms of the 1990s, a show set at a sports bar in Cleveland. Lorin disdained the company of his fellow thespians, preferring instead to hang out in the writers' room. There, he'd sip Earl Grey tea and talk about his days at the Royal Academy of Dramatic Art. He'd dish about Kenneth Branagh and Emma Thompson and Dame Judi Dench, until the writers' assistant would stick her head through the doorway and say—in Big Dave's recounting—"Whenever you're ready, Mr. Chatsworth, they've finally got the sombrero on the pig."

"I need you to do me a favor," said Pete. He grabbed my wrist. His hand was icy. I leaned in close and took a whiff, bracing for the scent of booze or dope or something worse, but all I got was Tom's of Maine toothpaste and Dial. His sleek blond hair was neatly combed, his blue eyes weren't bloodshot, and the pupils looked to be of normal size. Pete's face was as pleasant as pie, a generically handsome assortment of features that could be used to sell anything from cars to banks to jokes. He was a safe choice, a guy who was compelling enough without being risky or edgy, and I'd stopped worrying about him the moment he'd been cast. Clearly, that had been a mistake.

"Here's the thing," Pete began. His Adam's apple bobbed, and I heard the click when he swallowed. "I'm more of an auditory learner than a reader." He paused here and gave me his Level Six charming smile. Level One, I knew, was what he went around with most of the time, the grin he'd reflexively give to the cashier in the commissary and the girl whose job it was to pat powder on his cheeks. His charm ascended all the way to Level Ten, but that was reserved for the presidents of networks and, possibly, nations. "So, the way I get my lines is, I have my acting teacher, or a friend, or someone, read them to me until I've got them down."

He paused, looking at me expectantly. I stared at him, wondering, briefly, guiltily, whether Pete could read at all. I was thinking of a story I'd heard about Keshia Knight Pulliam, who'd been just six when she'd been cast as little Rudy on *The Cosby Show*. During table reads, she'd sit on her father-slash-manager's lap, and he'd whisper her lines into her ear. One wintry day, instead of giving her the line, her father, sick with a cold, had coughed. Keshia, ever dutiful, had replicated the cough instead of the line. Bill Cosby had looked down the table, widened his eyes, and said in his drollest tone, "That one's broken."

"So . . . you need me to read you your lines at the table?"

Pete put his hand on my arm and ratcheted his smile up to Level Seven. "It's just for the table read. I'll have all my lines by the network run-through. I promise. This is just part of my process."

I thought fast, while grabbing his hand so that he couldn't retreat back into his dressing room and waste even more of our time. Nobody expected an actor to be off-book at the table read. Plenty of actors took their time learning their lines, knowing that scripts could change right up until the moment shooting actually commenced, not wanting to peak at a run-through or a rehearsal, days before the audience arrived. Besides, however weird Pete's request seemed, I didn't have time to worry about it. I had to get him to the stage, by any means necessary.

"Fine," I said. "Let's get going, though. We're late."

He turned his grin up to Level Eight. "You're my hero."

We hustled out of his dressing room and race-walked to the soundstage, a gigantic, echoing room with bleachers for two hundred on one side and forty-foot-high ceilings crisscrossed with metal support beams and ladders and lights. At the table, I quickly rearranged the placards so that Pete was sitting on my left. As the room settled down, I got to my feet. I'd seen the Daves do this a hundred times, before each table read for *Bunk Eight*. Now it was my turn. I straightened up and smoothed my hair, feeling a back-to-school kind of excitement. My hands were tingling, my face was flushed, and in spite of everything, all my fears and disappointments and everything that had gone wrong so far, I found myself smiling.

I looked down the table, to my right, where Chad sat at one

end, with Cady and Penny Weaver, each with a script on the table, with the words THE NEXT BEST THING, WRITTEN BY RUTH SAUNDERS in front of them. I looked out at the sea of faces until I found my grandmother, with Maurice sitting beside her. Then I began.

"Everyone!" I said. "Welcome to the first of hopefully many, many table reads for *The Next Best Thing*!" The applause started slowly and then got louder. The executives were clapping; the actors were hooting; Chad actually cracked a smile. In her seat three rows back, my grandma was dabbing away tears. "It's my pleasure to introduce our amazing cast. In the starring role of Daphne, last name To Be Determined, we have the irresistible Cady Stratton!" Cady got to her feet and sketched a curtsy. "Playing Brad Dermansky, we have the charming Pete Paxton!" Pete gave the room a salute. "In the role of Nana Trudy, the lovely and talented Penny Weaver!" Penny, who had bright-red hair and china-doll features, blew a kiss. "Playing Veronica King, the estimable Taryn Montaine!" Taryn had a puzzled frown on her face as she gave her little wave. It was evil of me, but I'd picked out that word, *estimable*, precisely because I knew that Taryn would have no idea what it meant.

"Our pilot is directed by the Emmy Award–winning Chad Garson!" Chad, in the process of unwrapping another piece of gum, took the time to briefly lift his head. *Never mind him*, I thought, and intoned the phrase that had kicked off every show on every network since time untold: "And now, without further ado, the table read of *The Next Best Thing*, Episode 101: Pilot!" More applause. I sat down. The actors flipped their scripts open—Penny, I saw, had reprinted her lines in twenty-four-point typeface, while Cady's pages were scribbled over with hot-pink and lime-green highlighter and dotted with Post-it notes. Pete's script was, as I'd suspected, dismayingly pristine, and Taryn had done the actor's trick of drawing a line through everyone's words but her own. *Bullshit, bullshit, bullshit, me,* was how Big Dave described that move. "Everyone ready?" I asked quietly. They nodded. We began.

The first scene, a toned-down version of Nana's getting kicked out of her ailing beau's house, went smoothly. People laughed at Nana's barbed insults to her boyfriend's three sons, and while I hadn't been able to get rid of every awful sex addict/Viagra joke, I'd rewritten enough to make it clear that Nana got the best of the middle-aged boys. In the crowd, I could see my own grandmother laughing as Penny read her lines, which meant that I'd fixed it enough that she'd be able to watch it on TV and brag about it to her friends without disowning me.

Then it was time for Pete's scene, back at the apartment, the moment when he'd be meeting Daphne. I whispered his first line, which was "Hey, babe." Pete looked at me, frowning. "What?"

I jerked my chin toward the page, then up at him, and whispered more urgently, "Hey, babe."

"Oh, oh, right!" he said, and patted my arm. "Jeez. For a minute there I thought you were coming on to me!" He widened his eyes, giving the executives a *who, me?* smile. They ate it up, laughing and clapping. Then Pete said, "Hey, babe," in the sleaziest, most construction-worker-with-his-hand-down-his-pants tone I could have conjured. Cady sat up straight. "Excuse me?" she said, in a high, quavering voice. "Are you speaking to me?"

"Nobody else here," I whispered. "Nobody else here," Pete said. "You new in town?" I whispered. "You new?" said Pete. "Because I haven't seen you around."

That wasn't what I'd written, but it was close enough, and Cady slid right into her next line. "My grandmother and I just moved here. We're in 6A."

"And I'm in the basement," I whispered to Pete. "I'm the handyman. Anything you need fixed, any lightbulbs burnt out, anything you need, you know, loosened, tightened . . ."

Pete read the line back flawlessly. Cady gave a prim shudder. "I think we're okay on the loosening and tightening front," she said. Without waiting for me to feed him his next line, Pete gave a dazzling smile.

"If anything changes . . ." he said, and lifted his hand to his ear in the universal gesture for "call me." Laughter rippled through the room, and I scribbled a note to change the line from what I'd written—"give me a call"—to what Pete had just done.

"I have to go now," Cady blurted, and Pete hollered, "I hate to see you go, but I love to watch you leave." It wasn't on the page, but got a big laugh. I wrote it down and turned the page, and we were back in the apartment, where Nana was primping for a date and waiting to find out how Daphne's first day at work had gone. As soon as Penny started reading her lines, Pete sagged back in his seat. Beneath his shock of shiny hair, his face was pale, and when I put my hand on his shoulder, I could feel him tremble. "Pete? Are you okay? Do you need some water?" I whispered.

He managed a smile. "Nah, I'm good. Just a little stage fright."

That was puzzling. We weren't even onstage, insofar as our sets were still in the process of being built. Performing in front of executives had to be nerve-racking, but these were the people who'd already liked Pete well enough to give him the role, which should have calmed him down. What if Pete fell apart in front of an audience? Hollywood was full of actors like that, people who could perform flawlessly when it was just the crew and the camera, but who'd experience professional vapor lock when the audience filed into its seats.

At the other end of the table, Penny Weaver was winding up

the speech I'd written imagining that Annie Tait would be the one to read it. "You're going to let some plumber whose tattoos probably have their own Facebook page talk to you like that?" she demanded. "Honey, no. I didn't raise a dishrag. You get back out there and you stake your claim! You plant your flag! You set up that StairMaster!"

"I don't know," Cady whimpered. Her hesitation, her obvious fear, should have made the audience want to give Daphne a firm shake and a pep talk. Given Cady's emaciation, it probably made the audience want to give her a sandwich. I scribbled myself a note in the script—*fix this*—as Penny's tone shifted from strident to sweet. At the table, she reached over to touch Cady's chin. "Everyone's scared," she said gently, "but not everyone's brave enough to say so."

At the other end of the table, Taryn was getting ready for her big moment, squinting at her script, Botoxed brow attempting and failing to furrow. I smiled to myself. It was petty, and maybe pointless, but I'd taken care to use every SAT word I knew in describing Taryn's speech and actions. When she met Daphne, she was supposed to glance at her *combatively*, and deliver her first line *stonily*, after which she'd *lope* out of the bathroom . . . and I was ninety-nine percent sure that she had absolutely no idea what any of those words meant, unless Rob had bought her a dictionary as a push prize.

Even though she might not have known the adverbs, Taryn had at least learned her lines, and the back-and-forth with Cady went smoothly. You got a sense of Daphne's strength and generosity, the kindness she extended to strangers, the way she beat up on herself. If I just listened, it was fine, but when I watched sunny, skinny Cady acting awkward and insecure, it didn't work at all. *More rewrites*, I thought, and began scribbling notes on my script.

We swung into Act Three. Nana went on her date. Daphne

charmed the pastry chef, flirted with a customer, and impressed her new friend Veronica with her humor, determination, and ability to fold napkins into swans. Back at the apartment building, she knocked briskly on Brad Dermansky's door. "My pipes need cleaning," she announced. "And there's a piece of exercise equipment that I need your help with." Pete gave her a lazy grin . . . and I got so caught up in the moment that I forgot to feed him his line.

"Baby, I will clean those pipes right now," Pete improvised. It got a big laugh. Unfortunately, it was in no way related to what he was supposed to say, which was "I've got company."

"But I've got company," I whispered.

"But I've got some people over," Pete said, waggling his eyebrows. "You, uh, want to join us? Come on in, maybe look at my etchings?"

In the front row, Lisa was laughing. Beside her, Joan smiled sweetly, and Tariq wore the expression of a man who'd just learned that his stage-four cancer had gone into miraculous remission.

"No, thanks," Cady said, back on script, in a frosty tone. "I have plans with my grandmother."

"Of course you do," I whispered.

"Bring her, too," said Pete.

Cady shot me a desperate look. I nodded at the script. "I'll expect to see you first thing tomorrow morning," she said, reading the line as I'd written it.

"I'll be there," said Pete, which was close enough. Then there was the final scene, the tag, the thirty seconds of show that would run alongside the credits. It ended with Cady saying, "This has been an interesting day," and Nana lifting her glass in a toast to "many interesting tomorrows," and Daphne's final "We're all right for now."

There was a beat of silence. Then, as if we'd choreographed

the move, all of us, the actors and the directors and me, raised
our heads as the executives started clapping. Pete squeezed my
hand. Grandma blew me a kiss. I let my eyes roam past the audience, toward a seated figure by the door. It was Dave, in his
wheelchair. My heart lifted. *He's here for me.* As I watched, he
lifted one hand, doffed an invisible hat, and mouthed two words:
nice job. He must have sneaked in during the read, I thought
as I tentatively waved back. I was out of my chair and halfway
around the table, wanting to go to him, to ask him how it had
been, if the show could still be saved in spite of everything, and
if he'd been thinking about me the way I'd been thinking about
him, whether I'd made a total fool of myself, and if, maybe, he
could have feelings for me after all, before remembering that I
needed to thank everyone for coming and tell them that I'd see
them all soon . . . and after that there were a million things that
needed doing.

There'd be notes from the executives, then a preproduction
meeting about all of the details that went into each show. My
costume designer would need to know what Daphne and Veronica should wear to work at the restaurant; the set decorator
would ask how many cookbooks should be in Nana's kitchen,
and whether they should look worn or new or somewhere in
between. I'd have to tell the assistant director how many extras
to hire as restaurant diners, and what ages and races and genders
they should be. Props would need to know what color teapot
Nana should have, and whether we'd see a glimpse of Brad's
apartment when he opened the door, and what I'd imagined the
audience seeing in the basement storage lockers. There would
be all of these questions, and dozens more, and I would have to
answer every one of them . . . but for now, all I wanted to do was
bask. I'd pulled it off; I'd actually made it happen. Something
I'd dreamed up was actually going to be on TV. And if it wasn't
exactly the way I'd dreamed it, if one actor looked nothing like

the character I'd imagined, another couldn't read, and the third was my worst enemy, well, compromise was part of the deal. I'd wanted this, I told myself . . . and now I had what I wanted, and I would do my best to enjoy it.

By the time I could take a breath and another look around, an hour had sped by. The actors were back in their dressing rooms; the writers were back in the bungalow, working on the script. The executives had moved on to their next table read, a few buildings down . . . and the back of the soundstage was empty, as if Dave had never been there at all.

NINETEEN

Two weeks later, I stood next to Big Dave backstage at a different Burbank soundstage for the network's West Coast up-fronts, the night they'd unveil their new fall shows to ad buyers and foreign broadcasters and the press. I was all dressed up in a silk top, pants, and ballet flats. Dave, in a three-piece suit, a French-cuffed shirt, and a wide silk tie in alternating stripes of raspberry and plum, had a clipboard in his hand and a frown on his face. As actresses paraded past us, waiting to be introduced and go onstage and take their bows, he shook his head, murmured things like "That won't work," and scribbled on the page.

"Cut it out," I said as the actress closest to his whisper stared at him and then tugged at the hem of her dress. "You're going to give someone an eating disorder."

"That's the point," he said as the actresses, hearing the name of their show, paraded through the curtains, and another group of hunks and beauties took their place. Dave eyed them each, up and down, and then shook his head and started scribbling again. "No," he said, loudly enough to be heard over the blare of the pop music and the applause of the assembled ad buyers and television reporters. "No, no, I'm afraid that just won't do."

"Dave," I hissed as one actress licked her lips and another fiddled with her bra strap. I nodded at the ladies. "Ignore him,"

I said. "He's doing a bit." The actresses smiled anxiously, but I knew they weren't ignoring Dave. Maybe they knew who he was—powerful showrunner, potential employer, creator of *Bunk Eight*. More likely, they were trained to preen for any men whose eyes chanced upon them, to believe that their job in life was to arouse them, and to worry when the evidence suggested that they'd failed.

"Oh, my," Dave murmured as the actresses, show ponies in short dresses and stilettos, trotted by. "That's unfortunate."

I slapped his arm with the silver clutch I'd borrowed from my grandmother. I thought I'd looked nice when I'd left the house, with my hair blown out and my arms and legs smoothed with a sugar scrub, but here, among the actresses, I felt like an elephant surrounded by gorgeous girl acrobats, enormous and ungainly and altogether different. "Cut it out." To change the subject, I said, "Oh, thank God, there's Cady."

Dave's eyes lit up. I stifled a groan. Among the up-and-coming starlets of L.A., competitive underdressing—showing as much skin as possible without courting arrest for public indecency—was a well-established practice. Taryn had arrived in a handkerchief-size skirt that barely covered her panties—assuming, of course, that she was wearing panties—and a cropped top that skimmed her belly button. "Hi-i-i!" she'd said, air-kissing me before vanishing into the hair and makeup suite the network had set up on the stage next door. I'd poked my head in to take a look at the dozens of makeup artists and hairstylists, waiting behind chairs set in front of lightbulb-ringed mirrors, next to palettes of cosmetics, rows of bottles of hair-care products, and all manner of brushes and sponges, foam rollers, and flatirons. An hour later Taryn had emerged with her hair curled and piled high, sparkly pink lips and gold-toned eyelids. She was so beautiful, stunning even in this crowd of stunners . . . . and I knew, from a "Body After Baby" feature in one of the gossip magazines, that the bits concealed by her outfit looked just as good as everything on display.

As I watched, Taryn sauntered over to the open bar, ordered a vodka tonic with lime, ignored the trays of appetizers that waiters carried through the crowds, and began working the room with a professional's poised nonchalance, laying her hand on a male executive's forearm, air-kissing a female producer's cheek. I'd kept an eye on her, watching her work, and then looked at the time and gone backstage to wait for Cady, who was waving at me as she hurried over. I exhaled, checking out her short, sheer minidress and towering sandals made of spiked black leather that wrapped around her calves almost to her knees. *Okay, that's not so bad,* I thought. In contrast to the skintight ensembles the other young actresses were sporting, Cady's dress had a flowing cut and a high, almost chaste neckline. If you were willing to ignore her nipples, poking at the silk like a pair of pencil erasers, and how the dress stopped halfway down her thighs, it was perfectly appropriate, even conservative. Then she'd turned around. "Oh, my," Dave breathed as we saw that the back of the billowy dress dipped so low that it exposed the small of her back, the top of her buttocks, and a solid inch of ass-crack.

Big Dave, beaming like Christmas had come early, snapped a picture with his cell phone. "God, I love Hollywood," he'd said.

"Don't you dare tweet that," I told him, slapping his forearm again. Pete Paxton greeted his costar with a wolfish grin. Penny was scowling—she looked lovely in a dusty-rose dress of ruched and pleated silk, but in this crowd she had to be feeling her age. I gave Cady a weak smile. "Wow," I said to my star. "It's pretty easy to tell which women are the writers and which ones are the actresses." Thinking: *The writers are the ones who remembered their underpants.* Cady raised her eyebrows, indicating that she had no idea what I was talking about and didn't care to learn. Then she pulled out her phone, snapped the day's sixth self-portrait, and posted it on Twitter. *Oh, well*, I thought. *At least it's a shot of her front side.*

I pulled out my own phone and glanced at the time. In ten minutes we'd do our little appearance. After that, I'd decided I would mingle for an hour, not a minute less and not a minute longer. At nine o'clock there was an *L.A. Law* marathon on Lifetime, and I intended to be at home, on the couch, when it started.

The cast of *Bunk Eight* trotted into the backstage corral: Whitney Marx, the beautiful lead, and Carolee Rogers, recently cast as her rival, and Willa London, the new bad girl in town. Whitney and Carolee greeted Dave with squeals and hugs, embracing him as if he were a long-lost uncle welcoming them off the boat and into America. Willa gave him a heavy-lidded glare.

"Here we go," said Dave, as the announcer, sounding like a man on the verge of an orgasm, or possibly a stroke, shouted, "And now, the cast and creator of the returning hit series *Bunk Eight!*"

"Let's move," said Dave.

"Yes, massa," Willa drawled. When Dave returned, I stood on my tiptoes to speak into his ear.

"What's up with Willa?"

He grimaced. "She hates white people."

"Good times."

"You know it, sister." Dave sighed, watching Willa, her flawless body displayed in billowing harem pants and a jeweled cropped top, stomp out of the holding area. "I thought we were hiring Halle Berry. Turns out she's Malcolm X. The very first day, she shows up in my office. Wants to know who all the white people at the table read are."

"The executives?" I guessed, remembering all the table reads I'd attended.

"Right-o-rama. Not much I can do about that. Then she tells me she's counted up how many people of color there are—how many cameramen, how many extras—and how many of them are Jewish."

"How would she even know?" I wondered.

"Last names," said Dave. "Of course, the irony is, we're probably more diverse than most of the shows out there." I nodded. *Bunk Eight*'s house director, the man who shot the majority of the shows, was Lannie Dawson, a black man as experienced and respected as Chad. There were two black writers, a black set designer, and a Hispanic assistant director. "So I explain to her that of course we care, and of course we've noticed, and we're doing the best we can to hire people of color, but there just aren't that many of them, and the good ones have their choice of any job they want, and she's giving it right back, talking about my unexamined privilege and how I'm not trying hard enough, and finally, I say, 'Okay, Rosa Parks,' and she looks at me"—Dave leaned close, lowering his voice—"and says, 'Was Rosa Parks one of the girls in the *Charlie's Angels* remake?'"

I closed my eyes. There were no words.

Dave tucked his clipboard under his arm, loosened his tie, and turned to me. "Never mind my privilege problem. I invited you here for a reason," he said.

"You didn't invite me here," I pointed out. "The network did."

He waved one big hand dismissively. "Me, network. It's all the same. We need to talk."

"What now?" In five minutes, I'd be onstage with my cast, and then we'd both have to work, glad-handing foreign reporters and big shots who bought ad time for tampons and Swiffers and weight-loss programs.

"Now." He turned to me, for once managing to look serious. "What is going on with you and my boy?"

I tried to keep my face expressionless. "What do you mean?"

"Every time I mention you, he gets this look." Dave gave a wince that made it seem as if lunch hadn't agreed with him. "And I know he's barely been to your set all week."

"Everything's fine," I said. "He was there for the table read. I've got everything under control."

"Ruth," he said. "Talk to your daddy." He put one heavy hand on my shoulder. "I know you can't be happy about Taryn. The network cast the girl who stole your man away."

"It wasn't like that," I said, blushing. "And really, the issue with Taryn isn't our history. The issue is, she's not very good."

Dave kept talking. "And you had to replace Annie, who we all loved, and you've got the whole Cady situation."

"She's not wearing underpants," I blurted as another clutch of actresses came teetering by.

"I noticed," Dave replied. "So did the shooter from *People* magazine. And don't tell me everything's fine. I know what's going on." He looked at me, for once not tossing off a joke or telling a funny story or doing his impression of his father trying to pass a kidney stone.

I didn't answer. Vaguely, I was aware of movement around me, actresses stepping onto the stage, more actresses taking their place. I heard fabric rustling, heels clicking, fingers snapping, very close to my face. "Um, hello? Earth to Ruthie? Come on! We're up!" Taryn Montaine's breath smelled like olives, and she was standing so close I knew that, if I looked, I'd be able to see the scars from the face-lift she'd lied about having.

"You broke his heart," said Dave . . . but before I could think of what to say, I heard the announcer's voice.

"And now!" he shouted, as the music—"Do You Really Want

More?"—played even louder. I knew the clip they'd show by heart. I'd picked out each scene and edited it myself. There was Nana getting dumped, Cady getting fired, Cady on her Roller-blades, Nana holding Cady's chin in her hand, promising her a big life, the life her mother would have wanted her to have. "The stars and executive producer of the debut comedy *The Next Best Thing*!"

"I have to go," I whispered to Dave, and stepped through the red velvet curtains to stand onstage with the bright lights in my eyes and the cast on either side of me, letting the music and applause wash over me like water.

As soon as I climbed down the steps, my girl-stars gliding ahead of me and Pete ambling behind, Big Dave grabbed me by the elbow and steered me to an empty cocktail table in a corner. "I am going to get you a drink," he announced. "And you are going to tell me what's going on, and we are going to fix this."

I shook my head. I'd already decided that I could give him only the vaguest outline of the situation. I wasn't going to betray Dave's privacy or embarrass myself. Besides, what Dave had said couldn't be true. I hadn't broken Dave's heart. It wasn't possible. By the time Big Dave came back, with two glasses full of clear liquid and ice and wedges of lime, and a plate full of skewered chicken and slices of sushi, I had a speech planned.

"I had a crush on him, and we kind of hooked up, but it's not going to go anywhere," I said. Dave set the plates on the table and put a glass in front of me. I took a sip, tasting sugar and tequila. "So it's really no big deal. Things might be a little tense for a little while, but I'm sure it's not going to cause any problems in the long term."

There, I thought. *Done*. Except Big Dave still wasn't talking. He ate a chunk of a sushi roll, eased chicken off its wooden toothpick with his teeth, chewed, and swallowed. He patted his lips with a napkin and smoothed his hair. Then, finally, he repeated his line from backstage. "You broke his heart."

I shook my head, feeling breathless. "No."

"He told me. Well, not exactly, but he told me you guys fooled around and then you got out of there so fast it was like your ass was on fire and your hair was catching." He gave me a hard look. "If you didn't want to be with a guy in a wheelchair, you shouldn't have started up with him in the first place."

"If I . . . I didn't want . . ." I couldn't process what he was telling me. I could barely speak. "Dave thinks I don't want him because he's in a wheelchair?"

"What else could it be?" Dave asked.

"How about, he already has a girlfriend? How about, I don't want to be the other woman?"

Big Dave waved one big hand dismissively. "The Shazia thing's just for show. He's in love with you."

My heart was swelling. I felt like I'd been pumped full of helium; like at any moment I might lift up off of my chair and start floating. "He is?"

"Duh. And you," he said, shaking one long finger in my face, "should not have hurt him."

"I didn't leave because of the wheelchair." I dropped my voice, my face burning. "It was Rob. Rob didn't want me, and I thought Dave wouldn't, either, once he came to his senses. I thought he was just being nice."

"One dumb-ass model-fucker breaks your heart and you think we're all dogs?" Big Dave shook his head, looking disappointed. "You don't think Dave's any better than Rob Curtis?"

"So he . . . he likes me?"

Dave shook his head, rolling his eyes as if he couldn't believe my folly. "Don't get all junior high on me now. Of course he likes you. You're both smart and funny. You care about the same things, and you're from the same place. Which, now that I think about it, might be the problem. New England. Frickin' Puritans. Repression and witch hunts." He paused, thinking, and then pulled his iPhone from the front pocket of his shirt, which had his initials embroidered in lilac-colored thread on the cuffs. "Question: Could there be a show about a modern-day witch hunt? Maybe set it in Salem, Massachusetts?" Satisfied, he put the phone back in his pocket and said, "Go to him."

"And do what?"

"I don't know. You tell stories for a living. Tell him how you feel. Tell him you're sorry you ran away. Tell him you have herpes."

"What?"

Dave smiled, pleased with himself. "And then tell him you don't, and he'll be so relieved he'll probably propose right on the spot." He looked at me with a puppy-dog expression. "Can I marry you guys? I'll get Internet-ordained and everything."

"One step at a time." I couldn't believe this. I was blushing so hard that my face felt like it might burst into flames. The tablecloth and the billowy white drapes on the wall would catch. Many dead actresses would have to be identified by their dental work or their breast implants' serial numbers. Dave snatched another fistful of food from a passing waiter's tray, then laid his free hand on my shoulder. "Go to him," he said again.

I shook my head. "I need to think."

"No, you don't. You need to get in your Prius and drive over the mountain and tell him how you feel."

I could imagine doing it. I could also imagine Dave opening the door, and seeing Shazia standing behind him . . . or worse, Dave saying politely that he was flattered, but that it was too late . . . or that Big Dave had gotten it wrong, and he'd done what he'd done to comfort me in what was clearly my hour of need; that he didn't like me like that.

"Hey, Ruth!" Cady and Taryn glided toward our table, a pair of goddesses who'd descended from Mount Olympus to walk among the mortals. Cady grabbed my hand as Taryn assumed a hip-sprung pose and batted her long lashes at Big Dave. "We're going dancing. Want to come?"

I blinked at her, at both of them, wondering if they were kidding, if this was some kind of mean joke on the ugly show-runner. Then I chided myself for being cynical, and I thought with longing of my couch, the blanket Grandma had knitted, the *L.A. Law* marathon, how I'd take off my skirt and my Spanx and sink into the quiet of the sofa for what was going to be one of my last nights alone with my grandmother.

"Go to him," Big Dave said. His voice was quiet but insistent.

"I will," I said . . . but I knew that I wouldn't—at least not yet, not until I had some sign, not until I was sure.

I watched Taryn and Cady go, arms linked, laughing, attracting stares with each step. "He doesn't want that," said Big Dave, reading my mind. "He wants you."

"Okay," I said, and slipped my valet ticket out of my clutch. Now or never. Grab for that ring or spend the rest of my life wondering. "Okay."

TWENTY

Dave answered the door before the bell had finished chiming. "Ruthie?" he said, staring at me.

"Hi." I hadn't called or emailed or texted to tell him I was coming. I hadn't wanted to lose my nerve.

"What are you doing here?" he asked.

"I came to apologize. For leaving last time. I didn't mean . . ."

Before I could finish, he'd wheeled a few steps backward, beckoning me inside. He was the most casually dressed I'd seen him, in sweatpants and a plain blue T-shirt, and his feet were bare. "It's fine," he said. "You look very nice. Were you at up-fronts? Everything go okay?"

"Everything was fine," I said, leaving aside for the time being the matter of Cady's ass crevice. "But what I did wasn't fine."

"It's okay," he said again. "Not every girl dreams of Prince Charming riding up in a wheelchair instead of a white horse. I get it."

"No! No, you don't! It's not that at all. I don't care about the wheelchair. I just thought . . . I mean, with Shazia, and all the women before her, you'd come to your senses, and you'd look at me—"

"And see what?" Dave was gazing at me steadily.

Tears sprang to my eyes. "You know," I whispered, and touched my cheek. "You can have anyone. Why would you want me?"

"Because you make me laugh," he said promptly. I couldn't keep from giving a hiccupping sob as two tears trickled down my face. He reached up and took my hands. "Ruthie. I like you so much. When you left . . ." He was looking at me, his face so open, so boyishly hopeful, that it broke my heart. "I thought, *Okay. I'm not what she wants, and she deserves better.*"

"There's nobody better than you!" I went down on my knees and wrapped my arms around his shoulders. He sat there not moving, not returning my embrace. "I thought you didn't want me," I said.

"So it's all a big misunderstanding?" Slowly I felt one of his hands rise until his palm was settled against the small of my back, and then he was pulling me closer.

"Like on a TV show," I said. "Where everyone but the man and the woman know they're in love."

"Sam and Diane."

"Maddie and David."

"Captain Picard and Data."

"You totally just made that up."

"Maybe," he said, and reached down and lifted me up into his lap, as if I were as tiny as a young girl. In that moment, I was back in the hospital, in bed, bandaged and in pain. The room was dark except for the glow of the television set, the theme music from *The Golden Girls. Thank you for being a friend,* I heard—the ring tone I'd assigned my grandmother's calls. In my memory, I could feel the warmth of my grandmother's body beside me, and could smell Camay soap and cigarettes and finally I could let myself sleep, stop fighting the maddening itch of my flesh knitting itself together. I could stop thinking about whatever shot or stitches or surgery came next. In the darkness, in that bed, with my programs and someone who loved me nearby, I was safe. This was like that . . . only better.

I wrapped my arms around his neck as he began wheeling us down the hall. "Why do birds suddenly appear? Every time you are near," he sang in a low and tuneful voice.

I raised my head, looking at him. "Are you singing?"

He didn't answer. He just kept singing. "Just like me," he continued, as we made our way toward the back of the house. "They long to . . . touch your ass." He reached underneath me and gave my bottom a squeeze. At the touch of a button, the glass doors slid open, and then we were outside, in the warm, sweet-smelling night, right in front of the pool. Dave's eyes seemed to darken as he looked at me. "Stand up," he said.

"Do I have to let you go?"

"Just for a minute."

I got off his lap and stood before him. He reached out, grasping the hem of my dress. "Put your arms up."

I felt the muscles of my belly quiver and tighten. He had one hand on my dress. With the other, he reached around and, with a featherlight touch of one fingertip, stroked my spine from the small of my back to the top of my ass.

Oh my God. "Dave," I said weakly. I was trying to picture how my industrial-strength bicycle shorts would look, but before I could think, Dave's fingers were underneath the hem, and my Spanx were on the ground, on top of my dress, and I was standing there, in (thank God) my good black lace bra and panties.

Dave took my hand, brought it to his lips, and kissed it. I could feel his tongue on my knuckles and my knees got weak.

"Follow me," he said, and wheeled away into the pool house. The shower—really, it was more of a wet room, all in azure-and-turquoise tile—was large enough to accommodate a basketball team. There was a built-in bench, that oversize showerhead, nozzles everywhere. Dave turned on the water, adjusting the dials. The room began to fill with steam.

"Come here." Dave's voice was thick and husky, deeper than I'd heard it, and his eyes were intent on my body.

"What are you doing?"

"What I should have done the last time you were over here swimming. I'm not going to let you run away from me this time." He reached for me and took both my hands. "I love you, Ruthie."

I closed my eyes. I didn't answer. I couldn't speak. I thought about Rob. I thought about Gary. I thought about my grandmother, telling me not to be the same fool twice. Then Dave was sliding my panties down my legs, with his face so close I could feel his breath on my skin. I felt his hands on my thighs and his tongue, making its way down my belly, and I forgot everything, every man I'd ever known, every piece of advice I'd ever been given, as he slipped one finger inside of me.

"God, you're so wet," he whispered. He pulled out his finger—I mewled in protest—then he grabbed me around my waist and settled me on his lap. "Lean back," he whispered. I did, letting my head rest against his shoulder as he pushed the cups of my bra down, lifting my breasts up and out, brushing them with his fingertips, then pinching the nipples, first the left one, then the right.

"Oh, God," I groaned. I was squirming in his lap, wanting his fingers back inside of me, wanting to feel his skin against mine. He was kissing my ear, nibbling at the lobe, then moving his lips down the side of my neck, nipping me gently with his teeth, then kissing me.

"My Ruthie."

My eyes filled with tears. That was all I wanted—to be his Ruthie, his girl. "Please," I whispered. "Oh, please."

"You want this?" His voice was soft. "You want me?"

"Please," I said again, and started to cry. *I'm so ugly. I don't deserve you. You could never love me.* I tried to stand, seized, once again, by the impulse to run before I got hurt, but he held me in place in his lap. He was so strong . . . even broken, even crippled, so strong. He pulled me against his chest, all warm skin and hair and muscle. "Please don't."

"Don't what?" he breathed in my ear, biting my lobe again.

"Please don't break my heart," I whispered.

"Never," he said, trailing tiny kisses down my neck, over the scars on my shoulder, the puckered pink flesh that I always kept covered. "I'll never break your heart. I want to take care of you, for as long as you'll let me."

"Okay," I whispered, thinking, *This isn't happening. This is some other girl's fairy tale, someone else's happy ending.*

"Stand up."

For a moment, I wasn't sure my legs would work—they were so wobbly, and I was so wet. Dave gave me a gentle push, and I was on my feet.

He gripped my hips, then reached around, brushing my clitoris with the ball of his thumb. I groaned, pushing against him, thinking, *More, more, oh, God, more.*

"Get in the shower." On shaky legs, I did as he commanded. "Stand against the glass. I want to look at you." I pushed myself forward, arching my back, feeling the cool glass on my breasts, the warm water beating down on my skin, my hair, raining down my back. On the other side of the glass, I could see him taking me in, all of me—my breasts, my thighs, my skin, my scars—and I saw nothing on his face except love, adoration, excitement. It was the way Maurice looked at my grandmother, the way my father looked at my mother in the wedding picture that I kept and carried and put on the set, the way Big Dave, for all his teasing, looked at Molly, his wife, and Paul and Claire, my married writing team, looked at each other when they thought no one was looking at them.

"You are so beautiful," he said.

"Come in here with me."

"Be patient."

I nodded, dizzy with arousal, loving the way he was taking charge, telling me what to do with none of Gary's fretful delicacy, his questions of *Is this all right?* I'd never imagined anything like this, never imagined feeling this way.

"Spread your legs. Close your eyes." I did what he told me. Over the concussive beat of the spray, pulsing from the jets, I imagined that I could hear his chair inching forward, clothes hitting the ground . . . and then Dave was sitting on the bench behind me. One of his hands was gripping my bottom. He slid the forefinger of his other hand inside of me, then pulled it out, brushing it against my clit. I felt my thighs and belly clenching, felt my orgasm spiraling up from deep inside of me. Just when I was trembling on the brink, eyes shut, mouth open, he pulled his hand away.

"No," I groaned as he reached up and held my breasts, cupping them firmly, then tugging at the nipples.

"Sit on my lap," he whispered, and he kissed me, his tongue slipping into my mouth, the water pounding down on top of us.

"Dave," I said. "I love you."

He slipped one finger inside of me, then two . . . and then, with his free hand, he pulled the shower nozzle out of its holster. I felt the teasing brush of the water on my neck, my shoulders, my breasts, as I leaned my head back against his shoulder. "Oh," I said as I felt the water pulsing between my legs. "Oh, God."

"Now," he breathed in my ear, his fingers working between my legs, his lips against my neck. "Now."

"Oh," I said. It felt like I was lighting up, from my toes to my calves to my knees, my thighs, my hips, my belly, all of me filling with fire. I managed to say his name once, and then as the spasms shook my body, I couldn't say anything at all.

When I could move again, I turned around and looked at him. "Oh my God," I whispered. "What was that?"

Dave was looking at me with something like wonder on his face. "Bedroom," he said hoarsely, and I pushed myself up and out of the water, and held his hand as we hurried into the house, me on my bare feet and Dave on his wheels, both of us moving as fast as we could.

TWENTY-ONE

When I woke up the next morning Dave was propped on one elbow, looking at me. "Money's on the bedside table," he said. I felt my heart stop. "I'm kidding," Dave said, and started to laugh, his familiar dry *Heh heh heh.* "Oh, my Lord, the look on your face!"

"You're hilarious," I said, and whacked him with a pillow. "Have you ever thought about comedy?"

He grabbed my hand and pushed it up over my head. He was so strong. I could still hardly believe it. My body was still ringing like a struck chime. I wondered what he was experiencing, if he felt the way I did, at least in the parts of his body that could still feel. Maybe sex was just more intellectual when you had no sensation from the waist down. I'd have to ask him about it. I wasn't sure, but I thought we'd have time.

But before I could ask him anything, there was something I needed answered.

"Dave," I said. "What about Shazia?"

He tucked my head under his arm, kissed my cheek, and said, "Shazia and I aren't really a couple."

I gaped at him. "What do you mean?"

"She's gay."

My mouth dropped open. "What?"

"Her parents are born-again Christians. Super-conservative. She has a partner, a talent manager, and they live a very private life. But she's not ready to be out. Because of her parents, mostly."

"So you're . . . what? Her beard?"

He nodded, slightly shamefaced.

"That is so old-school," I murmured. "But don't you want . . ." I groped for the words. "Haven't you been lonely?"

He shook his head. "I have the writers' room."

Me, I thought. *You have me.* "But what did you do about . . ." I stopped, remembering what Big Dave had said, back during my first week of work. "He pays for escorts," Big Dave had announced, tossing his light saber from one hand to the other. "Which is painful for a penny-pinching WASP from New England. First, there's the shame of admitting you even want to have sex. Then there's the pain of having to pay for it."

"You probably saw the swimsuits in the pool house," he began. I swallowed. For a moment, I was tempted to tell him to stop, to ask him not to say any more, certain that I didn't want to hear what was coming.

"Sometimes I have women over. Escorts," he said, in case I couldn't fill in that blank on my own. "I watch them swim. And then sometimes I watch them do other things I tell them to do."

Other things. Oh, boy. I pictured beautiful women gliding through the water like mermaids, shedding their swimsuits as they went. I imagined them in the shower, with the handheld nozzles, maneuvering their bodies against the glass as Dave told them what to do. "So you're a director," I said, and laughed at his expression, surprised and amused.

"I never really thought of it that way."

"Was this what you liked before the accident?" I asked.

Dave's brow furrowed. "Interesting question," he said. "I'm not sure. I hadn't had a lot of girlfriends before then."

"Why not?"

"Oh, I was shy. And I was short. Runt of the litter." He shook his head. "It bothered me when I was younger. Before I knew I'd spend the rest of my life sitting down." He cupped my cheek, smiling fondly. "So do you think you're ready for an introduction into the wonderful world of catheters and Viagra?"

"I've seen the ads for Cialis," I told him. "The one with the old dude and the lady in the bathtubs. It looks like fun. What's the big deal?"

"For starters, you have to take it two hours in advance of when you expect there to be . . . activity. I'm not an optimist, but I can't tell you the number of times I've gone to sleep on my back."

I laughed as I looked at him, with his hair uncharacteristically mussed, in a plain white T-shirt and plaid pajama bottoms. His hair was thinning on top, and his upper and lower bodies looked as if they belonged to two different people, a fitness buff grafted on top of a couch-bound grandpa, and I loved him so completely, loved every part of him, the way his ears were a little pointed on top, the light brown hair on his forearms and on his toes. I fitted my body against his, smelling soap, the hay-and-sunshine smell of his skin. In the morning light, his eyes were clear and pale blue, and I could see the ghost of freckles on his nose. I touched his cheek with my fingertips and was encouraged when he didn't move away.

"So what now?"

"Get up," he said, and swatted my rump lightly. "I'll toast you a bagel. Then you'd better get to work." He glanced at his phone, plugged in on the table next to his bed. "And I should, too."

"Can't we both just call in sick?" His hand was still on my bottom, and I felt myself start to flush, remembering the night before: *Touch yourself there. Let me see you. Keep your eyes open. Look at me.*

I reached for him, pulling him close, letting my mouth linger on the underside of his jaw. He flipped me over and eased me onto my back, and I wondered, with a dizzy, wonderful lurching feeling, if we were going to start again. With Gary, the sex was over when he was . . . but now, blissful possibilities unfolded in my mind. What was sex like with someone for whom there wasn't necessarily the end point of an orgasm? I couldn't wait to find out.

But, instead of kissing me or fondling my breasts, Dave lay down beside me, tracing the scars on my shoulder with his finger.

"Did it hurt?" he asked. His voice was so full of concern that my eyes prickled.

"The operations did. The accident, I can't remember." I looked down at his legs. "How about you?"

"Ah," he said. "Did Big Dave ever tell you the story?"

"He told me a little. I know that you were in a sailboat, and you got hit by a guy who was in a powerboat, and he was drunk when he hit you. He'd been in trouble before, and he went to jail."

"Ten years. Down to eight, with time off for good behavior. Go forth and sin no more." Dave paused. "He said it was a blessing."

This was news that hadn't appeared in the paper, news that Big Dave had not shared. "You talked to him?"

"We were pen pals, I guess you could say. When he was in jail. He earned his GED, got about halfway toward a bachelor's degree, and he finished it at CCCC—that's Cape Cod Community College—after he was out." He gave me his small, tucked-in smile. "And I got a year-long deferral from law school and came out here."

"Lucky for me," I said, and took his hand.

"Lucky for me," Dave said. "If it hadn't been for the accident, then Craig—that's the guy who hit me—would never have gotten his college degree, never gotten sober, never met his wife, and I'd be another miserable lawyer."

"So you're saying . . ." I rolled away from him, propped myself up on one elbow, and looked down at his dear, handsome face. In her bed in the corner, Pocket stood up, yawning as she stretched.

"I remember," Dave continued, "one of my philosophy professors once said that 'Why do we suffer?' is the question that's driven every religion that's ever lasted."

"So what's the answer?" I asked. "Why do we suffer? What does it mean? What is it for?"

Dave thought for a moment, his eyes on the ceiling, fingers drumming on the comforter. "I don't remember," he said. "I think I dropped the class." He shook his head at the memory of his college-age self. "I only signed up in the first place because I thought I was in love with this girl, and she was a philosophy major."

I tucked myself against him, my head on his chest, my hip against his hip, my strong, tanned legs hooked over his pale, thin ones.

"Maybe it's like running. You do it because it feels so good when it stops. Maybe there's suffering because it makes us appreciate the good things more."

He bent down and kissed my forehead, gathering me against him. My body stirred in response. I could feel that familiar heady thrum between my legs, and I shivered, wondering if we'd have time for more.

"Want that bagel?" he asked, looking at the time again.

"Are you buying?"

"In the kitchen," he said, and used his arms and shoulders to swing himself out of the bed and into the chair. "Come along."

I found one of his T-shirts and a pair of boxers in the dresser drawer and pulled them on, then walked down the sunny hallway, with Pocket trotting briskly behind me, thinking that maybe everything balanced. There was suffering, and there was joy, and maybe, just maybe, amid the wreckage of what I'd thought I wanted most, there was still a chance for me to grab some happiness, to snatch victory from the jaws of defeat.

TWENTY-TWO

After the director rolled his eyes and yelled, "Cut!"; after the warm-up guy hollered, "That's a thank you and good night" and played "Hit the Road, Jack"; after the studio audience filed out the doors; after the actors had taken their final bows and driven off into the night, I went back to the writers' room.

It was almost two in the morning. The bungalow was dark and deserted. The cleaning crew had come and gone, tossing the pizza boxes and plastic cups we'd used to drink a Champagne toast before showtime. I scavenged a clean cup from the pantry, found the bottle of Scotch that the Daves had sent over, gift-wrapped, that morning, and sat at my desk with the lights off, the computer displaying its coruscating screensaver, waves of color rolling from violet to blue and back again. I could hear a breeze through the windows, and the refrigerator's clicks and churns. The rooms smelled like furniture polish and fresh flowers—everyone's agent had sent bouquets that morning, and the outer office was filled with enough roses and lilies to stock a funeral. I spun the bottle cap loose and poured myself a shot. It burned going down, first painfully, then pleasantly. I refilled the cup, leaned back in my chair, and lifted it in a toast. "Here's to me," I said, and swallowed.

I felt wired and jittery, exhausted and exhilarated, and underneath all that, deeply, deeply afraid. I was afraid that the show was turning into a disaster and that there was no way for me to stop it, to stem the tide or turn the ship or hit REBOOT and start things over again. I was Mickey in the sorcerer's hat, and the brooms had danced away from me. All I could do was wring my hands and watch them go, and worry that what I was putting out into the universe not only would fail to comfort the girls I'd imagined, the girls like me, but would actively harm them.

I took another swallow of Scotch, rocked back in my chair, and shook my head. Having survived the development process, the pilot shoot, the test results, and the decisions that had followed, having fired Annie Tait and dealt with Cady's weight loss and Pete's crippling stage fright, I thought I'd been prepared for every species of trouble that could come with today's pilot reshoots, with an audience in the seats, executives in the green-room, picking at their catered dinners, and my gum-chewing director tanned and rested and ready to earn his pay (three times as much per episode as I was getting—I'd checked).

I'd arrived at the lot early that morning, my car freshly vacuumed, hair straightened, makeup on, wearing the short-sleeved black cotton dress with a mock turtleneck that I'd bought for the occasion, carrying the lunch that Dave had packed for me, my body still ringing from our morning's session in the shower. I strode across the parking lot and knocked on Cady's dressing-room door, waiting for her wan "What?" before I stepped inside.

Cady was standing in front of the mirror, in paint, as I'd learned the actors said when they were made up for the cameras, and in costume: the navy-blue skirt, high-heeled pumps, and a white blouse with a froth of flounces covering the buttons that she'd worn in the first scene, the one at the restaurant in Boston, right before she got fired. Underneath the clothes she'd worn six weeks ago, Cady wore a padded corset, which returned her body to an approximation of what it had once been. Her waist, cinched by a dark-blue leather belt, was still tiny, but she'd been amplified fore and aft, with the curves of her bosoms straining the buttons of the blouse, and a bottom round and ripe as a peach pushing at the seams of the skirt.

"You look . . ." I was about to say *amazing*. True, it was padding, a Hollywood lie, but Cady appeared just the way I'd hoped she would when I'd imagined the character, cute and curvy and, if you didn't look too long at her scrawny, corded neck, or the sharp angles of her cheeks and her jaw, absolutely adorable. We had, after tense negotiation and lengthy phone calls, reached a compromise: She'd wear the padding for the first three episodes, then a little less padding for the next two, and so forth, until she wasn't wearing anything extra at all. It wasn't what I wanted. It wasn't what Cady wanted. It was only the best we could do.

"You look beautiful," I said.

"I look *awful*," said Cady, and burst into tears. She turned away from the mirror and collapsed onto the couch, sobbing and, undoubtedly, ruining the work it had taken the makeup artist an hour and a half to complete. Her mother shot me the look of You Have Made My Child Suffer and I Will See You Burn in Hell, then knelt beside her daughter, patting Cady's shoulders and talking quietly. *Awful*, I thought as my fingertips went to my cheek. Cady Stratton wouldn't know awful if it sat on her face . . . and here she was, whining about how horrible it was to wear padding that made her look no worse than normal, like the girl she'd been for most of her life.

"It's like, I worked so hard . . . not to be that girl anymore," Cady gasped between sobs. "And . . . now . . . I . . . have . . . to . . . be . . . her . . . again!"

I couldn't keep from shaking my head. It was crazy. Even with the padding, Cady was still smaller than the average woman in America. I wanted to grab her by the shoulders and shake her until her teeth rattled, tell her to quit crying, to grow up already, to do her job and play the part that she'd signed up to play. Instead, I patted her back, feeling the straps of the corset, stiff underneath her blouse.

"I know that this isn't what you want," I said as her mother continued to scowl at me. "But Cady, this is what you agreed to."

"I . . . can't . . . stand . . . to see . . . myself . . . this way!"

"You look beautiful!"

"I . . . look . . . disgusting!" The walls of the dressing room echoed with the sounds of her despair. She lifted her head and glared at me, looking me right in the eye . . . but no, I realized. That was wrong. She was looking me right in the scars. "I look like a fat, disgusting *freak!*"

"Oh, sweetie," said her mom. Cady's mother's name was Martha, and she'd worked at a Kroger supermarket when her children were young. When Cady had been cast on her first TV show, Martha had left her husband and younger children and moved to Los Angeles to be her daughter's manager. She'd spent the past decade on Cady's payroll, an unhealthy dynamic even for the most stable and well-adjusted of people, in whose company I wasn't sure Martha belonged. Now Martha lived in a town house in Toluca Lake that Cady had paid for. She wasn't a manager or an agent . . . more like a paid companion whose job—quote-unquote—was spending days with her daughter on the set. That, and shopping. As she hovered over Cady's prone and weeping form, I noted that Martha's sunglasses were Chanel, and her quilted white leather purse, on a length of gold chain, also sported the interlocking *C*s. She wore a Tory Burch caftan, white Prada jeans, and Kate Spade slides, all with their logos and brand names clearly visible. The Tiffany charm bracelet around her left wrist bore a silver heart engraved *Love Always, Cady*.

Cady sniffled. Martha glared at me, furious that I was upsetting her daughter, and, no doubt, terrified that the aforementioned upset might bring the gravy train to a grinding halt, that Cady would cry herself out of a job and she'd be back to slicing honey ham in Minnesota.

None of this was my concern. Cady's future, on the big screen or small, was none of my business. Nor were Martha's feelings. All I cared about was getting Cady Stratton to play the part I'd written, and that meant sucking it up and wearing the goddamn pads that pushed her all the way to a goddamn size eight.

"Cady," I began, "you look beautiful. A million girls in America would kill to look the way you do. And, like I keep saying, it's so important for those girls to see someone on TV, someone who's gorgeous and funny and smart . . ." *Or, at least, someone who can act smart on TV.* "A girl like you who's the star of the show," I concluded. At this point, I could recite the speech by heart. I'd given it to her, and to various executives, from Loud Lloyd on up the food chain, at least a dozen times in the weeks since brunch at The Alcove, making the case as to why skinny Cady Stratton needed to pretend to be at least slightly curvy, if only for the first few episodes.

"I hate this!" Cady wailed. "I can't stand it!"

Her mother grabbed me by the elbow and steered me outside. "Are you sure we have to do it this way?" she asked, the way she'd asked me sixteen times before. "Cady worked so hard to lose the weight. Can't you just let her be who she is?"

"Going forward, we can adjust the padding like we talked about, but for tonight she's got to wear it, so we have at least a chance of matching the way she looked in the pilot."

The two of us stared at each other, Martha in her thousands of dollars of designer finery, me in my clogs and the dress that I'd bought, online and on sale, on the off chance that anyone would be looking at me instead of at our stars when we taped.

"She's not happy," said Martha.

"I can see that. And I'm sorry. But this is the part—"

"That she signed up for. Right. She knows. We both know. You've made it very clear." Martha turned on her heel and slammed the dressing-room door behind her. Approximately ten seconds later, my telephone buzzed. It was Cady's manager, the breathy, useless Justin. I hit IGNORE and made my way to my third stop of the morning.

I knocked on the door of Pete's trailer. No answer. I banged louder. Still nothing. "Hey!" I hollered, aware that grips and makeup artists and assorted extras were all staring, along with the cute guy driving the forklift filled with potted plants to the soundstage next to ours, where they shot *It Grows On You*, a comedy about three women who worked at a family nursery in Maine.

"*Pete!*" I yelled, past shame, past caring, and pounded at the door until my hands stung. One of the makeup artists poked her head out of the room next door.

"Hey," she said. "You need a key?"

I took it gratefully and gave one final knock. "Pete!" I yelled. "It's Ruth! I'm coming in now!" I unlocked the door and stepped into a marijuana-scented sauna. The smoke was so thick I could barely see my feet, the air so warm that my face and back were instantly running with sweat, and the music—I thought it might have been Phish—was so loud that every note made my bones ache. "Pete?" I called, coughing and squinting, fanning at the fog. "Pete?"

"Hey! Ruth! I'm over here!" he hollered above the booming bass. I blinked . . . and there was Pete, clad in a skimpy Speedo and nothing else, his torso gleaming with sweat and his arms stretched over his head. As I watched, he windmilled his arms down into triangle pose.

"Bikram yoga!" he yelled. "Clears my head!"

I located the stereo and turned the music down. I spied a

tiny window and cranked it open. I found a joint, still lit and resting on the lip of the clamshell that Pete used as an ashtray, and pinched it out. Pete appeared not to notice as he proceeded through a series of sun salutations.

"I do my own practice," he said, positioning his right foot on the inside of his left thigh, then twisting his arms into a pretzel. "For a while, I was working with a yogini in Beverly Hills, but that got complicated." From his leer, I deduced that the complications had something to do with sex.

"We need you onstage in an hour," I told him, fanning at the air in a vain attempt to shoo the smoke out the window.

"No worries." He nodded toward the coffee table, where he'd set out the classic stoner's emergency kit: a bottle of Visine, a gallon jug filled with water, a towel, a Speed Stick, and the clothes, still in dry cleaner's plastic, that he was supposed to wear for the first scene. He gave me a cheeky grin. "You don't have to worry about me." His smile widened. "I hear you've got other things to worry about."

Reflexively I glanced at my phone, wondering why everyone on the show—the stars, their managers, their mothers—seemed to know what was going on before I did. In the five minutes since I'd left Cady's dressing room, I'd logged five missed calls, four from Team Cady and the fifth from Loud Lloyd. As I watched, the screen lit up with another incoming call, this one from Joan at the network. I hit IGNORE as the door to the back room of Pete's trailer opened and a face peeked out. I turned away, wanting to give him and his girl of the hour some privacy, but I'd seen enough to recognize Penny Weaver's bright-red hair and guilty face.

I spun around in shock. The door was shut. Pete stood there, wearing nothing but his Speedo and a shit-eating grin. "No," I said.

He shrugged modestly.

"No way," I said.

"It's show-mance," he said, eradicating any hopes that what I'd glimpsed was innocent, simply one actor generously sharing his space with his castmate.

I took him by the hand, the way Grandma had done with me when I was young, and dragged him, still mostly naked, out into the sun. "Listen to me," I hissed. "This is unacceptable."

He gave me a lazy shrug. "I like older women."

"She's seventy-two." At least that was what she admitted to. IMDB had her at seventy-four, the *Los Angeles Times* had printed that she was seventy-five. Was this some kind of dare? A bet? Was Pete trying to fill some kind of sexual bingo card?

"You ever read what Ben Franklin said about older women? 'In the dark, all cats are gray.'"

"You aren't a cat! And neither is Penny!"

"Whatever. Listen, don't worry. We're both grown-ups." He gave my shoulder a squeeze and then turned, walking back into his dressing room.

"But she's old enough to be your . . ." He waved at me, easing his dressing-room door shut. "Grandmother," I finished. Pete was gone, no one was listening, and my telephone was ringing again, with Loud Lloyd's name flashing on the screen. I didn't know whether to laugh, cry, or cut my losses and get in my car and start driving back to Hancock Park, maybe even back to Framingham. I lifted the phone to my ear. "Hello?"

I knew what he'd say before he said it: After sixteen times of telling Cady that she had to suck it up and play the part I'd written, the network had caved. Instead of redoing just the scenes with the recast Nana Trudy and the new characters the network had added, we'd be reshooting the entire pilot. "It's easier this way," Loud Lloyd boomed. *Easier for whom?* I wondered. Next door, my star was probably tearing off her padding, hugging her mother, and congratulating herself on how she'd defeated the hateful and foolishly stubborn showrunner, not caring that *The Next Best Thing* was now just another sitcom starring just another pretty thin girl.

"It's not such a big deal, really," Joan said when she got on the line. I didn't respond. She didn't seem to notice. "You need to look at this as a blessing in disguise. You'll get people tuning in just to see how Cady looks, or to figure out how she lost the weight."

"I'm going to have to get started on the rewrites," I said. There was no point in arguing, in making my case yet again. By now, I knew the sound of a done deal when I heard it. *Enjoy this,* I heard Dave saying in my head, back at the kickoff dinner, before things had started their downhill slide . . . and at that moment, I wished I could hit REWIND, send time spinning backward until I arrived at the moment when the story of Daphne and Nana existed only in my head. I wished it as fervently as I'd wished for the show to get picked up, what felt like such a long time ago.

"Take your time," said Joan, all sweet accommodation. "Just send the pages as soon as you've got them."

"Okay." I hung up and walked into the writers' bungalow, thinking longingly of the half-smoked joint in Pete's dressing room. That, of course, was when Taryn Montaine came around the corner, wearing stovepipe jeans and a racerback tank top that left her arms and shoulders bare. A broad-brimmed straw sunhat shadowed her face; sunglasses covered her eyes. On her left ring finger was a diamond the size of a smallish walnut. Her right hand was entwined with the fingers of her husband, Rob Curtis.

A jolt went through me, and my hand went reflexively to my hair, tugging it against my cheek. I hadn't seen Rob in person since our night together. I'd seen pictures in magazines, You-Tube videos, and interviews he'd done on red carpets, at Taryn's side. If I'd been hoping for physical devastation, a bald spot, weight gain, maybe the loss of a limb or two, I'd have been disappointed. Rob looked the way he always did—tanned and fit and handsome, with a curving, cynical smile. His hair was still dark and thick, his chest solid underneath his T-shirt. His jeans and unlaced black Chuck Taylors could have been the same pants and shoes he'd worn when we'd worked on *The Girls' Room*, but I knew that he ordered them in bulk and replaced them every six months. Once, I'd been the one to place the orders, sign for the boxes, unwrap the clothes and shoes, and recycle the cardboard. Once.

"Hi, boss!" Taryn called, making me think yet again that she hadn't bothered to learn my name.

"Hi, Taryn." Then, because I saw no way of avoiding it, I made myself face him. "Hi, Rob." I waited for my stomach to clench, for my face to get hot, for my eyes to start burning with shameful tears, but instead I felt nothing . . . nothing but the memory of Dave's arms around me, his lips against my neck, whispering, *Good morning, beautiful,* and me, not doubting for an instant that he meant it. *He doesn't get to win,* I thought, and straightened my back. I had a man, and I had a show, and he had nothing except a future with the unpleasant ditz he'd chosen over me.

He had the good grace to look embarrassed as he lifted a hand in greeting. "Hey, Ruth. Congratulations on everything."

"You, too," I said. Rob squirmed. He didn't look like the happily married husband and father, a TV writer on top of the world. He looked like a man with no job except holding his wife's purse while she went to work.

Taryn, meanwhile, was looking from her husband to me. "Omigod," she said. "Do you two know each other?"

"We worked together," I said. "I was a writer on *The Girls' Room* a while back."

You could almost hear the wheels turning ever so slowly as she considered what was clearly new information. "Omigod," she said again. "I remember you!"

"Great," I said, not adding that she'd found my face so offensive that she'd asked the showrunner to have someone else deliver her scripts to her dressing room.

Taryn was frowning, her brain, such as it was, still hard at work. "So, you were an assistant? And then you wrote for *The Girls' Room*? And then you wrote this show?"

"You got it."

"Ro-ob," she said, turning to her husband with a whine it was hard to imagine even the most besotted man could find charming. "Why don't you write me a show?"

His smile thinned, and his voice sounded strained as he answered, "That would be something, wouldn't it?"

"Then," she said, "we could be together every day!" She swung their linked hands upward, pretending to smack him in the nose, giggling. From the way he winced, I wondered how hard that fake smack had been. Then I wondered what he was doing here. Didn't he have work of his own, an office to go to? I was startled to realize that I didn't know the answer. I hadn't checked. I knew that *The Girls' Room* had been canceled after eight so-so seasons, but I hadn't taken the step of Googling to figure out where Rob had landed, or if he was working anywhere at all. Which meant that time had done what time was supposed to do. My wounds were healed. I'd moved on. It was almost enough to make me smile. It was the brightest moment of my day . . . that, and when we'd finally finished the reshoots, and my grandmother had gotten out of her seat in the front row with a bouquet of roses in her arms.

Standing on her tiptoes, in a vintage shirtwaist of crisp pale-blue cotton, she'd hugged me, whispering, "I'm so proud," in my ear. At that moment, whatever hard feelings were left between us, the lingering anger over my failure to be ecstatic about her

wedding, or the changes Nana Trudy's character had undergone, seemed to finally disappear. Grandma turned, with her
arm around my waist, guiding me to the center of the stage, into
the spotlight where the actors stood. "Hey, Ruthie!" said Pete,
amiable as ever. Cady had narrowed her eyes, clearly unhappy
about sharing the attention, and Taryn had shot us a poison-
ous glance before continuing to wave at the crowd. Grandma
ignored them both. She raised her voice over the audience members and extras, the blare of the music and the executives' conversation. "Everyone!" she'd yelled. "This is my granddaughter.
She wrote the show!" For one moment, I basked in the applause,
halfhearted and puzzled though it was, and let myself imagine
that things had gone better: that I'd gotten the star I'd wanted,
that Cady hadn't gotten skinny and then ruined multiple takes
by giggling and posing like she was at a photo shoot for *Playboy*,
that Pete, God love him, with his lines scribbled on his hands
and his wrists, hiding pages of his script in the newspaper he was
leafing through onstage, had learned the words he was supposed
to say.

Little victories. Small moments. I'd tucked my grandmother's roses into a vase and set them on my desk, a visible reminder
that this endeavor had not been a complete disaster. I had written a show that would be on TV. That was something. I poured
myself another drink and stared up at the poster on my wall.
There was Cady Stratton standing in the living room, one arm
flung over her head in carefree, girlish abandon. She wore an
apron and held a whisk in one hand and a mixing bowl tucked
against her hip. Penny Weaver stood slightly behind her, looking on with an expression of mingled anxiety and pride. Cady's
hips had been Photoshopped to reflect a compromise between
the girl I'd hired and the girl I'd wound up with (cost of said
digital manipulation: $30,000), and I'd spent three tense hours
on the phone with Penny's management, negotiating the size of

the font in which her name would appear, and precisely how far behind Cady she would be standing. "They're Going to Make It After All!" read the copy over their heads, in what I worried was a blatant and lawsuit-baiting rip-off of *The Mary Tyler Moore Show* (the executives had assured me it was fine). Underneath Cady's skirt was the title of the show: THE NEXT BEST THING. My name appeared nowhere on the poster, because people didn't tune in to TV shows because of their creators; they came for the same reasons they went to planetariums—in short, to see the stars.

I wandered out to my assistant's desk and sat in her chair. There was an economy-sized jar of Advil in her drawer. I took two, then a bottle of water from the pantry. My phone trilled in my purse.

"Ruthie?"

I felt myself smile, and suddenly everything I'd been worried about—the taping, the ratings, whether we'd last past our initial airing—didn't seem to matter as much. "Hey."

"You coming home?"

I grabbed my keys, my water, and flicked out the lights. "As soon as I can."

TWENTY-THREE

The first review of *The Next Best Thing* appeared in *Variety* the morning of our premiere. "*The Next Best Thing*," read the headline. "If the Title's True, We're All in Trouble." I was at home, in my bedroom, where I'd returned after spending two nights in a row at Dave's house, telling myself that I needed to play at least the tiniest bit hard to get. Besides, he had his poker game, and I could watch *Grey's Anatomy* with my grandmother, let her feed me, and smile, looking smug, when she asked about my "young man."

I clicked away from the page as fast as I could and collapsed onto my bed, the very spot where I'd gotten the news about our pickup, with my fists pressed against my eyes, trying to un-see what I'd seen. Then, feeling numb, I made my way to my car, put my cell phone on speaker, and dialed Two Daves Productions as I began my drive to the lot. "Help," I said when Big Dave got on the line.

"Oh, Jesus," he said in disgust. "Are you reading the reviews? Have we taught you nothing?"

"Where are you? Can I stop by the offices?"

"I'm meeting Dave at a thing," said Big Dave. "Pitch meeting."

"*Time-Share*?" I asked.

"Huh? Oh, no. It's a new reality show. Scripted reality. Well, semi-scripted. *Butterface.*"

I pulled onto the freeway. "Please tell me you're kidding."

"Nope. It's *The Biggest Loser* meets *Extreme Makeover* meets *The Bachelor.* Twelve women with great bodies but, um, less attractive facial features live in a house together, where they compete for dates and plastic surgery."

"And this is going to be a Two Daves show?"

"Hey, listen, if we're involved, at least it won't be totally degrading. And quit with the reviews! They don't matter," he said. "People just tune in because they want to see the stars, or because someone told them it was interesting."

"*Butterface.*"

"Shut up," said Dave. "Word of mouth matters. Ad campaigns matter. Name recognition matters. Not reviews. Not for TV."

"I know." I pulled onto the exit for Ventura Boulevard and then stopped at the light. "So how bad is it?"

"Hang on," Dave grumbled. I waited, my heart beating painfully, while he accessed his iPhone and then hummed as he read. "It's actually not terrible," he finally reported. "I've seen worse. The *Times* thinks you're solid. *Variety*, not so much."

"So is there any kind of consensus?" I asked, thinking that if all the critics said the same thing—that Cady was terrible, that Penny was written too broadly, that the music wasn't right or the laugh track was too intrusive—it would actually be helpful. I could fix the things that everyone agreed were wrong. But as I suspected and Dave confirmed, there was no agreement among the half-dozen outlets that had reviewed the pilot. A few of the critics had loved Cady's performance; a few had found it grating and lazy. For everyone who'd written that the show was cheesy and obvious, someone else had found it a charming throwback.

Everyone had picked on something different . . . and no one, I discerned, had said that it was great.

"Listen to this," said Dave. "The guy at the *L.A. Times* says that the writing has 'a tart sharpness' and 'a refreshing verve.' "

"Sounds like we're a grapefruit," I said. "And I feel a 'but.' "

"Do you want to read them yourself?" Dave demanded.

"I promise you, I do not," I said. The light changed, and I turned onto Ventura. My plan was to stop at Big Sugar Bakeshop to pick up a box of doughnut muffins for the writers' room, and get to my office early enough to sit with a cup of tea and figure out what I'd say to all the people who had probably seen the same reviews I'd heard by now. "See you at the party?"

"Wouldn't miss it," said Dave as I pulled up to the curb, plugged quarters into the meter, and walked into the store. The girl behind the counter smiled at me; the security guard, a guy named Cliff, didn't look at me like I had a communicable disease; and I was feeling almost cheerful by the time the writers showed up. I greeted them with a calm look on my face and a box of baked goods in my hands. The truth was, the reviews might have been truly devastating if I didn't know that at the end of the day I could go home to Dave and tell him all about it.

"So listen," I began. "I know that some of the reviews have been a little mixed, and I'm sure you guys all know that they don't really matter much. People in Connecticut or Ohio aren't going to tune in or not tune in because of what *Variety* says. They're going to tune in because they want to see Cady Stratton looking skinny, or because Pete Paxton's a hottie, or because the promos were funny, or whatever they normally watch on Wednesday nights is a rerun."

"Or because the batteries in their remote are dead, and they couldn't change the channel even if they wanted to," said George.

"Hey. People who can't figure out their remotes count, too.

And the bottom line is this: We can't worry about the things we can't control." I looked around the table, making eye contact with each one of them. "We did the best we could with what we had. And today we're going to write the best script we can, and have the best run-through we can, and the best party. The rest of it's out of our hands."

"Will there be a moon bounce?" asked Sam, who evidently had confused *launch party* with *rave*.

"No, but there will be an open bar, and a face painter." I'd been surprised to learn that the network was not throwing us a premiere party. I'd assumed that they'd footed the bill for the catered bashes I'd attended at the start of both seasons of *Bunk Eight* I'd been around for, but the Daves had been quick to inform me that they'd paid the bills themselves. The network couldn't afford to drop thousands of dollars on each new show, especially since the majority of them wouldn't last past a season. So I'd unlimbered my pen and my checkbook and invited everyone, cast and crew and writers and spouses and their kids, knowing, even though it hurt to think about it, that the party I was planning could be both a celebration and a farewell.

Qué será, será, I told myself as we worked through the morning, the atmosphere strangely quiet, charged and subdued, like the calm before a thunderstorm rolls in, as if we were a room full of prisoners awaiting the executioner's blade, or a phone call from the governor. When we broke for lunch, Reilly, my line producer, was waiting at my office door with folders in his hands. "We need to pick a goat," he said.

"Ah." Next week we'd be shooting an episode in which Daphne dated a self-righteous locavore, a fellow who raised his own chickens and made his own goat cheese. In my office, Reilly fanned out a bunch of eight-by-eleven photographs on my desk. I looked down at them, puzzled.

"The goats have head shots?" I asked.

"Yup," said Reilly, who was excellent at his job but did not have much of a sense of humor. "Any specific look we're going for?"

"Goat-like. Goatish. Goatka-esque."

"How about a particular color? Do you want one with horns? Does the gender of the goat matter?"

"Not really," I said. "You can pick."

Reilly frowned. "You don't want to watch their reels?"

I opened my mouth, then shut it. Of course the goats had reels. "You know what? Let's just stick to Hollywood tradition. Hire the skinniest one."

He left my office. I shook my head, ordered my lunch, and tapped out a text to Dave. *I just hired a goat.*

Replaced me already? he wrote back.

I grinned. *It's a very talented goat. Good look. Good manners.*

He's just using you, Dave wrote back. *I've seen the goats out here. I know how they operate. Give him a day, he'll be asking to be a series regular.*

I'll watch my back, I wrote. *See you tonight?*

I will be there, he wrote, and, beaming, I practically skipped back to the writers' room. We stayed until five and then I sent everyone home to take a break and get dressed for the party and the premiere.

Back at the apartment, my grandmother was waiting at the door, with her bulging makeup bag in her arms, like a doctor called out of bed to attend to a woman in labor. She shooed me into the shower, then had me sit at my desk with my damp hair twisted in a towel and the window shades open, to let in the last of the day's light.

"I hired a goat today," I said as she went to work on my face, smoothing moisturizer over my cheeks and forehead and then dabbing on foundation with a sponge. She peered at me, her eyes narrowed in concentration, her hair pinned up in mother-of-pearl combs, her good ruby earrings in her ears, Maurice's ring, which I was still getting used to seeing, on her finger.

"Are congratulations in order?"

"Who knows," I said, and shut my eyes so she could brush on sparkling bone-colored shadow. "Who knows about any of it?"

"Well, Maurice and I will keep a good thought."

"Mmm." I couldn't answer, because she was rubbing her homemade combination of brown sugar, kosher salt, and Vaseline on my lips, sloughing off dry skin. I wondered if she'd seen the reviews. I hoped that she hadn't.

Grandma went to work with her pencils and brushes, one hand gripping my chin lightly, moving my face this way and that. It could have been worse—so much worse. An acquaintance of mine named Ronni Josephson had written and was starring in a sitcom premiering right after *The Next Best Thing*. In spite of our publicist's best efforts, Ronni was the one who'd landed a Q and A in the *New York Times Magazine* that weekend. I'd been jealous, until I'd seen the piece. The first question the reporter had asked her was "Your fellow comics joke about how you slept your way to the top. Did you?" "Ouch," I'd said out loud, wondering whether the guy who'd written the piece had a sitcom or a novel or a screenplay in a box under his bed that he'd tried to sell and couldn't, whether he reflexively hated anyone who'd gotten what he wanted, or whether it was just the women he loathed. At least no one had accused me of getting my show on my back, while that interview ensured that the suspicion of having done just that would follow poor Ronni all the days of her life.

"What a jerk," Dave had said, reading the screen over my shoulder. He'd brushed his lips against the back of my neck so sweetly that for the next hour or so I forgot about the *Times* and poor, unfortunate Ronni.

Grandma tapped the tip of my nose with her brush—her signal that she was done. "Go take a look," she told me.

I walked to the mirror, in my white terry-cloth bathrobe and bare feet . . . and there I was. My eyes looked bigger and brighter, my lips were flushed and full, my lashes fluttered, sooty and mysterious, against my cheeks, but it was still my face: same not-quite-right eye, same stretched pink skin, same subtle wrongness to the angles of my jaw and the bones of my eye socket, which had been shattered then repaired. It was me, in other words: me at my best, but me, still. *And yet,* I thought. *And yet.* I'd gotten a show on the air, something thousands of writers (*like Rob,* my mind whispered cattily) dreamed of but never achieved. And I was in love.

"Ruthie?" I turned. Grandma was dressed in a knee-length gold sheath and high-heeled T-strapped shoes that matched the shade of the dress perfectly and shimmered in the twilight sun. The curtains stirred in the breeze. Beyond her, I could see the kitchen, the aloe and basil and parsley plants that grew on the ledge, my mother's orange kettle that Grandma had brought from Massachusetts, the picture of my parents on their wedding day on the wall. She was leaving me all the furniture, the dining-room table and chairs, the couches with their knitted throws, the heavy gold-gilt mirror. Maurice had agreed to let her do whatever she wanted to his place, whatever redecorating or renovation, and I knew from the binders she'd started putting together, the magazines I'd seen in the house, and the telephone calls to decorators I'd overheard, that she was looking forward to the chance.

She stood behind me on her tiptoes, with her hands on my shoulders. "We need to shake a tail feather."

"Ready in a minute," I said. I'd tried not to think about it, had kept myself so busy that I barely had time to think of anything, but this would be our last week together. On Saturday, Grandma would be Mrs. Maurice Goldsman, and when she returned from her honeymoon, she'd move into Maurice's house in

Brentwood. We'd been cautious around each other, on our best behavior, trying to pretend that nothing had happened and that nothing would change. As always, though, the truth was in her cooking. In the week before the premiere she'd prepared all my favorites: roast turkey, stuffed breast of veal, hoisin-roasted duck and grilled scallops skewered on branches of rosemary, potato latkes and matzoh ball soup, and had left what appeared to be a year's worth of foil-wrapped meals in the freezer.

On my bed, draped across my mother's old quilt, I found the outfit that Grandma had chosen: an A-line linen shift in pale pink, a long necklace of oversize golden beads, and a pair of gold sandals. *Princess shoes,* I'd called shoes like that when I was a little girl, and I would slip into my grandmother's closet to try on her high heels, to smell the ghost of her perfume and run my fingers along the handbags and hatboxes she kept in neat rows on her shelves.

"Beautiful," she pronounced, spritzing me with Shalimar after I stepped into the living room.

"I concur," said Maurice, who looked dapper in a dark-gray suit.

"I've got something for you," said my grandma . . . and then, a little shyly, she handed me a velvet drawstring bag. When I opened it, a pair of diamond drop earrings fell out, sparkling in my hand.

"Oh my God. They're beautiful. This is too much."

"I'm so proud of you, Ruthie. So proud."

I ducked my head. "I just wish the show was a little better." There were a thousand things I dreamed of having done differently—insisted on Annie Tait, banished Loud Lloyd's jokey monstrosity to the fiery pits of hell, somehow convinced Cady that looking like a normal girl would mean so much to the girls who'd be watching . . . but at least I knew I'd tried. If the show succeeded . . . or if, wonder of wonders, miracle of miracles, someday I had another shot at another show, I'd know better what to do, the battles to pick, the people to approach, the words to use. Maybe it would be better . . . or maybe it would go exactly the way things had with *The Next Best Thing*, being thwarted and heartbroken at every turn. It was like Big Dave's Magic 8-Ball, only instead of being customized to read *Fuck yeah*, each side of the triangle would read *Who can say?*

I slid the earrings into my ears and left the bag on the kitchen counter. Maurice held out his arms. I took the left one, Grandma took the right, and he escorted the two of us down to his car.

I'd decided to have the party on the lot, in the commissary. There was plenty of parking, everyone knew how to find it, and the room came equipped with six big television sets mounted on the walls. I got there early, stopped by the bar for a Daphne's Daiquiri (we were also offering Nana Trudy's Sweet Tea, and Brad's Home-brewed Beer). Then, like a bride in a receiving line, I stood by the door, waiting for the guests to arrive.

Cady showed up first, holding hands with her new boy-friend, a hockey player from Canada who was roughly three times her size and looked as if he was having trouble walking and chewing his tobacco at the same time. "Ruth!" she squealed, and flung herself, all bony limbs and pointy elbows, against my chest. I wondered if she'd seen any of the reviews that had called her performance *The Next Best Thing*'s biggest problem, but I knew we didn't have the kind of relationship where I could ask. "This is Lars." She linked her arm through his, revealing, as she did, that her billowy knee-length dress of Champagne satin was so radically slit up the sides that I could see her entire teacup-size breasts when she leaned forward. Internally, I rolled my eyes . . . and then I made myself stop. As much as I thought that Cady had every advantage over me, she was trapped, too. Time was her enemy in a way it would never be mine. In ten years, she'd have passed her sell-by date. She'd have to fight the old familiar battle, spending untold time and money to continue looking like she was in her twenties when she was in her thirties, then her forties. By the time she was in her fifties, she'd have to either give up and age gracefully or turn into one of those sad, stretch-faced women who'd auditioned for the Nana Trudy role.

Now she smiled up at a man whom she'd probably selected less for his conversation or the pleasure of his company than for his mass, which made her look tiny. "Lars plays hockey."

Lars grunted something that might have been a greeting or a death threat. Cady smiled at him sweetly. Lowering her voice, she whispered, "His English? Not so great."

"Nice to meet you. Go get a drink!" I gestured toward the bar. Cady giggled, snapped a shot of the room with her iPhone, and steered her barge-size boyfriend toward the booze.

Taryn breezed into the commissary next, sunglasses in place, towing Rob with her right hand, and an adorable little boy toddler with Rob's dark hair with her left. "Hi-i-i," she drawled, presenting her smooth cheek for an air kiss.

"Nice to see you," I said, and smiled at the happy couple. "Bar's right over there."

"Yummy," she said, and drifted away, leaving Rob standing awkwardly in front of me, with his little boy beside him. Rob had gotten dressed up for the occasion, in pants that were not denim but linen, and a shirt that had buttons and did not have anything ironic written on it, and the little guy had on a sweater-vest.

"Hey," he said.

"Hey," I responded. To think, the two of us had once written dialogue.

"This is Jackson."

I knelt down. "Hi, Jackson. I hope you have fun tonight."

The little boy didn't answer as his eyes took in my face. "There's a moon bounce," I said, pointing (I'd caved in to Sam's request after making him promise that he'd let whatever kids attended the party use it, too). Jackson raced away. I straightened up.

"So," Rob said, and jammed his hands in his pockets. "Is it everything you ever wanted?"

I smiled. With Dave in my life and my show on the air, for however long both of those things lasted, it actually was most of what I'd ever wanted. Love. Success. Enough money to throw a party like this and send my grandmother and Maurice on a ten-day honeymoon in Hawaii (my wedding gift—they didn't know yet). It wasn't perfect, of course—the show wasn't what I'd wanted, and it could get canceled, tomorrow Dave could dump me for a hotter, younger model—but, like Dave said, in this life you didn't get "perfect." And barring perfection, what I had was, to coin a phrase, the next best thing. "It's not bad. How about you? How's marriage? And parenthood?" I found, to my surprise, that I actually wanted to hear his answer, and that I hoped he was happy. I'd liked Rob once, liked him before I'd loved him. Then I'd hated him. Now I just felt mostly indifferent . . . and hadn't I read somewhere that the opposite of love was not hatred but indifference?

He gave a shrug. "Ah, you know. Ups and downs."

"Where are you working these days?" I asked him, thinking it would be a kindness if I changed the subject.

Evidently not. Rob shrugged once more, looking uncomfortable. "I'm doing a rewrite for Paramount. This action thing. It's a remake of a Japanese film. Will Smith was attached for a while, but . . ." He rocked back on his heels, then forward. "I had a pilot in the running at CBS, but it didn't get picked up."

"Ah. Well, you know. Try, try again. Are you going out for staffing jobs?"

He made a face. "I'm getting a little expensive."

I made a noncommittal noise, thinking that it would be the

absolute height of ridiculousness if Rob expected me to feel sorry for him. Then again, at his age, with his years of experience, he was probably too pricy for most writers' rooms to afford . . . and if he couldn't get a show of his own off the ground, his options were limited to screenwriting (or rewriting) and traipsing around after his wife.

"Hey, boss lady!" Both of us turned gratefully. Pete Paxton was ambling toward me, grinning, contented and possibly stoned. He was rolling with an entourage, his blond mom, blond sister and two blond brothers, and the obligatory beauty in a dress that advertised exactly the qualities that had attracted her TV-star boyfriend. I wondered if Penny Weaver had seen her yet and what would happen when she did. *Never mind*, I told myself. As of next week, the actors were officially not my problem anymore, and they wouldn't be until—if—we got picked up for a second season.

"We did good, huh?" said Pete, after trying and failing to engage me in a complicated handshake.

"We did."

"I'm feeling lucky," he said, hugging me. I wasn't, but I hugged him right back.

I waited, watching the time, as people drank and filled their plates. Just before eight-thirty, Dave came up behind me. He touched my hand, and I turned to him, beaming. I should have been nervous, my belly knotted, palms sweaty, on edge, counting the hours until the ratings came in, but all I could do was think about how desperately I wanted this all to be over so I could go back home with him, back to bed. "You ready?" he asked.

I nodded. "Ready as I'll ever be."

"Then go get 'em," he told me as Reilly the line producer hurried over with the microphone in his hand.

"Ruthie? It's time."

I took the microphone and stepped to the front of the room, next to one of the television sets that was broadcasting the show's title card.

"Hi. Welcome, everyone. Thank you all for being here." I waited until the room quieted down and then said, "I'm Ruth Saunders, your executive producer, and I want to start with the good news. We're airing the premiere episode of *The Next Best Thing* tonight, as you all know, so I'm happy to announce that there will be no more pilot reshoots."

Laughter and a few good-natured groans filled the room.

"But seriously. This was my first show, and I couldn't have asked for a better experience." *Or a worse one.* But never mind. I thanked my stars, thanked the crew, the writers, the executives, the studio that had given the show its first shot, the network that had put us on the air. I let my eyes wander, catching a glimpse of my grandma, Maurice's proud nod, Big Dave's grin. "So, before I embarrass myself or forget someone important, thank you all. Thank you all so much. And now . . ." Just like I'd practiced, I waved my remote at the first of the flat-screen TVs and watched them flare to life as the theme music swelled to fill the night.

TWENTY-FOUR

The Next Best Thing premiered on a Wednesday night. Ten days later, on a perfect Los Angeles afternoon, with a breeze that smelled of eucalyptus and salt blowing in from the ocean, and the sun shining and the sky a brilliant blue, my grandmother and her beloved were married. They stood in front of the fountain in the lobby of our apartment building, which had been decorated with tiny twinkling lights. Grandma wore an ivory silk sheath, a double strand of pearls, and peau de soie heels. Her hair had been drawn back into a sleek chignon, ornamented with a single calla lily tucked behind her right ear. A canopy of flowers, more creamy lilies and pale-violet orchids, stood in the center of the tiled floor, and fifty of the happy couple's friends and relations sat in ribbon-draped white wooden chairs in front of it.

Before the service began, Maurice pulled me aside. For a moment, I thought he was going to ask my permission for my grandmother's hand. Instead, he put both big hands on my shoulders, looked me in the eye, and said, "Your grandmother is so proud of you."

"Really? Even after everything?"

He smiled up at me, dentures gleaming in the sun. "It's Hollywood. She's been on enough shows to know how it goes. You did the best you could by her. Because of you, she'll live forever!"

More like three episodes, I thought, but I let him hug me, embracing me in his scent of Chanel for Men and soap and starch and the white rose pinned to his lapel.

Maurice's sons held two corners of the chuppah. The lawyer had a stony expression on his heavy features; the podiatrist looked amused. I held the third corner, and Maurice's great-grandchildren, two boys and a curly-haired girl in a white dress with a violet sash, giggled as they clutched the fourth. The rabbi, who moonlighted as an extra, was a friend of my grandmother's. His voice boomed theatrically through the lobby as he led the couple through the vows.

Do you, Maurice, promise to love this woman, to honor and cherish her, to always smoke your cigars on the balcony and never complain when she spends your money on organic produce? Do you, Rachel, promise to love this man, to honor and cherish him, to make sure he takes his Prilosec before you eat at El Coyote? Smiling into each other's eyes, hands clasped, they said *I do* and *I will.* After the rabbi pronounced them husband and wife, Grandma wrapped her hands around the back of Maurice's golf-tanned neck and pulled him close to kiss her. The audience clapped. The great-grandchildren whooped. Maurice stomped on a lightbulb wrapped in a napkin, crunching it resoundingly, and the cheers were so loud you would have thought we were a crowd of hundreds.

Maurice clasped Grandma's hand and started to lead her back down the aisle, but on the way Grandma stopped to give me a hug. I kissed her cheek, and she started to cry.

"Oh, don't," I said, even though I felt close to crying myself. "You'll ruin your makeup."

"I just want you to be happy!" Grandma said.

"I am," I told her. "Really." It wasn't a lie. I was wearing my pink dress, the one I'd worn to the premiere party, and, last week after work, I'd gone to the Hermès store in Beverly Hills and bought Dave a tie to match. He hadn't walked me up the aisle—he wasn't a groomsman, and it wasn't the kind of wedding that even had groomsmen—but he was sitting in the front row, in a navy-blue suit and the tie, and he'd given my hand a squeeze when the vows were done, then put a glass of Champagne in my hand. "I believe a toast is appropriate," he said.

I smiled and got to my feet.

"Ladies. Gentlemen. Actors," I began. A ripple of laughter made its way through the crowd. Dave looked up at me, pleased and proud, and I felt my heart melt, wondering whether I'd ever dreamed or imagined that I could be so happy. "Please leave your gifts on the table and your head shots with me." More laughter. I adjusted the glass in my hand. "As most of you know, my grandmother has taken care of me since I was three years old. She nurtured my dreams. She made me believe in myself. She moved across the country with me, away from everything she knew, because she believed in me, and she made me believe that I could write. But more than that, she made me believe . . ." My throat was closing. Dave gave my hand a reassuring squeeze, and I made myself go on. "That I was smart, and funny, and worthy, and beautiful." Across the room, I saw Maurice hand my grandmother a handkerchief, and I saw her wipe her eyes. I lifted my glass. "She gave me what every woman—every person—deserves. I've been so lucky to have her in my life, and Maurice, I know that you know how lucky you are to have her in yours, and how happy you make her." I lifted my glass high. "A toast to my grandmother, Rachel Scheft, the best and bravest woman I know, who deserves every happiness."

"And a speaking role in a major motion picture!" someone called, and everyone laughed. I took a sip of my Champagne, and the mariachi band struck up what sounded suspiciously like "La Macarena" as Dave and I found a quiet place at the side of the fountain.

"Did I do okay?"

"Perfect. Are you hungry?"

There was a taco truck parked outside, with servers handing out carnitas dusted with cilantro and wedges of grilled pineapple, and chicken enchiladas, and sugared, cinnamon-dusted churros. On the tables were pitchers of white sangria, with chunks of peaches and sliced sugared grapes. An open bar was set up in one corner, and the band in another. Children raced around the fountain barefoot, waving sparklers, and couples danced. Even Maurice's sons didn't look miserable. "Awesome party," said Sam, who ambled by with a burrito in one hand and a bottle of Dos Equis in the other.

"Congratulations," said Nancy, trailing happily after Sam. She'd made my grandmother a lei out of purple-and-white blossoms, and Grandma had slipped it over her head after the vows.

Dave and I filled our plates, and then I took a seat on the edge of the fountain. Tonight my grandmother and Maurice would sleep at the Regent Beverly Wilshire in the same room my grandmother and I had shared our first night out here, when Hollywood was all bright lights and possibilities. Maurice knew about the honeymoon, and I'd had the tickets and itinerary delivered to their room, along with Champagne and chocolate-dipped strawberries. Tomorrow they'd be flying to Hawaii. From now on, I was on my own, a single lady . . . a single lady with a boyfriend who loved her. I bent down to dip my fingertips in the fountain water, smiling. If things wrapped up before the sun went down, Dave and I could take a swim before dinner.

"Did you see *Variety*?" he asked.

When I shook my head, Dave reached into his breast pocket and unfolded the page he'd clipped. Sure enough, there it was. "Maurice Goldsman, a retired financial adviser, and Rachel Scheft, an actress who has appeared in shows from *ER* to *Cougar Town*, are to be married on Saturday afternoon . . ."

"Good God," I said, and shook my head, laughing.

"You're in there, too," Dave said. I kept reading. "Scheft is the grandmother of Ruth Saunders, creator, executive producer, and showrunner of the recently debuted ABS sitcom *The Next Best Thing*."

I shook my head again, impressed by a woman wily enough to turn her own wedding announcement into a commercial for her granddaughter's show.

Dave took my hand. "Are you doing all right?"

I nodded. "I'm good. I'll miss her . . ." I didn't want to say more, didn't want to tell him how empty my apartment and my life would feel without her. It was a first-world problem if ever there was one.

"So tell me this," said Dave. "Is it everything you thought it would be?"

I knew what he was asking about and considered my answer. "It's different," I finally said. I'd thought about it a lot since Rob had asked the same question, trying to digest the reviews and the network's notes and what I was seeing every day, onstage and in the writers' room. After all of that thinking, I had slowly arrived at the conclusion that there was no real way to change the show's direction. Not this season, not at the four-shows-in-five-weeks pace the network demanded, where there was barely time to grab a shower and a few hours' sleep after one episode wrapped before we'd have to be back on set to get started on the next one.

The stars weren't going to be replaced. Cady was much more valuable than I was, and if it came down to it, the network would rather make *The Next Best Thing* without me than without her. Pete wasn't going to get any more consistent about his line readings—if the acting coach we'd finally hired hadn't gotten him up to speed by now, it was probably never going to happen. Taryn would do her Taryn thing, blond and gorgeous and funny enough of the time, no more, no less. The best shows, the ones I'd grown up loving, the ones I admired as an adult, took a whole season, sometimes more than one, to come into their own, to find their tone and rhythm, their own particular language and look. We would not have that luxury. It was counterintuitive—if great television needed time to happen, why not give all shows that time? But the truth was, in this cutthroat climate, with cable channels and on-demand playback and entertainment available on every iPad and cell phone, no network was willing to wait. Either you were a hit right out of the gate, or you demonstrated the strong potential to be a hit, sooner rather than later. If neither of these things was true, then you were done.

Dave nodded toward the center of the room as the band swung into a bouncy version of "Wonderful Tonight." The dance floor cleared. Maurice led my grandma to the center of the room. In front of the fountain, they posed, facing each other, hand in hand. Then, to claps from the grown-ups and cheers from the children, they began to dance. They shimmied and twisted, Maurice's hands in her hands and then on her waist as she twirled, flushed and laughing, with her pinned hair coming loose and blossoms raining down onto the tiles. "Christ," Maurice's son the lawyer muttered, "Dad's hip can't take this." His brother clapped him on the back. "Lighten up, Howie. Let him have some fun."

Grandma and her husband stood, facing each other, kicking left, kicking right. Then Grandma started laughing, and Maurice opened his arms. He pulled her into a bear hug and they rocked back and forth, holding each other tight. *Be happy,* I thought. All that she wanted for me was all that I wanted for her.

"Ruthie!" Grandma called. She was laughing, beckoning, stretching out her hand toward me. "Dave! Come dance!"

I looked down at Dave, who shrugged and gave me his tucked-in smile. He wheeled himself forward and then faced me gravely. Setting his hands on the wheels, he moved precisely, just as Maurice had: first left, then right. Grandma and Maurice stepped back, and the rest of the crowd followed them, forming a circle. Dave wheeled around me and then tilted on his back wheels. "Spin!" he called, and twirled himself in a circle. I spun, laughing until we were facing each other again, left and right and left again. Then he grabbed my hands and pulled me until I landed in his lap. When he kissed me, my grandmother was the first to start clapping. Then Maurice joined her, then Maurice's podiatrist son and his wife, and then the whole room was applauding.

"Come here," said Dave, and kissed me again, and I thought at that moment I had everything I'd ever wanted: a show on the air, a man who loved me. Maybe none of it would last—in the back of my mind, I could hear Dave saying drily, *You don't get perfect*—but I was going to grab this happiness and hold it as tightly as I could. I was going to enjoy it for as long as it lasted.

"If it's good news, there will be a lot of people on the call," said Dave. "If it's bad news, you might not hear anything."

"What do you mean?" I'd asked, paddling through the shallow end and curling myself into his arms. It was three weeks after my grandmother's wedding. That night, the fourth episode of *The Next Best Thing* would air.

Dave had traced my cheek and then my shoulder, and he'd said, "I mean, you might end up reading it online."

I'd shaken my head, not believing it. It wasn't until later, when I was in the shower, that I thought about what he'd said. Could it be true? Even in the hard, cold, impersonal world of Hollywood, the idea that you'd learn the fate of your show on the Internet, before any of the executives in charge had the good manners to call you, seemed unbelievable, completely outside the realm of basic human decency.

The Next Best Thing had premiered to solid ratings, numbers that were good, not great. The network's bean counters and publicity people had tried to put the best possible spin on things, slicing the demographic pie into slivers so they could claim that we'd won the night with women between eighteen and twenty-four, that we'd attracted a significant number of men between eighteen and forty (most of them, I thought, had tuned in to get a look at the slimmed-down Cady), and that we had improved significantly, if not tremendously, on the ratings of the show in the same time slot the previous fall. For that first week, hope had filled the air.

Then our ratings had dipped during the second week and had fallen even lower during Week Three. Not even the most ambitious spin could make things sound better. By then most of the websites that tracked such things had us on their death watches, and I could feel the blade hovering above our neck.

The writers and the actors were home, waiting for the word. They would remain under contract for another three weeks, during which time we were supposed to get the news about whether we'd be making more episodes or not. Still, when Sam, my writer-slash-toilet-paper-tweeter, had called and asked, diffidently, whether it was okay for him to interview for another possible staffing job, I'd told him to go for it. Better a bird in hand, I'd said, and he'd said, "Just so you know, I really had a good time working for you."

I told myself that I knew what was coming. I'd thought that I was ready for it. Part of me had been bracing for cancellation since Cady had come sashaying toward me at The Alcove, or maybe even since the Loud Lloyd had leaned on me to replace the Nana Trudy scene I'd written with his own work. Still, I felt my skin bristle with goose bumps when my telephone buzzed as I was strolling down Ventura Boulevard. My plan had been to take a walk, do some window-shopping, treat myself to an hour browsing in Bookstar, an iced coffee and a pedicure. When I looked at the screen, I saw that Sam and Nancy had both texted me. *Deadline sez we're canceled,* Sam had written. *U hear?*

I hadn't heard, but I clicked the link to the link he'd included, which took me to a Web site claiming that *The Next Best Thing* was one of three new underperforming sitcoms that ABS had axed that morning. My heart clenched, and I slumped down onto a bench beneath a bus shelter, staring at the story, trying to make the words say something different. When they refused, I dialed Dave.

"*Deadline* says we're canceled, but nobody's called me."

"Oh, Ruth. I'm sorry," he said.

"But maybe it's not true! I mean, they'd call me, right? Someone from the studio? Lloyd or Lisa or Shelly would call. Someone. They wouldn't just let me find out like this, would they?" I heard the answer in his silence, the same one Shakespeare's Prince Hal had given when his friend said, "Banish Fat Jack, and banish all the world." *"I do. I will."*

They did. They would. My call waiting beeped. I looked at the screen and saw Shelly's name flashing. That was when I knew for sure.

I had expected, when the moment came, to feel any number of things: terror, sorrow, anger that things hadn't gone my way. Instead I found myself numb and ashamed, as if I'd left the house naked and every passerby could look at me and know exactly what was happening: *Girl, Getting Fired.* "It's Shelly. I have to take this," I said.

"Hang in there," Dave said, and paused. "I love you."

Warmth suffused my body, flowing from the crown of my head down to my toes. "Love you, too." I swallowed hard, a girl clinging to a trapeze with sweaty hands, swinging between exultation and despair.

"Ruth? Hold for Shelly, please," chirped Shelly's assistant. Then Shelly herself came on the line.

"Ruth Saunders," she said sadly. "Oh, cookie. I'm so sorry. I wish I didn't have to make this call."

"Yeah." Anger was making a belated arrival, cutting through the cotton that had wrapped my limbs. It was unforgivably embarrassing, the network's making me learn this way, in public, with half the bloggers in Hollywood finding out before I had.

"Look," said my agent, talking fast. "For a first time out, you had a great run. You got a show picked up and on the air. The reviews were solid. That's an achievement. You grew so much, and you did a great job, and that's what people are going to remember. Anyone we want to set a meeting with is going to be happy to sit down with us. I know you probably feel like shit—"

"Not really," I said, remembering Dave's *I love you.*

Shelly didn't pause. "But this is a good thing. Seriously. Trust me. You're going to be fine. Better than fine. Let's set a lunch later this week. We'll regroup and figure out our next move."

"Okay," I said. We hung up, and I sat on the bench with my phone in my hand, watching the screen flash. The network called. Then the studio. I let all the executives talk to my voice mail. I'd be able to speak to them at some point, but first I wanted to try to ensure that my actors didn't learn the bad news the way I had.

I called them all: first Cady, then Pete, then Penny, then Taryn. I had a brief conversation with Pete and left messages for the rest of them, following up with texts. *I am so sorry,* I wrote. *So grateful for your hard work,* I said. *Hope we'll get to do it again someday soon. THANK YOU.*

When that was done, I put my phone into my purse and sat still, head tilted back, eyes shut, the sun warm in my hair. I tried to remember the good parts, the way my heart had swelled at the first meeting at the network, where someone had taped signs reading THE NEXT BEST THING to the conference-room doors.

The time we'd all gone out for pizza the night before we shot our first episode, when Cady had picked bits of sausage and strings of cheese off her slice with her fingertips and sent her butterscotch budino back without taking a bite. Spending my days in the writers' room, in the rollicking company of a half-dozen people who delighted in making one another laugh. I pictured Sam, tugging morosely at his shoulder-length locks, saying, "I haven't gotten laid since my last haircut," and Paul, without missing a beat, asking, "Who's your barber?" I'd had friends. I'd had fun. I'd gotten to tell a story to the world, and if it hadn't gone exactly the way I'd wanted, well, that was a story, too.

My telephone rang with a number I didn't recognize, and on a whim I decided to answer. "Hello?"

"Ruth Saunders? This is Alice Michaels from ABS." Ah. My old friend Lumpy Alice, the sleepy sack of potatoes in a dress. Vince Raymer's old assistant, the one who'd gotten Dave stuck in the bathroom before getting promoted and becoming one of the cadre of executives who sometimes seemed bent on nothing less than the complete destruction of the show I'd dreamed of.

I thought about playing dumb, pretending I had no idea why she was calling. But two wrongs wouldn't make a right. I decided to make it easy on Alice, to spare her the awkwardness. Besides, if she hadn't been too lazy to find out whether her building was wheelchair-friendly, maybe Dave and I would never have gotten together. Maybe I should write her a thank-you note. "If you're calling to tell me we're canceled, I already know."

Alice didn't answer. Nor did she pause to say that she was sorry. "We'll need you to turn in your keys and your ID by the end of the business day, and sign off on the last budget."

Oh, I thought, *oh, you are so not getting a thank-you note.* It was unbelievable. On a day when a bunch of funny, smart, talented writers and performers, not to mention cameramen and crew, wardrobe ladies, hair and makeup artists and the craft-service guys had all lost their jobs, this slow-moving, sullen mediocrity with no discernible wit or sense of humor had kept hers. She'd probably be getting a promotion. She was like a cockroach in a nuclear war, the thing you couldn't crush and couldn't kill. Showrunners would rise and fall, the tectonic plates would shift, California would slide into the ocean, and Lumpy Alice would outlive us all. She'd probably run a network someday. It was unfair, so unfair. *Better to die on your feet than live on your knees,* Big Dave had been fond of saying . . . and here I was, dead on my knees. I'd done everything they'd wanted. We'd been canceled anyhow.

"You need my keys?" I asked Alice.

"That's correct."

I shut my eyes. Later, I thought, I would get my toenails painted bright red, and I'd drink iced coffee with sweetened condensed milk. I'd pick up something for dinner, chicken sausages or turkey burgers, and Dave would cook outside while I mashed potatoes and sautéed spinach in the kitchen. We'd eat by the pool, and I'd light citronella candles to keep the bugs at bay. Later, once the meal was finished and the dishes were cleared, we would swim together. On Saturday morning I'd go to the flea market on Melrose with my grandmother and her husband, and on Sunday afternoon, I'd go hiking in Runyon Canyon. I had enough money saved to survive for a year, maybe even two. I could pay my rent and my health insurance and my car loan, maybe even take an actual vacation, without touching my principal, the money from the insurance settlement, and what I'd put away while I'd been working. Maybe someday I'd make another television show, or maybe I'd be happier writing episodes of someone else's and letting the actors and the executives and the ratings and reviews be their problem, not mine. Maybe I'd go back to helping kids with their college essays, only instead of helping just the ones whose parents could write me thousand-dollar checks, I'd also do it for kids who couldn't afford my services.

My call waiting beeped, and I looked down. SECURITY, said the screen. "Goodbye, Alice," I said, and answered the second call. "Hello?"

"Ruthie?" It took me a minute to place the voice. It belonged to Cliff, the middle-aged man in the white shirt and brown pants who stood in the security booth and lifted up the gate to let me onto the lot every morning, the one who called, "Hey, showrunner!" as I steered my Prius past his window. "It's Cliff, from the gate. I saw *Deadline*. Is it true?"

"True," I said, amused by the idea that even the security guards kept up with industry news.

"Aw, shit. Listen. I just wanted to tell you how sorry I am."

"Wow. Thank you. I appreciate that."

"I've worked here a long time. I've seen a lot of asshats. Pardon my French."

"Thank you," I said, trying my best to keep my voice steady. "You know, it happens. And we had fun."

"That's what really matters. You be good now," he told me. "I bet I'll see you again." *I'm not so sure,* I thought as I hung up the phone and pulled my ID and office keys out of my bag, weighing them in my hand. A thought was slowly forming in the back of my mind, a radical idea, something that could get me in trouble . . . but something that could be amazing, provided I could pull it off.

Somewhere, in the depths of my hard drive, I still had the version of the script I'd turned in to the network, the script before I'd rewritten it for a slimmed-down Cady and removed any references to Daphne's size, before I'd added Pete's character and Taryn's character and the scene where the grandma gets so cruelly dumped. Somewhere, on my contact list, I still had phone numbers for Annie Tait, and Carter DeVries, my favorite of the three potential Daphnes. Before I could think twice or second-guess myself, I dialed Ginger's number. Lucky for me, my most senior writer answered on the first ring.

"You want to do what?" she asked, sounding dubious but not immediately dismissive.

"The sets are still up." I wasn't actually positive that this was true, but it had to be too soon for anyone to have taken them down. Eventually, other set designers would come by to scavenge our walls and furniture, the same way we'd taken the bits of other shows' sets—a wall here, a door there, a window reputed to be from Arnold's bedroom on *Diff'rent Strokes*—but I didn't think it had happened yet. "The props, the lights, the costumes . . ." Cady's clothes wouldn't fit Carter, but never mind. "Everything's still there. We'll do it in one night. One take per scene. We'll shoot it on flip-cams and find someone to edit it . . ."

"Why not our guys?"

"I don't want to get them involved," I said. "The fewer people, the better."

"I think," said Ginger, "you should at least give everyone the option of being involved if they want."

"The option of committing professional suicide?" I asked, only half joking.

Ginger sounded somber. "You know, you're not the only one who noticed when there was a difference between what we wanted in the room and what happened on the air. You're not the only one who's been through this wringer. If you want a do-over, I think you owe people the option of deciding for themselves if they want to be part of it."

My face felt hot. I swallowed hard before I said, "Right. Of course. I'll start making calls."

"Let me call the editors. You call the writers."

"What about the actors? No, you know what? Never mind. I'll handle that part." I found myself on my feet, arms swinging as I walked. I hadn't felt so energized and excited since I'd gotten the green-light call, and even then, it had been enthusiasm tempered with pragmatism, excitement mixed with the realities of the situation. Now there were no constraints, no realities, no advertisers to impress or executives to appease, no critics, no ratings. No compromises. "If we actually do this, what's the worst thing that could happen?"

"We could get in trouble with the network," Ginger said. "They still own the show and all the characters."

"They canceled us," I pointed out. "What do they care? I say we go for it. We shoot it, we edit it, we put it up on YouTube. It'll be like a thank-you note to the six people who were watching. And I'll actually be able to see it the way it was meant to be."

Ginger didn't answer. I waited, feeling dizzy with a combination of excitement and terror. "I bet my dad could do the lighting," she finally said. "When's this going down?"

"Tonight," I said. Word was out already, and if we waited any longer, the door would swing shut. Whether or not the network began dismantling our sets, the guards and the producers from other shows on the lot would know that we had no business being there unless we'd come to clear out our desks. I paced along the strip of grass between the sidewalk and the street, my head filling with plans, figuring out what we'd need and who to call and whether it was even possible to pull this off. "And then come meet me in the writers' room. Before we do anything else, I've got to see if my keys still work."

Carter DeVries's agent said it was either the dumbest or the gutsiest thing she'd ever heard. Then she refused to ask her client if she was interested. "It's fine for you to go burn bridges, but Carter's got a new one-woman thing she's working on, and she's up for a part on a new scripted reality show. I'm not going to jeopardize that."

"Is it *Butterface*?" The agent didn't answer. I cringed, thinking of Carter, of whom Lanny had drawled, *I wouldn't fuck her*, on some stupid joke of a reality show, competing to become pretty enough so that men who didn't deserve her in the first place would find her desirable. "Just tell her to call me. If she thinks it's crazy, she can tell me no."

"I'm not crazy," the agent retorted, "whether she is or not. So no. I'm sorry. I feel for you. But I can't let my client sign up for this."

Fine, I thought. *There's more than one way to skin a cat.* I tracked down Carter on Facebook, and she didn't think it was crazy. She thought it sounded amazing. She even agreed to bring her own wardrobe—the outfit Daphne wears to work at the restaurants in Boston and Miami, the casual clothes she'd wear in the apartment—and to see if she could recruit a friend to do hair and makeup.

"I can't pay you," I said. Then I thought: *If I'm putting my own career on the line, why not spend my own money?* "You know what? I totally can pay you. I can pay you a thousand dollars." I could offer everyone else whatever their rate would have been for one night's work, and so what if that depleted my reserves? I had all this cash I'd been saving for a rainy day, and if this didn't qualify, nothing ever would.

"I'm there," Carter said. "And by the way, I would have done this for free pizza and a bag of Skittles. This is going to be awesome!"

So we had our Daphne. Penny Weaver had left for the Maldives, her manager coolly informed me, and I didn't think Annie Tait would welcome my call. "Let me get Mom on the phone," said Ginger, who'd joined me in the writers' room, our war room, with a sack full of takeout from Chin Chin and her laptop. I'd printed out a dozen copies of the original pilot script, plus a contact list of all 186 people who'd had a hand in the show's creation, and the two of us were working the phones.

"Do you think she'll do it?"

Ginger pursed her lips and widened her eyes. "My mother? Are you kidding? I think she's probably in her car circling the executive parking lot right now, just waiting for someone to remember she's alive. So yes, I think she'll do it." She paused. "What about your grandma?"

"Honestly? I think she'd rather watch than act."

"Give her a line," Ginger advised, and I promised that I would.

"Now. Who's going to play Brad?" I asked, figuring that whoever we found would probably do a better job of learning his lines than Pete Paxton had.

"I'll bet Sam would be good."

"Sam the writer? Our Sam?"

"He did that video," she said. Her fingers rattled over the keyboard, and there was Sam, getting escorted out of a Lululemon store as he sang the praises of the cashier's "Bikram booty," which he rhymed with "spin-class cutie."

"You call him. I'll get extras," I said, and dialed my grandmother's number, and said the words I suspected she lived to hear. "Grandma, I need your help."

"Name it," she said.

"Do you think you can get about twenty extras to come to the Radford lot tonight at nine o'clock? I need . . ." I glanced at my script and the notes I'd made. "All ages and ethnicities, for the restaurant scene, another six for the apartment building . . ."

"Ruth Rachel Saunders, what are you up to?" she asked.

I was smiling, grinning from ear to ear, as happy as I'd been at work since this process had begun. "We're putting on a show."

"Well, then, you'll need an audience," she said. "Leave it to me."

I called Cliff, the security guard, and told him that there'd be people coming through the gates that night for what I described as a farewell party for *The Next Best Thing*. Then I called all the writers. "More pilot reshoots?" asked George. "You promised us we were done with all that."

"This is special," I said. I explained to him, like I'd explained to everyone else, what the plan was, what we'd do and how we'd do it. "If you don't want to be part of this, I completely understand."

"You can Alan Smithee me?" he asked—Hollywood code for leaving his name off the credits or giving him a pseudonym.

"Whatever you want," I said. "But we were a team. We were a team when we did this, and I want us to be a team if we're going to try to do it right."

"Gotcha," he said. "I'm in."

By six o'clock the pizzas and drinks I'd ordered had arrived, and Carter, and her friend Matt the makeup artist, who'd gone to work on our cast: Carter as Daphne, Leanna Fairfax as Nana Trudy, Sam King as Brad Dermansky and Sam's girlfriend Debbie in Taryn Montaine's part. We'd gotten the guy who'd played one of Nana's boyfriend's evil sons to double as Daphne's soon-to-be-ex, Phil. My grandmother happily agreed to her one-line role; then she'd sit in the audience and take it all in. I'd wanted to call in a skeleton crew to handle the lights and the props and the cameras, knowing the kind of trouble people could get into with the network and their unions for doing what I'd planned on, but somehow, the word had gotten out.

By the time I poked my head through the elephant doors and took a look at the stage, Reilly, my line producer, was sweeping the floor, and Abby, the prop master, was lining up vases and teapots and making sure Cady's Rollerblades fit Carter. The actors were running their lines. George and Paul were fiddling with the lights. My plan had been to film with cell phones, and with the handheld digital camera Paul and Claire had bought after their daughter was born, and I felt my throat tighten when three of the four cameramen quietly arrived and took their spots behind their rigs.

"You guys don't have to do this," I said.

"Ah, there was nothing good on cable tonight," said Matty, who tended to speak for the rest of them. "You gonna call Chad?"

I shuddered at the thought. "I don't think he'd be interested," I said. I also didn't think that Chad would work for anything less than his quote of $75,000, and while I could afford to spend some money on this insanity, I couldn't afford that.

"So you're in charge?"

"I guess so. What a cliché. Turns out what I really want to do is direct." I looked at my phone, checking the time, as my grandmother led her friends into the bleachers and then rounded up the ones who'd be extras and started telling them where to sit or stand and what to do. It was just after nine o'clock. My plan was to begin the shoot at ten. I'd already called Dave and said I'd be spending the night at my grandmother's, that she was having a minor surgical procedure performed early the next morning and had asked me to drive her and wait to bring her home.

"She doesn't want her husband?" Dave had asked.

"It's a girl thing," I'd answered, suspecting that any intimation of the female anatomy—my grandmother's in particular—would head off follow-up questions. It was the first lie of our relationship, but I felt okay about telling it. If Dave found out what I was doing, he'd either try to talk me out of it or drive down here to help. This was, I had decided, my show and mine alone. If I got in trouble, well, my show had been canceled already, but I couldn't risk getting Dave in a bad spot with the network. "Come home when you can," he said, and I felt my heart leap. Was his place where I lived now? "I miss you," he said, and I told him that I'd see him soon.

At 9:45, we were ready to go. The actors were in costume, the cameras were loaded, the lights, rigged and run by Ginger's spry-looking eighty-year-old father, were shining brightly onto the apartment set. Sam was getting into character, swaggering around backstage like he was twenty percent more muscular than he was in real life, and Leanna Fairfax was fussing with her wig, murmuring her lines under her breath. *Your mother didn't want you to have a little life, Daphne. She wanted the world for you.*

I stuck my head outside the stage doors, certain that we were on the verge of being busted. At any moment security guards with flashlights and walkie-talkies and cell phones connecting them to Chauncey McLaughlin himself would shut us down and drag me off to showrunner prison. So far, though, the night was quiet, with just the usual cars and pedestrians moving around the lot, a breeze rustling the palm fronds, the Los Angeles river flowing through the concrete channel behind the bungalows. Was it possible that we'd get away with this? I thought of Big Dave's Magic 8-Ball: No matter how you shook it, all signs always pointed to yes.

"Hey, Ruthie?" Ginger was calling me. "You gonna say something before we get started?"

"I hadn't planned on it."

"Oh, come on. Give us a speech!"

"Speech!" called Sam, and then Nancy and the rest of the writers took up the chant, and I found myself center stage, under the lights, in front of the camera.

"Wait, she needs makeup!" Grandma said as I took a seat in the couch of the apartment set. Carter's friend hurried over with concealer and foundation and pots of powder and color. "Beautiful eyes," he said as he lined and shadowed them, one hand resting lightly on my scarred cheek. "By the way, I think this is fantastic. Like, let's put on a show!"

"I wish," I said, and didn't continue. I wished that I'd stood up for Carter and fought harder for Annie Tait; that I'd figured out how to get a decent performance out of Pete Paxton and that

I'd told the network to find another show, possibly even another planet, for Taryn Montaine to inhabit. It was too late for any of that, but maybe this could be at least a gesture toward making it right.

"All set," said Matt.

"On three," said Ginger's father. The cast and crew and extras gathered around. I watched Ginger's dad lift three fingers, then two, then one.

"Good evening. My name is Ruth Saunders. I'm the creator of the show some of you may have seen, a show called *The Next Best Thing* that starred Cady Stratton and Penny Weaver, and ran for three episodes on ABS this fall." I should have been nervous. I hated being photographed, couldn't stand being on-camera. Day to day, if I stayed away from mirrors and glass and anything that might give me back my reflection, I could imagine—as long as I wasn't meeting new people—that I looked fine . . . and of course, I always gave the stage a wide berth on shoot nights because I was terrified at the thought of even just my elbow or the back of my head accidentally appearing on TV. Tonight felt different. Maybe it was adrenaline, or the combination of despair over being canceled and the audacity of hijacking the sets and the show, but I felt as calm as if I were sitting in my own chair, in my own apartment, talking to friends.

"I think I speak for everyone involved in *The Next Best Thing* when I tell you that we are proud of the work we did. But as anyone who's worked out here will tell you, television's full of compromises. *The Next Best Thing* was supposed to be the story of a regular girl and her grandma trying to make it in Miami . . . two normal women in search of happy lives. When we cast Cady Stratton, she was that regular girl, but by the time we started shooting . . ." I lifted my hands, palms open, toward the sky. "Things had changed. By the time we started shooting, the show I wrote wasn't the show that ended up on the air. It happens.

Out here, it happens a lot." I swallowed. With the lights shining, I couldn't see any of the other people on the set, so I had no idea whether they were laughing, or rolling their eyes at how naive I'd been, or just ignoring me completely. I tugged my hair against the side of my face. Then I made myself stop. *Warts and all,* I thought.

"Anyhow. We're here in Studio City, on the ABS lot, on the set of *The Next Best Thing,* which is probably going to be struck tomorrow. We've gone rogue, I guess you could say. We've got Carter DeVries playing the role of Daphne Dannhauser. In the role of Daphne's Nana Trudy, we're lucky enough to have Leeanna Fairfax, whose daughter, Ginger, was one of our writers. Sam King, another writer, is going to play the role of Brad Dermansky, and my grandmother, Rachel Scheft, appears in the opening scene. And now, without further ado, we're going to start shooting the pilot of *The Next Best Thing, 2.0: The Next Next Best Thing.*"

"*The Best Thing!*" someone called . . . and I smiled and said, "*The Best Thing.*"

We shot from ten o'clock at night until two in the morning. I kept my promise to do one take per scene, except for the scene we had to do over, after Carter wiped out on her Rollerblades and the cameras hadn't caught her fall.

Ginger and I walked the tapes over to the editing bay, where her friend Kevin sat, sipping Red Bull. "You gonna want music with this?" he asked, pulling out his earbuds and letting them rest around his neck.

"Anything that's in the public domain," said Ginger.

I looked at her. "We're worrying about the legal stuff now?"

She shrugged. "I'm okay if ABS gets pissed, but I'd rather not spend the rest of my life in court with Coldplay."

Kevin said something under his breath.

"Pardon me?"

"I could score it for you. I've got some original stuff."

"That would be excellent," I said. Kevin swigged from his bottle and then plugged in his earbuds. "See you in the morning," he said.

Back onstage, there was a party going on. Someone had brought wine, and someone else had picked up a case of beer. Music played from the speakers, boxes of pizza were strewn across the apartment set, and on a table in the restaurant set, some extras were playing a noisy game of quarters. George offered a solemn high-five. Nancy shook my hand. Ginger hugged me.

"That was fun."

"It was." By now I was so tired I felt dry-eyed and shaky, and doubts were starting to creep in. I couldn't get fired—that had already happened—but what if I got blacklisted and ended up never working again? When Sam handed me a beer, I took it and drank half of it down, fast. A few beers later, I'd decided that maybe not working in television again wouldn't be such a terrible thing.

"Title sequence!" said Nancy, and pressed a button on her phone. I looked at her screen and laughed in delight when I saw what she and George and Paul and Claire had been working on in the greenroom while we shot: a twenty-second stop-motion masterpiece in which a dozen frosted cupcakes chased one another around a table before calming down and spelling out the words *The Next Best Thing, 2.0* and *Created by Ruth Saunders.*

"You guys are the best," I said, and hugged her.

"We all already filed for unemployment," Sam explained.

"Don't worry. I'll disavow you. This one is all on me."

TWENTY-FIVE

I took my time cleaning out my office, piling my books and scripts and photographs into a box, cleaning up my computer's hard drive, erasing the Internet history, trashing drafts of scripts and memos and emails I'd sent, making sure I wasn't leaving anything behind. When I was done, I curled up on the couch to grab a few hours of sleep. I woke up at seven, took a shower, changed into the clothes I'd kept in my desk drawer, packed my towel and last night's outfit in my gym bag, and locked the door behind me, leaving my keys in an envelope in the mailbox outside the bungalow door. When I was halfway to my car, my telephone rang. It was Kevin, calling to say that he'd emailed me his final cut.

The doors to our set were still unlocked. I took a seat on Nana Trudy's couch, pulled my laptop out, downloaded the file, and watched, impressed, almost amazed at what we'd done. If it wasn't a professionally produced half hour of television, it was so close that casual viewers would have a hard time telling the difference. Kevin had spliced in the title sequence and added my intro, and had our theme music playing as the show began. I watched it straight through, laughing, wiping tears from my eyes, knowing that I could not objectively say whether it was good or bad or even in English. I had lived my own version of the story—girl and grandma cut their ties, move to a strange new world, and try to make it. I'd lived it, then written it, and rewritten it, over and over, and taped it once, then again, and then a third time last night. After draft after draft and take after take, weeks of editing and reediting, and then last night's fast, frenzied, seat-of-our-pants shoot, all the words and actions had turned into Kabuki and nonsense. Whether it was decent TV, whether it was funny, would be for other people to decide. I logged on to YouTube, my finger hovering over the UPLOAD button. "What the hell," I murmured, and hit the button that would send our show—my show—out into the world.

Then I went to *The Next Best Thing*'s Twitter account and typed what would probably be the account's final tweets. "*The Next Best Thing* was axed yesterday. Thanks if you watched. Want to see it the way we dreamed it?" I added the link and posted the same message to the show's Facebook fan page. Finally I packed up my laptop and walked through the empty stage. There was the living room, so like the one I'd grown up in back in Massachusetts. There was the restaurant's kitchen, the hostess stand, the ladies' room, the places where Daphne was to have had her misadventures, her setbacks, her triumphs. There, on an end table in the apartment set, was my parents' wedding photograph, the two of them impossibly young, impossibly happy.

This is where the magic happens, I thought, and pulled out my phone, snapping pictures of everything so I would always remember. At least now I knew I'd done what I could. I'd given it my best shot, I'd created something I could be proud of, and even if ABS pulled the video down thirty seconds after realizing it was there, the evidence would live on my hard drive forever. All things considered, it was a happy ending, I decided. I put my parents' picture in my bag and walked offstage, letting the door slam shut behind me.

* * *

"Ruth?"

"Sleeping," I said, and rolled over, with my eyes squeezed shut.

"Honey, it's ten o'clock at night."

"Tired," I insisted. I'd gotten back to Dave's place a little after nine o'clock in the morning. There, I'd cooked us an enormous breakfast, scrambling a half-dozen eggs with chives and cheddar cheese, toasting four slices of bread, pouring a pitcher of orange juice, and slicing brick-size wedges of coffee cake. We'd eaten together, and when he'd asked how my grandmother's procedure had gone, I'd chirped, "Just fine," before piling the dishes in the sink and crawling into bed without washing my face or changing my clothes. There I'd stayed, sound asleep, for the past nine hours.

Now Dave was shaking my shoulder, fully dressed and in his chair, looking at me with an expression somewhere between bemused and impressed. "You could have told me what you were doing. I could have helped."

So word was out. "I wanted . . ." I said, and yawned. ". . . you to keep your hands clean. So one of us could eat lunch in this town again."

"I don't think that's going to be a problem."

I sat up and rubbed my eyes. "Huh?"

"What do you want first? The good news or the bad news?"

"Bad news," I said. I'd always been a pessimist, or maybe the accident had made me one.

He folded his hands in his lap. "Okay. ABS's attorneys sent you what I'm guessing is a cease-and-desist letter. A process server stopped by. I told him you were sleeping. He said he'd come back."

"I got served!" I said, and giggled. It was what I'd expected, no more and no less. "I should call my lawyer." I swung my legs onto the floor, thinking. "I don't actually have a lawyer. Do you know anyone?" I was walking toward the front door, where I'd left my laptop, trying to remember my password for YouTube, thinking that the faster I took down the video, the less trouble I'd be in.

Dave came wheeling after me. "Wait. Don't you want the good news?"

"Okay."

"The show's already gotten more than two hundred thousand hits." I stopped in the middle of the hallway. Dave rolled up behind me, still talking. "Carter DeVries and *The Next Best Thing* have been trending on Twitter all day. Shelly's been calling for hours. You've gotten interview requests from the *Today* show, *Good Morning America, Deadline Hollywood, Variety,* the *Hollywood Reporter . . ."*

"Not *Variety,*" I said. "They gave us a bad review." I went to the end of the hall and found my bag, which I'd left on the floor, underneath the Warhol. I unzipped my laptop's case and unfurled the plug, carrying them both to the living room. Dave wheeled forward, bumping my hip with his chair, forcing me to stop.

"Hey!" I said, and swatted at him. Then I yawned again. Everything felt like a dream.

"Ruth," he said, and took my hands, "I don't think you get it. You've gone viral. Everyone in Hollywood is talking about *The Next Best Thing.* And you got a call from the head of the CW. They're interested in picking up the show, with Carter as the star."

I waved my hand, not letting myself get excited. "It won't happen. They say they'd do it the way I want, but they've got advertisers to answer to, same as ABS. They'd want a thin girl, and a big name to play Nana Trudy."

Dave was shaking his head. "I don't think so. I think now

that everyone's seen the potential—what the show could have been—they'll want to do it right. Especially since you put the network on notice. If they mess it up, people will have a template to look at. They'll know how it should have been."

I sat back down on the white linen couch, with my legs curled underneath me. The room was so beautiful, every time I was there I just wanted to sit and look, to flip through the stacks of art books or mix myself something grown-up from the drinks cart. "Could it even happen? Would ABS turn over the rights? What if they decide they want a do-over?"

"Would that be the worst thing in the world?" Dave asked.

I didn't answer. The truth was, I wasn't sure I wanted to go through that process again: the auditions, the rejections, the inevitable compromises, the way, last night excepted, the thing you wrote was never the thing you ended up shooting; what you dreamed was never what you got.

"Cady's going to kill me," I said.

"Hey," said Dave. "She had her shot. It's not your fault she wanted to get skinny. Or that she wasn't as good as Carter." He smiled, remembering something. "Sam, your writer, called, too. He says his rates have gone up and to call his manager's manager's manager if you need him."

I started laughing. I couldn't help it. Then I leaned my head on his shoulder. "So what would you do?" I asked. "If you were me."

"If I had a chance to do exactly the show I wanted? If I had a guarantee that I could cast whoever I wanted, that I'd have final cut? Are you kidding?" He looked so handsome with his faintly freckled skin, his light-brown hair; and I loved him so much, his calm, steady nature, his good humor, his competence and even temper, his strength. "I can't believe you did this. I think you're amazing."

I smiled at him. "Do I have to decide right now?"

Dave considered, looking at me more intently. "I bet it can wait an hour or two."

"Come to bed," I said, and a few minutes later we were chest to chest, face to face, with his lips on mine, with the covers over our heads, in a world we'd made for two. Let the process servers ring the doorbell, let my in-box overflow, let the the agents and managers and reporters call until my voice mail was too full to even take their messages. For the next little while, I had everything I wanted, right in this bed.

helped me find the perfect happy ending. To everyone who reads my books, indulges my tweets about *The Bachelor*, or takes the time to visit my Facebook page, keep up with my blog posts, or read my short stories, my deepest thanks. None of this would be possible without you.

SIMON &
SCHUSTER

Jennifer Weiner
Fly Away Home

When Sylvie Serfer met Richard Woodruff in law school, she had wild
curls, wide hips and lots of opinions. Decades later, Sylvie has remade
herself as the ideal politician's wife - her hair dyed and straightened, her
hippie-chick wardrobe replaced by tailored suits. At fifty-seven, she
ruefully acknowledges that her job is staying twenty pounds thinner
than she was in her twenties and tending to her senator husband.

Lizzie, the Woodruffs' youngest daughter, is a recovering addict, whose
mantra HALT (Hungry? Angry? Lonely? Tired?) helps her keep her life
under control. Still, at twenty-four, trouble always seems to find her.

Diana, an emergency room physician, has everything Lizzie failed to
achieve - a husband, a young son, the perfect home - and yet she's
trapped in a loveless marriage. With temptation waiting in one of the
ER's exam rooms, she finds herself craving more.

When Richard's extra-marital affair makes headlines, the three women
are drawn into the painful glare of the national spotlight. Once the press
conference is over, each is forced to reconsider her life, who
she is and who she is meant to be.

Paperback ISBN 978-1-84739-025-7
Ebook ISBN 978-0-85720-068-6

SIMON &
SCHUSTER

Jennifer Weiner
Best Friends Forever

Addie Downs and Valerie Adler will be best friends
forever. At least that's what nine-year-old Addie believes
when Val moves into the house across the street. But in
the wake of betrayal during their teenage years, Val is
swept into the popular crowd, while mousy, sullen
Addie becomes her school's scapegoat.

Fifteen years on, Val has found a measure of fame and
fortune as the local weathergirl. Addie, meanwhile, lives
alone in her parents' house, looking after her troubled
brother and trying to meet Prince Charming on the
internet. She's just returned from Bad Date No. 6, when
she hears a knock at her door. There, on the step, is her
long-gone best friend, blood on the sleeve of her coat.
'Something terrible has happened,' Val tells Addie. 'Can
you help me?'

'The brilliant author of *Good in Bed* has come up trumps
again... beautifully written with humour and warmth'
Daily Mail

Paperback ISBN 978-1-84739-023-3
Ebook ISBN 978-0-85720-024-2

ACKNOWLEDGMENTS

As hard as it is for me to believe, what you hold in your hands is my tenth book . . . the tenth book I've written with the help and encouragement and guidance of my wonderful agent, Joanna Pulcini, and my amazing editor, Greer Hendricks.

All those years ago, when I was a young woman with a full-time job and a manuscript for a book called *Good in Bed*, I remember hoping that some agent somewhere would be interested, and that she'd be able to get some editor somewhere to bite. I could never have imagined ending up as part of such a great team, with two smart, funny women who became not just colleagues but friends.

I am also lucky enough to be published by some of the best in the business: Judith Curr, publisher of Atria Books, and Carolyn Reidy, CEO and president of Simon & Schuster.

Marcy Engelman, my publicist, is another woman I was lucky to find, and am lucky to have in my corner and call my friend. She and Dana Gidney Fetaya and Emily Gambir work so hard to make sure the world knows about my books, and I'm so impressed by them, and grateful for everything they do.

Special thanks to Greer's assistant, Sarah Cantin, and Joanna's assistant, Katherine Hennes, for their patience and enthusiasm, and to the team at Atria, who publish me so well: Chris Lloreda, Lisa Sciambra, Craig Dean, Lisa Keim, Hillary Tisman, and Julia Scribner.

Nancy Inglis has the ungrateful task of copyediting my books and saving me from myself. Anna Dorfman gave this book its beautiful cover, and my friend Andrea Cipriani Mecchi, who takes my author photos, somehow makes me look good, too.

At Simon & Schuster UK, I'm grateful for the support of Suzanne Baboneau, Ian Chapman, Maxine Hitchcock, and Nigel Stoneman.

Jessica Bartolo and her team at Greater Talent Network make my speaking engagements a joy. I am also grateful to the fine work of DriveSavers Data Recovery in Novato, California, especially Chris Lyons, Joe Novoa, and Bodhi Nadler. Fellow writers—if you ever turn on your computer on Deadline Day, only to be greeted with a gray screen, a question mark, and an ominous clicking noise, these guys will save your life.

On the West Coast, I am grateful to the executives at ABC Studios and ABC Family, who let me explore the world of television, and to the writers, cast, and crew of the short-lived and deeply missed *State of Georgia*, who gave me a chance and an education. This book is dedicated to my brothers Jake and Joe, who handle my Hollywood business and take care of me as if I was their sister.

Anyone who is lucky enough to spend ten minutes in her company knows that my assistant, Meghan Burnett, is cheerful and funny and kind. She and Terri Gottlieb, who takes care of my daughters when she's not performing miracles in the kitchen and the garden, make my writing life a pleasure.

I'm grateful to the support of my family and my friends, in real life and online. I owe a special debt to Bill Syken, who